AMBER KNIGHTLY

DEMON IN THE DARK

◆ IMMORTALLY ◆
FORBIDDEN SERIES

WHITE CARDINAL
PUBLISHING

WHITE CARDINAL
PUBLISHING

Demon in the Dark

First edition March 12, 2024

10 9 8 7 6 5 4 3 2 1

ISBN 979-8-9898078-1-9
ISBN 979-8-9898078-0-2

Printed in U.S.A.

GLOSSARY OF TERMS

Abaddon: Hovard dimension. No outsiders have ever set foot here and lived to tell about it.

Amare: the Fae realm.

Crol: immortal troll-like creatures with a love for bashing. Not seen as the brightest of the immortal race. Believe in honor and keeping oaths.

Deity: immortal beings of unknown origins. Said to know all and see all. Often insane of nature. Extremely rare and hard to find. Revered as Gods or Goddesses.

Demon: immortal beings fueled by a singular goal, usually destruction. Drinking the blood of a purebred demon and reciting a spell might grant the drinker some of a demon's characteristics, or cause death.

Dragole: often described as half gargoyle/half dragon. Have the ability to become stone.

Dryad: immortals with the ability to manipulate plants. Often live in tree houses.

Eabrith: immortals with power over certain elements.

Elite: mortal soldiers with a sole purpose to abolish the immortal race. Have been known to hold immortals for experimentation.

Fae: immortal beings with unknown origins. They are known for their trickery, deception, and lustful appetites. They reside in another dimension called *Amare*. Known talents include glamour and time alteration. Their blood is poisonous to all immortals. Said to be devoid of any human emotion.

Guardian: mortal protectors of the portals to *Shrodah*. *Keepers* can open portals at will. *Seers* can see into the future. *Protectors* have increased strength and are trained in combat. *Scribes* specialize in runes and language translation.

Hirx: immortal, Goddess like beings that love sex and often have sadistic personalities. Rare. Gain energy to perform spells through sex, can heal immortals of wounds that would kill them, and can see into an immortal's essence.

Hovard: immortal thieves know to steal babies. Live in a dimension called Abaddon. Often described as cloaked hunters that fly. Their true appearance is unknown as none have seen under their cloaks, but are said to be nothing but bones. Said to be bringers of death. Contract killers. Once marked by a Hovard, none survive.

Kurs: immortal shifters that can take the form of any animal and have been known to work as spies.

Lifeblood: a term used by vampires that means "mate."

Lykae: immortal beings with the ability to transform into a wolf under a full moon, or transform at will once mated. Their bite and blood is poisonous to vampires.

Mate: term used to describe an immortal's companion/lover. Most immortals only have one mate in a lifetime and they feel no sexual arousal or companionship toward others once mated. Will protect their mate with their life, and often die if their mate dies.

Mercenary: immortal contract killers

Provean: term used to describe immortals.

Province: term used to describe the immortal world on

earth. While not separate from humans, immortals have their own laws within the Province, including keeping immortals a secret.

Raudskinna: a book said to house the strengths and weaknesses of every Provean in the Province, as well as the location of any item or artifact the reader may be trying to find. Seems to have a mind of its own and the language frequently changes.

Shaga: rare mortals that have the ability to fertilize immortals, allowing any immortal to bare children.

Shrodah: a dimension that houses immortal beings of the foulest, basest sort. Often thought to only house purebred demons. The equivalent of the mortal word 'hell.'

Slig: slender, immortal beings that steal the life force from others from their dreams, often by planting sexual images in their head until death.

Sylph: rare immortals known for their unique skills in tracking.

Vampire: immortal beings that live on blood and die every morning until dusk. Once mated: they can only feed from their *Lifeblood* and die if their *Lifeblood* dies (through lack of nourishment), can teleport short distances, and walk in sunlight. Corrupt vampires are called *venal*.

Venal Vampire: a vampire thought to be corrupted with no regard for mortal or immortal life and only lives for their next kill. Solitary creatures. Terms "insane" and "bloodlust" are often associated with venal vampires.

Witch: mortal beings that can pull power from the energy around them to perform magic spells. Often become immortal once their skill reaches a level that they can successfully cast the *vita* spell.

Womnot: immortal, cannibalistic creatures that feed on flesh. Resemble that of an upright capybara. A single bite can turn the infected into a mindless cannibalistic scourge with no known cure if they survive.

To all my naughty book sisters.

Demon in the Dark

IMMORTALLY FORBIDDEN SERIES

AMBER KNIGHTLY

WHITE CARDINAL PUBLISHING

Chapter 1

Stay...fucking...calm. He could do this.

Khaine adjusted the book in his hands, shuffling it from one to the other before he stepped through the double doors of Bastian's study.

The silence was overwhelming. Discarding his leather jacket on the chesterfield in front of the fireplace, Khaine heaved a breath. Trying to force his demon side back in its cage did nothing, it rattled the bars inside him.

"The Witch give you trouble?"

The deep voice slammed into Khaine.

Bastian stood by his liquor cabinet, his back to Khaine, filling a crystal glass. Remembering Bastian standing in that same place twenty years ago, doing that very same thing, threatened what little resolve Khaine had left. He shouldn't have come.

"Nothing I couldn't handle," he said.

The smell of burning aspen from the fireplace wafted to his

nose, bringing with it more memories. Khaine smashed them into a pile of broken pieces, then swept it to a deserted corner of his mind. If only they would stay there.

"You should have come to me sooner. Four weeks, Khaine. It doesn't take four goddamn weeks to get here."

Khaine *knew* that, but what was four extra weeks compared to twenty years? The last time they spoke, Bastian's efforts had done little to ease Khaine's conscience. How many times would his oldest friend tell him it wasn't his fault?

He shook with violence. Too damn many.

Khaine rolled his shoulders, desperately trying to keep his demon half from surfacing, and walked the length of Bastian's study. He dropped the book on Bastian's desk. "There, you have it. Do something with it. Tell me where to find a portal."

Bastian swirled the liquid in his glass, then downed the contents in a single swallow before turning to Khaine. Khaine inwardly cringed as Bastian's eyes faded to a bottomless black the second their gazes locked, right before Bastian gave him that damn disapproving once-over.

"Fuck. You look like hell."

Khaine *felt* like hell.

"I smell blood," Bastian said, one eyebrow cocked in question. He inhaled as his eyes shifted back to their brilliant, blue hue.

Khaine adjusted his shirt. Of course Bastian smelled blood on him, he hadn't bothered changing. He sported the same shirt and jeans from the club, Lesters, hadn't troubled himself to shave in weeks, and... Khaine combed his fingers through his hair, now reaching his shoulders, and flinched when several strands were ripped out.

Remnants of blood had matted his hair. No wonder Bastian's demon had surfaced.

"Did you have to kill them all?"

He glanced at Bastian and scowled. "They got in my way." Besides, he didn't kill *everyone* at Lesters. One got away. There was no need to ask how Bastian knew of his escapade. Word traveled fast among Proveans, and with an immortal escaping his clutches that night, he would be surprised if the Province wasn't already scrying for him.

Let them come, he thought. What he wouldn't give to sink his claws into immortal flesh. *Any* immortal flesh. Something to feed his fucking demon. He was getting restless.

As if on cue, his demon side thrashed those steel bars inside him.

"Your eyes darken," Bastian whispered.

Khaine would have missed those words if not for his excellent hearing, and not just the words, but the threat Bastian laced in them. Khaine balled his fists as Bastian's eyes shifted to black. Bastian was likely feeding off Khaine's rollercoaster of emotions, and that only made things worse.

"Watch yourself, old friend," Khaine said. Fight me, he thought.

"Cage your demon." Bastian gripped the crystal glass as if ready to use it as a weapon. "Whatever angered you, it wasn't me. I'm not the one you want to fight."

Wasn't he? Fighting Bastian's demon form would no doubt silence his need for bloodshed. Bastian was his friend, the only one he had left. No, he didn't *want* to fight him.

But the need!

Khaine dug his nails into his palms, the pain calming him. A slight rumble stole through him as he slid his demon half back into the confines of its cage. Bastian tucked away his beast, donning a resemblance of normal.

As if all was well.

Filling another crystal glass with a bronze liquid, perhaps whiskey, Bastian handed it to him. As if nothing had changed. As if Raiden wasn't rotting in Shrodah, a demon's Hell, suffering a torture neither of them could comprehend. *Soon, brother.*

Khaine took the glass. *Gods, let it be whiskey.* Tossing back the drink, he relished in the slight burn as it slid down his throat. Malted barley swirled with a hint of oak on his tongue. It warmed his empty stomach.

Bastian set his glass on the ornate, leather-topped desk and flipped open the Raudskinna's cover. Khaine eyed the mahogany wood paneling of Bastian's study, the cream wallpaper scaling half the wall above the wainscoting, even the ornamental lighting hung in metal globes over the desk; anywhere but down at the book before Bastian. He didn't have to look to know the intricate, dark runes marking Bastian's neck were pulsating with the electrifying contact. Khaine's did the same every time he touched the book. Or that Bastian's eyes were darkening with each word they traced. His own eyes had glazed to black the first time he'd looked at it.

Four weeks he'd had the book. That was four weeks he'd contemplated the gold-leaf cover, wishing he could read the blasted thing, searching for anyone but Bastian that might help. If he had come to Bastian sooner, they would be further along in getting Raiden back. Time was running out; that was the only reason Khaine returned.

"Why didn't you come to me sooner?"

Khaine gritted his teeth, staring at the Hans Memling painting in front of him. It depicted a demon in Hell with a man trapped inside its skin, sinking its claws into mortal flesh. *Fitting.*

"Thought I could decipher it," he said.

The Raudskinna was said to hold the darkest magic known to any immortal, as well as the origins, strengths, and weaknesses of every Provean—immortal creatures that lived among the mortal race, and Khaine couldn't read a damn word of it. Not one...fucking...word.

He wondered if his and Bastian's twisted kind were in that book. Perhaps he would ask Bastian one day once Raiden was free. Half demon. Half human. How many such abominations existed? As far as they knew, they were the first and last of their race.

"This doesn't mean you will get him back," Bastian said, half whispering as his palms caressed the worn, parchment pages. He placed the Raudskinna on a sheet of glass lining his desk. "You know that, right?"

Something about Bastian's voice, the undertone of lost hope, pricked at the edges of Khaine's mind. It was as if Bastian were telling him to give up, but leaving Raiden in Shrodah would make him a failure.

Failure. It bounced in his head as if solidifying just how little he'd been hanging on. *Failure.* With one word, all the measures he'd taken to calm himself came crumbling down.

Just like that.

Khaine crushed the crystal glass in his hand and embedded a single shard in Bastian's neck. He moved too fast for Bastian to react; too fast for him to contemplate his own actions. One moment Bastian was standing before him, and the next he was pressed tight against the wall with a fragment of glass impaled above the collar of his shirt, Khaine's hand locked around his neck. Bastian's black blood sprayed Khaine's bared fangs as he dangled by his throat next to the painting. Khaine felt his demon half come to the forefront. He didn't care whose blood it was, as long as he got a taste of it.

"Calm yourself," Bastian choked out.

Fuck calm! Need death. Violence. Fight me! He squeezed harder.

Bastian retracted his claws from Khaine's hand around his throat, putting his palm up. A sign of submission. He should let him go.

He *couldn't*.

A thick cloud clogged his vision. All he could see was the blood around Bastian's neck and his claws digging into soft flesh. He snarled with pleasure.

Yes, this is what I need!

The glinting of steel caught Khaine's eye. He felt the tip of the knife a second before realizing Bastian held it against his ribs. Without warning, Bastian twisted the blade deep, just barely missing his lung. Khaine closed his eyes and forced his claws to release, the pain calming him.

"I'm *not* your enemy," Bastian ground through clenched fangs.

"Then stop acting like it's pointless!" Khaine's voice bounded through the room, stabbing his ears with a thunderous tempo. He pulled the knife from between his ribs and shucked it across the study.

"You want me to help you? Let me!" Bastian wiped the

blood from his neck, the wounds already healed. "You can't do this on your own. I can help you. Stop showing up only when you hit a wall and *let me help you*."

Khaine glowered at him, disregarding his own wound. It, too, had closed. What was a little more blood soaking his clothes? He licked his lips. The metallic taste of blood had become too familiar.

Forcing his demon back in the pits, he retreated a few steps. *Breathe.* Khaine ground the words through his lips, ignoring how alien they felt. "I apologize." He'd have to work harder at keeping himself calm. "Can you read it?"

Bastian studied him; his eyes still black. Khaine forced a smile.

I'm calm. I'm calm.

"You're scowling. My demon still senses you as a threat."

"I'm not scowling!" Khaine ran a hand over his face. Fuck, he was scowling. "It was supposed to be a smile."

"You don't *know* how to smile."

"Fine." Khaine shoved his thoughts into a padded box and locked it. Masking his face into what he hoped was a visage of indifference, he said, "Can. You. Read it?"

Gods, he was walking a razor's edge.

Pain. Violence. Death.

He gritted his teeth. *Shut up.* Not that the demon part of him ever listened. Deep breath. In. Out. It didn't help that he *was* the demon, even if he liked to think otherwise.

Bastian twisted his neck, his black hair swirling with the motion. He shuddered as his bones cracked but forced his demon to obey, his eyes once again a soft blue.

"I need time," Bastian said after length. "I haven't read this language since before the turn." Walking back to his desk, he leaned over the book, his muscles tense.

Khaine didn't miss the way a corner of Bastian's silk, maroon dress shirt fell unyielding from his black slacks, now scattered with drops of blood. Or the way his midnight-black hair, usually kept short, now dusted his neck; unkempt and awry. Not even the slight stubble his friend sported that said he'd forgotten to shave. Khaine recognized his guilt was leaking into Bastian. It didn't look like the last twenty years had been kind to him either.

Khaine told himself he should care, but he didn't. Raiden was all that mattered to him. Once he had his brother back from Hell, perhaps things would be as before. He and Bastian were like brothers, once. He'd die for the man under any other circumstances, just not before Raiden was free.

Khaine cleared his throat. "How long?"

Bastian's forehead furrowed as he thumbed through a few pages in silence. His eyes darted over the words as if trying to pry the meaning from the cryptic text. Few could read Téagu Dás. Khaine only learned a few words, but Bastian's father had worked with him for years, sitting him in front of the fire for hours each night, forcing him to memorize half-dead and long-forgotten languages. It was Bastian's duty as a Scribe. It had come easy to him before becoming a demon, before that knowledge was stolen from him. His mind had soaked up tiny details of every language faster than most men could do in decades. But not anymore.

"It will take some time, but I'm sure the location of a portal is here. The description of the rune should be as well."

"I can't wait any longer. I need something, now." Khaine

pursed his lips and paced along the seam of the carpet, his jaw clenched. Bits of broken glass crunched into the soft fibers under his feet. He wanted this over with; his brother back in their presence.

"These words are faded and of a language I haven't seen in some time. There's nothing I can do with this, right now." Bastian flipped the cover closed.

Just like that.

An insistent pounding worked its way through Khaine's head. His body shook with rage, his demon half threatening to come forth without his consent. Balling his hands into fists and forcing his claws into his palms was all he could do to hold himself at bay. Black blood pooled in the center of each hand. He didn't *fucking* care what it took! He wanted Raiden back. Having to live with the guilt of sentencing his brother to Shrodah for the last four centuries had already taken its toll.

Finding out his brother could be saved from those soul-snaring pits was almost his undoing.

What had become of his brother in that time? He knew what awaited a demon in Shrodah. Fires that never let you die. Water that filled your lungs but never let you drown. Forests of creatures so foul they skinned you alive, only letting you heal so they could do it again. Raiden's mind would be irreversibly shattered if he didn't find a way to bring him back. And it was that very fear that had been plaguing Khaine's dreams with nightmares he found himself desperately needing a release from. Even the guilt of dragging Bastian into this world, his problems, ate at Khaine every time he saw him. He wanted nothing more than to leave Bastian to his own life. He told himself he didn't need him.

Over the years, Khaine's rage had become his only friend; a welcomed ally. The demon part of him, the half he loathed, became the brother he'd lost. Bastian didn't belong in this fight. He was better than Khaine, better than them all. He'd *tried* to stay away. But Khaine *did* need him. Not being able to read the damn book had proved that. There was nobody else.

Bastian sidestepped to stand in front of him, his movements almost unnoticeable, and narrowed his eyes. "He's my brother too. Maybe not by blood, but I would do anything to get him back. Don't you fucking push me away! I'm not a Guardian, anymore. I wasn't the one that left us to die. You're not alone in this. We'll bring Raiden back."

A Guardian? No, that line was wiped out ages ago.

Pity, Khaine thought. What he wouldn't give to rip their hearts out one by one for renouncing them.

"Calm yourself," Bastian said. "I said I can help, and I can." He skirted his desk, pulled out a drawer, retrieved a single piece of paper along with a small rectangular box, and handed the paper to Khaine.

Khaine unfolded it. "Coordinates?" What was he supposed to do with these?

"Pembine, Wisconsin. The Lykae split the land there with the vampires."

Khaine clenched his teeth. "Get to the point."

"There's been rumor there's a tomb on their land. One of the immortals I questioned called it a dilapidated ruin with symbols on it."

"What makes you think it's a portal?"

"I'll try to translate the Raudskinna and find a portal, maybe even the rune needed to open it. You can keep yourself busy by checking out those coordinates."

"A wild goose chase." Khaine crushed the paper.

"It's not a wild goose chase. Besides, it's Lykae and vampire territory."

"Point?"

Bastian threw up his hands. "Immortals."

Khaine raised a brow.

"For fuck sakes! Go kill something."

His demon half leaped at the thought. *Kill, yes!* At least in this, they agreed. Killing was something he could focus on. Demons had to have something to aim for or they were less than nothing. The purebreds that came out of Shrodah dedicated themselves to destruction and misery, maiming and killing for nothing but sport.

Khaine and Bastian weren't pure demons, but half-breeds of their human selves. They retained their mortal form and way of thinking but were immortal to the core, demons that needed substance, purpose, and while they were hard to kill, there were still ways for a demon to die. A demon without a purpose never lived long. Most found a way to end their miserable existence. A fact Khaine had almost become the victim of.

"Fine. Just translate that book," Khaine said. Going to Wisconsin sounded more appealing than being stuck in this study for days, waiting on Bastian to decipher the text. The smell of fresh wood and leather was fucking with his head.

Besides, maybe he would get lucky and the rumors would be true.

"You'll need something of Raiden's for him to pass the gateway alive." Bastian handed him the small box he took from his desk. "Here. Take it."

Khaine reached for the box. His hand stalled twice before he forced it to take the tiny container. He didn't need to open it. A desolate part of him already knew what lay inside.

"Thought one day you might want it back."

Khaine clenched his jaw, compelling himself not to demolish the wood. "I told you to destroy it."

Bastian sighed. "Well, it's a damn good thing I didn't. We never thought Raiden could still be alive, never thought he could come home. Maybe I held onto hope." He sounded just as defeated as Khaine felt.

Khaine tucked the box into his pants' pocket. He wouldn't look at what was in it, it would only tear him apart. His muscles were tired, his mind threatening to fail him with each passing night. Khaine glanced at his tattered, black cotton shirt, his faded jeans that were stained with the blood of several Provean races—they had gotten in his way when he'd told them it wasn't wise—and almost cringed when the hair he'd forgotten to cut fell over his harsh face. What he must look like in Bastian's eyes. No wonder Bastian regarded him like he had. Scrubbing his chin, Khaine brushed his calloused fingers over the scratchy stubble he'd neglected.

"I'll call you when I get there," he told Bastian. He grabbed his coat from the Chesterfield and burst through the double doors of the study before Bastian could say another word.

His chest tightened. Khaine took a deep breath; felt the world closing in around him. Bastian didn't need to suffer this guilt with him. He took the help from him when there was no one else, and nothing more.

Khaine uncrumpled the paper the moment he cleared the

front door into the cool night, his jaw stiff. The coordinates Bastian gave him were a hard three-days drive from Bedal, Washington. That gave him plenty of time to ponder every possible scenario that awaited him; to set his mind to something else. The Lykae and the vampires were fierce creatures, but they held no chance against him when it came to getting his brother back. He was a hard-washed demon on a mission.

Nothing was going to stop him when that moment came. *Nothing.*

Chapter 2

Skye held her breath as the woman on the television ducked around a rock. The cave in this movie was gloomy. Bones lay strewn around the woman's feet as spiders crawled over damp, jagged stones. Blood splattered the woman's arms and hair with the entrails of one of her dead friends hanging off her shoulder.

Jade reached over and stole some popcorn from Brooke's lap, dropping most of it before popping the rest in her mouth.

Skye cringed as the woman on the screen peeked her head out from where she was hiding.

Big mistake!

Skye gripped the material in her lap, the florescent silk half-pinned with fishnet patches. Her goal had been to finish cutting and pinning the fabric so it could be sewn, but then Caden showed up with another demon flick.

"Stupid woman," Caden yelled. "Run for your dead friend.

At least he had a gun. Oh my gosh, not that way. Yes, pick up the rock. What the heck are you doing! Don't *throw* it. Now it knows you're there!"

Caden turned to them. "Can you believe this woman!"

"Run, damnit! It's coming," Jade cried.

The grotesque demon, with skin falling from its silvery-gray face and claws the size and shape of twisted metal, gnashed its teeth while the woman darted from one dark corner to another.

Brooke curtained her long, red hair onto her face as if shielding her eyes, the motion casting loose strands over Skye's lap. "Gah! Tell me when she's dead. I can't watch."

Skye gripped the half-finished skirt in her lap, her heart pounding, the woman drawing nearer to the cave's exit. *She has to make it!*

Caden stood and unsheathed her sword. She pointed it toward the screen and shrieked when the demon came down on the panicked woman in the movie, her tight leather catsuit shimmering in the television's reflection. "Hit him! No... What are you doing? Ah, damnit, now you've been bit. What the fuck are you going to do now?"

The woman on the television twisted on the wet ground, grabbing a nearby rock and bashing the demon in the head with it. Blood poured from the wound, momentarily blinding the creature.

Jumping from her spot on the couch, Skye hardly noticed the half-pinned skirt tumbling to the carpet. "That's it, hit it! Kill it!"

The woman could do this, Skye thought. She could beat the demon. Excitement flared inside her. Someone was going to win!

The demon screeched in pain on the screen, thick green slime oozing from its head before it released the woman's leg. She scrambled to her feet, tossing the rock to run again as her brunette hair matted against her face.

"No... Don't leave the rock. Turn around," Caden shouted. "Kill it before it gets up."

Skye winced when the demon attacked the woman once more. She thought she heard the woman's head pop after she tripped over a crack in the rocks, dirt spraying into her eyes and blocking her line of sight when she fell. Blood gushed from the woman's skull down the dirt-encrusted lines of her face. Abruptly, the frame switched to the cave's entrance where the woman could be seen reaching toward it as if begging it to drag her to freedom.

No... It can't end like this!

Skye watched the demon burrow its teeth into the woman's leg and she screamed — or was that her? — but it was too late. The demon dragged her backward and out of sight, no doubt killing her like it did all her friends.

Skye stood in awe when the screen went black and the credits began to roll.

That's it? That's how it ends?

Sinking back into the brown, suede sofa, Skye crossed her arms and glared at Caden. "You said this would be a better movie. Your exact words were, '*Someone* will live this time.' That woman looked far from being alive."

Caden sheathed her sword and threw up her hands, her long brown hair pulled back in a snug ponytail and bouncing about her shoulders. "Well, she *would* have lived if she wasn't so naive."

Skye smirked. "Not everyone can be as badass as you, Cad."

She had to give the woman in the movie credit for living as long as she did without actually defending herself. Not even *she* could do that. She also had to admit, she kind of liked these Indie movies Caden came back with. All of them were about demons, and not only that, they even managed to get the demon's anatomy and looks close to the real thing. It made it easier for her to get into what was happening, but only if the people in the movies didn't die at the end or end up in love.

Most movies about demons now were embarrassing. Romances? Gah! Who in their right mind could love something so foul?

Not her, that was for sure.

If Skye had to sit through another movie where the demon was the hero and the woman couldn't help but fawn over him, she thought she might retch. No, she *would* retch. Demons in the real world were nothing less than hideous, self-indulgent, predatory killers that hunted people down for their own amusement. She didn't spend the better part of her adolescent life, and *all* of her adult life, killing demons that managed to break free from Hell, however few there had been, just to get sucked into some sappy love story that could never be true.

She'd rather spend the remainder of her life in an insane asylum, just like her mother had, than watch another demon romance.

Skye reached over and brushed Brooke's hair from her face, unfurling the strands from Jade's lap. "It's over. You can look now."

"Why do we watch this stuff?" Brooke fussed. "It's not like

we can't watch a demon attack a woman in real life. Hellooo! You're a Guardian, remember? We have all the demons we need right under our feet. No shortage of attacking in that department."

"It's not the same," Jade said. She brushed the popcorn bits from her gray sweats and readjusted a blue knit blanket over her lap. Her short, black hair bounced with the motion, jostling some of the hair-sprayed spikes loose. "Besides, that portal only opens once a year, *if* that," she groaned.

Caden shrugged her shoulders. "We'll just call these little movies research. You know, for next time. Who knows, maybe one of us will need to defend ourselves against the next solstice breakout by bashing in a demon's skull with a rock." Her eyes lit up with the thought.

Skye scrunched her face at that. "God, I hope not."

It took Skye years to learn how to use a sword properly, finally able to wield one with confidence. If she had to return to basic training, she was afraid it would hamper her progress. She'd worked so hard with Caden's help, just learning to defend herself without blowing something up. They all liked to think of her as the ticking time bomb.

Not true.

It wasn't her fault she accidentally caused a little destruction when she was afraid. Or at times, she reminded herself, opened a portal that let loose a nine-foot-tall demon to smack its lips and think the guy presently sharing her bed looked like a tasty midnight treat.

But, that only happened once. Skye couldn't thank Caden enough for rushing in and slicing the thing to pieces. Skye hadn't known how or why it had happened. Being able to defend herself had become a top priority. She'd rue the day she ever had to live through that, again.

"I think I've had enough blood with all these movies you bring home, Cad," Brooke said.

Caden arched a brow. "Whatever. It's about time you got over your damn blood phobia. You're a mercenary for God sakes! How the hell do you even do your job?"

Brooke glared at her, small currents of electricity pulsing through the palms of her hands and sparking in the air above them.

Skye ran her fingers through her blonde hair before pulling it back to secure it. "Come on. She's just trying to rile you up." It was like a pissing contest between the two. She decided it best to change the subject before Caden and Brooke dived into their normal "who was the better mercenary" argument and their newly patched stone wall took another beating. "Has anyone heard from Mckenzie?"

Glancing down, Skye noticed her own trail of popcorn hitchhikers and escorted the crumbs from her breasts, knocking them onto her loose, baby-blue jeweled shorts. She brushed the bits onto the floor, then promptly saved the skirt she'd been pinning off the carpet and placed it on the side table. Jade was so going to love it when she was done!

The television began a parade of orange lights across the screen when the credits drummed to a close, the movie switching back to the main menu. The room was still dimly lit. Skye clapped her hands to turn on the lamp, the shadows cast over the stone walls of their home scurrying out of sight. Light bounced off the glass of the TV stand and sent a glare over a poster of Milla Jovovich.

Now *that* was a badass woman.

Well, at least in the movies.

The steady hum of the generator in the next room now mixed with the quiet stream of music emanating from the TV. Installing the generator a few years back was the best decision they ever made. The dark catacombs of their slowly decaying hideout seemed a lot less dreadful when floodlit with electric fixtures.

Seeming to ignore Brooke, Caden plopped down in the black rocker, decorated with iron-on patches of the Powerpuff Girls, and used one of her knives to pick dirt from under her nails. "Haven't heard from Mckenzie since she left weeks ago. I hope she finds that girl okay. You sure you haven't sensed the girl since Mckenzie went looking?"

"No," Jade said.

Right after Jade had a vision of a Guardian in distress, Mckenzie rushed off to find her. She was the best tracker they knew. If anybody needed found, Mckenzie was the woman for the job. Being a Sylph, she could find and track anybody or anything with ease, even over hundreds of miles, and her immortality meant nothing would stop her in the process.

Sylphs were revered creatures in the Province—the name immortals gave themselves; the name that governed all factions. They were rare, which meant Mckenzie always had other immortals pining for her, as well as the mortals that called themselves the Elite.

Skye could only imagine what the girl was going through. When she first came into her own confusing ability, Skye had no idea what it was or why she was blowing things up for no apparent reason. Actually, she *still* had no clue, except for the fact that it seemed to be linked to fear. She was lucky Caden had been there with her, helping her get past the worst of it and understand how to control herself better.

The worst part? It had brought her mother's words back to searing life. Being told her mother was a whack-job that had reoccurring hallucinations was one thing. Being told they were real and that she was a Guardian born to protect portals to Hell was completely different, and a revelation like that held a lot more merit when Skye suddenly turned into her own freak. The immortal world had been dumped on her overnight, and she'd had to learn how to survive in it. She'd had to learn fast that you either rolled over and died, or you started kicking and clawing the shit out of whatever tried to bring you down.

Caden had been there for Skye when their foster parents threatened to kick her out, accusing her of destroying things with her bare hands. Not once had Caden questioned why Skye was the way she was, but that was because Caden had skeletons in her past as well.

"I'm sure she'll find her," Brooke said. She eased off the couch and arched her back, stretching her limbs. Her elbow caught Jade's forehead by accident, Brooke's ankle-length red hair crowding her view. She quickly bent to run her hand over it. "I'm sorry. I didn't mean to…"

Jade's face was stark white, her eyes hollow and face frozen.

Skye frowned and slid over next to her, brushing the back of her knuckles along Jade's face. "Jade?" She jerked her hand back from Jade's icy skin. "She's cold, again."

Caden joined Brooke to stand in front of Jade, examining her features. "Jade, honey. You in there?"

Nothing.

An uncertainty filled Skye. Jade didn't freeze like this often. On the few occasions she had, nothing good had followed.

A loud shriek broke through Jade's lips and Skye jumped, quickly trying to calm her racing heart. It would do Jade no good for Skye to flip out, now.

Jade's eyes darted frantically about the living room as if seeing nothing and something at the same time. Working double-time, her hands flailed in front of her as though trying to fight off some unseen attacker. She caught Skye in the face, forcing Skye to scramble out of reach.

Oh, god. Here we go, again.

This one seemed worse than the others they had witnessed in the past. What was Jade seeing? What could cause such a strong woman to appear as though death were gripping her and dragging her down to Hell? Was it the other Guardian? Had something happened to Mckenzie?

Please, don't let it be Mckenzie.

The hair on the back of Skye's neck stood on end. Jade often saw things that came to pass, like the vision before Mckenzie rushed off, but this one was different. Whatever Jade was seeing behind her eyes was bad. Memories of her mother's final hours rose in the back of Skye's mind.

The panicked shrieks that echoed down white corridors. The doctors jamming needles into her arms trying to calm her. Those last moments of pure torture where she hysterically bashed her head against the brick wall, knocking herself unconscious. Her mother had shared Jade's ability, and the way it ended for her mother would be forever fused in Skye's mind.

"Jade!" Skye tossed one of the couch's pillows at her, trying to jostle her enough to snap her out of her trance.

It didn't help. The pillow landed in Jade's lap and she clutched it in a full-fledged vise grip. There had to be some way to snap her out of it.

Brooke raised her palms, small electrical currents shooting through the tips of her fingers.

"Whoa," Caden said. "Slow down there, Sparky."

"Well, somebody has to do something."

Skye grabbed one of Jade's hands from the pillow and squeezed, anything to get her attention. Just as Skye was about to toss another pillow, Jade sucked air into her hoarse lungs, releasing the pillow in her lap along with Skye's hand. She shifted her legs, folding her knees to her chest to rock back and forth like a cornered child, sweat beading on her forehead. Tears streamed down her face.

Skye wanted to comfort her but didn't know how. Instead, she smoothed back some of the spikes on Jade's head and brushed the tears from her eyes, hoping the small movements might ease whatever horror her mind had bestowed on her.

"What did you see?" she asked.

Jade babbled incoherently, stringing syllables together that didn't fit. Her head shook back and forth like she was desperately trying to toss the vision out. Caden moved forward and rested her hand on Jade's shoulder trying to calm her enough for them to make out words, but Skye didn't think that was helping either.

Skye couldn't understand anything Jade was saying, watching Jade's fingers toy with the blanket in her lap with a nervous gesture. Some of the color was coming back to Jade's face, but barely.

"Shh. It's okay," Caden said. "Tell us what you saw. Was it

Mckenzie? Has something happened?"

It seemed Caden had been thinking the same thing.

Skye tucked the blanket in Jade's lap up to her waist, stilling her fingers. It couldn't be that bad, could it? Jade's visions before Mckenzie took off were only fleeting images of Brooke dropping a glass of water, seeing it shatter on the concrete floor, and then a premonition of their homemade waterline breaking. Those had been weeks ago. Even the vision Jade saw of the Guardian hadn't rendered her mute.

No, something was wrong. The more Jade's face paled, the more it reminded Skye of her mother's 'visions' before she whisked herself away trying to make them stop.

They never had. It had only been the beginning, and nothing in the book Skye's mother had left for her could shed light on why. She remembered her mother getting worse over the course of a few weeks. Screaming in her sleep, then during the day, then eventually... By the time Skye was old enough to understand what was happening, to believe the stories her mother tried to tell her, her mother was too far gone to do more than beg Skye to protect some portal she knew nothing about.

"Protect it! It's your job, now. Don't let that demon take it from you!"

Let a demon take it from her? She hadn't even known what portal her mother was raging about. Thinking back on that comment made her want to laugh. Now that she found herself living above said portal, what made her mother think a demon would ever take it from her? And why would that moment cause such a panic?

That was years ago, Skye. Get ahold of yourself. She shook her head and tried to focus on Jade.

Jade wiped a tear from her eye and took a few measured breaths as though forcing herself to be calm. She looked anything but calm when huddled in a ball of terror. The spikes on her head began to lay flat as Skye continued to brush her hair with her fingers. It didn't look like whatever she had witnessed wanted to be comforted by the motion, so she dropped her hand.

"Not Mckenzie... Skye..."

Me? What did Jade see about her? Surely, she wasn't in any trouble, was she? Her mother's words snaked up her throat again, choking her. She swallowed to keep herself from screaming. Fear wouldn't help anybody, right now.

"I s-saw it," Jade sobbed. "I s-saw what your m-mom was talking about. The d-dea...demon..."

Skye shook her head, on the verge of denying it all before she stopped herself. She'd spent her entire life trying not to think about her mother's premonition; a demon killing her. And that's all it had been, a premonition. A bout of hysterical laughter threatened to consume her and she cleared her throat. Her? Killed by a demon? She was supposed to live out her whole life, be the next hit clothing designer, figure out her damn emotional problem, and then find... What? A Provean to marry? A mortal?

Her hands clammy, she rubbed them on Jade's blanket, absently pulling it into her lap. Be calm, she told herself. Deep breath. In. Out.

Just because Jade was having the same vision, didn't mean it was going to happen anytime soon, if at all.

She caught Caden eyeing her, a look of pity and worry mixing on Caden's face.

"Are you sure?" Caden asked, turning her gaze back to Jade.

Jade pivoted on the couch to face Skye. "I'm sorry. I saw the demon...attack you. I s-saw...I saw you laying in a p-pool of blood, its gray skin and claws..." She looked like she was barely holding it in, her throat working double-time.

Skye swallowed. "Did you see when?"

Gah! Why would you want to know that? But, she did. It was something her mother never got a chance to tell her before she died. She'd merely assumed it would be soon because her mother's visions came to pass shortly after. And later, when months had past, she concluded it had been a hoax on her mother's failing mind. It never happened. Skye still lived with that possibility in the back of her mind, but *nothing ever happened.*

"I don't k-know, b-but soon. You looked the same as you do now. B-but..."

Her teeth were chattering, the cold-shakes kicking in.

"But what?" Skye pressed. God, she needed to know. If it was true and there was a way to stop it from happening, she had to try. Maybe this was a sign that she was to take action.

Why else would she be given two warnings, or be told of her death by two different people, if she wasn't meant to prevent it?

No, this wasn't going to happen, she told herself. Just because her mother had foretold the same thing coming to pass meant nothing. It had taken Skye years to convince herself that the vision might be wrong.

Seeming calmer, Jade cleared her throat. "You weren't here. You were gone."

"Gone?"

"Like you had left on a mission. By *yourself*."

That didn't make any sense. She never went anywhere alone. Her power, or whatever the hell it was, was still too volatile. Why would she take off on her own when she knew how damaging one little slip of her emotions could be? While she could control herself better, calming herself, she still feared it getting away from her at the wrong moment.

What if someone attacked her in the middle of a crowd and she panicked? How many people would she kill? Or what if she got scared at a club for some reason and destroyed the whole building, people and all? No, that wasn't like her. She wouldn't go anywhere without at least Caden for help.

See, her mind chided. Irrefutable proof this curse hanging over her life couldn't be true.

Not only that, but with Jade barely able to control her ability, it was best they both stuck around to guard the portal hiding under their stone fortress, *together*. Skye would never leave Jade alone with that responsibility. If anything happened to the portal, there was no telling what the consequences might be. With Caden, Brooke, and Mckenzie frequently taking off on one mercenary gig or another, that left Jade and Skye.

"You know I would never leave like that." She gave Jade a weak smile trying to smooth away her tears. It wasn't her fault some higher power gave Jade the gift of sight. Well, maybe not so much a gift, Skye thought.

"There's more," Jade said. Her color had come back, the shakes subsiding. "There was this...clock."

"A clock?" Skye scrunched her face.

"Like...a watch. I'm not sure. It was black, the face of it

broken. But it had this band around it. There was a date on it, or beside it? I don't know, but it felt wrong."

"Wrong, how?" Brooke asked.

"Like time wasn't the same. Or maybe it *was* the same..." Jade pressed her fingers to her temples. "Again, I don't know."

"It's okay," Skye said.

"There was a number. A ten. I kept seeing it. And then there was this man, but not a man. He came here." Jade closed her eyes and shook her head while they all waited for her to gather the memory. "The ten seemed important somehow. I kept seeing it, over and over again. It felt like time itself."

Jade shook her head, again. "Weeks? No, that isn't right. Days? Time didn't seem much different. Days...yes. Ten days." She opened her eyes and looked at Skye. "Ten days after the man comes..."

Skye tried to smile, tried to level her breathing.

"That's when I saw the demon," Jade continued. "Ten days after the man that isn't a man comes, you leave, and then the demon..."

"Kills me," Skye finished. None of that made any sense.

Caden's forehead creased. "Maybe it's a fluke. A man that isn't a man? What if your vision doesn't come true for once?"

One could only hope. Those were Skye's exact thoughts as well. It was too unlike her.

Taking a deep breath, Jade let it out. "Maybe you're right. Stranger things have happened."

"Besides," Caden said, turning a smile on Skye, "We've known about this vision your mom had for a while, now. It's been years, right? Everything Jade sees happens within moments of her seeing it. She's never been able to see into the future that far. Do you see any men, here? And ten days is a long time. You can't say it will happen for sure. Even if it's true, there's plenty of time to stop it. It's not like some man is just going to walk in here, you know."

Skye couldn't help but wonder at that. A man in their hide-out?

"And if not," Caden said, "Brooke can always zap you back to life."

Brooke shot Caden a look of pure horror. "You know I don't have that kind of power. I can only zap small things back to life. And even then, it doesn't always work out right."

Caden rolled her eyes. "It was a joke. I was trying to lighten the mood." Straightening the knives along her right thigh, she groaned. "In any case, I'll go down to the basement and check on the portal, just to make everyone feel better."

Skye wanted to stay and comfort Jade more, but she needed to see the portal with her own eyes. "I'll come with you." She wasn't going to simply sit around if her life was on the line. What if what Caden said was true? They had never had an opportunity to prevent Jade's visions from happening. It *had* been years since her mother's prediction. If it *was* true, maybe she had done something in that time to stop it from happening. If so, she could do it again. The only way a demon was ever going to get near her was if something happened to the portal; if the gateway faltered and demons were allowed access to the human realm.

At least, that's what some of her mother's ramblings had said would happen if a portal ever fell. The rest of her journal had been barely readable, like the parts about a Guardian's power.

"I'm sure you have nothing to worry about, Skye," Brooke chimed in. "Jade *did* say you weren't here, so as long as you don't leave, everything should be fine."

So, what was she supposed to do? Never leave again because her next adventure would be her last? She was being held back because of something inside her she knew nothing about, and now this?

She was getting her confidence back; had begun arguing her case with Caden and the others. After years of being on the sideline, practically her whole life, Skye wanted to get out there, explore, become a mercenary or start her own clothing line... Something, anything but be stuck in some dilapidated ruin they called home. With another Guardian about to be around, she would finally be able to leave on occasion knowing Jade wouldn't be alone. She could go with Caden and Mckenzie on missions and not get left behind, or set up shop somewhere and sell her clothing.

Well, that's the way it *would* have gone. Now she was to be stuck here? Indefinitely? All in the name of staying alive? Jade said ten days after some man came, she would leave and that's when the demon would kill her. Ten days *after*.

There's nothing to worry about, she told herself. She could fight this. She could win. There was no way in hell Skye was going to end up like that woman in the movie. She was *not* a pushover, and if some demon thought she was going to just die peacefully...well, they had best think again. If she had to dig in her heels and claw her way through a hoard of demon slime, that's exactly what she would do, but she would *not* be caged like an animal.

Her mother's vision was wrong. Jade's vision was wrong.

She wasn't going to die, and she definitely wasn't going down without a fight. Even if Jade was right, she had plenty of time to figure this out.

If whatever demon Jade and her mother saw standing over her lifeless body wasn't a hoax, she'd make it wish it had never crossed her path. There wasn't a demon in the world she wouldn't kill.

Chapter 3

Khaine stood transfixed, gaping at the stone archway before him.

Impossible.

Symbols swirled and danced along the outer edge, illuminated by the magic they held. He brushed his palm along the left side and traced the column around to the back. The middle was barren, a blank space where a gateway would rest when the portal was open. Save for a few minuscule chips of stone that had fallen to the marbled floor, the portal was intact; operational.

Impossible, his mind seethed again.

All this time searching and the fucking Lykae had one under their noses?

Rage threatened to ensue him, but he held it at bay, able to push those vile thoughts aside because he was finally here. All those years of searching; over.

He was getting Raiden back.

As soon as Bastian deciphered the last rune required for the ritual and the planets aligned…

Khaine pressed his hands to either side of the archway and hung his head. He shouldn't get his hopes up so soon. The planets wouldn't be in the right formation for over a week. That was ten days and six hours. Bastian had said he would have the translation of the rune, but still…

His nails dug into the stone. Anything could fucking happen before the planets aligned. *Anything* that hadn't already.

Why didn't the Lykae meet him when he crossed into their territory? He knew their kind were daft, but he never expected them to be that ignorant. There was no resistance as he treaded the woods, determination mapping his way. The trees had been eerily quiet. While that hadn't unsettled him, it had pulled his demon from the pits. He'd been ready to lash out if necessary.

Lash out, his mind reverberated in his ears. Anticipation was clouding his actions; he needed to stay attentive. A part of him wished the Lykae *had* crossed his path. Ridding himself of this pent-up frustration, this ever-growing pit of abhorrence and ferocity, would have schooled him enough to focus. That was the sole reason Bastian sent him here. He couldn't have known there would be a portal still standing. No, he'd sent him to kill something and calm himself.

Instead, Khaine had made it to the underground tomb without interference. He'd thought he'd sensed a presence to the North, but he'd let it go, in no hurry to delve into matters he didn't serve. When he came upon the stone fortress, falling and savagely kissed by time, there were no lights or signs anybody had been there in ages.

Brush had molded itself like vines along the outer rock, twining up the stone only to fall away and hang. On one side, what was once a window was now bedding itself on the bottom blanket of ground where dust had sat for so long it became piles of dirt collecting along the wall like trim. The tomb was well hidden, surrounded by thick trees on all sides. If one weren't looking for it directly, it might never have been found.

There was a slight hum he thought might have been a generator, but who would squat in such a place? It was Lykae land. The Lykae didn't live in such crumbled conditions. They had actual homes. But then again, they weren't known for leaving their territory unguarded, either.

Khaine had shoved his predatory instincts aside and entered the large underground chamber through an outside access. When he laid eyes on the gateway, all caution had left him.

Lifting his head, Khaine surveyed the scattered debris around him, his mind heavy with sleep.

I'll sleep when my brother is in my fucking arms. There would be only nightmares to greet him, anyway.

Trash littered the white marble around the slate archway. There was a perfectly clean circle under him, stretching three feet in either direction like it had been swept back to keep the portal uncontaminated.

More signs of another's presence?

Someone had been here, recently.

Cans and wrappers strung themselves over concrete benches and lay wasting away in towering alcoves. Mold consumed the musky atmosphere, the smell of mice seeping into what remaining air was left. Several strategic mirrors on the far wall were angled to catch light from the hole he entered through, but bits of glass lay strewn around the dust under them. With what was left, they caught some of the last rays of sun from outside, illuminating areas with beams of orange and red; enough for his predator to see without trouble.

Winter was catching up fast, which meant the sun had fallen under the woods only moments ago. The moon would still offer the mirror ample reflection and being underground meant the cold night would be mostly diverted. He could stay here tonight and fetch supplies in the morning from the nearby town. He would defend this portal with his life. He couldn't believe it was still standing.

Kicking some of the trash aside for a place to rest, he stilled when a sound echoed over the high walls. His senses went into overdrive; hammering at him. His demon half rose to the surface, unguarded, unchecked. It stirred under his skin, forcing a guttural sound from his throat. Khaine slunk into the shadows. A beam of light bounced down a hall on the other end of the enormous space as footsteps rang close behind.

The Lykae?

No, he didn't smell the danger of another immortal. Whoever they were, these beings were mortal. Perhaps deviant teenagers looking for a place to party, he thought. Mortals were predictable.

Shadowing himself behind a large pillar of stone, Khaine waited in silence, his demon on edge, barely slumbering. He'd wait these trespassers out, or if need be, uncage his monster if they posed a threat. There wasn't a mortal alive that could best him. Half the Province was already on his tail. Even they hadn't overpowered him, but he wasn't worried about himself. His insides reeled with the thought of losing the one thing he'd just found. Nothing would be tearing it down, ripping it from his grip. His brother would be walking out of the portal's glassy surface one way or another.

Soon, brother.

Khaine had already caused them all so much pain in the past. He *needed* to get this right; redeem himself.

Shifting his feet, keeping his eyes trained on the intruder's entrance, Khaine steadied the thick soles of his hiking boots before they knocked the aluminum cans strewn around him. Voices reverberated from the tunnel and ricocheted throughout the enormous hollow chamber.

Female?

His jaw slackened when two women emerged, flashlights darting bright light over every ghostly crevice. Sucking himself back when the rays flickered over the column he stood behind, Khaine braced his palm against the cold surface to peer out. He glared at them.

What the fuck were they doing here? And why alone? There was no sign of someone with them, no other voices drifting close behind. When did mortal women venture into the woods to explore an abandoned temple by themselves, at night, no less? Had they grown that naive since the last time he encountered them?

Khaine watched the two enter the darkening space, their gazes on everything as if expecting carnage to impinge on their presence. He narrowed his eyes. The two women were quiet, pensive, nearing the portal with slow, cautious steps.

Too close for comfort. He clenched his fists.

Khaine assessed them, one dressed in a full leather suit, her brown hair tightly restrained high at the back of her head. Her leather boots clicked along the marble, taking precautions not to disturb the surrounding trash.

Maybe there was a party. A costume party?

Something pulled his gaze to the other female. Khaine's eyes snapped to her and held, drinking in the sight. She was facing the other woman, but what he could see of her was riveting. Her blonde hair reflected the flashlight she darted around her, golden strands highlighting champaign waves as it twirled around her back, bound by a small band against her neck. Moonlight gathered on the glittering jewels of her blue shirt, the slight fabric accentuating her smooth, creamy skin.

His eyes dipped lower to her bottom, covered in formfitting black shorts that revealed more than they wanted to cover; small sequins stitched around the back pockets and shining as they bounced with her movements.

Khaine dug his nails into the column beside him to still himself.

When was the last time a woman roused him so methodically?

She was saying something, but damn if he could hear.

Her legs were parted, ever so slightly, just enough for him to wedge himself between them if he chose. Khaine gritted his teeth at the thought of burying himself there, taking his release along with her. How long had it been? Ten years? A hundred? His mind could no longer think, let alone fathom anything besides tasting her sweet womanhood.

"...Skye...demon..."

Fuck, she bent over. What he wouldn't give to wrap his arms

around her waist and stake his claim on her.

Palming his shaft through his jeans, that only succeeded in arousing him more, Khaine clenched the stone column, his nails cutting into the hardened surface, lengthening with his rising tremor of excitement.

Focus, you fool!

Demon?

What were they saying?

Why was this female affecting him so much?

Shaking his head, Khaine drummed down his raging arousal to listen. What did these mortals know of demons?

Gods, if only she would turn around. What would her face be like?

"Everything will be okay, Skye," the brunette said, twisting in a shadowed corner behind the portal. He couldn't see her frame anymore, but his senses told him exactly where she was. It didn't matter anyway; his eyes were riveted to the other woman.

His cock pulsed and he reached his hand into his dark-blue jeans to adjust himself, gain more room.

Khaine played the name across his tongue; Skye. How fitting, he thought. She looked like a storm about to arise. The back of her was exquisite.

Turn around.

"You don't know that," she said. "Even you know Jade has never been wrong. And what about my mom?"

The brunette emerged from behind the portal, out of the dim light to point at its surface. "Look, it's still standing."

"C'mon, Caden. You know that means nothing. What if a demon comes out? We don't know enough to say it won't.

Then what?"

A demon? So, he hadn't been mishearing them. Testing them with his instinct again, he still didn't sense anything immortal about them. There was confidence in the way they held themselves, but nothing otherworldly.

"Then we kill it," Caden, the brunette he now noticed had a sword strapped to her back, said.

He froze.

No, it wasn't possible. Khaine tried to calm himself. He closed his eyes for several long moments, gritting his teeth. Blood seeped into his mouth as he bit into his cheek. Could they indeed be Guardians? That cast had been killed off hundreds of years ago. After the demon prince murdered their village, it had dispatched demons all over the world to exterminate any Guardians remaining. He was sure none had survived. It was a miracle the remaining portals hadn't fallen as well.

If these were true Guardians, they would likely kill him on site for being what he was. His jaw ticked, the stone wall beside him crumbling under the force of his hand. Shards of concrete tumbled to his feet, echoing in the enormous chamber. His eyes snapped open.

Guardians. Kill them!

They were the reason Raiden sat rotting in Hell! The reason they were cast out from their village and told never to return!

What had their people said to them?

"If ye come back, ye twill meet death. Be gone, foul demons!"

That's right, he reminded himself. When Raiden had then tried to warn them, they attacked him instead. Khaine had been too late. They were all too late.

How differently things would be if their own people hadn't

abandoned them!

Shifting his attention back to the two, he froze. They were peering in his direction, the sound of his sudden outburst no doubt grasping their curiosity. Khaine molded himself into the darkness and hung his head, willing his body to blend with the surrounding shadows. He waited in silence, utterly motionless, only relaxing his shoulders when they seemed to disregard the noise and move again, the sound of their movements spurring him.

He looked back to see Skye taking measured steps toward the portal and reaching her hand to run along one of the runes, her back to him once more. Her voice was a whisper, as if speaking the words alone would cause the ceiling to part and lightning to rain down on her for her treachery. "What if we destroyed it?"

He tensed. No breath came to him.

"We can't say for sure what will happen. Maybe nothing."

They mean to take Raiden away from you!

Calm yourself, he thought. Breathe. No. Guardians would never do such a thing.

He'd kill them before they got the chance.

Kill them anyway! They forsook you!

Caden eyed the portal as well, a look of hope marking her features.

Stop them!

His back straightened, his nostrils flaring. The stiff muscles in his legs shifted, causing his boot to collide with a metal can beside him. Khaine gritted his teeth at the careless mistake.

Be still!

The women whirled back toward him, Caden with her

sword drawn in his exact location and Skye sliding behind her, her flashlight beaming over the wall beside him. Caden's eyes scanned where he stood, but it still didn't seem either of them could see him. Not surprising. People only noticed him if he wanted them to. They were mortal; a mortal's eyesight could never match a demon's.

Caden inched forward, her flashlight darting rays of light. "Who's there?"

His nails dug deeper, pain setting in as one broke off. Khaine shifted to the side in case their eyesight was keener than he thought.

"A rat. Let's get this over with, Cad. I don't know what else to do. It's worth a try. Jade said ten days after this man. What if her vision *is* right? Or what if she got it wrong and it's ten days from now? I can't live in fear for the next ten days, maybe longer. Maybe my mom was also wrong and nothing will come from destroying the portal. You saw her journal, it was hard to read *anything* useful. Besides, maybe *you* were right and her vision was meant to be stopped. What if it's the only way?"

Khaine peered out from the column. Caden stood in silence, still assessing his shadowed corner.

Turn back, Guardian. This isn't your fight.

Skye touched her arm and she relaxed.

"We can't be sure nothing bad will happen," Caden said.

"Do you have a better idea?"

"She said you weren't here. Destroying the portal might not stop it from happening. A lot can happen in ten days."

"What am I supposed to do? Hide out like a coward? *Wait* for something to happen? That's not who I want to be, and you know it." Her voice rose an octave as she spoke.

There was a fire to her that Khaine found himself drawn to. What did she think was going to happen to her?

"I'm done hiding," Skye said, this time a whisper. "It's time for me to *do* something."

"And you think destroying this portal is the answer?"

Skye threw her hands up. "I don't know what the answer is. As far as I know, they're both wrong."

"Are you sure? This portal is the only reason we're here. Protecting it was the only thing your mom ever asked of you. What if destroying it makes things worse?"

They paused for a long moment, so long his muscles locked as he awaited their next move.

Skye bit her bottom lip and nodded. "Let's give it a try. I never asked to protect it anyway."

Don't do it.

"Fine," Caden sighed, seeming to reluctantly cave. "It's your portal; your decision."

"What's the worst that could happen?"

"The sky could open, demons could rain down on us, bust through the stone ceiling, and kill us all?"

"That's not helping, Cad. Besides, according to Jade, my time isn't up, yet."

"Yet, being the key word, there." Caden propped her sword against one column. "C'mon," she said, pushing on one of the stones. "Won't know until we try."

They meant it? They were going to destroy his last shot at getting his brother back.

Not a godsdamn chance in hell!

Khaine kicked the litter by his feet aside, pushing himself from the wall to glare at them. Their eyes widened as he strolled forward, backing them away from the portal and snarling. Distance, his mind churned. *Keep them away.* Nothing was getting between him and the stone archway now at his back.

Khaine's eyes connected with Skye's. He hadn't bothered to look at them when she'd turned around, had been too preoccupied with their plans. Now?

Fuck, her appearance almost made him falter. He side-stepped to hide his break in stride.

Stray strands of hair covered her left cheek, swaying around her stormy, blue eyes. They seemed to swirl with gray clouds, dancing against the white light she was pointing at him. Yes, her name suited her.

Khaine trailed his eyes down her small nose, landing on her slightly parted lips. What would it feel like to have those soft edges part around his cock?

Gods, he was growing hard again just thinking of it.

Thinking of a Guardian giving you release?

Khaine shook his head and growled.

Never!

Skye repositioned herself to stand by Caden, grabbing a knife he hadn't noticed from Caden's right thigh. His mind had been too preoccupied to assess them. Not anymore. If they meant the portal harm; they were a threat. He didn't entertain threats lightly.

What the Gods had granted him with; two tokens in one laughable move. A portal to bring back his brother, and Guardians, the means to his revenge.

Now that his thoughts were clear, Khaine could see the arsenal of weapons strapped to Caden's body. The sword in her hand that she'd expertly grasped from the portal's side when he appeared, knives down both thighs, and he thought he caught a glimpse of a pistol strapped to her lower back. Mortal or not, she meant business.

It didn't escape him that Skye was sporting a *lack* of weapons. Save for the knife now pointing at his chest, she was unarmed. Not that any of their weapons could harm a demon such as him.

Well, the sword could, should it grace his neck in the right spot and cut deep enough.

Not likely.

"What is your business, here?" he growled. He couldn't wrap his mind around the plans he overheard. A true Guardian would never destroy a portal on purpose. They knew what that would bring.

What did it matter? Who cared what their motivation was? He had two Guardians standing only yards away, his brother's escape at his back. Why was he stalling? Had it been so long that one fucking woman had him acting against his instincts?

"Could ask you the same thing," Caden spat.

Skye elbowed Caden in the side, whispering something in her ear. Even with his keen hearing, the only words he could pick out were 'man' and 'in our hideout'.

He disregarded their side talk and stifled a laugh, pacing a short distance in front of the portal's arched opening. He kept his movements light and voice even. "I'm staking my claim. This tomb belongs to me, now."

Skye scowled at that, perfect white teeth glinting behind her full lips. "That would mean you were here first, but you weren't."

His lips curled. Then it *was* a generator he'd heard. They

were living here?

How could he be so fucking stupid? Of course they were. Guardians stayed as close as possible to the portals they protected. How many others were here? Ten? Fifty?

Not for long, he thought. He would slaughter them all.

Then why aren't you making a move?

Frustrated by his own thoughts, Khaine spread his stance, ready for them to attack if they thought they could. Let them try, his mind seethed. The exertion of raw power would dwindle the storm rocking him. Not being stopped by the Lykae on the way in had his demon begging for something to kill. He twisted, his hand rising to rest along the stone beside him, letting them know who this tomb now belonged to. They wanted to destroy it? They'd have to get through him, first.

Caden smiled and addressed Skye in a sweet voice, never taking her eyes from him. "What's our play?"

Skye didn't hesitate. "Straight for the head. Slice clean through. No holding back."

He smirked. "Are you sure that will kill me?"

Skye narrowed her eyes at him. "Mortal or immortal, decapitation kills anything."

So, she wanted to play? Why did the notion excite him?

Kill them and be done with it!

Reaching his right arm above his head, Khaine gripped his blade, hidden by a rune, masked in invisibility. One of his favorites. "Reconsider."

That one word, layered in his demon's many voices, would cause any Provean to scatter.

He gripped the hilt as Skye took a step to the side. "Not a chance," she said.

"You wish to fight? Tell me, how do you see this ending?"

"You die," Skye said, her voice matter-of-fact.

His lips curled. Him? Die? "Have it your way."

Caden lashed out first. She sliced her blade through the air with precision, her body fluent and speed unexpected. Nothing that mattered. He dodged the blow, turning on his heels to keep them both in his sights. Caden swung again, this time clipping his shoulder when he unsheathed his sword. Khaine heard his blade clang against the steel of hers when she brought it back up, hammering it down on him with what would have been a fatal blow, but he pivoted at the last minute and caught Skye about to sink her knife into his back.

Khaine shoved her aside with his forearm as Caden's sword came down on his other arm. He winced at the pain, then dodged another blow and swung his blade.

Skye was getting back to her feet, charging him. He ducked her attack and called on his demon, his speed increasing. He kept the beast caged, only drawing subtle amounts of strength.

He never revealed his true power to an enemy until it was too late, for them.

Caden jammed the heel of her boot into his side, sending him crashing backward against the portal. He fell to the ground.

Him, on his back?

Fuck subtle!

Why was he encouraging this madness? He shouldn't be playing this game. He could kill them in one move!

Black blood trickled down his arm.

Both women stood mere paces away, Skye with an innocent smile and Caden's face smug. Their flashlights had been scattered to separate corners of the room, pillowing their attacks with light. He got back to his feet, moving in a way that was more animal than man. It unnerved people. Gave him the edge. They regarded him instantly, assessing his next move.

"Had enough?" Caden asked.

Khaine shook the excess blood from his arm, the cut already healed. Caden seemed to follow the motion.

"Not mortal, then?"

Skye narrowed her eyes. "Doesn't matter. We'll still take your head."

He grinned. "Will you, now? It would seem I have the edge, human."

Before he could blink, Skye launched a knife at him, hitting him in the leg. It stuck deep, the tip embedded in bone, and anger blurred his vision. She would think to catch him off guard!

His demon half pounded his chest, demanding retribution. Who was he to deny his monster revenge?

Gritting his teeth, Khaine pulled the knife free and shucked it aside. He dove for Skye. She was the least armed, now. He could take her by surprise, use her as leverage, kill the other and finish Skye off last, but she seemed to anticipate his move as he punched Caden in the chest and watched her fall. Skye rolled from his grasp at the last second, sending him staggering back. *Not enough.* She'd made a valuable mistake.

He turned when she moved around him, failing to gauge his speed like she should, like one versed in immortality might presume. Snatching Skye's arm, he pulled her into his body.

And stilled.

Fire snaked up his right side, burning his chest with searing intensity. As a reflex, he gripped her arm harder while she lashed out. His eyes caught hers and she sucked in a breath.

Pain! Sweet, pulsating pain. Khaine's teeth sharpened in his mouth, cutting his lip. He fought to breathe around the fire in his chest, but blood collected in the back of his throat, momentarily choking him. His claws sharpened, his back straining to keep his demon side tucked securely in its cage. His cock surged at the pleasure racking him.

No! It couldn't be. This wasn't happening. Not now.

Words danced in the back of his head, one more than the others.

—Mate—

No! Not her; not this.

She was a Guardian, the only thing he despised more than demons.

Kill her!

No, that wasn't right. Protect her, his mind shouted. *Protect your female!*

Khaine closed his eyes and shook his head.

Fuck! This wasn't the time or place. All these years and some higher power chose *now* to grace him with his mate?

A punishment, his mind churned.

He opened his eyes, astounded. His female. His *Guardian* female, that currently had a knife edged at his throat. She must have stolen it from Caden's thigh before he attacked. Her eyes darted from his teeth, to his eyes—that were sure to be black—to his shoulder where Caden had sliced his flesh. He could see the moment her mind realized what gripped her, his black blood not helping his cause.

Fear arrested her features and she called out. "Caden!"

Before Khaine could react, a sudden blast hit him square in the chest, knocking him into the air. Too shocked to catch himself, Khaine roared as he fell. His back slammed down on a concrete bench. His spine snapped, bone grinding against itself. The sound of it rocked him, the feel of it debilitating, but he couldn't move. He was dumbfounded, stunned, and angered beyond reason.

He'd just found his mate, and she'd tried to kill him.

Chapter 4

A tingle worked up Khaine's legs.

He severed something. From an explosion?

She means to kill you!

Bits of rubble came down around him. His ears were ringing, he could only see the debris falling, couldn't hear it or move from its path. A chunk of stone collided with his forehead, knocking his head to the side. Another connected with his wrist, instantly crushing the bone. Blood pooled over his brows, the warmth of it seeping into his eyes before he wiped it away with his other hand to clear his vision. It would be several moments for his back to heal enough for him to move and the dust encasing the room to settle. It smelled of burnt clay and seared varnish, choking him. Khaine cried out as the bone in his wrist popped, healed, popped again.

What the fuck did she do to him?

A female's moan in the distance.

Shouting.

More Guardians?

I'll kill them all!

Propping himself off his back with his elbow, Khaine maneuvered himself enough to ease the pain. Jerking his torso to the left, his back snapped, whatever he'd severed starting to heal. A burning sensation engulfed his legs as the blood flow returned all at once.

Doesn't fucking matter!

Bellowing a sound of pure rage, he pushed himself off the concrete bench and stumbled to unsteady legs, ignoring the agony the motion caused. His eyes caught sight of Skye, the dusted air clearing, her silhouette visible through the wall of smoke. She was leaning over Caden, blood dripping from Caden's head, soaking away the dirt to stain the white marble hidden under years of soil. He could smell it, see the dark liquid.

Skye seemed unharmed.

Anger boiled inside him. Why did he care? She'd tried to kill him. A *Guardian* had gotten the better of him. His *mate* had tried to kill him.

Stepping forward, intent on exacting his revenge, a shift in the air turned his gaze to the right.

Khaine froze.

"No..."

His heart sank, his mind unable to comprehend the sight. Black smoke gathered, twirling in the air above a layer of rubble. Stone columns lay in a pile where the portal once stood, blasted to bits while the smoke above it began to solidify. It grouped into a single shape before his eyes.

It was gone. The portal; destroyed. She'd done this. Somehow blew it up. Any second now, demons would have their freedom, but all he could do was stare at the spot where the gateway had been not moments before. Khaine shouted, the sound bouncing around the large chamber, his corded neck swinging his head around in search of his blade.

The black smoke collided and formed a rippling surface. Voices hammered him from the other side of the room, but he couldn't focus on them right now. He needed his fucking sword.

A tentacle emerged from the dark watery abyss, snaking out to test its new realm. Khaine peered at the crumbled remains of the bench he'd crushed, spotting the glinting of steel under a large chunk of rock. He reached for it as the first demon pushed itself through the glassy void.

The demon, gray leathery skin and eyes the shape of hammers, shook out the spikes running along its skeletal body. Khaine reached down with both arms, wedging his foot in a small crevice before gripping the black onyx handle of his sword. Dark eyes found his movements, disregarding the other voices in the chamber with him.

Mate. Mortal. Protect!

He needed to slaughter this demon before it noticed Skye. Pushing the rock with his foot, the large stone dislodged itself, giving him enough access to grasp his blade and pull it free.

Just in time.

The demon charged Khaine as another emerged close behind. Followed by another, and another. There were too many. He couldn't fight them all at once and get to Skye before the demons did. Something hammered his insides.

Fear?

Frantically, Khaine's eyes scanned the space where Skye sat, relieved to see others had gathered around her and Caden.

More mortals?

More Guardians?

Doesn't matter, he gritted to himself.

Fuck, he couldn't be sure, though. The demons now surrounding him were clouding his senses. He couldn't smell anything but immortal, rotting flesh.

"Skye!" Khaine called out to her, hoping to get her attention. She was bending over Caden with her head hung low, not moving. He didn't know if she was aware of the threat so close to her. Female Guardians couldn't defend themselves against an attack like this; at least not with so few numbers.

The steel of his blade sliced through the air, his gaze riveted back to the demon barreling toward him. It caught the creature's neck and cut a straight line clean through. Bone cracked, blood spraying his eyes. His demon half laughed, that bitter sound channeling straight through him. Disregarding the head that fell to his feet, Khaine swung again at the second while more filed out of the portal's entrance. If he could get to the remains, there was a rune that would seal the gateway, preventing more from coming through. If not, the portal would remain open until dawn when the first rays of light sealed its void. That was hours away, and thousands of lower cast would be free.

But he needed to keep his demon caged. Letting his beast loose would serve nothing. He needed to be rational, attentive, and seal off the portal before more demons got out. His body was still healing, and the pain told him that changing to his demon form wouldn't make that better.

Khaine shifted on his feet, the rubber soles of his boots dancing effortlessly among the rubble. Something to his right caught the moonlight filtering over the mirror and his eyes pivoted.

Mistake!

A demon, claws sharp and pointed, sliced his left arm, cutting the skin all the way to bone. He roared and jammed the blunt end of his blade into the demon's jaw, knocking it back enough to swing a fatal blow. Its head toppled to the ground before he chanced another glance at what had caught his attention.

Skye stood with two other females, Caden's sword in her hands while she lashed out at a pair of demons. The other females followed suit.

What the fuck is she doing!

She was going to get herself killed! She was a mortal female, no match for what she was fighting. He should punish her for being so naive.

Khaine needed to get to the portal; now.

Bashing his way through the throng of demons, Khaine managed to get close enough to see the pillar he would need to inscribe the rune on laying under a pile of rubble, but he couldn't etch the symbol and battle the hoard at the same time.

Lightening laced the air around him, sparks flying past him and hitting any demon that emerged from the crumbled remains of the portal. He couldn't make sense of the origin.

More demons emerged, uncaring of the lightning lashing them, their unnatural frames funneling around the chamber. The graveling sound of teeth gnashing drew his mind to focus.

Several now huddled in an alcove off to one side, seeming to assess their attacker's next move. He followed the eyes of one, landing its blackened gaze on the women trying to fight them off, and he jammed his elbow into the demon about to latch onto his right arm, spinning around with his sword outstretched. It connected with the demon's head before he spun again and bashed the hilt into another's throat.

The motion crippled the creature and Khaine reached out with his left arm before the demon could recover, gripped its neck, and sank his claws deep. Thick, black blood sprayed Khaine's eyes as he ripped its throat out, roaring at the satisfaction. There were too many.

More came, surrounding him. Skye's shouts rose above the chaos, drowning out his thundering heart. He couldn't do this on his own, not in mortal form. He would never be able to kill the hoard of demons, etch the symbol, and save Skye at the same time. He would lose.

Never!

Rage engulfed him, blocking out all possibilities of failure. It no longer mattered if his body was still healing, he would fight through the pain. Khaine opened the cage and let his demon take over. His back convulsed, his chest tightening. He jammed his claws into an oncoming demon and tore its heart free.

Hunger. Fury. This was what he was. A monster.

His sword became a second arm to him, pulverizing anything in his path. Demons fell at his feet, heads ripped from their shoulders. Another advanced on him, then fell. Then another... No, it too fell. He was fighting them back, but more came, the portal all but pushing them out of its glossy depths, now. He had to close it.

Ignoring his mind's cries for blood, Khaine slaughtered his way toward the crumbled remains. Another walked into his path, snarling. He sliced it to pieces, but not before a second swung at his abdomen, cutting him.

Good, he thought. He'd need the blood.

Khaine gripped his side, filling his hand with his black blood while he fought to hold the demon attacking him at bay. At the last minute, Khaine fell to his back by the column, shoving his sword out in front of him before the demon delivered a fatal strike. The steel stabbed the creature in the neck. It wasn't enough to sever its head, but enough to keep the demon back with a boot on its chest while he ran his blood-soaked fingers along the pillar's surface.

In moments, the rune was cast and the portal began to close.

Kicking at the demon littering his blade, Khaine dislodged his sword from its neck and swung to sever its head. Getting back to his feet, adrenaline fueled him, giving him enough strength to cut through three others, making his way toward Skye and the females fighting beside her.

She was still standing.

Aw gripped him. She was a woman, a mere mortal, holding her ground against the demons surrounding her. Then she was stupid, Khaine seethed. Even the others aiding her, fighting them back, had no idea what they were doing. The demons dropped at their feet as he continued his advance, but their idiocy was palpable.

What the fuck was his female thinking! Yes, he'd definitely punish her for this.

When the last one in his path had fallen, Khaine sprinted

forward and sliced the head off the remaining demon about to sink its teeth into Skye's arm. Its head fell at her feet and rolled to a stop by her slipper-covered foot.

Black blood covered her hair, falling in waves down her face and chest. The other two females seemed to just notice him, and one, ankle-length red hair lowlighted with the demon's remains, held her arm across Skye's stomach to back her away. Currents sprang from her palms as her eyes bore into him.

An Eabrith. She was the source of the lightning.

Khaine heaved several breaths to calm his racing heart. He felt the demon shadowing his features subside, tucking itself away again.

As his adrenaline ebbed, another feeling crept in to take its place.

He turned his head back to the portal, the destroyed portal, and gritted his teeth. His mate, the one female chosen for him, had just destroyed his chances of getting Raiden back. She'd taken it from him, ripped it from his grasp.

She thought she knew fear?

Make her pay!

No, that's not what he wanted.

Protect her!

Fog clouded his mind, unable to let him think.

She's yours, his mind played out to him. *Claim her.*

Yes, she *was* his. The possibility of his brother being stolen from him had him clutching the hilt of his sword with an iron grip and grinding his teeth, but the higher powers had given him something in return. *Revenge.*

If Bastian couldn't uncover the remaining locations and discover the rune in time...

He had a mate, now. A Guardian. His for the taking. Given to *him*. He'd take his release anyway he could get it.

Sheathing his sword against his back, Khaine ran one hand over the symbol on his right arm, placing his blade back under the rune's protection. He eyed Skye standing behind the woman and growled, a sliver of a smile etching across his face. "You're mine."

The red-haired female took another step back, shielding Skye from his grasp. "You're a..."

"Demon," he finished for her. "And I'm taking my mate."

Running his palm along the tattooed rune on his left shoulder, he reached out and snatched Skye's arm before the woman could react, moving too fast for any of them to see. In an instant, they both became invisible, her cries no longer reaching her friend's ears. It was a convenient rune, one that masked his sight and sound, letting him venture unseen and unheard.

It affected anybody he touched, but it was a rune he could only use every few days. Today seemed fitting.

He bent to Skye's ear and whispered, not caring if his voice dripped vengeance. "Blast me like you did again, *mate*, and I'll take my retribution out on your body next."

His cock pulsed at the thought.

He was sure she understood when she gasped, going still in his arms.

Good, he thought. Khaine whisked her toward the opening he came through, keeping his hand tight around her waist when she climbed out in front of him. The females at his back screamed her name, but it wasn't going to do them any good. There was nothing that could save his mate, now. She was his, and he didn't give up his things easily. Revenge had never seemed sweeter.

Chapter 5

Lightning laced the dark sky when they emerged from the tomb. At first, Skye had thought Brooke was the cause, but the bolts had been otherworldly, low-lit with flashes of blue and green, then drastically altered with dark hues of red. She hadn't known what they were but assumed they had something to do with the portal. Not caring to ask the demon if he knew something about them, Skye had turned her attention to more pressing matters, like the fact that he'd kidnapped her.

"A man that isn't a man," she mumbled.

She dug in her heels, pulling on her captor's arm. Her bunny slippers slid against her feet. They were preventing her from gaining a proper grip. It didn't help to have demon blood oozing out the back, squishing in the soles every time she took a step. Fucking gross!

Skye briefly wondered how she had kept them on during

the fight, but apparently, one's wardrobe took care of itself in extreme circumstances when not thinking about it. She was thinking about it, now.

Her hair was matted against her neck, creating an uncomfortable feeling, and the further he dragged her, the more agitated she became. This had gone on long enough.

Caden was back there, lying in her own blood because Skye's damned emotions had run the gauntlet again. Had she really thought she could control her fear better? How wrong she had been, and now Caden was probably dead. Just one look at the demon and everything she'd worked so hard for had been undone. Caden had been breathing when Skye left her on the ground, but what if her injuries were more severe?

She tried once more to pull her arm from Khaine's grip of death, her agitation taking on a life of its own. Any minute now, she would be clawing at his back like a banshee.

When he didn't budge, merely kept dragging her along like she was some reluctant dog, Skye snapped, pulling back on her arm so hard she thought it might pop from the socket. "Stop!"

He did then, turning and backing her against a nearby tree, driving her with his large frame. His voice dripped hatred when he snarled, "do not think to tell me what to do."

Blood was smeared along his jaw, wiped across his eyes, and muddied his blonde hair to a dark, marbled paste.

"You can't just kidnap me. I don't even know who you are!"

He jerked a step back and regarded her, his eyes flashing to black. Good! She hit a nerve.

Quickly regaining himself, he tilted his head to one side, gliding that raven gaze over the swell of her breasts. Unashamed. Brazen. She wanted to cover herself, hide the effects of cold air across her nipples, but he trailed his eyes back to hers and held them.

"My name is Khaine Reeves," he scowled, "and I can do whatever the fuck I please with my mate."

Why did he seem so *displeased* with the notion?

"I'm. Not. Your. Mate," she gritted.

Khaine. Where had she heard that name before?

Realization hit her square in the stomach. Mckenzie. She'd mentioned him, the half human, half demon that murdered an entire immortal bar trying to track down a single Witch. He had to be the most hated immortal in the Province. Even Mckenzie wanted to sink her claws into him. She'd barely been able to make it out alive, the only one who had, or so she'd relayed to all of them when she returned from her last excavation. Not a purebred demon, then. A half-bread. His visage resembled that of a man now, not a creature.

"You *are* my mate, *Guardian*."

"How do you know what I am?"

They made it a point to keep their faction secret since they didn't know much about themselves, which meant they knew even less about their weaknesses. As far as they knew, her and Jade were the last of their kind. To survive in the Province, you either had to be known for your ruthlessness, or damned good at faking it.

Suffice it to say, Skye hadn't survived by being ruthless.

Instead of answering, Khaine gripped her arm again and continued his tirade of dragging her through the dark trees. The blood that had long since dried to a crusty canvas along her arm didn't seem to sway him.

Skye peered down at her slippers and scrunched her face.

Mud and twigs had gathered around the outer edges of the bunny's noses, hitching an unwelcome ride. The once-white fur was now entirely muddled with demon blood, and she thought she caught a glimpse of flesh hanging off one side of her right shoe. She couldn't be sure though, with the lack of light to see by, but if they weren't already ruined, he wasn't helping the cause.

Who was she kidding? Blood didn't just wash out! Those weren't shadows being cast over her feet. Or her jeweled shorts.

Oh God, my shorts!

It had taken her days to hand stitch all the jewels and even longer just to find the fur to even *make* the slippers.

That's beside the point, she told herself. He had no right to drag her along!

"Let me go! You're ruining my slippers. I can't even see where I'm going."

"*You* ruined your slippers when you destroyed the portal. Or do you need a reminder of the damage you've caused?" His deep voice dripped with hatred.

Skye shrieked as Khaine shifted his hold and picked her up, throwing her over his shoulder like she weighed nothing. When he settled her over his ridged back, she beat on the curve of his spine and screamed. "Help!"

"Yell all you want. We're miles from your little tomb. Nobody will hear you out here."

"Where are you taking me?" She gave up her struggle, allowing him to relax and hopefully loosen his grip.

A low rumble vibrated through his body, seeping through her chest. He seemed angry. What did *he* have to be angry about? She was the one slung over a demon's shoulder, being dragged through the darkness against her will.

Well, she was being carried through the darkness against her will, and on the verge of now *losing* a slipper. It was almost too much, like the fact that she had damn near single-handedly destroyed the one thing her mother begged her to protect. Okay, maybe the demon was right. It *had* been her fault, and maybe she *had* decided to destroy it, anyway. But still... Let the demon take it from her? Ha! She didn't have to. She practically gave it to him right before blasting it to bits.

And to make her situation worse? She'd just been kidnapped by a demon. *A man that isn't a man.* Skye could hardly process that information. And not only was Khaine a demon, he claimed she was his mate.

The fuck I am. No way in hell was she going to be this thing's mate. Skye pounded her fist into his back as hard as she could.

He twisted his head and inhaled.

Did he just smell her?

"Put me down!" she wailed.

This had gone on long enough. All she wanted was to make sure Caden was okay, *gods, please let her be alive,* take a nice hot shower, and gouge out any traces of Khaine from her mind.

Khaine shifted his hold, startling her. Skye landed in the dirt, her back splayed over damp patches of grass. Before she could move away, Khaine was on top of her, blocking her from escaping. He snarled and dipped his head to her neck, breathing deeply.

Did all demons have a fetish for smell? She couldn't exactly speculate, since every demon she'd ever come across never lived long enough. She'd never encountered a half-bread before. Where was her sword when she needed it?

Skye lashed out with her right hand, but he caught it, pinning it above her head. When she tried to strike him with her left, he grasped that one as well, restraining it with the other.

Her heart thudded in her chest and her body strained to get free.

The stubble along Khaine's jaw brushed her face. "You smell of a storm, too." He shuddered.

What the hell does that mean?

Skye could feel his chest heaving above her as he took in her scent. Apparently, being covered in demon slime had a trivial effect on his mounting excitement.

She felt him press his growing shaft to her thigh and grind his hips. The bulge in his jeans pulsed, stilling Skye and causing a surge of heat to flare between her legs.

His rich smell engulfed her, a mix of old wood and scotch. It was masculine, causing her insides to react like never before. When Khaine threaded his fingers with hers, she hardly noticed his grip loosening. Despite the muck covering every inch of him, there was something erotic about the way his body moved over her, the way his breath sent a warm shiver down her sides.

It was all she could do to keep herself from turning into him, letting his lips brush across her aching mouth.

No, wasn't going to happen. This was wrong. Why was her body responding?

He turned his head then, rising above her to peer down, his eyes locking on her lips. They were fully black, blending with the blood on his face, making him look every bit the demon she knew he was.

Half demon, she told herself. *A man that isn't a man.*

Despite being trapped by the thing she feared most, her body seemed to answer to him, her legs spreading beneath him and her breasts rising to his chest of their own accord.

"Let me go," she breathed, not sure she meant it.

When had she ever been beneath a man in this way?

"Why?" His voice husky, Khaine bent down and licked a trail along the skin of her neck. "I smell your arousal."

Uh-huh, she thought.

Wait, no. Not aroused!

His hand slid down her arm, brushing the sensitive skin with his callused palm, gliding to the hem of her shirt and easing under. She sucked in air at the contact, his fingers splaying over her stomach, working their way to her breasts. Her hips rocked to meet his groin. The feel of his hands on her skin sent electric jolts through her body.

"Wait."

Khaine groaned in her ear, the deep sound sending another jolt of pleasure through her. "Never, female. You're mine."

His. Right.

No, wait. Not his!

What was she doing? She hadn't spent her entire life trying to gain her independence for someone to come and take it from her. He thought he owned her?

She wasn't a fucking object.

Gah! The nerve of him. That was all it took to snap her brain out of whatever trance it had fallen into. Skye thrashed her body underneath his. "Let. Me. Go."

Khaine gripped her wrists tighter and growled. "Do I sicken you, female?" His even white teeth flashed in the moon's dim glow as he shifted himself to face her, his fangs grasping her attention.

"You're a demon," she voiced, breathless, as if that should give him his answer. How could Skye forget that? She was laying on the ground, under a demon, getting aroused by the prospect. She should cast herself into a pit of fire to burn away the feeling of his breath on her, his mouth working over her flesh. Of course he sickened her!

"Half demon," he grated.

"A demon is a demon."

He snarled, his voice clipped. "And what of you, Guardian? I should kill you for being what you are."

She might not know much about the Province and the beings that inhabit it, but she *did* know a thing or two about mates. Every immortal had one, and some waited thousands of years to find theirs. Skye also knew that no immortal could ever harm their mate. While some called them different things, they all revered them as the same priceless treasure. To lose a mate was the same as losing one's life. Few were able to continue living after that, and many ended their suffering shortly after.

Skye lifted her chin. "You can't hurt me."

His face twisted with what looked like rage, but he released her wrists and bounded to his feet as though she'd scolded him. Moving a few yards away, he began to pace by a large cottonwood. The moon hovering above the trees offered enough light to gauge his features and she took the opportunity to look her fill.

If he wasn't a demon, she would have been lost in the sight of him. Despite being fresh from a battle with blood covering every inch of his body, he was still a sight to behold. His thick, dark-blonde hair, slightly curled and falling about his shoulders, tapered to dense strands around his face and danced as he repeatedly ran his fingers through it, completely uncaring when they got entangled in dried gore.

His black T-shirt was cut across his stomach, but there wasn't a single injury on the smooth surface underneath. Whatever damage he'd sustained had already healed. Only black shapes that disappeared behind the material graced his skin, now. Likely more tattoos similar to the ones running up both arms, full sleeves that seemed to intertwine with one another. They appeared to be symbols, much like the ones that used to mark the portal.

His muscles were honed, with broad shoulders and strong caves. Whatever this man did for a living seemed to work for him. He could easily break her if he wanted. There was nothing to stop him from killing her, despite some inner voice demanding the opposite.

Skye could see why the Province hadn't captured him yet, and likely never would.

She should tread carefully. Just because she knew immortals never hurt their mates, didn't mean this man couldn't prove her wrong.

So, he's a man, now?

Skye shook her head and looked away, but she couldn't keep her eyes from Khaine long.

As if abruptly realizing she was still there, Khaine stopped his pacing and faced her. "Why do you find me lacking?"

He seemed to frown at his own question as if he didn't mean to ask it.

"What?"

He snarled. "Lacking. What other reason could you have for

not acknowledging what your body needs?"

Sex? He was angry because she didn't want to have sex with him?

"Ohh!" Standing, Skye dusted herself off, kicking away her slippers all together. "I don't sleep with demons. Get this through your thick, blood and ooze and...and...gore encrusted head! I won't *ever* have sex with you, mate or not."

It wasn't. Going. To happen. She saw what he was. Back at their hideout, when he had stalked up to them in his demon state, her mind had shot warning signals all through her body, hammering at her to both run and kill him at the same time. The only thing that had kept her standing was Brooke's arm across her stomach. How could she ever forget that?

His face had been masked with a shadow of something sinister under the surface, black blood slithering through the veins in his face, forming gray streaks that ran along his jaw with dark circles hovering under his black eyes. Fangs had hung from his sneering lips with blood dripping out one corner of his mouth. His body had been larger, muscles wider, stretching his clothes to the point where she thought they might rip apart from the strain. She even noted the set of claws; each one sharpened to a point. Even without the grey skin of a purebred, there had been no mistaking what he was.

No, she'd been careless to forget. Never again.

He was a demon; her a Guardian. The two didn't mix. It was just...forbidden. Whatever higher power thought this man should be mated to her was playing a sick game.

Besides, there would be no getting sexual with him or *any-body* else. There was a vivid memory floating around in the back of Skye's mind of the one time she *had* gotten sexual with someone, and they didn't even get to the good parts.

No, he'd be keeping his hands to himself or she'd find a way to take his head, sword or no sword.

Chapter 6

G ods, her smell was intoxicating. Khaine hadn't been able to think about anything but burying his shaft inside her after he caught a whiff of her sweet scent. When she'd demanded he put her down, he was driven to oblige.

She'd responded to him almost instantly. Her breasts had risen to brush provocatively against his chest and her legs had parted, just enough for him to position himself between them. Fuck, everything had been lost to him at that moment. He couldn't even remember what he'd said that upset her so un-expectedly.

Like his question. Why the fuck did it matter if she found him lacking? He wasn't here to entertain her idea of him; he was here to get his brother back, a mission she'd so easily wrecked.

But damn, the thought of being between her legs had his cock aching to be back there. What the fuck was happening to him? How could one woman steer his mind so wickedly?

Things had gotten out of hand. She'd somehow managed to derail him from his course for a moment, it wouldn't happen again. The second time a Guardian had gotten the better of him?

Khaine ground his teeth together and flared his nostrils.

That's right, his mind chided. A Guardian. He had just been humping his hips between her legs, about to rut in his pants. For a Guardian.

Khaine pounded his fist into the tree beside him, leaving a splintered hole. *Don't care.*

He should walk away from her, leave her alone and never see her again. If only it were that simple, he thought. *No* immortal had ever been able to abandon their mate. It was unheard of. They each had an unmistakable pull to them, one that proved impossible to ignore. Wherever their mate was, you could bet the immortal wasn't far away.

No, he was stuck with her, and he couldn't decide what sickened him more. What she was, or what she was to *him.*

Stalking over to Skye, Khaine gripped her left arm and pulled her to her feet, blocking the punches she thought she could land. He held her in place and glowered at her. Thick, matted strands of blood-soaked hair were caked onto the sides of her face, tussled in the back where frayed strands had come loose from the band against her neck. Even in the dim light of the moon, he could see her perfectly, his demon an expert at sight. Smeared marks that looked like black war paint muddled her once striking features, and still he found himself aroused by her.

A low growl broke free from his throat. He hated her, hated

her kind for what they did to them all those years ago. Nothing about this female should be waking his lusts. He wasn't a weak man, and he wouldn't let himself feel inadequate because she thought of him as such. Her view didn't matter. He had bigger things to contend with, like finding another portal before they were destroyed as well.

Khaine ran his calculating eyes over her body, not hiding his assessment of her. He hardened his face as though she repulsed him. "Understand this, woman. Your kind will never satisfy me. If I ever release seed in your presence, it's not something I couldn't do in another's. You're a disgusting breed with no honor, and I won't be brought to your level by thinking you don't feel the same."

Her features twisted. His words had hurt, but Skye didn't let them affect her long. She scowled and jerked her arm free from his hold. He'd lashed out, intent on making her suffer anyway he could, but it appeared this woman was too strong for his tactics.

So far.

He would break her before they were done.

Taking a step back, Skye inclined her chin. "If you find me so repulsive, then you have no need of me. I don't want to be your mate any more than you want me to be. Let me go."

He smirked. "Never."

"You don't understand. Caden is back there. She needs me!"

Pleading, now? For a mortal? Perhaps she wasn't as strong as he pegged her to be. In this, he could hurt her, and hurting her was only the beginning of his revenge. "You don't need her anymore."

"She's my family!"

"Your family?" he yelled. Right, because they were all what he despised. "You have no family, Guardian. You will *never* see them again. *I'm* your family, now."

Her words like a whispered warning, she stared straight into his eyes. "You don't understand. I *need* to go back. You can't keep me from them. I'll kill you."

Khaine laughed. "I welcome the try."

"How do you think this is going to go? I'll bend to you? Introduce you to everyone I love as mine? You're a demon. They would never accept you. To them, you're the disgusting breed."

"Ah!" Khaine grabbed her by the throat, his fangs inches from her face. "You *will* bend to me. I'll make you break, just like I did everyone else who crossed my path, female. You're not strong enough to escape me. You'll never be free of me. I'll send word of your death to your *family*. They'll never come looking for you. Face it, woman. I'm all you have. And just when you get used to having me around, I'll leave you on some deserted plain to spend the rest of your useless life alone."

Tears welled in her eyes, her cheeks flushing. There, he thought. Not strong at all. It'll be easy to break this one.

So why did her pained expression leave him with an overwhelming need to comfort her? The tear that fell from her right eye sent a stabbing sensation straight to his gut. He balled his fist where she couldn't see and released her, frowning.

Skye brushed a few loose strands of muddied hair from her face and did her best to harden her features, but he saw through it. She could act strong all she wanted, he knew better.

A vibration of sound drifting through the trees turned his head to the south. He thought it sounded male, like a sound of anguish, but it was too far for him to gauge its purpose. It didn't matter. He pivoted back to the woman before him.

Seeming to take a page from his book, Skye scowled at him and lowered her voice to a dare. "I welcome you to try."

Fascinating woman, he thought. Perhaps breaking her wouldn't be so simple. Her determination sent a feeling coursing through him he hadn't felt in some time. He stamped it down and buried it. He didn't have time for this. He needed to get back to his car and the sat phone laying on the passenger seat. Bastian would be awaiting his call, hopefully with good news.

Running his fingers through his own blood-encrusted hair, Khaine narrowed his eyes on her. "You can either walk of your own accord or be dragged by mine. Make your decision."

"I'm not going anywhere with you."

"So be it."

Before she could react, Khaine bent forward and hefted her onto his shoulder, her legs dangling under the grip above his chest. She protested, clawing at his back, trying to kick him in the face. The muscle in his bicep bulged, constricting the flow of blood to the smooth, creamy skin around her ankles, making it take on a bluish tint.

Another sound reverberated in the still night, coming from the same direction as the last. Khaine twisted with her in his hold. He tried to home in on it while she continued to rail at his shoulder blades.

"Be still!"

"Not a chance in hell!"

Movement through the tree to his left.

He couldn't hear around her pounding fists against his

backside. His agitation welled, throwing any patience out the window. Khaine brought his hand down on her bottom, palm cupped to lesson the impact. "Stop your squirming."

Her voice an octave higher than he would have liked, Skye shifted over his shoulder as if trying to face him from behind. "Did you just spank me?"

He raised his brows. Had he?

"Put me down, Khaine! I'll walk, okay. Just let me go."

Shifting her off his shoulder, he set her to her feet, not caring to catch her when she stumbled and landed in the dirt beside him. Khaine sniffed the air. They weren't alone, and this time, it wasn't mortals.

Khaine caught the distinct scent of an immortal close by, perhaps two.

"I'd rather walk than have your hands on—"

"Quiet!"

Something was headed right for them. Two somethings.

The Lykae?

Fuck. He was hoping he wouldn't have to deal with them. He thought it strange that he'd managed to traverse their territory without interference. It looked like his luck had run out.

"Get up," he gritted.

Not taking his eyes from the dark trees creating shadows in the distance, Khaine chanced a sideways glance at Skye beside him. She was looking in the same direction as him, all previous anger depleted.

"What do you see?"

Two large figures were moving in their direction. Definitely Lykae. There was no way her mortal eyes could see what he saw, not in this light, and not at that distance.

"Get up," he told her again. He might have to fight these two and didn't need her getting in the way.

Skye got to her feet and brushed dirt from her bottom. "I don't understand. I don't see…"

The two dark shapes moved closer, her eyes seeming to finally pick them out.

"Lykae," he said.

She moved in front of him. "They're coming this way."

"Get behind the tree and stay there."

Turning to face him, Skye smirked. "Why? It's you they won't like. You're in their territory. *We*, on the other hand, have a right to be here. McCain gave us his protection in return for keeping the portal under control."

He glowered at her. "Do as I say."

Gave them his protection? If the Guardians were under McCain's protection, the two Lykae could be here to take her from him.

They can fucking try.

The two Lykae stepped around a tree, close enough the moon shone over their features. Darren and Devain. He knew these two. They were right and left hand to the Lykae king. Next in line for the throne. Princes. McCain sent them on his most pressing missions. He had run into Darren, once; could probably take the Lykae if he had to. His brother, Devain, was another story. He was said to be devoid of a soul, completely vial and merciless. Hence the names; Darren the Cruel and Devain the Ruthless.

The McCoy brothers in one place? That was a rare oddity.

When Skye didn't show signs of moving, he pressed his hand to her shoulder and gave her a shove toward the tree beside them. She groaned but moved to stand behind it as the two Lykae strode up, their faces indifferent. Darren's eyes were blue, something he hadn't noticed during their last encounter.

That meant he'd found his mate.

Good, he thought. A possible weakness. Khaine chanced a look at his own weakness huddled in the dark beside him, a smirk on her face and arms crossed. She thought these two were going to save her? He slammed the door on his laughter, but not before it was replaced with thoughts of what made him think she was his weakness.

Despite Darren's blue eyes, his short, brown hair, that was slightly shaved on both sides, was still the same. His usual blue-jeans with strategic tears down both legs and maroon T-shirt hadn't changed either.

His brother, Devain, sported dark jeans with a black T-shirt, tucked behind what looked like an iron belt fashioned into the shape of scales. He had heard stories of how that belt was made, but none he believed.

With brown eyes and dark, brown hair shaved to a mohawk and slicked back with gel, Khaine could easily tell the two were brothers.

Another weakness, he thought.

Darren stopped a few feet from where Khaine stood, his eyebrows rising. "Khaine?"

Devain stepped beside his brother and narrowed his eyes. "The demon that murdered everyone at Lesters?"

"Aye."

"What of it, dog?" Khaine said. So what if he murdered everyone in that immortal club? The Witch shouldn't have angered him.

"There's a hefty price on your head," Devain said, his demeanor calm. "One we could easily collect."

"I don't think your brother would risk his mate for a payday." Khaine rose an eyebrow in Darren's direction. "If I'm not mistaken, your eyes have taken on a more *caged* glow." Darren scowled at him, so he smiled. "What's the matter, dog? Trouble with the misses?"

Darren flared his nostrils. "Let me kill him!"

Yes, let them try, his mind chided. Perhaps he could ease some of this tension Skye provoked.

Devain tilted his head, seeming to measure Khaine's worth. "What of you, demon? Tell me, does your mate return your interests?"

His head inclined to the tree Skye stood behind and Khaine followed his gaze. Lykae were known for their keen sense of smell. He likely picked her out based on the demon blood covering her from head to toe, but their eyes were equally acute. They could have spotted her long before they approached. As for pegging her as his mate? A lucky guess. His scent was probably all over her.

"Leave her out of this," he growled.

"McCain offered his protection to these women. If she wishes to be free of you, it's our duty to see her safely home."

Skye stepped away from the tree, then. "How did you know where I was? Did Caden send you?"

Her eyes looked hopeful. Khaine fought the urge to strangle her again. Still thinking about that damn mortal?

Darren stood, tense.

"Sorry, lass," Devain said, the tone in his voice delving to a warmer note when addressing her. "We were simply in the area."

He'd cut his fucking tongue out.

"Who are we to stand in the demon's way when he's found his mate?" Darren asked.

Khaine watched the exchange of looks between the two Lykae in silence. It seemed the brothers had had a falling out. To his advantage?

He took a step toward Skye, just in case.

Devain eyed him. Trying to gage his intentions? When he looked over at Skye, apparently non-pulsed to see her covered in blood, he nodded. "It would seem my brother wants to give you a pass, demon, but these lands are private. The vampires would have no second thoughts helping us with your escort out of them. See to it that you don't wander into our territory again."

"Just like that?" Skye said. "You're going to let him leave with me? You don't understand. I *can't* go with him. What about my family?"

"We'll see to it they know you're safe."

"Safe?" she squawked. "He's a demon."

Khaine growled at her and she grew quiet.

Darren shot him a look of understanding. How the fuck could he possibly understand?

"Consider this a boon, demon. I'll collect on it later," Darren said.

He stalked off, headed back toward what Khaine could only assume was the Lykae's clan, his shoulders rigid.

Devain seemed to be waiting for Khaine to acknowledge the agreement, so he nodded, sealing the deal. They would let him walk this time, but that meant he owed the pair a favor in the future. Not a problem, he thought. He wouldn't be coming back to these parts.

He watched Devain follow his brother back the way they came, cutting through the shadows and out of sight in seconds. Skye stood beside him, her jaw clenched.

"Some form of protection," she mumbled.

"Let's go."

"You can't force me to go with you," she groaned.

Khaine cocked his eye, reminding her of all the times he already had. Her shoulders slumped in defeat, but she followed him as he made his way back toward town where he would find his car waiting. He had things to do. She could bristle all she wanted, and while she was at it, tell him what her power was.

That blast that she knocked him with back at the tomb was rare. He hadn't struck on it before because his mind was a ball of chaos, but it seeped into his thoughts the moment Darren and Devain acknowledged what she was. In all his years, he'd only seen one Guardian with that anomaly. The woman had been taken away and never seen again. Some said she was killed because her destructive nature was too volatile. Others said they let her live but told her never to return.

All Khaine knew was that it meant she had another power deep down that she hadn't learned to tap into yet, and he was going to find out what it was. His mate would keep no secretes from him. He'd learn all he could about her, then use it against her.

And if he got another taste of her? That was just a plus.

He concluded that she was given to him for a reason and he was going to capitalize on that at every opportunity, whether it be revenge or sating his desires. Before this journey was over and Raiden was back from Shrodah, he told himself he'd do both.

Chapter 7

Caden clenched her teeth and let Jade continue smearing the ointment on her head, globbing it in her hair. She tried to rub her sweaty palms against her legs, but the leather of her catsuit made her hands slide across the surface instead.

The overhead light in the kitchen was killing her eyes. She fought Jade's hold on her forehead to look down. God, did her blood condition suck sometimes. Not only did she feel weak, but every time Caden moved her head even the slightest, she thought she might retch. Her stomach was a twisted knot of nausea.

"Don't move," Jade said.

"I'm trying," she gritted.

Jade brushed her finger on a sensitive area and Caden winced. "Ow."

"Sorry, but you won't let me stitch this up."

"We don't have time for stitches. We should be out there,

looking for her."

"I told you I would lead, get a good distance toward them and you could follow later," Mckenzie said.

"Not a chance in hell. Give me five minutes and I'm coming with you. If she's been kidnapped by who you say..."

Mckenzie had made it back with the girl only moments after that demon took off with Skye. As soon as Caden was conscious, Mckenzie tried to leave, head them off before they got too far. Caden wasn't letting Mckenzie leave without her. No fucking way. She would be good enough to go in a second, she'd thought.

That second had turned into an hour, then two. Now? Caden glanced at the clock on the wall and groaned. "Hurry up, Jade."

"I'm going as fast as I can."

Brooke leaned against the far wall, her red hair braided down her side like Rapunzel. "Are you sure it's this Khaine guy that took her?"

Mckenzie picked at the dirt under her claws, a bored tick. "Blonde hair, medium-length with a slight curl, dark, brown eyes, stubble along his jaw cause the bastard can't shave, six feet tall, built like a tank, tattoos all over his body... Oh, and a demon. Did I get all that?"

Brooke groaned. "Fine. But he *did* claim she was his mate. Immortals can't hurt their mates."

"That doesn't mean we're leaving her with him," Caden said behind clenched teeth. "How could you be so wrong, Jade?"

"I'm sorry. I didn't know."

"She was just kidnapped by this 'man that isn't a man.' You said she had ten days *after* he came."

"The visions aren't always clear. I didn't know," she ground out. "Now we do."

"And now she's out there with him. Ten days. Are you *sure* about that part?"

"Yes."

Caden flinched as Jade hit another sensitive spot. "Then that means we only have ten days left before..." She couldn't say it. Didn't even want to think about it. Damn their situation. If Jade would just hurry up.

"Was it him? Is Khaine the demon that kills her?"

Jade paused. "I don't know."

"What do you mean you don't know?" Brooke asked.

"I...can't be sure."

"We're going to kill him," Caden said.

"I've been waiting a long time to sink my claws into him," Mckenzie cut in. "He murdered those immortals like it was nothing. Granted, they were low-class beings, easily dispatched, but that didn't give him the right. If anybody is killing the demon, I'm first."

Her voice was laced with a hint of reprisal. This had been on her to-do list ever since she got back from that trip four weeks ago, waiting for the right opportunity. If not for Skye, and herself begging Mckenzie to wait, she'd be out there right now, looking, tracking him to whatever safe corner of the world he thought he could hide in and clawing his insides out.

Jade grabbed a roll of gauze from the med kit and tried to unwind it with her free hand, dropping it on the kitchen floor. It bounced over the roll of laminate they had laid down to cover the dirt. Caden bent to retrieve it from her position on the stool.

"Don't move!" Jade cried. "I just got the skin back in place. Stay facing me."

"I got it!" Sophie exclaimed, hopping off the counter by the sink and scurrying over to the ball of gauze by the mini-fridge.

It didn't appear anything could set the nine-year-old on edge. She had been a big ball of joy ever since Mckenzie brought her back, and attached to Mckenzie like she was her mother. Caden had a sneaking feeling that something had happened while they were gone, but neither of them had said anything about their trip. Not that they'd had a chance. Something in Mckenzie was also different, though. Every time she peered at the girl, some part of her softened. Mckenzie? Soften? Not a chance in hell.

Caden didn't even know what the girl's ability was. So far, she didn't seem to have visions or an innate ability to blow things up.

Plus and double plus, she thought.

"Here you go!"

"Thanks, Sophie."

Caden sat still while Jade wrapped the gauze around her head.

"There. How does that feel?"

"Completely. Fucking. Awesome."

"It looks pretty damn good, Cad," Mckenzie chimed in, the corners of her mouth twitching. "Bleach your catsuit and you have your Halloween costume."

Now she was cracking jokes? What had happened while they were away?

Sophie scrunched her face, seeming to not understand the reference. She bounced back and forth between her neon-green shoes, her lip quirked and mind searching. "I get it," she said at last. "A mummy!"

"Yes, Sophie," Mckenzie smiled. "A mummy."

Sophie ran over to Mckenzie and pulled on her black, leather skirt. "Can I be a mummy for Halloween? Do you think Cas would be one, too?"

Caden swiveled on the stool. "Who's Cas?"

Mckenzie straightened and then turned what looked like a mother's trained eye on Sophie. "Sophie..."

"Oh, right. Sorry. I forgot."

"It's nobody," Mckenzie said.

Right. It didn't sound like a nobody, but Caden had other things to worry about besides drilling Mckenzie on some mystery person. Skye had been alone with that demon for almost three hours, now. They were likely miles away, if not out of town already.

"Get my sword. I'm ready."

She slinked off the stool and then gave the surrounding light time to settle. Even with the dark rocks encasing them on either side, decaying and dull, the overheads still seemed too bright in the small room.

"Can I please go?"

"We talked about this, Sophie. You need to stay here with Jade and Brooke. They'll take care of you."

"Why can't I stay with Cas?"

Another pointed look from Mckenzie. Caden raised her brows at her.

"He's not here right now. You stay with them and I'll be back soon."

He? Who had Mckenzie met?

Mckenzie's phone went off and she pulled it out. "A message from Devain."

"It can wait," Caden said.

Mckenzie's face turned molten. There were few ways to thoroughly anger her beyond reason, and a text message usually wasn't one of them.

"What does it say?"

Mckenzie read the message, her voice a steel razor. "We intercepted Khaine Reeves with your sister Skye. He's promised not to harm her. They headed East."

"Are you fucking kidding me!" Caden rubbed her head and tried to calm herself. The sudden rush of blood to her head did little to ease the dizziness.

"He must have bargained with something if they let him go," Mckenzie said.

It didn't matter. None of it mattered. Not right now, anyway. McCain would hear about it later, though. He'd offered them protection. How was letting their sister go with Khaine protection?

Mckenzie tucked her phone away. "We don't need their help to get her back. Are you sure you're up for this?"

Caden wasn't sure of anything. There was a splitting jolt of pain reverberating in her head, her hands were clammy, and every time she moved, she thought the room was moving with her. She'd lost too much blood, but she wasn't leaving Skye out there alone. She had to be terrified! Although, terrified in Skye's case might not be a bad thing. It could help her escape.

"I'm fine. Let's go."

Mckenzie was right, they didn't need the McCoy brothers. Mckenzie reached over a chair against the wall and retrieved

Caden's sword from the makeshift counter. Caden had used it as a plainer to scrape away at dead tree limbs, enough to fashion a workable surface. Aside from that, they had a fireplace that Brooke knocked in, using her lightning to blast a hole through the six feet of stone so they could cook food in a cast-iron pot. Jade dubbed it her Witch's pot, even though she wasn't a Witch.

Caden took her sword and sheathed it. "If something happens, go to the Lykae. McCain still promised to help if we needed it. Just doesn't seem to extend outside of our property," she ground out.

"Right," Brooke said. "And what about you? What are you going to do?"

Was she serious?

"Find Skye."

Brooke rolled her eyes. "And Khaine?"

Mckenzie strapped a set of knives to each leg under her leather skirt, then belted on her leather breastplate. "Khaine's as good as dead."

As soon as Caden replenished enough blood to not feel woozy, with her and Mckenzie, that demon wouldn't know what hit him. She hadn't protected Skye this long just to let her die. With Jade's recent vision...

There wasn't much time. Skye was with a *demon*.

She hardened her face and strolled out of the front entrance to their fortress. The only good demon was a dead demon. She'd make him wish Skye had done the honors. As it stood, her and Mckenzie would play it out as long as possible. How many times could he regenerate his dick, she thought?

Chapter 8

Skye was in deep shit, now. If everything else Jade said was true, which at this point she would bet money on it, that meant she only had ten days left.

Skye leaned against Khaine's black BMW M4. She saw this car in a magazine not long ago. When all she had was time—and she wasn't fretting over a new clothing project—she'd often sit and read the Teen Vogue magazines they'd stashed. This car had been pictured in one of their full-page advertisements, complete with a full description and specs. With the upgrades, it came with an eighty-thousand-dollar price tag, and being his, it felt damn good to rest her bloodied backside on it. What she really wanted to do was pet it and purr in its ear.

Not to a demon's car, she told herself. How in the hell did a demon end up with an M4, anyway? Under any other circumstance, she would have been drooling over the sleek, black finish. Instead, she bounced up and down, letting her crusty clothes and pocket sequins gouge a few marks. Take that, demon!

Khaine peered out from under the trunk's hood and glared at her, his hand resting on the side. "This car is new."

Like that made a difference, she thought. Skye snorted. In fact, that made her tactics better! Having to repaint this car would serve him right for kidnapping her. Not only that, but her favorite bunny slippers had been lost and the clothes she wore, that took her weeks to stitch with all the tiny blue sequins—some that were now missing—were beyond repair. Blood stained; there would be no getting it out. Black or not, they were ruined.

"So?" she said, her arms crossed.

For the last two hours, she'd done nothing but demand he let her go. Eventually, her demands had turned into pleas, then persuasive arguments. At one point, he'd cut her off to ask what her power was, to which she grew confused and answered with another round of pleading. He hadn't budged. She even tried to make a run for it, waited until he'd dropped his guard and poured all the energy she had left into throwing one foot in front of the other. The damn Neanderthal had actually let her run for a couple hundred flipping feet before he tackled her, shoved his body over hers, and in a voice that made her stomach do happy somersaults, said things she refused to ever acknowledge.

It was at that point that she entertained the idea of telling him *why* he needed to let her go. She squashed that thought before it could fester. She didn't trust him, and with the way he was acting toward her, she figured he wouldn't care.

Fine, she'd bristled. If she was going to be stuck with him, she was damn sure going to make it the most unpleasant experience he ever had. But, realizing she wasn't going to get away from him had made other thoughts creep into her mind.

He was a demon, and despite her being his mate, that gave her no reassurance that he wouldn't be the one to do her in. The better part of her life had been spent with the understanding that a demon would, possibly, one day kill her, and now here she was, in the presence of a demon, being forced to follow him blindly. Ten days, she told herself. He could be the one to kill her in ten days. That was *if* Jade hadn't been wrong about that, too.

While he'd made a call on a sat phone he retrieved from the passenger seat, that Skye desperately needed to get her hands on, Skye had tried to convince herself that he was only *half* demon, but somehow, she thought that wouldn't matter. She then worked her brain over the events that took place back at the hideout, trying to replay every aspect of him. There was a key piece she was missing.

Slanting a look toward the back of the car, she tsked.

"Was that your demon?"

When silence followed, Skye elaborated. "Back there, when you...changed."

The thick arms along each tree shook with a gentle huff of wind, making a rustling sound all around them. The woods were dark, and before her eyes had adjusted to their new lighting, she'd been able to see in them fine. Now? Shadows seemed to taunt her, just out of reach.

Khaine slammed the trunk closed and stepped around the side of the car. Two clean shirts were gripped tight in one hand

and a jug of water in the other. His expression guarded, he inclined his head. "Yes."

"So, you don't have their gray skin?"

His eyes narrowed. "I retain a human form, simply growing larger and more defined. At times when I'm fully turned, a hint of a monster can be seen hovering over my features, but nothing like a pure demon."

She thought back to what her mother had told her. Parts of her brain had closed that memory off when she was fourteen, deeming it too much for her to handle. She had only retained bits and pieces of that conversation.

"Skye, I need you to listen."

"What is it, Mom?"

"Do you remember what I told you about my dreams?"

She set the coloring book down on the floor of her mom's room and peered up at her sitting on the bed. "That they're real? That you can see things that are going to happen and that's why you came here."

The memory fogged, closing off and coming back like it had skipped a full chapter.

"A demon?"

"I see it standing over you in one of my dreams."

"What does it look like?"

She had never seen a demon before and had no idea what to expect. A part of her wanted to toss her mother's dream aside, but she knew better. After witnessing one of her visions come to life, she no longer thought of them as schizophrenic episodes like the doctors did.

"It'll come out of nowhere. You won't be able to fight this one."

That was it. As far as she could recall, her mother never told her what the demon looked like, only that she wouldn't be able to fight it and that it would come out of nowhere. Khaine had come out of nowhere, but he hadn't posed himself as a threat. Not yet, anyway. Surely that meant he wasn't the one, right?

And Jade? What had she told her?

"I s-saw...I saw you laying in a p-pool of blood, its gray skin and claws..."

Right. Gray skin and claws. All purebred demons had the same leathery skin and sharp, gray claws. Khaine might have had claws, but she thought his were black, and his skin had been the same hue as it was before his demon had emerged, the only dark cast coming from the veins streaking under the surface.

That could only mean he *wouldn't* be the demon that killed her.

Skye glanced at him and tried to determine if that was good or not. She still wasn't safe with him, not entirely, and that didn't change the way she felt about him.

His eyes were on her as if trying to gauge what her questions entailed. He seemed to know there was a hidden reason she wasn't telling him, and that's exactly the way it would stay.

Eyeing him, he looked worn standing in the parking lot, his shoulders slumped and fingers gripped tight around the contents in either hand.

She also noted that he was presently *not* sporting the blood-stained shirt he'd had on, and his pants had been changed. That must have been what he was doing behind the back of his car while she stood there trying to add as many scratches in it as she could.

He'd parked his car under a street lamp that sat off the main road and down a slope, far enough back that any traffic traveling through this area couldn't see, but close enough to hear anything that went by. At this time of night, Pembine was all but closed down, the streets rolled up until dawn. With a total population of one-thousand people, there wouldn't likely be anybody out this late. The perfect area for Lykae and vampires to settle.

Under the crackling glow of light, Skye ran her eyes along his bare chest. Tattoos etched their way up his torso and connected to the full sleeves down either arm. She'd known they were there from the glimpse she got back in the woods, but knowing and seeing were two different things. Staring at him now, she was sure his tattoos were symbols. They were identical to the ones that ran along the outer edge of the portal, but some she had never seen before. Each one looked to be imbued with some form of magic. They swirled on his skin, the black shapes twisting with hints of blue and green that reflected under the light, making them look metallic if you stared long enough.

He knew about the existence of Guardians, the symbols on his body were almost identical to those on the portal; what else might this demon know about her kind? Was it possible he knew more than her?

Skye ran her eyes back over his muscles. They were impeccably refined and looked like he had spent years doing manual labor, but she knew that wasn't the case. A man like him would have been a warrior to his people.

Would have been, in a prior life. She didn't know much about how one became like him, but surely he wasn't born a monster. In fact, it was impossible. Most immortals were incapable of having children. Although...there were a few. It's not like she ever put two demons together to see if they could have a child.

She followed the slight dip in his abdomen down to the ridge of his jeans where it disappeared under the fabric. No underwear. At least, none she could see. If he *were* wearing underwear, they were tucked so low they didn't register. There was a trail of hair from his navel that no doubt ran all the way to his shaft. Demon or not, this man had been made with precision, sculpted from perfection. In any other circumstance, Skye would have welcomed being his mate.

"Look your fill, Guardian?"

Her gaze shot to his and her cheeks grew warm. His eyebrows drawn tight, he thinned his lips and glared at her. His voice had sounded strained, a hint of annoyance under the surface. The heat in her face blazed like an inferno as he watched her.

He might not be the demon that was destined to kill her, but she *definitely* wasn't safe with him. Her damn biological clock was hammering at the space between her legs, begging her to fill it with this male. Apparently, her inner woman didn't recognize what he really was, under all that impeccably polished muscle.

No, not safe with him at all!

Besides, what had he said to her? That she was a disgusting breed? He hated her as much as she did him, the only difference was she had a good reason. Her mother had drilled it into her the best she could that demons were not to be trusted. She was a Guardian. It was her job to kill demons.

And yet, this one still lived! There must be something wrong with her, she grimaced.

What had she ever done to him to make him hate her? They had never met before tonight. Was it the fact that demons were supposed to fear Guardians?

Though, he didn't appear to fear her so much as despise her existence. There had to be some other reason.

Khaine tossed one of the shirts to her and she caught it, his arms flexing as he uncapped the jug of water. Setting it on the shadowed pavement beside his feet, he took the other clean, black shirt and ripped it down the middle on both sides. The fabric gave like paper between his hands.

He bent and placed one half of the shirt by the jug, then picked up the container and poured a liberal amount on the torn material, using it to clean the worst of the blood from his face. Dousing the cotton with another generous chug, he rubbed it over his arms and neck, wiping away what remaining blood was left. He then turned the jug over his head and used his other hand to wash what he could from his hair, slinging it side to side to shake off the excess. Black tinted water cascaded over his shoulders, trailing down his sides before he could soak it up. When he was done, there was hardly anything still showing. There were patches in the crevices of his ears and a few streaks lowlighted under his chin, but nothing too noticeable. His tattoos helped to conceal anything he had missed. Khaine wrung out the piece of cloth and dried himself the best he could.

Watching a man clean himself had never seemed so fascinating. The way the water molded itself to his skin with tiny drops darting away from the pack. She wondered if his skin was as soft as the water made it look. Would he enjoy her running her hands over his chest like that?

Skye mentally slapped herself.

"Get yourself cleaned up," he ordered.

His words shook her out of her fantasy and she darted her eyes back to his. "With what?"

He capped the jug and tossed it to her along with the other half of the shirt he'd ripped in half. She caught the jug, managing to keep a sure grip on the undamaged shirt in her hand. The shirt Khaine had cleaned himself with landed by her feet. She bent to pick it up.

Skye cast him a bewildered look, then surveyed the contents she held.

"You've got to be joking," she half said under her breath.

"Take off your clothes. You can wear the shirt I gave you. Use the water to wash out your hair."

"And if I don't?"

Open mouth, insert foot, she thought. All he had to do was speak and whatever fantasy she might have been having about him was ripped to shreds. His cocky attitude and demanding demeanor was already making her weary. As much as she would love to get cleaned up, this wasn't what she had in mind. A nice hot bath, complete with shampoo and conditioner, sounded more welcoming than a jug of cold water poured over her body in the middle of September. For this time of year, the weather usually dropped to the thirties at night.

Thank God for that warm front, she thought.

Still, at fifty degrees, with her limbs already fighting to stay warm, dumping water on herself didn't sound appealing.

Khaine grumbled. "I told you, this car is new."

"And the seats are leather," she shot back. He could easily wipe them off later.

His agitation seemed to rise a notch. With his forehead creased, the thick muscles in his neck bulged. "Either you wash yourself and change before getting in, or you ride in the trunk."

He was glaring at her as if demanding she see reason. In fact, all he had done so far was command her to do this or order her to do that. Skye glowered at him.

Irritating demon!

"Fine," she gritted through clenched teeth.

Scratching the outside of his car was one thing, sliding onto the leather seats with all the dirt and filth covering her from head to toe? Sacrilege. Even she had limits.

And riding in the trunk of a car was one of them.

She had to admit, it would also be nice to clean off some of the blood and grime.

She pulled on the band that held her hair in place, wincing when the tangled mess got caught and several strands were ripped from her head.

Khaine's gaze bore into her, one hand tightly fisted at his side.

Skye paused, waiting for him to turn around so she could remove her clothes.

He wasn't moving.

"You don't need to watch me undress," she ground out.

His eyes shifted, black seeping in and soaking up the dark, brown color, the whites shadowing to a deep gray. He cocked an eyebrow. "You mean the way you watched me? Don't think I didn't notice your eyes toying with me, Guardian. You'll be showing me soon enough, while I drive my cock into your sweet folds. I won't have this between us."

She flushed. Arrogant demon!

"I already told you, I'm not sleeping with you." Was never going to happen.

His face hardened. "You're mine by right."

"I might be your mate, but I'm *not yours*. I could never love someone like you."

"Love?" he said, his nostrils flaring. "Who said anything about love? I don't need love to satisfy my urges."

No, of course not. She highly doubted he knew what love was. He could hardly need something he'd never known.

She, on the other hand, *did* know what love was. Despite her mother giving her up, she had still shown her more love than most kids ever got in a lifetime. She was able to visit her mother at the mental institute, her doctors thinking it might help her mother find reality. She taught her that love wasn't hurtful and selfish, the two qualities Khaine seemed to have in abundance.

"Another reason you and I won't ever happen. The first person I have sex with will want me for more than my body."

"First?" he said, a hint of disbelief in his voice. He regarded her incredulously.

Skye flinched, a swath of heat quickly building in her cheeks. She hadn't meant to say that. He had no business knowing anything about her sex life, or lack thereof. If he didn't have such a way of irritating her beyond reason, to the point that she forgot her tongue... She scowled at him.

No matter, Skye didn't need to justify anything. She had her reasons for remaining pure, like the fear of randomly opening another portal. She would never forget the sight of that boy's mangled body.

Khaine shook his head, his forehead creased.

Wait a minute. She wanted to punish him? What better way to do that than let him see what he would never have? She had never been a bashful person. She'd had no problem taking it all off for the *best-in-show* contest at the last nightclub Caden took her to. Man, had that crowd gone wild. Granted, she'd had a few to drink and Caden had briefly disappeared to the ladies' room, which meant she wasn't there to advise her differently, but still, had she ever rocked that night! Skye could make this demon *wish* she would spread her legs for him. At least, she thought she could. If she played her cards right, she could wrap him around her finger so tight he would do anything for her. She'd watched Caden do it plenty of times to get them out of sticky situations, like a speeding ticket.

How hard could it be? Just because she wasn't versed in that area personally, didn't mean she hadn't watched Caden use that same tactic. If it worked for Caden, why not her? What could go wrong?

Skye discarded the jug of water on the asphalt and rested the torn shirt on top. Time to show this demon what he'd be missing, she thought.

Chapter 9

K haine balled his sweaty palms. She was a virgin? No man had ever touched her, his mind repeated. How could that be?

She had to be in her twenties. By the Gods, he would be her first.

No. She told him he would never have her. Because he would never love her?

Laughable. Khaine could never love a Guardian. Her people had taken everything from him!

Skye bent down and set the jug of water on the pavement, her unkempt hair knotted in a bloodied mass around her face. She righted herself and smiled, the outer rim of her mouth turned up in a sadistically provocative curve. He frowned.

What was she playing at?

The last hour had been nothing but her pleading with him to let her go.

Wasn't going to happen.

Tilting her head, Skye crossed her arms in front of her stomach and fingered the hem of her shirt. His heart stopped. Her luscious lips spread as she watched him with a heated glow. Seductive. Tantalizing.

Light spilled over her, warm radiance from above. The lamppost danced beams of yellow over her golden hair, the dark blood that had matted pieces together making her look forbidden; a creature about to strike him down. Her stormy, blue eyes seemed to size up her target.

Him. He was her target. Let her strike, he thought. He would gladly be her prey to get a glimpse of her.

He flicked his hungry gaze over her breasts, covered by the wispy fabric. He'd felt those mounds under his chest when he lay atop her in the woods. So soft. So pleasing.

He needed to see them.

He still wasn't breathing?

Don't need air!

Khaine forced himself to become rigid, as though one simple movement would change her mind.

He might be the prey, but he was innately aware of the predator nearby, stalking him, honing in. She thought she could outsmart him? He'd let her play whatever little game she was playing, revel in every moment of it. Soak it up. Take it in.

"What would you give for this?"

Slowly, Skye pulled the hem upward, revealing inch by agonizing inch of her creamy skin. Her hips that dipped sensually under her black shorts.

Khaine's cock surged to life.

Her perfectly flat stomach.

Gods, how he would love to run his palms over her smooth flesh.

Her navel, that small ring he wanted nothing more than to tongue. What sounds would she make? Khaine froze, his shoulders stiff and cock growing painfully hard. Would she moan? Scream?

Yes, scream. He'd make her yell his name while he brought her release. He could be the man that ruined her for all others. Would take her beneath him, bury his cock deep inside her.

Fuck. She lifted the fabric higher still. He shuddered. Khaine's eyes soaked up the sight before him. His demon half shifted, excitement fueling the jailed beast. *Let me see.* Then, to the rim of her breasts, those ravenous, plump curves on the verge of spilling out.

Something ringing.

Don't fucking care.

She pressed her forearms into her sides, pulling up on the shirt and squeezing her breasts together at the same time, creating the most erotic image he'd ever seen. One more inch and they would spill out for his greedy gaze to rake over.

Left as they were and he could imagine shoving his cock between them, pumping his shaft in and out of that tempting crevice below the fabric. Would she delight in bringing him to come that way? He imagined she would.

His demon half vibrated under the surface.

—Claim her—

Not yet. His nails sharpened and he dug them into his palms, relishing in the blood that pooled there. Pain. It kept him grounded. He feared that any minute he wouldn't be able to hold himself back.

The ringing was persistent now, a buzz in his ear.

Khaine ignored it.

He had to see her breasts, to devour them with his fervent gaze. Perhaps there was a hint of sorcery in her bloodline. He was enthralled. Had he thought himself *pretending* to be her prey? Just a little higher, he pleaded. There had to be something amiss, some anomaly to her body that would break this spell she'd cast on him.

"What would you give," she whispered, her lips parted in a sensual smile.

His mouth opened before he could think. "Anything," Khaine said.

"Anything?" Her voice was that of a siren.

She hiked her shirt higher still and Khaine ground his teeth, his breath lost.

What breath? He hadn't any.

Perfection.

Fuck, she was exquisite. His back strained from his cemented position, standing in front of his female while she lifted the material over her head and discarded it. He stifled a groan, his gaze locked to those two delicious mounds.

No anomaly. Nothing to deter his searing gaze from her body. She was every bit the storm he thought her to be, and she was somehow slamming those waves right at him. Yes, a sorcerous, he thought.

Ah, fuck. Her hands ran a sensual line to her shorts, edging under the waistband. He sucked in a rapid breath. Air filled his lungs, his heart thundering. Sweat beaded on his forehead as he fought to keep control of himself. Khaine scrubbed at the stubble on his face.

He took a step, faltered, stilled himself from moving further.

"Pull them down," he hissed. He needed to see what beauty those shorts covered. Would she have on white cotton underwear or a black lacy thong? Would her skin be completely shaved, or would she have hair for him to run his fingers through?

Another stutter step. His cock was hard as stone, now. Any more pressure and the pain alone would do him in.

Another blasted ring!

"Are you going to get that?" she asked, her voice sultry.

"Fuck the phone," he yelled. "Remove them."

Skye grinned and adjusted her hold, sliding her thumbs into the front and pushing them down. Just before she was about to reveal the garment underneath, she stopped and covered her breasts with one arm snug across her chest.

His frown deepened. "Why did you stop?"

She cocked her head. "There will be an understanding between us," she said, all level of sexuality stripped from her voice. Her eyes darkened. "I'm a woman that needs things, and I won't be treated like a caged animal you think you have to carry along. You agree to start treating me with some respect, and I'll finish gliding these fingers," she waggled the waistband of her shorts, "down all the way."

He growled. Clever woman. Had he thought he could underestimate her?

No, he knew she was playing him, and still he fell into her trap.

Never again.

She wanted him to be awash in her. Wanted him to lose himself so she could change the game to her advantage. And it had almost worked!

Clever, indeed.

"Wash yourself in peace, then."

Khaine gave her his back. He wouldn't be brought to a Guardian's level. She had just revealed a new piece to her game, he'd be ready for it the next time she wanted to toy with him. Khaine hid a full smile when she groaned her disappointment at his decision, then frowned. The movement felt alien to him. When was the last time he had smiled?

He scowled at the darkened woods. Apparently, her nails had dug deeper than he thought.

The sat phone in the pocket of his jeans rang. The first thing he had done when they reached his prized car was call Bastian. He hadn't answered.

Retrieving the small device from his pants, Khaine punched the green button and lifted it to his ear. A rustling sound on the other end greeted him, a gurgle of noise, then Bastian breaking through the momentary chaos.

"I've been trying to reach you."

"Likewise," he said, wondering what Bastian was doing to cause such a ruckus.

A similar rustling sounded behind him. A splash of water over cloth.

Was she naked?

He *wouldn't* look. She was no doubt eyeing him. He could feel her urging him to turn around. One more glance so she could work another spell on him.

He locked his jaw. Wasn't going to fucking happen.

"What happened to the portal?"

Bastian's question brought him back to why he was here.

His inner demon thrashed its steel bars, ramming its entire weight against them. Rage. That was what he was. He was a monster that had lost sight of his goal. Over a female?

Raiden would be turning in Hell! How could a woman make him forget about his own brother? He would never choose her over him. *Never.*

"It was destroyed," he snarled.

By the female standing behind me, he grated in silence. How could he forget that?

"I know. How could I miss the lightning show?" Bastian paused, a hint of accusation in his voice. "Destroyed how?"

What could he say? That his mate had tried to kill him the second he realized she was his? That she blasted the portal to bits in the process?

Instead of answering a question he didn't know how, Khaine asked one of his own. "Do you have the location of another portal or not?"

Silence.

Bastian was no doubt debating on whether to peruse his own answer.

Bastian was a cold and calculated man. He never did or said anything without a reason. There was no matter his brain couldn't solve, no problem he couldn't fix. As a former Scribe to the Guardians, his mind had years of practice sifting through details to find the one needed. He seemed to be doing that now, trying to deem if how the portal was destroyed held merit.

Khaine waited with all the patience of a child, fuming for a response. Behind him, the sounds of water splashing over the torn shirt had his cock dancing again. Gods, those breasts.

He hadn't touched, let alone seen a female's naked body in a very long time. He could hear her washing herself, running the cloth over her body, pouring the water over her hair, it splattering to the pavement below.

Her nipples would be hard in the cool night's air. Tiny beads he could wrap his tongue around.

"I have not."

Bastian's voice startled him. "Have not, what?" Khaine asked.

Another length of silence.

"Found another portal," Bastian said. "You're distant."

A blast of fury worked up Khaine's spine, pillowing in his mind, driving his thoughts to a dangerous place. He strode to the lamppost and jammed his knuckles into the solid surface, relishing in the pain, releasing his temper in one full swing of his fist. The pole careened to the asphalt, crashing hard against the ground and breaking the light. Darkness crept in to take its place, the sound of shattering glass echoing through the trees.

He turned his gaze to Skye. His eyes easily found her still standing by his car, her expression one of shock and uncertainty. She stood with the torn material over her body, hair wet, eyes searching. The moment she found him, he let her see the ferocity she'd evoked. Because of her, his mind was a chaotic mess of thoughts. He had never lost sight of his course.

Khaine poured every ounce of lust into that one look. All the things he would do to her. The ways she would satisfy him. She gasped, her eyes seeming to adjust to the lightlessness enough, her fingers toying with the cloth, then he gave her his back again. She would do well not to play with his demon.

He heard her quickly dress into the shirt he gave her.

"I need that portal."

"The words in this text are elusive and there's no guarantee I would send you to a portal still standing."

Khaine groaned. So close, yet so far. "Tell me what you *do* know."

"I can have the rune ready when the time comes, but I won't be able to get the portal's location."

Khaine walked the distance of the parking lot and slammed his fist into a nearby tree. The trunk cracked.

"Calm yourself," Bastian said. "There's another way."

He froze, the muscles in his back easing. "Tell me."

"The Raudskinna mentions a deity, a goddess that sees and hears all. There is some detail here about how to call on her, though the description of her nature is vague. This deity could either skin you alive and weave a new dress from your entrails, or watch as you dance on your head."

Neither of those outcomes sounded delightful, but if this particular deity knew all, she could tell him the location of another portal, perhaps take him directly to it. "How do I call on this deity?"

"It says there is a relic used to summon her dimension. A small magic pendant made of blue diamond that swirls with stars. You would need to find it." Irritation skirted his voice. "I heard of such a thing once, though I can't recall who possessed it."

A magic pendant made of blue diamond? Swirling with stars? Khaine knew of it, had seen such a thing not long ago in the hands of a Hirx, a goddess-like immortal being that was skilled in all things sexual and sadistic. Asha was her name. She never let the jewel out of her sight. It always hung from her neck on a chain.

"Done," he said. "Asha has it." He had dealt with Asha in the past, she would oblige him.

"Asha?" There was a questionable note in his voice. "She's not one to trifle with."

Khaine knew that.

Bastian seemed to let it go. "I will have the rune ready, but there's more," Bastian said before Khaine could hang up.

Khaine waited, the corner of his jaw ticking with anticipation.

"The rune isn't all that's needed for Raiden to be allowed out of Shrodah."

What was one more measly obstacle? He'd see it done and Raiden would be back at his side.

"The book depicts the sacrificial stone."

"A sacrifice? No matter," Khaine said. "What kind of sacrifice?"

Bastian sighed on the other end of the line. "A Guardian."

Silence.

Khaine took a breath, let it out, took another.

Turning, he took in Skye's state. The shirt he gave her hung over her bottom, enough to conceal anything underneath. It was all he'd had to give her. He only brought two shirts with him. One she wore and the other he'd ripped to shreds so they could clean themselves. Her hair was wet and disheveled, but she otherwise appeared clean enough to not stain his seats.

Skye stood by the driver's side door, rubbing her arms against the chill. A shiver worked over her body. Khaine walked to her and around the front of his car, stopping by the passenger door to open it. "Get in."

"Get in?" Bastian repeated.

"Not you," he said to the phone.

"Where are we going?" Skye asked.

Instead of answer, Khaine barred his teeth.

"You have a female with you?" he heard Bastian say on the other end of the line. Khaine ignored him.

When he thought sure Skye would protest, she eased herself around the front of his car and climbed in. He slammed the door shut and made his way back to the driver's side.

Khaine hung his head.

"Khaine?"

"I'm here."

A pause. "Perhaps it's time to consider Raiden gone."

Never!

"He's not gone."

"The Guardians are dead."

Not true! There was one sitting in the passenger seat of his car.

"Without a Guardian…"

"No matter," Khaine said. "I have it handled."

"But the line—"

"I'll take care of it," Khaine gritted. "I'll call you when I reach Asha."

Khaine hit the red button on the SAT phone, ending the call. He then stood there, unsure of what to do next. There was a Guardian sitting in his car, his mate, and he would have to sacrifice her to get Raiden back. Khaine trusted Bastian, believed he would never lie about something so important.

He would have to kill his mate.

No. There had to be another way. He could turn back, take

another of her family. Khaine knew Skye would never forgive him.

Now you care?

It doesn't matter, he told himself, pounding his fist into the hood of his car. There wasn't enough time. He would find another way, and if not...

Raiden was everything to him. He hung his head. He would get his brother back, no matter the cost.

Chapter 10

The silence stretched, ushering Skye's thoughts toward treacherous territory. Trees flew by in a blur outside her window, Khaine effortlessly maneuvering the car at an alarming speed down deserted roads. She'd nonchalantly glanced over at one point to see him doing one hundred.

He'd been quiet. *Too* quiet. After getting in the driver's seat and backing out of the small parking lot, nothing else had been said. Was this a new approach from the overbearing demon?

Who had been on the phone? What had they talked about? And why couldn't he have left the phone someplace she could get to it?

Perhaps she shouldn't have played with him. The way he'd taken out that metal post like it was nothing, then sent that chilling glare over her...

Khaine's head was focused forward, the headlights beaming out over the road barely bouncing a few stray strands of light back into the car, but she could see his eyes drifting over her lap where the shirt hardly covered her. Squirming, Skye pulled the material down as far as it would go before it forced her shoulders with it. Her bottom was stuck to the black, leather seat and made a rubbing noise when she moved, shifting the shirt under it.

His head shot to that spot on her seat.

Maybe trying to play him as she had, hadn't been such a good plan. She'd blame Caden for her lack of direction the next time she saw her.

If she ever saw her, she told herself. For all Skye knew, Caden was dead, had bled out because of her reckless control. She remembered Caden lying on the floor in her own blood. If only she could call, could see her. Anything to know she was alive. The only two that had a phone were Mckenzie and Brooke, and calling Mckenzie would not end well. Mckenzie didn't need any more distractions while trying to track the Guardian in Jade's vision. If she could get the phone from Khaine and call Brooke...

Stupid, demon!

No, there would be no calling, not now, anyway. She would just have to hope that Caden was alive and well. Not wanting to get lost in that dark ravine, Skye shoved it from her mind and pushed back the tears.

She needed to get away from Khaine. She also suspected he would never let her go, being his mate at all. No, she *knew* he would never let her go. Skye would have to kill him.

Memories of the way his eyes had raked over her body floated by her window while she stared out at seemingly nothing.

His eyes, black as night, had held tiny flecks of gold that had glimmered in the darkness. The way he'd fisted his hands when he thought she wasn't looking, or worked his Adam's apple at the sight of her exposed breasts.

What the fuck had she been thinking?

Suddenly uncomfortable in her own skin, Skye gripped the shirt Khaine had given her to wear and tried not to smack herself for being so stupid. Her face grew hot sitting so close to him in the confined space. He was a demon. A *mated* demon. Did he have the same need to claim her like the Lykae did? Would he attack her if she provoked him too much? Had he been thinking that very thing while she undressed for him?

How bad that would have been.

Mckenzie had described what a Lykae went through when they found their mates; an uncontrollable need to *claim* them.

Yeah, Skye knew what *that* meant.

If Khaine had the same instinct, toying with him, giving him a glimpse of herself, had likely fueled his need to a devastatingly high level. He would take any opportunity to have sex with her, and then her emotions would skyrocket and she'd end up opening another portal without knowing.

What would happen if he found out she could open portals, even if her emotions ran the show? Would he break her and let his kind loose on the world? She'd managed to derail him when he'd tried to ask, but how long could she keep that secret if she gave in?

Though, she reminded herself, Khaine had been human at one point. Maybe he didn't see them as his kind. Most immortals couldn't have children, so a demon impregnating a human was likely impossible. Which begged the question, *how* had he become a demon?

Then again, she'd destroyed the portal. Didn't that mean that any demons on the other side were no longer capable of coming through? Did destroying the portal mean she destroyed *all* demons on the other side?

Was that his reason for hating her? After all, Khaine was still a demon, whether he had been human at one point or not, and he *had* been after that portal. Why?

"Why did you say the portal was yours?"

A silhouette of trees lined either side of the abandoned stretch of highway. The road he had taken wasn't used much by travelers, and because of such, wasn't maintained to the same set of standards. Potholes littered the asphalt in droves, making his high-speed driving unnerve her. She wouldn't let it get to her. Fear wasn't a good thing.

Skye kept her face forward but could hear the distinct sound of the leather steering wheel as he gripped it between his palms.

"Was," he corrected.

"What did you want with it?"

She felt his head whip toward her and she met his chilling look, keeping the road ahead in her peripheral vision.

"So, you wish to speak with me, now? What happened to letting you go?"

She scowled at him. "Maybe I just want to know if more of your kind will come looking for the portal."

Khaine laughed, genuinely laughed, and the atmosphere in the car dropped to a staggering low. Unnerved at being so close to him, Skye shifted her weight as far as she could so that her right side was plastered against the passenger door. She could pull the chrome handle and try to make a great escape, even though the vehicle was barreling down the road at a killing speed. Hastily recasting that option, Skye made a fist, ready to punch him square in the jaw, and perhaps take control of the steering wheel while he recovered.

He was immortal. The only way to kill an immortal was by cutting off their head. That wasn't something she could manage without her sword, but she could sure as hell wound him enough to get back to the others before he caught up to her.

Maybe. It wasn't like she had any other options.

Watching the road ahead, Skye counted the seconds, waiting for a long straightaway to come up. Trying to derail a car on winding roads would be suicide. Perhaps her whole idea was suicide, but a straightaway seemed like the better option.

"You destroyed the portal." His words cut the still air like a razor. "What other being would come looking for something useless? Because of you, I'm forced to find another."

Another?

There were other portals out there? How did she not know this? Better question: how did Khaine?

She wasn't going to give him the impression that he knew more than she did, so swallowed that last question. He already thought of her as naive. What would he think if he learned she knew almost nothing about her own kind?

Scrunching her face, Skye mentally beat herself for that thought. She didn't care what he thought of her. In a few moments, it wouldn't matter anyway.

To keep him distracted, Skye tried to keep him talking. The more his attention was on her, the less control he would have when she struck, whether that was good or bad. "And how do you plan to do that? Why not let me go? You don't need me to find another portal."

The look he sent her made her feel like she had mysteriously sprouted another head. His dark blonde hair shadowed the slight stubble on his face in the dim light, making him look as menacing as she suspected he was.

"You're my mate. Do you not know what that means?"

"You can't tell me that you're literally incapable of letting me go."

Khaine shook his head. His deep voice rebounded around her. "Believe me, Guardian. I don't *want* you here. Your kind should be dead, and if not for this damn voice telling me otherwise, you would be."

Yup, she'd have to kill him. The first chance she got her hands on a sword sharp enough. Too bad he didn't still have the one on his back. Maybe she could get it out of the trunk.

"Fine," she gritted, turning her attention back to the road ahead. "How do you plan to find this other portal?"

Did he know where the others were?

Another damn corner. How many were on this route? Of course he picked the scenic way, with winding mountain passes. Taking the highway would have been illogical, after all. Skye rolled her eyes.

"A deity," was all he said.

When the silence stretched again, Skye tsked. "Do you care to elaborate?"

"Do you know what a deity is?"

"No." And don't care, she thought. Just keep talking.

Khaine cast her a curious glance.

Frustrated, she tucked a strand of tangled hair behind her ear. "I'm a mortal. Just because I know some of your world, doesn't mean I know all of it."

He shifted his eyes back to the road, taking another dark corner. A frown etched across his chiseled face, the glow from the center console drifting a slight beam over his features.

"It's a god of sorts. There is a rumor that they had a hand in the making of all immortals; that we're their children. It's said that they know all and see all, therefore would be able to direct me to one of the last two portals standing."

"Last two? So, there are others?"

Another curious glance. "Do you know nothing of your kind?"

"Maybe I'm merely testing you to see how much *you* know."

Not true! Skye hadn't a clue of what he was saying. Plus and double-plus for her. Gain information from him, then kill him.

Caden would be so proud.

Khaine raised a brow at her and she scolded herself. She'd said too much. When he faced the road again, she felt her quick reply had covered her ass.

"There used to be thirteen altogether. Now there's only two."

"What happened to the others?"

His face hardened, his eyes glazing over with a subtle darkness. "They were destroyed."

He didn't like this subject. Something about it had his shoulders tense and bare chest heaving shallow breaths.

Skye changed the subject back to this deity while he maneuvered the car around another bend, straightening the wheel when the road ahead smoothed. All she had to do now was make sure he was distracted. "So, this deity knows everything?"

Balling her fist, Skye readied herself for the blow, picking a spot square in the middle of his nose where her fist would cause the most damage. Tensing her upper arm, she prepared to strike.

"They see the past, future, and present."

Skye froze. Future. She played that word over her tongue in silence, her hand still firmly cupped in a fist. Did that mean this so-called deity could help her? Seeing the future would mean she could see the moment of Skye's death. Could she also tell her how to prevent it?

A sliver of hope crawled up her spine.

This deity would also be able to tell her if Caden was still alive. Skye could finally take back her life, not have to depend on other people to save her all the time.

"Your eyes lighten. This matters to you."

She released her grip and shoved those thoughts from her mind, plastering an inscrutable look on her face. "So," she said, waving a hand in the air, "this deity can tell a person things that are going to happen and how to prevent them?"

"Yes."

And he wanted to find this deity; to get the means of locating another portal. What was *his* reason?

"Why do you want to find another portal?"

"Tell me why this deity's abilities matter to you, first."

Wasn't going to happen.

As if reading that thought, Khaine turned his attention to another and said, "then you will accompany me?"

"Only to see this deity."

Another brow went up and something in his eyes sent another shiver over her body.

"How long until we get there?" she said. Being so close to Khaine was fucking with her head. The fact that his chest was completely bare and she could picture running her hands along his corded muscles, didn't help.

"Four hours. There is a nightclub in Evanston, Illinois I need to stop at. A friend there has something I need."

"What?"

"For someone who was begging me to let her go," he cocked his eye at her, "and plotting to wreck this car in an attempt to escape..."

Skye felt the heat rise in her face, again.

"...you sure have a lot of questions." Khaine glared at her. "A relic to open another dimension where we'll find this deity."

"Another dimension," Skye stuttered. She'd never been to another dimension before. The thought almost excited her.

Calm yourself, she said. It wouldn't do her any good to get all worked up, now. Not that it was fear she was feeling.

This was perfect! She could travel with Khaine to find this relic, stay with him long enough to get to the other dimension—and possibly learn how to find the deity—and then she could kill him, figure out how to stop the vision from happening, and be back home before the ten days was up. She had a plan! That was more than she had before this demon crashed into her life.

Scratch that. In no way would she give Khaine that credit. It was because of *her* that she was going to live. Khaine wouldn't have anything to do with it.

Khaine watched Skye, curled up in the passenger seat while he downshifted the car into fifth gear and took another darkened bend, the RPMs of his prized possession hitting the seven-thousands as he slowed into the turn, then used the car's weight to pull it through. He shifted back to sixth and leveled out.

She'd fallen asleep an hour ago, with her head rested against the corner of her seat, facing the tinted glass with one leg tucked under her thigh.

Sleeping.

A Guardian was sleeping next to him. In his car. Half clothed. *Alive.*

While he still harbored a feeling of hate toward her, something had changed. He no longer had an undeniable urge to kill her. He'd learned something about her.

She was a Guardian, yes, but she also knew little to nothing about her kind. Skye knew about the portal she was protecting, but that seemed to be where her knowledge ended. A far as he knew, she knew nothing about the past of her people. Nothing about the other portals. The more he thought about it, the more he got the impression that she likely didn't know anything about whatever power she possessed either.

And none of that mattered.

He would have to kill her. It didn't matter what she was to him; his mate. Not knowing what she was didn't make her any less innocent toward the wrongs of her kind. They were all the same. Selfish.

He had no doubt that she would stab him in the back the first chance she got. She had already plotted to kill him!

The moment Khaine had mentioned where they were going and why, her eyes had lit up. There was something the deity could offer her; something she couldn't get by another means.

He would take it from her.

What would Bastian say to him if he showed up without Raiden and a Guardian mate in tow? All those years they had spent hating Guardians for the pain they caused them. Bastian would do the same. He would take everything she held dear and crush it beneath him. She was a mortal. Skye would die one day, long before him, and again he would be without a mate. There was no logical reason for him to get used to what she was, or for him to accept her presence. What was he supposed to do? Turn her?

He gripped the steering wheel. That's not something he could do himself. You needed pure demon's blood for it to work, and the process of becoming a demon didn't guarantee the mortal came out of it alive. A fact he knew all too well.

A bolt of pain laced his chest. Skye. Dead. Gone forever.

Khaine slammed his fist into the console of his BMW, leaving a large hole where the heater vent used to be.

Fuck!

Now he would have to get that fixed.

Bits of plastic littered his groin and he turned his head to see if his outburst had woken the mortal beside him.

Nothing. She was still out. Soundless.

Soon, he told himself. Temptest was only another one-hundred-and-eighty-four-miles away now, off Lake Shore Blvd in Evanston, Illinois. At this rate, they'd get there by two in the morning; long before closing time for the immortal nightclub. He was having second thoughts, doubting whether Asha would welcome him into her place of business. He hadn't left things on good terms with the Hirx.

That didn't matter. Khaine would get the relic from her by any means necessary.

He peered at Skye again. And what was he to do with his mate? *Could* he kill her? The answer was simple. He would do whatever it took.

His eyes hung lazily on the leather seat where her ass was, hidden from view under his shirt that seemed to swallow her. Khaine scrubbed his bare chest. Asha's club serviced the more erogenous clientele. Taking her in there, dressed as she was, hair disheveled, lips full and sensuous, eyes naturally shadowed from what appeared to be exhaustion, and so much smooth, inviting skin showing... Immortals would be throwing themselves at her.

Never!

She was *his*. It didn't matter how short her life *might* be, how little time he *might* have with her; no immortal would be putting their hands on her. As much as he hated to admit it, they were going to have to stop and find her more suitable attire. He could also get a change of clothes while he was at it. The better he looked for Asha, the more she might be inclined to give him the relic. All he needed to do was borrow it.

Getting clothes for himself and Skye meant taking an exit toward Howard, Wisconsin and delaying their arrival. He didn't want to waste more time than needed, but this was a necessary stop.

Khaine pressed his foot to the gas pedal and narrowed his eyes along the darkened road, looking for the first signs of an exit to take. If Skye remained sleeping when they arrived—which would mean less time arguing with the stubborn woman—and he kicked up his speed, he could still make it to Evanston before sunrise when Asha was known to take her nightly catch back to bed.

If Khaine used another rune to keep Skye unaware of the little detour, he'd be putting them both at risk, forced to recover that much more energy before he could use another. That would mean days of being vulnerable. He'd weigh his options carefully when the moment came.

A large green sign came into view, the headlights beaming over *Howard* plastered on the front in bold, white letters and a mile marker showing the exit coming up fast. He downshifted and prepared to turn off.

Chapter 11

"**N**o." Was he serious? No way in hell was she putting that on.

Khaine thrust the pile of clothes at her again and growled. The black "dress" he'd picked out, floor-length and complete with bright red and yellow flowers embellishing the top half, was crumpled in his fist along with the red and black, checkerboard coat, gold stitches swirled on every square. Together, they would cover her completely from head to toe in an ensemble fit for a dynasty princess. Skye had nothing against formal Chinese clothing, but she would never be caught dead wearing it. Red alone wasn't her color. Yellow? Good, God! Blue. Give her blue any day and she was ecstatic.

It also didn't escape her notice that the stitching was poor quality. She could do better on her portable sewing machine. In the dark.

Lights flickered behind Khaine on the stone building. They

were standing outside a bar called Temptest. The neon-purple sign hung at an angle above the back door, casting a glow out over several rows of cars. There were too many to count. The size of the building didn't look near large enough to hold that many patrons, but according to Khaine, it housed a secret immortal nightclub underneath.

She'd heard of this place from Mckenzie. Not in detail, but enough to know never to come here, and yet here she was.

At first, Khaine had tried persuading her to wear the outfit he held, telling her what her lack of clothing would insinuate to the bar's particular clientele.

She'd snorted and promptly informed him she'd dressed in less before, to which he immediately changed his persuasion back to his normal demanding tactics.

Figured.

"We're going to an immortal nightclub," he told her.

"You said that," Skye gritted, fully aware of exactly how many times in the past thirty minutes he'd repeated that same one-line response to her refusals. Like he thought that would make a difference. She already told him it didn't. It *wouldn't*.

Wearing nothing but his shirt was far better than that thing he kept shoving at her. She promptly told him exactly where he could stick the dress, in expert detail.

Skye surveyed the crammed lot around them. Who knew how long they had been here before he nudged her awake. The moment she came to, she'd slammed her fists into his chest and launched her foot into his shin thinking he was attacking her. Skye had done everything she could to calm her thundering heart, to gather her emotions before they caused her to explode. Literally.

She'd dreamt about the demon, about him standing over her lifeless body. A part of her still wasn't sure Khaine wouldn't be the one to kill her. There were too many factors at play. Looking into his eyes when she woke was like replaying her death in her dream.

All those years she'd spent learning to control herself were slowly being undone by the demon. She needed to focus. So why was that so damn hard to do? She couldn't even sleep with him around, and yet, she had.

When had she passed out? *Why* had she passed out?

The last thing Skye remembered was Khaine slamming his fist into the dash of his precious BMW; the same car he demanded she be clean in out of fear for his damned leather seats. Skye had scarcely held back the flinch, keeping her head turned, pretending to be asleep.

But pretending didn't reenergize the body. She'd tried everything humanly possible to rid her mind of recent events so she could get *real* sleep. Her body was exhausted, her mind fighting with the force of a cannon to find rest, but knowing Khaine was so close made sleep impossible. The more Skye had tried not to think of the demon, the more her brain replayed images of him between her legs.

Traitor.

When he took the off-ramp headed toward Howard, Wisconsin, she'd remained still. He'd pulled the car over in a Burlington Coat Factory parking lot and then...

There was nothing after that. She'd been wide awake, her curiosity making her more attentive to the things going on around her. One minute she was sitting there, her head against the glass, staring out at the dim lights illuminating the empty lot and trees planted in concrete dividers, and then nothing until waking to Khaine nudging her.

She narrowed her eyes at him. "You did something to me."

"Put on the clothes."

"What did you do? Spell me to sleep?"

"Put them on!"

"What did you do to me!"

Skye took a deep breath. Arguing with the demon was making her crazed. She needed to stay calm. Her mother's vision, Jade's vision, still hung like a noose around her neck. The longer she stayed away from the safety of their tomb, the closer she was to death. She had to get to the deity, find a way to stop herself from dying, and Khaine was her golden ticket. Whatever relic he needed was inside that bar. All she had to do was bade her time until she could learn what she needed to know and steal the relic from him.

Khaine paced a short distance in front of her, back and forth like a predator, the wad of what he called acceptable clothing still balled in one hand. There was a glint in his black eyes. A reflection from the bar's sign? And the slight curve to his lips... Smiling?

"Do you ever do what you're told?" he asked.

"Do you ever answer a question with anything *other* than another question? Oh wait, that's right," she said, positively fuming, "you just demand that people do what you want. Get another ragdoll."

"Put them on," he sighed.

"What. Did. You. Do to me," Skye repeated through clenched teeth.

Khaine thrust his fingers through his hair, his nostrils flaring. "Will you put the clothes on?"

"Are we actually going to make a deal?"

He growled, flashing her his impeccably straight white teeth. Even like this, snarling at her, his eyes black obsidian and the undercurrents of a demon thrumming through his veins, he was still a sight to behold. Perhaps even more so, she was startled to realize.

Skye shook her head. *Focus.*

It wouldn't do her any good to ogle him, even if he was the sexiest man she had ever laid eyes on. She could still feel him grinding his cock between her thighs. She could come like that.

Focus!

Skye mentally shook herself.

This bothered him. She could see the demon wasn't used to compromise, had probably never known a moment of concession in his entire life, and if she was a betting woman, she would peg that as being an extremely long time, but this was *her* life on the line.

Knowing how he had made her sleep was information she could use against him in the future. The near future, she told herself. It had to be one of his tattoos. Which one was it? How did it work? *Could* she use it on him if she needed to?

That last question was at the top of her *need-to-know* list.

"I know your tattoos are spells. They look the same as the symbols on the portal."

"Destroyed portal," he corrected with a growl.

"Fine," she gritted, "*destroyed* portal. Tell me which one you used to make me sleep, and *how* you used it, and I'll wear that..." She couldn't say it, couldn't even fathom forming the words. Skye spat it out like it singed her tongue. "...dress. But

I'm *not* wearing the coat."

Khaine seemed to contemplate her offer, his eyes narrowed and lips thin. The darkness in his gaze receded as he turned his head away, his brows furrowed in thought. Water splashed in the distance, beyond a set of trees that walled off the parking lot from the many boats tied to small wooden docks on the lake. Lake Michigan. He'd driven to Illinois with her helpless and unaware in the passenger seat.

That was unacceptable.

The prospect of what he could have done to her hung in the back of her mind. She hadn't felt so vulnerable in a long time.

She took a breath. Pine leaves and maple bark. If she closed her eyes, she could picture home.

"How to use it is off the table," he said after length, pivoting back to face her, his now brown eyes sweeping her in long strokes that made the gold flecks in them shimmer. "You would no doubt try to use it against me at the earliest opportunity."

Aggravating demon! Skye shifted from one foot to the next, trying not to snarl, herself, her bare feet dancing over the asphalt. She wrapped her arms around herself to ward off the cold. It was always colder by the water.

She thought for a moment. What else could she bargain for?

"Fine," she said. "Tell me *how* you know them. I know the symbols on the portal..." He snarled. She corrected herself before they launched into another mantra. "...destroyed portal, are connected to your tattoos. Tell me how and who taught them to you."

He knew of her world, what she was, and for some reason, that unsettled her. How many other Proveans knew about her? She wasn't immortal. That alone was a disadvantage. Her and Caden had deemed that the existence of Guardians be kept secret a long time ago. Being mortal was bad enough, but being mortal *and* powerless? The Province wasn't known to be subtle or forgiving.

The only reason the Lykae knew about the portal and what it did was because it was on their land. They didn't know that it was a Guardian's job to protect it. Well, hers and Jades. They only knew that they could.

Khaine ran his palm over his black cotton shirt. He'd changed while she'd slept. Skye was startled to realize that almost...*almost* disappointed her. She could get used to staring at his bare chest. Those tattoos that trailed up his sides, across his toned stomach, over his broad chest, and down his muscled arms, made her want to run her fingers in the same line.

Traitor.

His dark blonde hair was now completely free of demon blood, unlike the patches that still clung to her own where she didn't rinse it out enough, and his face had been groomed to a clean shave, the stubble gone. That also disappointed her. The black shirt gripped his tight shoulders and he now sported what looked like a brand-new pair of Diesel jeans. She knew they had to be knockoffs, but the way they hugged his thighs and rode low on his hips, she didn't care.

His sword, which had previously been hidden on his back before the fight at the hideout, was now visible over his left shoulder, the hilt a polished, black obsidian. Skye had noticed it back in the tomb, the way it wasn't there one moment and there the next. More magic. She would *not* ask why he didn't feel the need to hide it, here. He wouldn't tell her, anyway.

There wasn't a point.

She didn't think there was an outfit he could wear that would make him look bad. He probably didn't think about what he was putting on, just grabbed something off the rack and changed. He'd even traded his hiking boots for black Timberlands. She, on the other hand, was still barefoot.

And did the demon have shoes for her to wear? No.

Bastard.

His outfit should be illegal, she thought. It pissed her off; the fact that he looked so good. But more than that, he claimed she was his mate, and yet he couldn't be bothered to get shoes for his mate.

Everything she had ever been told about mates made his actions confusing. Mated immortals were supposed to cherish their mates, care for them, *love* them. Khaine seemed to despise her existence. One more reason she needed to get as far away from him as possible.

"Well," Skye said, tapping one bare foot against the ground. "What's it going to be?"

She pulled the long shirt Khaine gave her down. Or tried to. It sprang back to just below the most important bits. If he didn't want to compromise, she'd hike it up and walk right into that immortal bar as she was, cursing him the whole way.

Let's see the demon argue, then.

A soft breeze broke through the trees and she suppressed a shiver. Damn cold. Khaine regarded her, something dancing in his eyes she hadn't seen before. The black in his gaze had faded to a deep brown, one corner of his lips curling into a slight grin.

"I'll tell you what tattoo I used for the dress…" He paused, the gold specs in his eyes dancing over her. His lips curved in a way that made her stomach do little somersaults. "...and I'll tell you where I learned it for a kiss."

She forgot to breathe. The heated glow in Khaine's eyes bore into her.

No.

No way in hell. That had "bad idea" written all over it.

Khaine smirked.

Shit, her heart was racing. The damn demon could probably hear it. All immortals had amped hearing. Heat flooded her face, the cold from the lake flushed out by warm shivers up her arms and sides. Deep breath.

"I'm not kissing you." Was that her scratchy voice?

"Afraid, then? Fine, where I learned it doesn't matter."

He tossed the dress at her. She caught it as he pointed to a tattoo on his lower left arm, just above the elbow. A series of circles stitched together with stars and jagged lines.

"This one," he said, his face smug. "Put on the dress."

Ooh! She wasn't afraid!

Okay, maybe a little afraid. But it obviously wasn't sheer terror or certain things would be exploding, right now. Excitement twisted in her stomach. She couldn't let him know how much he affected her, though. To kiss the demon? Oh, she'd thought about it. He hadn't tried to kiss her back in the woods, had done just about everything *but* kiss her. What would he taste like? What would it be like to run her hands up his sculpted chest, twine her fingers in his hair, twist her tongue with his?

Skye clicked her tongue against her teeth. She'd never been kissed by a man like him. If a man like him ever had the nerve to approach her, she would likely run screaming in the other direction. It was only a kiss. It's not like he was asking her to have sex with him. Besides, she didn't plan on being around him much longer. The answer to all her problems was somewhere inside that building. If everything went as planned, she wouldn't be anywhere near the demon in the next hour.

Shit! She was considering it. Skye rubbed her hand on his shirt and gripped the seam, tilting her head. Why deny herself this opportunity? What could it hurt, really?

"One kiss? Nothing more?"

"Nothing more," he said, his eyes held on her lips.

This was a *really* bad idea, but his answer could tell her more than she needed to know. About him. About who in the Province knew of Guardians. It wasn't good form to kill your enemy before learning their secrets. Words her sisters lived by. Mercenary code.

Her heart drummed in her chest. "Okay, one kiss." She cleared her throat and took a step forward.

Khaine shook his head. "No."

"No?"

"Not here. A time and place of my choosing."

She frowned. "That wasn't part of the deal."

"I said a kiss. I never said when or where."

Why not now, she almost whined. What was he playing at? She needed to get closer. He was too far to be strangled.

"Fine," she huffed. "A time and place of your choosing." She didn't plan on being around for it, anyway. "Who taught you the rune?"

"A Guardian."

Skye waited for him to elaborate. He didn't.

"And...where was this Guardian?"

The slight breeze banking off the water hit her again, the heat from her body subsiding. Goosebumps rose on her arms. The smell of rain hit her nose, the chilly air gathering moisture from the lake as it picked up speed.

Cocking his head, Khaine smiled. "Standing by a burning hut, melting in the fire like the rest of his kind."

That told her nothing! His kind? Guardians? Did Khaine kill them? They obviously hadn't all died. Where were the other Guardians? Did he know where they were? There was so much he could tell her!

His face twisted in what appeared to be grief, but the shadow of emotion on his face was gone before she could be sure. Only a cold, hard demon stared at her, now.

"Put on the dress," he said, his voice rough and careless.

Khaine leaned against a blue Prius and folded his arms over his chest, the shadows over his face only broken by the light emanating off a lamppost to the west.

"Are there any others that know of my kind?"

He tilted his head. Would he answer her question? Or would the infuriating demon try to bargain for more? Bargain for more, no doubt.

He was silent for so long she thought sure he wouldn't answer.

"One."

"One?" She could live with that. As long as the entire Province remained clueless, there couldn't be any harm in one knowing what she was.

"Who—"

"Put on the dress."

That was it. He'd shut her down. Skye wanted to ask more,

but his eyes told her he wouldn't be giving her anything else. He'd surprised her by acknowledging what he had.

She sighed. "Turn around."

Instead of moving, he planted his feet, waiting. His gaze bore into her, searing the shirt from her chest as he cocked one eyebrow.

No. Skye wasn't being sucked into this game. She wouldn't be undressing for him, again. Not now. Not ever. She'd learned her lesson. If he wanted to play cold and heartless, she could do the same. Better, even.

Scowling at him, Skye grasped the handle of his BMW behind her, pulled open the door, skirted around it, and climbed into the passenger seat. The deep sound of Khaine's laughter filled her ears as she closed the door, then locked it for good measure. Khaine's laugh rumbled low in her stomach, twisting her insides like a caress.

Ignoring how much he affected her, Skye turned away from the window and stripped off his shirt in private. Demon, meet tinted glass, she thought.

Chapter 12

Khaine pressed his hand to the swell of Skye's back as they walked through the basement's double doors. She shrugged it off and glared at him. He'd angered her. Again.

And yet again, the feeling it left behind was one he didn't want to focus on. He didn't care. Why should he care about her kind after what the Guardians had done to them? Why should he care about her when he might have to kill her?

He'd let her walk on her own, for now, but if any of the creatures in this bar wanted to gamble with their lives, walking would be the least of her worries. He was a wanted immortal, hunted by immortals, and presently entering an immortal bar. The irony.

It was cruel of him to trick her. He'd known it before setting the trap, but it was no less than what she'd done to him; giving him a glimpse of what he wanted and then telling him he would never have it. She was his mate. *Given* to *him*.

Khaine had answered her question and at the same time, told her nothing. He would still be getting that kiss. He would kiss her so thoroughly she wouldn't be able to deny him. His demon half was rattling the steel bars inside him trying to get to her. A first.

Perhaps his demon side recognized her as its mate?

No. Khaine shook his head to clear that thought. His demon had never known anything but violence.

He adjusted his Movado watch, a slight quiver in his stomach. Telling her as little as he did had sparked a painful reminder of his father's friend. Jonah had taught Khaine the sleeping rune when he was a boy and nightmares of the portal being destroyed, of demons burning their village to the ground, haunted him. And in the end, they *did* burn it to the ground. Jonah and all.

Soon, he thought. Raiden would be back at his side and all would be well.

He frowned at Skye. Would all be well without his mate beside him?

Khaine pushed through the second set of double doors and into the underground club. Music hit him like a wave, crashing and rolling over his chest. It was loud, the bass alone vibrating the maroon-painted walls. Pictures hung along an overhead beam inside the dim entryway. Framed posters of scotch and beer, glasses filled with drinks he had only ever heard of, and foods mortals would be wise to never eat, hung inches apart above their heads and down each column on either side of them. When he tried to tell Skye of Temptest's brand of customer, he was incapable of it. The bar served the Province's most particular guests. Immortals with a stout taste for laced blood, delivered to them by unaware mortals with an equally strong taste for sex. Orgy didn't begin to describe those who partook.

Khaine flexed his right shoulder, relishing in the feel of his blade at his back. Walk into this place without it? Not a chance. It wasn't customary for immortals to tote their weapons into this club, but being who he was, he considered it suicide *not* to. He was tapped out, drained. The spell he'd used to persuade Skye to sleep, plus the little he'd done to tamper with the security inside the store, had left him without magic. He wasn't a Witch. He couldn't use magic whenever it fancied him. It would be days for him to regain enough strength to use another rune. He couldn't hide his sword if he wanted to.

Skye's eyes were wide, trying to see everything all at once. Khaine had been here several times while acclimating himself to his new status in the Province. It had been over a century since then. He forced himself to see it anew.

Naked women and men, their bodies bloody, writhed in the far corner under a blacklight. Creatures with talons and horns tossed back drinks at the illuminated bar. Black tiles stretched a path around the center tables to the back where the light was so scarce, he knew she wouldn't be able to see the Womnots, small cannibalistic creatures that looked like Capybaras, entertaining themselves on sliced flesh they were picking off a corpse. The top floor railing had been covered with tinted glass, but what twisted behind in the shadows was unmistakable.

Temptest didn't discriminate against any creature, and so they came in droves.

Vampires, Eabriths, Kurses, and Crols. Even the retched Fae

were known to visit for a time, entertaining themselves on mortal endeavors.

"*This* is where you wanted to go? This is where we'll find the relic?" She sounded eager.

Skye's heart sped up. He found himself locked on the rise and fall of her breasts. He wanted to see them, again. Touch them. He followed her line of sight to a silhouette of a woman on the top floor kneeling before a man, but it wasn't pleasure she was giving him. He could hear it, Skye's heart, even over the music. The sudden thunder in her chest. She cleared her throat.

Khaine shook himself, his eyes soaking up the atmosphere as if for the first time. What the fuck was wrong with him? He should never have brought her here. Her stormy eyes regarded everything like an innocent virgin. Because she *was*. He should leave with her. Take her away from this place.

Hell, he could lock her in the trunk of the car and be back before anything happened to her. She shouldn't be here.

As if to solidify his claim, a Slig hunched over a naked mortal man and crooned in his ear, sucking the life from him through his dreams. The man would never know anything but the last erotic show the Slig gave him in his mind.

A low growl escaped him before he could stamp it down. Despite the loud beat reverberating around them, Skye turned her head at the sound. He met her gleaming eyes and glowered, his fists balled. Suddenly he cared what a Guardian might see? He couldn't. He *wouldn't*. Raiden was counting on him. She would never mean more to him than his own brother, he reminded himself. Let her look her fill.

He was only here for the amulet. They would be out of this

place before he knew it.

"I need to speak to a friend." He yelled to be heard over the thumping rhythm. Her mortal ears weren't as good as a demon's.

"Does this friend have the relic? Does the relic open this other dimension?"

Khaine thought about lying to her, but what was the point? They would be traveling to this other dimension together. Her fate was sealed. There was no escaping him, now.

The excitement in her voice compelled him to answer. "Yes and yes."

Her eyes lit up, the storm hovering around her irises a sudden brilliant blue, and she smiled. Khaine gapped at her. For one blasted moment, she was all he could see. It was the first time he had seen her smile, *really* smile. It was beauty like he'd never known. Not even his home in Scotland had evoked such a feeling. The way her lips hovered inches apart, her teeth a hairbreadth away from touching. She fingered the fabric of the dress he'd stolen for her and he almost forgot how to breathe. Did he think this dress would serve to make her less noticeable? He'd errored.

The dress firmly graced her hips, taunting him with images of his hands doing the same, the red and yellow flowers around the top cupped her breasts so tight he thought they might spill over, and even with the dress's length, he could still see the shape of her legs under the fabric. Could still imagine himself between them. Could still *feel* himself between them.

He'd admired her, standing there in nothing but his shirt outside the club, her defiance. No one had ever defied him. Not even Bastian dared to cross him like she had so many times, already. She had a fire in her like nothing he'd ever seen. Women in his time were weak and docile. Not Skye. Not his mate. She was every bit as bold and fearless as he'd hoped she would be. When he'd entertained himself on visions of his future mate, before he knew of a way to bring his brother back from Shrodah, she was what he'd imagined. He could almost get used to the idea of her as his mate. Happy.

Khaine groaned inwardly. And that thought made him ignorant. Skye would kill him the first chance he gave her. It was in her Guardian blood. A Guardian ever save a demon? Never. He'd been on the blunt end of their hate. He knew firsthand a Guardian's wrath.

"Khaine?"

His name rolling from her lips brought him back to her eyes. She'd asked him something.

"This friend," she said again. "Do you see them?"

Right. Deity. Relic.

Asha.

Khaine scanned the crowd in search of her. Two tables behind a Dragole, he spotted her, sitting with her legs wrapped around a Hovard's waist. The Hovard's black robes concealed death underneath. They were immortal hunters. Contract killers. They often kept to their own race, but it seemed this one had other wants, tonight.

Khaine nudged Skye's arm, motioning her to follow. He didn't dare wrap an arm around her. Touching her would only excite him more.

Several patrons chatting by the bar stopped to acknowledge their entrance. Keep calm, he told himself. *Fuck calm. Fight them!* Khaine locked his demon side down before it could escape. These immortals posed no threat.

Yet.

They kept walking, passed the orgy, around the tables, and toward Asha in the back.

A man, curly black hair that dusted his shoulders and a slight beard along his jaw, turned to them from the far end of the bar. Khaine stayed his focus, but he noticed the man. The others had resumed their conversation; this one was watching their every move. Khaine set his shoulders as the man rose and hardened his features to ice. If the man advanced...

Skye must have sensed a shift in him. "What's wrong?" she asked, shouting at him to be heard over the loud, thumping music. They were close to the dance floor now, the song beating against them. Bodies mashed together in a heated dance, most naked and not dancing at all.

He leaned toward her ear to be heard. "Stay beside me."

"You're a wanted man. I'd be safer if I *wasn't* beside you."

So, she knew about what he'd done, and she hadn't been more afraid of him? His woman was surprising him more and more.

"I'm a man, now?"

She clamped her jaw and he barely kept himself from smiling.

The man approached, reeking of immortality the closer he got. Then again, this entire club reeked of immortality. It didn't escape his notice the number of high-class Proveans, here. He had a price on his head. Every immortal in this building was now an enemy.

The man, with dark-green jeans, a green shirt, and black boots lined in green trim, locked his gaze on Khaine. His eyes were a dark green and fading with each step he took toward them. A Dryad.

Dryads could manipulate plant matter, make trees grow in any direction they wanted at any speed they wanted, and were known for their love of green. They were forest creatures.

"Khaine Reeves," the Dryad sneered. He wasn't shouting, but Khaine could hear him just fine. "You have no business being here, demon."

Khaine squared his chin and ushered Skye closer with his arm over her shoulder, suddenly not caring if he touched her or not. She surprised him by not objecting. "Could say the same to you. You're a long way from home."

He seemed unconcerned. "My name is Castello Collier."

"Should that mean something to me?"

Voices in the club had grown quiet, Khaine's voice ringing out over the crowd. Several immortals turned their heads to catch the conversation, the music at his back waning. This wasn't good.

Castello snarled. "It should. You hurt someone of mine in Calgary. You have a lot of nerve walking in here after what you did. A lot of immortals lost their lives that night. Or have you forgotten?"

Khaine smiled. A hundred eyes regarded them from all corners of the club. Skye tensed beside him and his demon rumbled. "How could I? They screamed so pathetically as I ripped out their throats, the sound alone amused me."

Several voices, whispers in the dark room, hovered in the air around them.

That's Khaine Reeves.

The immortal murderer.

There's a price on his head.
Should kill him, we should.

"Watch it, demon. A lot of immortals in this club, tonight. These aren't low-class beings you can easily dispatch."

The tone in Castello's voice was only a hint toward what he seemed to have planned, had likely fantasized about. The club fell completely silent. Not a sound. Khaine turned his head. The DJ had left.

He pivoted back to Castello, his hold still resting on Skye's shoulder. It was feather-light, waiting to see if the Dryad would strike. Castello stood only feet away.

"And not a one would dare engage me," Khaine said. "I'm here to see the owner, Asha. She would never allow it."

Khaine let her name ring out over the crowd but never took his eyes from Castello.

He knows Asha?
Another plaything.

Khaine flinched. He didn't want Skye to know the things they had done in the past. Or the things they almost did.

As if on cue, Asha broke free of her catch and glided over to where they stood. Her long, purple-toned black hair swayed around her ankles, curled in such a way that it seemed to dance like a curtain.

"Khaine," she purred. "It's been too long."

Khaine dropped his arm from Skye's shoulder. "It has. I've missed you." He tried to hide the lie in his voice. If Asha noticed, she didn't comment.

Her catch glided away into another dark corner, likely sulking. Capturing Asha's attention was a rare and lethal aphrodisiac.

It was the word 'lethal' that had kept Khaine from falling victim to her.

"What brings you to my club?"

Asha's golden eyes, flakes of blue and sea-green, fluttered over him. She stood a foot under his own height, shorter even than Skye, but her short frame was a contradiction to her immense appetite. If her eyes licking over his flesh wasn't enough of an indication of her needs, she slid one of her long, red nails over another, using the edge as a sharpener. They hadn't been painted but dyed with a permanent blood-coated stain.

Even dressed as she was, her top a translucent net of diamond jewels that barely covered her nipples, and a skirt made of fine-knit silk that showed nothing but a trail of hair underneath, she was nothing compared to his mate. There was a time when Khaine would have been aroused by her, *had* been aroused by her, but not anymore.

He frowned, but quickly hid the motion with a quirk of his lips.

Where Asha was a seductive goddess, Skye was the storm he desperately wanted to crash over him. The Hirx didn't compare. If Khaine needed any reminder as to what Skye was to him, he had it. His mate. The only woman he wanted to bury his cock in.

Khaine let that thought show, turning it into a smile he directed at Asha. "I thought we might pass some time, together."

The amulet he came for dipped between her breasts, a large blue diamond with smaller white diamonds set around the stone and snaking into a chain around her neck. It had more value than any other jewel of its color and was rumored to be the most expensive necklace in the world. Even more so, since the middle had been cut with a rare star. Several fakes had been made since its discovery, but the one around her neck was authentic. The way the center danced with imbued magic said as much.

Castello cracked his knuckles. "This demon murdered an entire immortal bar. There's a bigger price on his head than any of us can count. Let me kill him."

"Kill him?" Asha gasped. "I couldn't kill a lover."

"Lover?" Skye said, eyeing him.

Don't, Khaine thought. If Asha knew Skye was his mate, she would never entertain him. He needed her to entertain him. He needed her to willingly give him the amulet. If he tried to fight her in her own club, neither of them would make it out alive. And stealing the necklace would prove impossible.

"Who's your friend, Khaine?" Asha kept her eyes glued to him, her voice scathing. She didn't acknowledge those she deemed less than her.

"Nobody." He shot the hasty reply at her before she thought Skye was of any importance.

Skye flinched. He gritted his teeth, ignoring however the fuck that made him feel. Did it anger her? Was she jealous?

"It's been weeks since what he did. He deserves to be punished." Castello glared at him.

"Punished," Asha said. "Perhaps." She turned to Castello. "Leave us."

"Goddess—"

"I said leave us!" The hair twirling around Asha's frame glowed with purple streaks that hadn't been there before, her nails dripped with a poison only her anger brought on, and her eyes had turned a brilliant white.

Castello scowled at him. "This isn't over, demon." He turned to walk away.

Khaine released the nails digging into his palm but set his jaw as Castello laid eyes on Skye.

Walk away, Dryad. He had business to attend to, tonight. He couldn't thwart his plans by murdering another immortal sanctuary. If this immortal posed a threat to her, he'd attack. If Khaine attacked, nothing good would follow.

And since when did her life matter to him? As much as he wanted to deny it, her life *did* matter. *Still think you can kill her?*

Castello kept walking and Khaine relaxed his shoulders.

Asha spoke to Skye, her eyes still holding his. "You too, my darling. Leave us."

Her appearance had returned to her normal façade, but the note in Asha's voice made Khaine want to strangle her. It was a threat. If Skye didn't walk away, right now, they would both die.

Skye turned her head to him. He couldn't acknowledge her. If he gave Asha the impression that Skye mattered, this would all be over. His dismissal of her had to be done. He would rather scoop her up, let the whole club know who she belonged to, and leave this place. His demon sunk claws into the walls of his mind.

Khaine kept his voice even, his tone flat and uncaring. "Go."

He could *feel* her eyes digging into him. Without a word, she walked toward the bar.

Toward Castello.

She was trailing behind the fucking Dryad. Creatures followed her with eyes he would rip from their skulls. The club erupted into murmurs, most of them comments about her mortality. What they could do with her mortality. How they could pleasure themselves with her mortality. He'd just denied her in front of everyone.

Thoughts of ripping out their tongues bombarded him.

Khaine fought the urge to stalk to her side and demand to know why she chose *that* direction. She could have gone anywhere in the club. Hell, she could have waited for him at the entrance, in the *fucking* car. The need to stake his claim on her was palpable.

No. Khaine watched her from his peripheral vision. She'd chosen to follow the Dryad back to the bar and *sit next to him*.

His demon thrashed his insides and he gritted his teeth. *Claim her!* She couldn't know what she was toying with.

"Have you finally come back to me, demon?" Asha's voice was enticing, the vibrant sound pouring over him. She raked her nails down his left arm. "Your eyes darken. Does the memory of our time together beguile another?"

Never.

His eyes darkened because his female was sitting next to the same Dryad that threatened his life. One wrong move on Castello's part and their coming here would go from a simple retrieval to a dangerous game of *kill the immortal tree-hugger.*

Khaine forced himself to focus on the task at hand. "Perhaps."

Asha's golden eyes lightened, flecks of blue and green sheening in their depths. "Come, demon. Sit with me."

She motioned toward a Kurs in the far corner and the creature took over the DJ's place, reviving the musical thunder. Immortals left and right resumed their conversations, the sudden noise overwhelming after such silence.

Khaine followed her, keeping Skye in his sights. His wants torn, he sat in the chair across from Asha and grinned. It was time to get that amulet. The faster he got it, the faster he could be back at Skye's side.

"Remove your sword, demon. There is no threat, here."

No threat? Glancing at Skye sitting by Castello, Khaine grimaced. If only that were true.

He didn't want to offend Asha, though, so removed the strap across his chest and leaned his sword against his chair.

"Tell me why you've come."

Asha's eyes were searching him. He rested his forearms on the table and leaned forward. "Perhaps I only sought to be in your presence."

"You flatter me, demon." Her hair snaked under the table and rubbed his calf. "But that is not the reason. Tell me."

Khaine sighed. He was hoping to avoid this. It would have been easier for him to entice her to give him the amulet instead of outright asking for it.

"The amulet." He motioned to her necklace. "It's a gateway key."

"Perhaps."

Asha's hair folded under his pant leg and brushed against his skin. He hardly suppressed a shudder. He didn't want her touching him. He wanted Skye touching him. Asha could work her magic for now; he'd cut her hair off later.

"You want it."

It wasn't a question, but Khaine nodded anyway. If she didn't give it to him freely, he would be forced to take it from her. Calgary wouldn't be the only immortal club he was forced to slaughter to get his brother back if that happened, and this club wasn't filled with lesser beings.

"I wish to borrow it to get to the dimension it opens and back."

"Why?" she asked.

"The destination has value to me."

Asha regarded him with all the resemblance of a cat in heat. She licked one of her crimson nails and smiled. That motion alone could cause an unmated immortal to fall into her trap. He should know. He almost had.

Not this time, though. His mate was only yards away.

Sitting next to *another man.*

"What will you give me for its use, demon? My appetite is ravenous, this eve."

Khaine narrowed his eyes on the Hirx. What would he give for the amulet that could take him to the only being able to aid in his brother's freedom?

"Anything."

Chapter 13

Skye let her feet carry her in the only direction she could think of, to the bar where Castello had retreated. Her thoughts numb, she slumped on the stool next to him and without thinking, gazed at Khaine and Asha sitting snug in the dim lights.

He'd dismissed her. In front of everyone.

She didn't miss the eruption of voices that had followed.

He'd dismissed his *mate*.

Nobody else in the club could know she was the demon's mate, but *she* knew it. She didn't think such a thing was possible. Skye didn't want to admit it, but his blatant disregard of her had hurt. She should have left and gone back to the car. Hell, she could have left the *city* and he wouldn't have cared. His eyes had been glued to Asha. Why did the thought make her want to cry?

Don't you dare feel sadness over him, she told herself. There would be no leaving, now. It didn't escape her notice that Asha had an expensive-looking jewel draped around her neck.

The relic.

That had to be what Khaine came for. That meant it was what *she* came for, and she'd be taking it from him as soon as he got his filthy, demon claws on it.

Bastard.

"You're with the demon."

Skye pivoted on the stool and peered at Castello. His deep, angered voice cut through the resounding music. His dark green eyes were beginning to take on the black shade of his curly hair. Black stubble lined his cheeks and jaw. He was a good-looking man. An immortal. Khaine had called him a Dryad.

Her traitorous eyes drifted back to Khaine and Asha. Did she think the Dryad was a handsome man? Khaine could melt her in her shoes, if she were wearing any.

Not!

Skye contemplated finding a Witch to curse him with green ogre skin and pompous pores.

"You have a lot of nerve coming over here," Castello said.

His gaze was murderous. Skye could see all the ways he was envisioning hurting her for standing by Khaine's side, and he wasn't even looking at her, anymore. The demon must have done something unforgivable. Then again, this was Khaine they were talking about. He couldn't seem to do anything but.

"If you're trying to decide if I matter to him and you can use me as leverage for whatever revenge you have planned, don't bother. I don't matter."

Castello's voice had been laced with nothing but hatred and

detestation, but if Skye could spit venom, her voice was just that.

Castello's eyes softened as he looked at her. "I noticed."

She returned her stare to Khaine and Asha. They were sitting on opposite sides of a table, surrounded by blacklights hanging in white shades, their faces a finger's width apart. Any closer and they would be kissing.

"You look like you could use a drink."

She forced her attention back to the man beside her, Castello, who was presently sliding a glass of opaque, pink liquid her way. The drink stopped in front of her. It sloshed but held its contents. She hadn't even heard him order anything.

"No worries," he said. He tossed back a similar drink and upturned the cup on the bar. "It's safe for mortals."

Gee, that washed away all her uncertainties.

"What is it?"

The tempo of the music picked up its pace. Immortals danced and ground their bodies together to the beat.

"Sex on the Beach. Although, I believe they call it Wicked Kiss, here." Castello was watching her with rapt amusement now, but so was every other immortal sitting, and standing, within feet of her. It almost unnerved her. It wasn't unheard of for a mortal to know and understand the ways of immortals, but for one to attend an immortal nightclub and appear to have a drink with one of the patrons without being an appetizer to some twisted game? Outlandish.

Chancing another glance at the happy couple she wanted to throttle, she took a strong swig. Orange and peach burst in her mouth, dancing in tune with the music on her tongue. Her fingers closed around the glass and she sipped again, relishing in the heady smell of vodka. If this *was* Sex on the Beach, it was the best damn version she'd ever had.

Asha's hair twirled around Khaine's leg. She should hack it off, use Khaine's own sword for the pleasure of it.

"In a few moments, you won't matter to him," Castello said beside her. He stared at the wall of liquor in front of him, dark hair a shimmer in the blue overhangs. The worn wood of the bar-top grated under her arm.

Before he could get the wrong impression, Skye plastered a scowl on her face and shrugged her shoulders. "Matter to him? He doesn't matter to *me*."

A painful jolt kicked her in the stomach.

She would *not* watch them. Skye turned on the stool and faced the mirror lining the back of the bar. Blue LEDs drooped around a tall sheet of glass, illuminating her poor excuse of a reflection. Her hair was a mess, not like Asha's shimmering, black and purple mane. Her dress was a size too small around her waist and nothing like the stunning assemble barely covering the Goddess's body. Her breasts, though snug in the dress's fringed top, were a size too small on her frame, whereas the Hirx's breasts were full and large, practically spilling out of her top. There were even black circles under Skye's eyes she hoped to god were a consequence of no sleep and not leftover demon innards. No wonder Khaine had denied her. There was no comparison between her and the Hirx.

Skye downed the rest of her drink and slammed the cup upside down on the bar.

Castello raised a brow and smiled.

"He hurt someone close to me, too. At that bar," Skye said.

Mckenzie had been wanting to fine-tune every inch of

Khaine with her claws ever since. She'd made it out. The *only* one who'd made it out.

Castello watched her for so long she thought she might have sprouted horns to match her current state. "Mckenzie?"

Her eyes widened. "You know her?"

"You could say that. We crossed paths a few weeks ago. Split ways on her return."

When Castello had mentioned Khaine hurting someone he cared about at the club, Skye just assumed Khaine had killed them.

"Return? You mean she's back in town?"

He smiled. "Last I checked."

Mckenzie was back! That could only mean one thing. She was out there, right now, hunting Skye down. If Khaine was anywhere around when she caught up...

She looked toward their table. Asha was running her nails over the table between them, her breasts all but spilling out on the surface. Khaine smiled at Asha and she tried not to flinch.

He'd never smiled at her like that.

That's because he hates you, she reminded herself. For no reason. She was his mate, and he hated her.

His lips quirked in a way that made her want to run her tongue over them. His eyes were black obsidian, looking at the Goddess before him. Soaking her up. She already knew his eyes by now. The only time they changed like that was when she angered him or aroused him.

Since he was presently smiling, she didn't think anger was the cause this time.

Was he imagining all the ways he would please the Goddess?

She was the mate of an immortal demon that didn't want

her and would rather spend his time with another woman. Khaine had just confirmed how little she mattered.

Not that she cared.

Get the amulet and be done with him, she told herself. Let Mckenzie have her way with him if there was anything left. She had bigger problems to contend with. Her life was days away from ending and she was sulking at a bar because a *demon* denied her.

Get a grip!

Skye forced her eyes away. "So, how do you know Mckenzie?"

Castello frowned and slammed back another drink the barkeep left before him, a Slig almost as thin as the column holding up a shelf of liquor. She'd been to a few clubs before with Caden and the others. Temptest seemed like a place she could let loose a little, if it wasn't for the ways mortals and immortals let loose.

Castello's voice was distant as he toyed with the empty glass. "Thought she was someone she isn't."

If she didn't know Mckenzie so well, that would have made less sense.

"You must be Skye," Castello said. "She mentioned her sisters. What are you doing in an immortal bar, and with that demon." He spat the last two words like it was a sacrilege to even speak them.

She sighed. "It's a long story. Suffice it to say, I have no choice. Besides, I don't plan on being around him long."

"Then you wouldn't mind if I killed him?" The corner of his lip quirked.

Asha moved from her seat and skirted the table. Standing

in front of Khaine, her jeweled skirt danced over his lap, right before she climbed on top of him.

"Not at all," Skye gritted, turning away from the pair.

Damn the demon.

"Do you have a phone?"

"A phone?" Castello seemed genuinely confused.

"If Mckenzie is back in town, I need to get a message to her." It would also be nice to know if Caden was alright.

"I have no phone. Sorry"

"No phone? What century are you living in?"

Castello smirked. "Now you sound like Mckenzie."

She turned to the barkeep. Maybe she could use the bar's phone. Or she could go back to the car and see if Khaine left the sat phone there. It's not like the demon would notice her gone. The Slig behind the bar turned bottles up in the air, pouring mixtures of different colored liquids into glasses. The creature handed them to the patrons without even moving from its position, its long, slender arms reaching several feet with ease. The immortals sitting next to Skye were still eyeing her with rapt amusement. That unnerved her the more she focused on it. This wasn't the place to be noticed. Not for a mortal.

Asking the barkeep for a phone didn't sound like a fun idea. Too much attention would be drawn to her. Sitting next to Castello seemed like the only thing keeping her from being a toy in this place.

Khaine probably had the sat phone in his pocket or locked it in the car. She could easily break a window to get it, but if Khaine got the relic while she was gone, she wouldn't have the slightest idea how to use it. She wasn't letting him out of her sight until he had his filthy claws on what she was after.

Skye scrunched her face and tried not to look at Khaine.

"Could you do me a favor?" she asked Castello, her voice rising to be heard over the loud beat of the music.

Castello nodded. "Anything for Mckenzie's sister."

She didn't know Castello, had no reason to trust him, but if he knew Mckenzie then maybe he could get a message to her. Mckenzie could be out there right now, on her way to this very bar. In fact, if she was back in town and Brooke or Jade had filled her in, that went from chance to certain. Caden would be with her if she wasn't dead.

Skye held back those treacherous thoughts and pressed on. "I didn't leave Mckenzie and the others in good standing. I think Caden might be hurt and if Mckenzie is back, she'll be looking for me. There's something I need to do so I can't wait for her. Could you get a message to Mckenzie for me?"

Skye didn't miss the way Castello's eyes lit up at the mention of him relaying information to Mckenzie. If she was a betting woman, it would seem Mckenzie meant something to him.

"I could," he said. "What happened? Are they all right?" Castello narrowed his eyes at her. "Did the demon hurt them?"

Shit. He already harbored a grudge toward Khaine. She didn't think it would be wise to give him another reason to want to murder him.

And what do you care, her inner conscience chided. He doesn't want you, remember?

"No. He didn't hurt them." Which wasn't a lie. Khaine wasn't the reason the portal was destroyed, Skye was.

"I'll get this message to her," Castello said.

"Thank you. Just tell them I'm safe and that I might have found a way to get rid of my...um...problem."

"Your problem?"

"Yes. My problem. Mckenzie will know what that means." That's if she stuck around long enough to get filled in on the situation. "Just tell her that I'll be back soon and not to worry."

Castello motioned for the barkeep and in a language she didn't understand, yelled a single word. Moments later, the barkeep outstretched its slender arm and set a piece of paper in front of Castello. An orange pen followed. An image of Slenderman rose in the back of her mind, making the hair on her arms stand up.

"Perhaps you should write it down," Castello said. "I've no doubt your message would be best coming from you."

He was right. Under the circumstances, it was highly unlikely that Mckenzie, and hopefully Caden, would trust anybody but her. Writing a message also seemed more appealing than dealing with Slenderman behind the bar, and calling Mckenzie would be nothing but questions she didn't have all the answers to. She could do this on her own. She just needed her sisters to know she was safe.

Skye scribbled down what she told Castello, trying not to make it sound like a forced note. She handed him the paper but couldn't let it go. Her eyes drifted behind Castello again, and everything else disappeared.

The bar hovered in silence, her focus locked on Khaine, on Asha, on their lips *connected* as she straddled his lap. He was kissing her.

Kissing.

She thought she knew hurt? He'd denied her in front of everyone, all but told her to get lost. It had hurt, for reasons she couldn't fathom, and now he was blatantly proving just how little she mattered.

He'd said she was his mate. Skye didn't want to be the demon's mate because he would never love her; probably didn't know what love was. But this? No immortal could toss their mate aside that easily, although possible to do so, but it was *impossible* for an immortal to sexually toss their mate aside, which meant only one thing.

He'd lied.

She hadn't wanted to come to that conclusion before and had blocked it as a possibility from her brain. She couldn't do that, now. There was no doubt in her mind; Skye wasn't his mate. She couldn't be.

For some reason, the realization of that hit her square in the stomach.

The paper in her hand felt heavy, hovering over the bar top between her and Castello.

Why lie?

What purpose did he have in pretending to be mated to her? Had he done it thinking she would spare his life?

Hadn't she? Skye narrowed her eyes. He'd confessed to her being his mate back in the tomb, and instead of killing him, she'd been too stunned and let him lead her away from her backup. He'd separated her from the herd like a wolf, and she'd *let* him, all because he'd professed to some unbreakable bond between them, and she'd been too stunned to use her head.

That didn't explain why he didn't let her go. Was he toying with her? Was this some fucking game to the demon?

The bastard didn't know pain. Did he think being blown up along with the portal was pain?

Skye had planned to steal the amulet from him and leave.

Now? Her hand went limp around the paper and it fell in front of Castello. Khaine's sword tilted against the table in front of him, practically begging her to use it.

Khaine's nails lengthened, black blades curling around Asha's waist, in her hair, his eyes a reflection of the void around them. They were locked together as though the only two in the building. Her stomach turned at her own stupidity.

Skye's gaze was fixated, the silence deafening. Nobody seemed to notice them.

Because nobody was looking. They seemed to all be focused in the same direction.

Skye pried her eyes away from Khaine and Asha, snapping herself out of the trance. She grasped that the silence she heard was because the DJ had abandoned his post, the conversations ceased, and not a soul was moving. The note she tried to give Castello lay ignored on the bar top. He was looking at something behind her, his eyes heated and muscles tense. Khaine and Asha parted lips as Skye followed the club's gaze to the entryway. Her heart dropped.

Leclain.

Chapter 14

S kye stared at Leclain.

The vampire stood under the archway by the front doors, dressed in black from head to toe. His hair was a thick mass of short strands on his head, his jaw was covered in trimmed, black stubble, and his eyes were red.

It was rumored the vampire had found his lifeblood, but that she had been killed before he could claim her. If that were true and he *had* claimed her, he wouldn't be alive. A vampire could only feed from their lifeblood once they tasted them. If a vampire's lifeblood died, the vampire would soon follow, starved of the blood they needed.

Leclain had never claimed her, but the loss of his lifeblood had changed him. A vampire's eyes only turned red when aroused or enraged, but Leclain's had been the color of blood ever since that day. The Province, when gathered in large groups of different races, spread rumors faster than mortals.

Skye never cared about those rumors, but if they held merit, it would explain the vampire's hate. It would also help explain his current allegiance. With Leclain standing in the presence of so many immortals, or *any* immortal, that only meant one thing.

"The Elite," Skye said.

Castello shot to his feet beside her, grabbing the note she wrote for him and stuffing it in his pocket. The stool he'd been sitting on tumbled to the ground. "Run."

The club bounded to its feet as one, erupting around her, scrambling to dark corners and other hidden exits. In walls. Behind pictures. Mirrors no longer served a purpose and were smashed to reveal tunnels; black holes leading to unknown places. It seemed Asha had planned for something like this to happen. The Elite didn't normally target clubs, but their brazen attempts at kidnapping immortals for their sick experiments had been getting brash. Their slapdash actions were foolhardy at best and meticulously executed at worst. Immortals were on edge, the Province in an uproar.

Men stormed the building, mortal men, guns swinging around their tight frames as bullets grazed every inch of the chaotic scene. Automatic weapons cut through the pandemonium. They wouldn't kill an immoral, but Skye wasn't immortal.

And she also wasn't leaving. Not until she had what she came for; the amulet.

Mortal men and women dropped to the ground unmoving, their naked bodies splayed across the dance floor as immortals trampled them in search of an exit.

Khaine was on his feet, his black eyes locked on Asha and

sword drawn. The blacklights collided with muzzle blasts around the room creating a strobe effect that blanketed the dance floor with patches of light, the screams of immortals being shot ringing out in tune. Skye tried to focus on Khaine and Asha. His entire body seemed to be blocking any bullets that might graze her in the uproar. She lost sight of them, ducking her head when a few stray bullets blasted a stool beside her. Her heart thundered in her chest. She tried to slow her breathing and remain calm.

Lights shattered all around Skye. She shoved at an immortal running past her and ducked under one of the tables. Furniture upturned in the roar of moving bodies. Debris littered her hair, thick chunks of wood splintering above her head. In the entryway of the club, Elite soldiers fanned their way into the darkening room and funneled up the stairway to the second floor. Bodies fell over the railing, some lifeless, others rebounding to their feet in a hurry. Leclain never moved, his stance even, red eyes focused toward the back. They had to be after a particular immortal.

The soldiers were following Leclain's line of sight to the Hovard at the rear of the building, surrounded by Womnots tearing each other to pieces in a panic. The screams were deafening in the smoke-riddled room. The immortals dropping all around her were nothing but collateral damage.

Someone grabbed her arm, pulled her from under the table, and dragged her behind the bar. Castello. Skye shielded her face with one arm as glass shattered and liquor filled her hair to mix with the remnants of shredded oak. She hung her head to protect her eyes.

"There's an exit to the right!" Castello pointed to a mirror that lay broken on the tile floor behind her. A tunnel descended into the darkness where it once hung. "Run to it!"

"I'm not leaving." Skye turned back to him, yelling to be heard over the ear-piercing blasts of gunfire and the mixture of immortals shouting, her adrenaline making her memory faulty. Castello would hear her over an explosion.

"You need to go! I can cover your escape."

Escape? Castello wasn't hearing her. She was *not* leaving.

Skye threw herself to the side as bullets punctured the bar, her only thought that of getting to Khaine.

Castello's long, curly hair shielded his green eyes and he pushed it back.

"Go!" Castello bellowed the command and shoved her toward the broken mirror, his eyes pleading.

Behind him in the darkened corridor, surrounded by foam rubble that once constituted couches, Khaine wrapped his forearm around Asha's waist and dodged a barrage of gunfire. Had he even looked at Skye since the Elite arrived? His mate whom he should be concerned for?

No. He was trying to save *her*.

Because Skye *wasn't* his mate.

She clenched her jaw. Frustration and anger replaced any trace of fear.

The amulet still hung around Asha's neck, the muzzle flashes around the room draping the jeweled surface in flares of light.

"I'm not leaving," Skye gritted. Without hesitation, she leaped what was left of the bar's counter and dashed across the room leaving Castello shouting behind her. She would get that amulet. She would dismiss Khaine as he had done to her, take it from him and be gone. Knocking furniture out of her path, Skye only stopped to catch her breath and wait for the next opening between her and the wall of bullets blocking her path to Khaine. Huddling by a partially intact stool, she counted the seconds and then ran.

Stop. Run. Stop. She made it across the bar in record time, not a single soldier paying her any attention. She kept her focus on Khaine, ignoring the dead bodies all around her, the blood turning to pools on top of the tile. She stopped by another half-demolished table and waited. There were only feet between her and them, now. She could picture her hands wrapping around his throat and squeezing.

The gunfire changed direction and she vaulted the table.

A millisecond away from reaching her prize, Skye tripped over a chair, the hem of her dress snagging on one of its legs, and crashed into an Elite soldier. She screamed, the sudden change of movement startling her. Their focus had been directed to the Hovard they were presently cornering, the bullets cutting through the room only a deterrent, but not anymore.

The gunfire stopped and every Elite soldier, that wasn't blocking the Hovard's escape, turned to her. The silence was consuming.

Skye took several long breaths to calm herself.

Even Khaine looked. For the first time since the Elite's arrival, Khaine's wide eyes were staring at her in horror. His hands trembled around his blade. Their current situation must have sunk in.

The demon feared being taken.

Not Skye. The Elite had no use for her, she was mortal. Besides, her life wasn't supposed to end like this.

The Elite soldier leaned down, his military hair a dark brown and emanating the smell of tobacco and sour caviar. It was strong. Skye could smell it over the remains of smoke drifting through the room, over the smell of charcoal and sulfur from so many shots being fired in such close quarters.

"What have we, here? A mortal?"

"Stop playing with your damn cock. Kill the bitch and come help us!"

The soldier jammed his gun to her forehead and smirked, the barrel so close she could make out M249 Saw engraved on the side. "You groupies can't seem to stay away. Lucky for you, I have the perfect solution to your problem." He drew back and aimed.

The first pull of the trigger would kill her. Skye stared straight into the barrel of the fully-automatic, belt-fed .556, and smiled. What did she have to lose?

"Tell me," Khaine roared.

Skye chanced a glance in their direction, hardly noticing her relief when the soldier turned his sights to Khaine.

"We should take the demon," he yelled over his shoulder.

Khaine ripped the amulet from Asha's neck and clutched it in his left hand.

"Press a drop of blood to the amulet's bottom star." Her voice was hoarse. Apparently, Khaine hadn't done a good job of keeping her out of danger. "Follow the river to the red water. The sky cave is the way."

She'd given him the map.

Skye turned back to the soldier and jammed her foot into his shin, taking advantage of his momentary distraction from Khaine's outburst. The soldier pulled the trigger as she dodged to the side, the barrage of bullets narrowly missing her head. Nobody moved, Asha kneeling by a tall, brick column, the club's clientele scattered to safety, and the Elite soldiers no doubt thinking a mere mortal posed no threat. The hell she didn't! It would be the last time they underestimated a mortal on a mission.

The soldier doubled over, clutching his leg. "Stupid bitch!"

Bolting to her feet before the others could come to their senses, Skye ran toward Khaine. The corner of his mouth turned up in a slow, satisfactory smile at her approach, but it wasn't him she was focused on. It was what he held.

The demon had no right to smile at her. He was clearly standing in front of the woman that really mattered to him.

Before Khaine could think to shield it, Skye snatched the amulet from his hand, a feeling of gratification gripping her when his smile turned to a frown, then a menacing growl as she dashed toward the exit Castello had pointed out. She didn't see the Dryad and hoped to God he had made it out alive, took his own advice and ran. The Elite soldiers turned back to the Hovard, seeming too busy to care for her escape. Good.

Skye skidded over the broken glass from the mirror and ducked through the dark tunnel.

Khaine would chase her. If the Elite didn't mow him down the second he moved, he would be right behind her in moments, but she didn't care. Sounds of gunfire erupted behind her, coming from the tunnel's entrance, and still, she ran. He might catch her. He might not. All she could think about was getting outside with the amulet and using it to escape.

Her heart pounding and lungs on fire, Skye sprinted around the tunnel's curved corners, never slowing. To keep from dropping the amulet in her haste, she secured it in the swell of her breasts, then watched it as she ran for a distance to make sure it wouldn't fall out. How long was this damn tunnel? It seemed to go on for miles, the dusted corridor only lit in places by discarded torches still burning. She wanted to jump with joy as light shone through an opening up ahead. Why did this moment remind her so much of that damn movie they watched?

"Stop!"

Khaine's deep voice bounced between the narrow walls, then echoed in the still night as she burst into a tall cove of trees. Torches lay discarded in a heap outside the tunnel, left to burn in the darkness; the light she had seen from inside.

It seemed Khaine had made it out without interference from the soldiers. It had taken him some time. Skye wondered if he'd stopped to tuck Asha someplace safe before coming after her.

Don't really care!

Was it bad form to secretly hope Asha had been mowed down by gunfire, later hauled off to some compound and dissected with tiny instruments?

In the distance, immortals shouted for mercy as shots rang out. She ran as fast as she could, her sides on fire. The tunnel must have doubled back around, the maze of it emerging not far from the club.

"Mate!"

Mate? He was still playing that lie?

Skye laughed at the absurdity of it then ducked under a low branch. She made a sharp left around another tree trying to ward him off. She carried herself as fast as her feet would allow, away from the club and the demon chasing her. His heavy footfalls grew nearer, the thunder of his boots beating against the ground closing in on her. Heaving for breath, Skye tore branches from trees and threw them behind her. The thick limbs she tore off scratched her palms before she could drop them. Several refused to break free and she cried out as they lashed her. She didn't have to stop him, only slow him down.

Dark shadows littered the forest around her making it hard to see. She couldn't run as fast as she needed to escape him or risk impaling herself on a branch, or worse, tripping over her own blasted feet and having Khaine catch her. That horrid realization hit her hard. He was going to catch up before she could open the dimension.

More tattered screams in the distance turned her heels south, back toward the riverfront by the club. Khaine followed her. The sweet smell of ozone in the air filled her nose with each gasp for breath. She was close to the river now, the mist in the air like fresh rain. She'd never had to run this fast or this far before. Had never had an immortal chasing her because she stole something it wanted.

And Khaine *really* wanted the amulet. He was a demon in the dark, hunting her.

His thunderous roar behind her shook her to her bones. What would he do if he caught her?

Kill her?

Skye forced back another laugh. Of course, he would. The hunter had no ties to its prey. She wasn't the gorgeous demon's mate.

"He's *not* gorgeous," Skye gritted through breaths as she poured the last ounce of her energy into a sprint toward the docks. "Follow me, you bastard."

"Stop, woman!"

Dizzy on adrenaline, and despite a lack of oxygen making it hard to speak, Skye laughed and shouted over her shoulder. "Never!" A smile broke through whatever fear she should be feeling. She was drunk on it, on Khaine chasing her, on knowing she had stolen something he desperately wanted.

He was almost on her. Skye hooked her foot and bent under a low branch mid-stride, skirting what looked like a bush on the other side. She couldn't tell! Shapes were distorting around her in the darkness, her lungs pushing out more air than they were taking in.

Wet, tropical hardwood bombarded her senses, relief rushing toward her in waves of boats lining the dock along the water.

Skye pleaded for the Elite soldiers to not be the same bunch she escaped in the club. Her limbs were burning, a steady cramp forging a pit in her right side. If they recognized her, she would have to run headlong back into the forest and take her chances facing Khaine alone.

Skye didn't want to face him, didn't want the lying demon anywhere near her. She could finish this journey on her own. She didn't need him or anybody else getting in her way!

Pebbled grass turned into a concrete walkway under her feet. Up ahead, amongst the overhanging lamps shining light onto the moisture-covered boardwalk, immortals thrashed in chains while Elite soldiers jammed their guns into their backs.

"Almost there, Skye," she said to herself.

Leclain. Skye stopped almost involuntarily at the sight of the vampire standing beside the group, and Khaine tackled her from behind.

Chapter 15

Skye tensed as Khaine spun her on the ground. His large palms gripped her shoulders as he dug her back into the pebbled cement.

"What is the meaning of this!" His disheveled hair fell into his black eyes. He shifted her side to side looking for the amulet.

Skye couldn't help it, she smiled. Ignorant demon.

As if suddenly realizing who stood not ten yards away, he lowered his voice and scowled at her. "Where is it?"

Right, because that mattered more to him. No care toward the scratches on each hand trickling blood. No care if she was going to catch her breath or die from a lack of oxygen.

Not his mate. Not his mate.

"Get off me, Khaine. We have nothing to say to each other."

Skye twisted her neck to see the group behind them. "Please, let this work."

"Let what—"

Taking a deep breath, she let it out full swing, ignoring the sudden pain in her chest it caused. "Help! Help! There's one over here, help me!"

Khaine strained above her and cupped a hand over her mouth, but it was too late. Leclain turned to them, the Elite soldiers following suit. She thrashed under the demon's weight trying to make it appear as though he were attacking her.

He is attacking you!

"Over here," they shouted.

Khaine did exactly as she had expected, he released her. He couldn't focus on her if his life was in jeopardy. No, not his life, but his freedom. The Elite wouldn't kill him, simply torture him for years trying to decide what made him tick.

Khaine rose to his feet, a hiss playing on his lips, his limbs stiff and slow. Like a cornered dog waiting for the opportune moment to attack, he kept his legs a half-breath apart and tucked his arms to his sides, eyes blending with the dark sky behind him. He looked worried, but Skye reminded herself that the demon wasn't to be trusted, and therefore the thin line of his lips and furrowed brow wasn't to be trusted either.

The Elite soldiers moved forward in a steady group. They were cautious, their guns at the ready.

"Get up," Khaine said. His black shirt stretched as his muscles tensed.

She did, not because he told her to, but because she'd fulfilled her purpose. Khaine would otherwise be indisposed for an undetermined amount of time, long enough for her to make her escape and be done with him. By the time she got back, alive, Khaine would be long gone.

Skye got to her feet, pulling the dress he bought her, and coerced her into wearing, back down around her caves. Blood from her hands streaked the thin material, the papercuts already scabbing.

She took a step back and retrieved the amulet from her breasts, clutching the chain in her hand.

Khaine glanced at her out of the corner of his eye. His predatory gaze narrowed. "Don't."

"I wish this could have gone another way."

Perhaps in another life, under different circumstances, her and Khaine could have had something together. Mate or no mate, she couldn't deny the sensations he caused. As it was, Khaine was a lying, manipulative demon, and she didn't have much life left.

Soldiers advanced on him. At a dozen feet away, they were the definition of intimidating. They had a demon in their sights, and they wouldn't be letting it go.

"Has my presence been so dissatisfying?"

He was desperate. His shoulders curled, his neck stiff. He would try to fight them. The moment they put their hands on him, he would lash out, but even with his enhanced speed and strength, Khaine didn't stand a chance against six fully trained men wielding automatic weapons. Her stomach did a little somersault.

Don't go getting soft on me, now.

He'd left her no choice.

Skye took another step back. "I'm sorry."

And just like that, his face changed. His thin lips curved into a snarl, his brows going from high arches to drawn slits that slanted above his black eyes. This was the demon she met back at the hideout, the demon that demanded everything be done his way or not at all. Who kidnapped her, degraded her, and left her to pick up the pieces. No, she didn't feel sorry for him. Not a fucking ounce of pity.

She had no use for a man like him in her life. Didn't *need* a man at all, she told herself.

"Don't move," he said.

"I know this must be hard for you," she chided, "but you can't just order—"

"For once," Khaine snapped, "do as you're told."

She froze. Something about his pale face and cold eyes said wrong. Was that panic in his voice?

Fear? Khaine was genuinely afraid, and suddenly angry. What did a demon have to fear? It was a ruse, it had to be. She'd have to be the dumbest woman alive to fall for another one of his tricks.

Skye shook her head and backed up, into a hard surface that wasn't there before. Large hands snaked up her arms, cold and heavy.

"Back away, Leclain," Khaine said.

That wasn't possible! The vampire had been too far away to reach her that fast, unless he... No, he couldn't have. Vampires could only teleport short distances once they fed from their Lifeblood. Leclain wouldn't be alive if he'd fed from his mate all those years ago. His mate had died. Vampires needed blood to survive. No mate meant no blood.

He'd been standing several hundred yards away not seconds ago as the soldiers descended on Khaine.

"I think I have something you want," Leclain said. His hands rubbed her shoulders, his accent digging a grave in her ears. "A mortal. Let's see how long she can scream."

Skye stood motionless. Her heart was hammering inside her ribs. She needed to calm herself down. There was no use in getting herself worked up, now.

Or was there?

Fear. That's what she needed. She needed to be afraid! One blast would send Leclain vaulting into the water. But damnit, she wasn't. Even with a vampire behind her, that had just threatened to kill her, she wasn't afraid. Startled, anxious, and frustrated beyond all reason, but not afraid. The Elite soldiers positioned themselves around Khaine, one breaking off to stand beside her and Leclain. Khaine growled and moved his body in a slow circle trying to keep everyone in his sights.

It wasn't supposed to happen this way. They were supposed to focus on Khaine, not her.

Skye couldn't let them take her. She bore down on her emotions, picturing all the things the Elite would do to her if taken. Electrocution, dissection, drowning. They would find the most enjoyable way to kill her and let everyone watch. Or worse, hand her off to some starving immortal and document what they did with a human.

And Caden. Gods, Caden. What would her sister learn had happened to her? And Jade? Brooke? Mckenzie? Would they find her body dumped in some heap of a trash pile, her hands and feet cut off, teeth removed?

Her fingers tingled. Khaine narrowed his eyes at her. Did he know what she planned to do?

He smirked. "Back away, Leclain. I don't think you're going to like what comes next. *Trust* me."

Skye let the tingle work up her arms, fueled by thoughts

of torture. Fueled by the thought of her sisters never seeing her again, of never knowing if Caden survived. She still wasn't afraid, but there was something inside her that wanted out; a light pressure in the palm of her hands. Leclain released her. The soldiers beside Khaine took a few steps back, the one beside her moving to stand with the others. That's right, Skye thought, back away.

Khaine looked at her and his eyes held something she hadn't seen before. Pride. He was proud? Of her?

Use it, a voice inside her said.

She took the energy in her fingers, in her arms, that had worked its way to her chest, and funneled it into one ball. She couldn't see it, but she *held* it, twirled it in her palms, and let it go.

Skye cringed, preparing herself for the blast, to run the moment Leclain and the others were immobile. Khaine unsheathed his sword and sliced the neck off a soldier beside him, tossing him to the ground and using him as a shield. She tensed, waiting.

Bits of blue and green flashed from her palms and collided mid-air. They tumbled in waves over themselves before settling together like an orb. It expanded in front of her, growing darker and larger.

She took a step back and watched it twirl before them, the realization of what she'd done sinking in.

Oh, no. She didn't blast them all; she created a portal!

The orb elongated, sucking matter from around it to feed itself. The darkness solidified, shimmering with lighter streaks of blue.

All around her, the air became stale, and still it grew until it was taller than her. Skye looked at Khaine huddled behind the dead soldier, stunned by what she had done. She'd created a portal, by herself.

He narrowed his seething eyes on her, all manner of pride washed from his demonic face. She'd kept this secret from him. If he didn't have plans to kill her before, it would seem his plans had changed.

Khaine jumped to his feet as the first demon emerged from the portal. Memories of that night in Vegas bombarded her, of that boy's mangled body laying across her bed. Khaine gripped his sword, and it was at that moment that Skye knew she had to escape before he could get his claws on her.

Leclain unsheathed the blade at his side and effortlessly sliced the demon's head off. The Elite soldiers panicked, another demon emerging from the portal and charging for them. They reached for Khaine, wrapped their hands around each arm, and tried to drag him back. He snatched one arm free and swung his sword, cutting the demon in two, his balance off from being pulled on and making his attack sloppy.

Both halves of the demon writhed on the damp boardwalk. They would continue moving, continue living as separate parts until the head was severed.

Leclain was busy fighting a pair of horned monsters behind her, and the remaining Elite, yards away, were ushering their immortal catches into several black SUVs. So far, nobody except for Khaine was paying her any attention, and the look in his black eyes sent a chill down her spine. What had she done?

"Take the demon," Leclain yelled.

Take the demon... Yes, this was her chance.

"What of the girl?" another shouted.

Khaine roared her name. She clutched the amulet in her hand and dove for the dead soldier.

"Don't let her escape," Leclain roared.

The star at the bottom center needed blood for the portal to open, and the dead soldier lying not even a yard away wouldn't be needing his anymore. Landing on the hard stone before him, Skye smeared her hand, amulet and all, into the still warm blood at the soldier's throat. Before she could stand, a light shot out from the blue diamond, growing larger than the portal at her back. She jumped to her feet, but a hand snatched her wrist and locked down.

"I have her," one of the soldiers shouted.

The hell he did. Skye jerked her arm back, taking the stunned soldier with it. Turning her whole body, she positioned the wide-eyed man in front of the demon's entrance and kicked him through the swirling surface. She thought he screamed, his mouth agape but soundless. She couldn't be sure as the portal expanded around him, sucking him in. She never tried to enter one before, had never thrown anything through its void. She had no idea what would happen. It seemed to feed on him, happy to be given life. As if that was all it wanted, the portal rippled and closed with a silent implosion.

She'd killed him. She'd never killed a person before. Demons were one thing. Mortals?

Too dumbfounded to move from where she stood, Skye turned in place, a full, slow circle, and faced the soldiers still holding Khaine. Her body was numb. No, she couldn't shut down. Not now. For the first time in her life, several eyes regarded her like a monster. They held a demon between them, that could, and *would* kill them without hesitation, and it was her they were staring at in horror.

None of them had moved. Leclain was gone, had made some grand escape. The portal to the other dimension hung not five feet away from her. She peered at Khaine and his demon blasted forth, no doubt knowing exactly what she planned. He thrashed and clawed at the soldiers holding him, his eyes dark, fangs gripping her attention from the black veins running through his face. His obsidian eyes locked on her.

He would kill her, here and now if she gave him the chance. She wasn't a murderer, never had been, but Khaine had no quarrels with the subject. She could see it in the chiseled arches of his brows. The thought of killing a man did something to her stomach she couldn't afford to process at the moment. Her first kill. Caden would be so proud!

The Elite soldiers were barely hanging on, dropping around Khaine as others took their place, men running to help their comrades.

Skye snapped herself out of her stupor and dove for the portal. Her life was on the line, and Khaine held the string. She wouldn't be the woman in that movie, ignorantly signing her own gravestone. She didn't care who she had killed or why. Her body bounded through the surface's resistance, Khaine's murderous bellow echoing close behind, but the soldiers wouldn't let go.

Landing in some form of dirt in a place she had never been, Skye pushed herself to her feet and ran.

Chapter 16

K haine struggled in the soldiers' hold, his black claws digging into flesh, his demon lashing out in a frenzy. They weren't stronger than him on their own, but together they held him down. They held. Him. Down. One shoved a gun to his head, commanding him to be still, but he was a demon. He didn't answer to mortal men.

"Should we go after her?" one of the men shouted.

His roar was deafening, almost drowning his thoughts.

Kill them!

Behind the smell of blood and fear and uncertainty standing over him, the portal was closing. His mind blanked, his limbs tearing as he tried to force them out of the Elite's hold. Rage clouded his sight, and still the portal grew smaller. Still, they pinned him down.

"Let her go. The commander will want to study this one."

"I can't hold him much longer!"

"Shoot him in the head!"

"That will kill him!"

If only, he thought.

"It won't kill him," a man beside him grated. "It will only knock him the fuck out for a time."

"Just shoot him!"

Wouldn't. Fucking. Happen.

Khaine ripped his right arm free, ignoring the searing pain of his muscles shredding, and grasped the gun by the barrel. He bent it in half as it went off, the earsplitting sound causing the soldiers to loosen their grip. The man behind the weapon fell, blood covering his mangled face where the blast backfired, small bits of shrapnel embedded in his skin. His screams filled the night. The others released him, save for one.

Khaine took the gun from the wounded man's fingers and bashed it through the skull of the only soldier still holding him. His head caved in seconds before he dropped to the brick boardwalk.

"Shoot him!"

They funneled around him as one group, drawing their weapons. Several fired before he could get to his feet, fire grazing his arms and shoulder, the pain excruciating.

He didn't fucking care!

Skye was getting away. Running. His mate, who lied to him, left him to die, and repeatedly tried to keep him from his brother, was just on the other side of that portal; escaping.

Khaine reached for his sword and was shot in the hand. He dropped the blade and fell to his knees. For the first time, he was afraid. His limbs shook as adrenaline drowned him. The possibility of losing had never occurred to him. If he didn't get through that portal, Raiden was lost.

"Don't move!"

Not moving meant death. Without thinking, Khaine gripped his sword, ignoring the jolt of agony as another bullet pierced his trembling hand. His heart pounding in his ears, he locked his fingers, stood, and swung with no destination in sight. Several thuds reverberated through his arm before the steel blade came to a stop and he fell. Blood singed his eyes and ran down his face.

He tried to push his demon back into its cage as he took a breath and wiped the blood from his eyes. Bodies all around him. The two soldiers still standing backed up a step, their guns discarded and too far to reach. They held their hands high as Khaine leaned against his blade.

Using his sword to stand, he turned toward the portal. Plucking the amulet from the dead soldier's neck so no more of their fucking kind could follow, Khaine blasted through the opening, wincing at the sudden rays of sun. The portal closed behind him.

He stumbled and fought for balance. Sand pooled between his fingers. He fell, righted himself, and took stock of his surroundings. Dust seared his lungs, choking him. Using his sword as a temporary crutch to stand, Khaine staggered in a slow circle.

It was too bright. He couldn't see a blasted thing!

"Skye!"

Khaine rubbed his eyes, his voice bounding around him, echoing. The sunlight faded as his demon half adjusted, slithering back to its cage.

"Skye!"

He could smell her. Khaine knew his mate's smell by now, had buried himself in it more than once. It reminded him of a place that no longer existed; home. Even covered in demon's blood, he could smell it on her; autumn leaves from a Gean tree. She was honey and oil; almonds roasting over a fire. There was no place his mate could run that he wouldn't follow.

By the Gods, he would follow her storm through Hell if that's what it took.

He pivoted to the West, his senses on high alert. The stench of rotting flesh smothered him, the sounds of teeth gnashing against bone. An animal devouring its kill. There was nothing that suggested she'd traveled in that direction.

Khaine turned his head to the East and inhaled a long breath. There. It was faint, but her scent filled his nose, his demon shuddering under the surface.

He sheathed his sword over one shoulder and took off at a sprint, chasing after her.

Sand rose into the stifling air as he picked up speed, tall shrubs folding their dead limbs into his path. Littered bones snapped under his boots with every step. This wasn't a dimension he had ever been to. It looked like a deserted, desert plain, dry and crumbling. Everything dead. In the distance, an open field stretched out where sand turned into thick, green pasture. Tall trees sprang from the ground and huddled their massive bodies close together; a forest of color. The desert behind him seemed desolate. If his mate was smart, she would have sought shelter in the forest. She was too weak to defend herself as a mortal, the forest would grant a greater advantage. He ran for it, following Skye's fragrance in the still air.

Khaine's demon thrummed in his veins. *Follow her. Find*

her.

A crack in the earth stopped him. He skidded to a halt as the sand beneath his boots ended. It slopped over a ravine. Bones scattered to the bottom, thrown over the edge with his abrupt stop, clattering against the rocks before hitting the water. He curled his fingers into fists.

"Skye!"

Across the canyon was the pasture and forest. Green grass, free of dead limbs and rotting carcasses, stretched along the side. The cliff's edges had blended together, hiding themselves at a distance. Any faster and he would have plummeted to the water below. On one side, sand as far as his demon sight could see. Heat swatted his back, the hot desert fanning over him. On the other, trees so tall and so dense there was no way to tell what lay beyond, or within. The temperature in front of him was cool and misty. It was like two different climates fighting for space with an invisible wall in the middle.

He smelled the air, again. She'd come this way. The river flowing hundreds of feet down ran through the canyon, seemed to drop, and then disappeared into the forest on the other side. That side looked level, gradually descending to the river.

His side was a crag.

If Skye overheard Asha, she would be following the water, which meant she had crossed the canyon. Somewhere in those woods was a river of red that led to the deity. The trees would offer shelter as she followed the water. Naive woman. What made her think she could make this journey on her own? There was no telling what kind of creatures inhabited this realm.

As if on cue, a bone-starved mix of a lizard and a dog hobbled up beside him, razer teeth and long, thin tongue pointing in his direction. Khaine bared his fangs and the creature slunk back into the stifling-hot dust storm.

Khaine licked the blood from his lips and studied the two sides. The heat of the desert prickled against his neck. He wiped a thin sheen of bloody sweat from his brow and calculated his odds. Every moment he stood here was a moment longer away from her. His mortal mate was traversing a dimension alone. The dangers she could face here were numerous. And what did he plan to do when he caught up to her? Kill her or save her?

How many other people had ever bested his demon? Bastian would never cross him like his mate did. Her defiance. Her determination to reach a goal he knew nothing about. Even if he could care for her, she would never return the favor. She didn't trust him. She'd lied about her power, kept that secret from him.

A warm tingle snaked up his arm, the muscles he tore healing themselves. Dried blood cracked in his palms where the bullet holes had closed. He fisted his hands, growling at the sharp slice of his claws cutting flesh.

He could jump it. It was far, but if he angled himself just right, he could make it to the other side.

Water rushed below him. The sound tunneled between the rocks like a tsunami.

Had she tried the same thing? Had she jumped?

Had she fallen?

Khaine cringed and roared her name. "Skye!"

No response. He would punish her; for lying to him about

her power, for running from him, for trying to have him killed, and most of all, for putting herself in danger.

If she was alive—

She's alive.

He couldn't fall down that path. She was alive. He would catch up to her and then never let her out of his sight again.

Khaine backed up, assessed the ravine ahead, and ran for it. He bounded through the dead brush, the branches scratching his arms, and leaped toward the other side.

It was too far.

Khaine realized he'd errored the moment he caught the ledge on the other side. His chest slammed against the surface, rocks stabbing his ribs and lashing his shirt to the skin underneath. His ribs cracked under the pressure. He kicked at the rocks, his claws digging into the dirt and overhanging roots as he fell a few meters toward the rapid water below. The rock he grabbed onto broke free and he quickly reached for another.

Khaine stopped for a moment, hanging on the edge of the cliff to catch his breath. There was no way she'd jumped. Perhaps went around. Fuck! If he had calmed himself enough to think for one blasted second, he could have sensed that. He could have followed her smell to whatever path she took to get across the canyon. All he'd been able to think about was him on one side, and her smell on the other.

He dropped his forehead against the cliff's edge and took a breath. His assumptions had been correct. She was going to kill him, but not by her own hand, by making him crazed enough to lose focus. He chanced a glance toward the top. The ledge wasn't that far. He looked down. Falling would kill even him.

Pulling himself to the top, Khaine used his forearms as leverage and tried to find something solid his boots could dig into. Black blood, mixed with sand and stone, covered the wall as he climbed. One foot and then another, one blasted, agonizing inch at a time.

He would punish her. As soon as he got to the top of this blasted ledge, he was going to find her and punish her. His demon half leaped at the thought.

Khaine reached for a protruding limb below the ledge and growled as it was ripped from the loose earth. He fought for his hold, his hand grasping at a blood-covered stone in a panic. His hand slipped and he shot his arm out for another.

He fell.

Chapter 17

Skye stopped to catch her breath. She couldn't run, anymore. A constant throb had taken over her right side, and a dull ache had settled in her chest. Khaine was gone.

"You have nothing to feel bad about," she said. So why did she?

The demon had lied to her, but realizing she wasn't Khaine's mate hadn't affected her as much as seeing his lips locked on Asha's.

He'd said he wanted to kiss her, and Skye had a feeling that being kissed by the demon would do things to her that only happened in erotic romances.

She groaned. Khaine had gotten under her skin. She shouldn't care about him. It was better this way. The Elite were probably loading him into one of their military vehicles by now, if they hadn't already.

"They can have him."

Kicking at a rock and sending it tumbling into the river, she took a deep breath. A sharp pain shot through her foot. Skye braced her right hand on a nearby tree, careful not to scratch off the tiny scabs on her palm, and lifted her foot. She turned it where she could see the bottom.

"Okay, not so bad."

Who was she kidding? It looked like someone had taken a hatchet and simultaneously scrapped and hacked at her sole at the same time. Maybe it was worse than it looked. More dirt than blood. She clenched her teeth together and set it back down on a patch of moss, careful not to step on anything jagged. If she *had* been Khaine's mate, the demon would have at least given her a pair of shoes. All the running she'd done to escape the blasted man had obviously taken its toll.

But she *wasn't* his mate. He'd made that perfectly clear.

By kissing the fucking Hirx.

She needed to get her head straight. It didn't matter how she felt about being his mate or not being his mate. She couldn't afford to lose sight of her own goal; to live.

The river running through this part of the forest was so clear she could see the multicolored stones lying on the bottom beneath the water. If she followed the bank, she felt certain it would lead her to the red water, which should be close to some sky cave, and finally, the deity.

Tall trees lined the bank with arms stretching in all directions. Bushes huddled together in large patches of green. The woods were thick with them, only letting light in above the water where the foliage was broken overhead. Several birds with large hollow eyes and snout beaks peaked out from under a branch, then went back to whatever they had been doing. As long as they paid her no attention, she could care less.

Skye limped to the river and one foot at a time, stepped into the cool stream. She stood there a moment, letting it wash away the worst of the blood and dirt as she replayed the events from Evanston, Illinois. She'd opened a portal. It might not have been on purpose, but she'd opened a portal! Something had to be different. Could she do it, again?

She held out her palms and examined them. Energy had pooled there before. She concentrated on her hands, willing that energy to build. Willing. Willing.

What the hell had she done differently? Sky closed her eyes and imagined the portal, the size, the colors, the depth of it. Nothing. She squeezed her eyes shut even harder, balling her hands into a fist and scrunching her face. "Portal. Portal. Portal."

She let her breath out with indignation. How absurd she must look. Glancing behind her proved nobody was laughing at her lame attempt. Maybe the higher powers were on her side after all.

She bent down and washed the blood from her hands. At least they didn't hurt, anymore.

It didn't matter, anyway. Opening a portal was the one thing she *didn't* want to do. Bending down again, Skye used her palms to gently caress the bottoms of her feet, cleaning them as best as she could, gritting her teeth against the slight pain. Washing them already made them feel ten times better. At least she could stand on them without wincing. Her dress sloshed around her ankles.

She decided to use the edge of the dress to clean her feet instead of her rough hands, hooking the material under each foot and using it as a sort of rag. A proper cleaning would fix them up in no time.

She could really use a shower right about now. Wood and liquor and blood was caked all over her, but she didn't want to stop for long. A quick cleanup was all she was going to get.

One of the large trees beside her extended a single limb out over the river, so Skye picked a few leaves. The air around her was humid, locking moisture against her skin. No bugs swarmed her face like they did back home. A plus for this dimension, she thought. She hated gnats. Shaking off one foot at a time, she wrapped the leaves around her feet before stepping back onto the riverbank.

The bottom of her dress was soaked through. It weighed around her legs, making them heavy. The damn thing had kept her from running at times and being rid of about twenty inches would be incredible. She could also use a few strips to secure the leaves to her feet and wrap them tight, keep dirt from getting into the wounds and make walking less of a chore. If only she had her sewing machine. Even the portable one. She could easily fashion actual shoes from the dress's material.

This was the first time she had ever been out on her own. A shocking realization, one that should have caused panic. Instead, she felt a sense of calm. By the Gods, she would *not* admit defeat. It didn't matter how much she wanted Caden and the others to share in this glorious moment with her, she was free. She *felt* free.

The tall trees. The bushes. The river. The humid, warm air. This was home. And yet, something was missing.

"And it's *not* Khaine." She wasn't even going to contemplate that the missing feeling she was having was due to her acceptance of the overbearing demon. A liar. A traitor. A user. No. She would prove to herself and everybody else that she could do this. On. Her. Own.

Skye leaned over and picked up a serrated rock. A torturous sound bounced through the trees around her, carried on the wind. It was so low she couldn't be sure if she heard a person or if it was simply her imagination. What if it was an animal? Were there animals in this dimension? So far, the only creatures she had seen were the two birds she wasn't sure counted. When no other sounds followed, she resumed her task, stabbing the sharpest part of the rock into the material above her thigh and using the saw-like edge to cut it from one side to the other. The bottom half fell to the ground around her legs. A cool breeze bathed her skin, fighting back the humidity all around her. She sighed. Better.

She quickly cut and shredded the material into strips, then secured the leaves to her feet by tying small knots. Not her best work, but it would do.

Another bellow reverberated through the trees, this time louder. She jolted upright at the noise. Whatever it was, it was getting closer, maybe being carried by the river.

Carried by the river. That flowed through a deep canyon she crossed. After entering this dimension through a portal nearby.

The demon portal she had opened had closed the second that soldier went through. Skye had been sure that this dimension's portal would close right behind her, preventing anyone from following. Except...

Shit!

How could she be so stupid?

Skye frantically dug between her breasts, then threw her head back and closed her eyes. She'd left the amulet behind. Some mercenary she was going to make; forgetting priceless artifacts and allowing the enemy to follow.

Any one of those Elite soldiers could have used it to open another portal.

Another sound of agony drifted downstream, this time familiar.

Shit and double shit.

Khaine.

Skye gritted her teeth, fighting the urge to scream into the woods around her. How did he get away from those soldiers? They'd had him surrounded. Had they hurt him?

Had they followed him?

"Skye!"

Oh, God. It sounded like he was in pain. And alone. Had he tried to cross the canyon at the widest point? How idiotic did he have to be? She'd had to follow the drop-off a quarter mile up to pass where the two sides were narrower. If Khaine had tried to jump at the widest point, he could have fallen.

"Skye!"

His voice was getting closer. Skye stood with the shredded dress around her feet and leaves tucked and tied into shoes. Her hair matted to her neck and sticking to her brow, she considered her options.

She should run, leave him behind. Wouldn't he do the same for her? Leave her for dead? He was angry with her, for no reason that she could conjure except not telling him about being able to open portals, accidentally, she added, since she couldn't open them willingly until back in Evanston—even that was an accident—and going back for him would be suicide. Besides, he'd lied to her, and not some little "the dog ate my homework" lie, but he lied about being mated to her. In the Province, that was the equivalent of a mortal woman telling her husband the baby was his, only for it to end up being the brother's.

He was obviously on the move, and if he could move on his own, then he wasn't in that bad of shape. Right?

Now she was contemplating letting him catch her? She couldn't be away from the demon for more than a couple hours without thinking about him. Wanting him to be okay. Wanting him to kiss her.

She'd gone insane. That was all there was to it. Insanity.

The demon could fend for himself.

Sighing, Skye brushed a strand of hair from her forehead, cringing when it pulled at her skin. No, that wasn't her. Leaving him for the Elite to haul off was one thing. They wouldn't outright kill him, giving him a chance to escape and live. But leaving him alone when there quite possibly wasn't another living soul around for miles? That was another. She didn't know the dangers of this dimension, and she wasn't wired that way.

Skye threw up her hands and groaned at the bright sky. She'd make sure the damn demon didn't get himself killed, even if only so she could do the deed herself later, and *then* run.

Again.

At this rate, she'd never reach mercenary status in Caden's eyes. Caden would have left his ass to fend for himself. So would Mckenzie, and Brooke. Hell, even Jade would have turned her back on him under the circumstances. Skye closed her eyes. She wanted to get away from him, had sent the Elite after him to serve her own purpose of escaping him for good, and now she was considering helping him?

"There's got to be something wrong with me," she said to the cool air.

"I t-thought the same thing," came the voice behind her. Skye whirled toward the sound, her eyes snapping open. Khaine leaned against a tree and heaved shallow breaths, a braided piece of torn shirt hanging from his right hand against the bark. "Why w-would the higher...powers give me...such an opportunity, then r-rip it away?"

"I was coming to help you."

He smirked. The left side of his face was broken, his ribs were positioned at an odd angle, his leg was twisted below his knee, and somewhere under all that black blood, there had to be skin. He *had* fallen, and far by the looks of it. Even with his hair and torn jeans being wet, telling her he had, in fact, floated down river, there was still so much blood seeping out. Khaine would continue healing until his wounds were gone completely, at least she thought, but it appeared he'd already been healing the worst of his injuries.

As if to solidify her claim, his jaw popped into an almost natural curve. A blood-soaked path of foliage trailed behind him.

"You ran." He rubbed his chin. "Again."

Skye scowled at him. "And you would have done the same if you were lied to."

"L-lied to. That's s-something you...do a l-lot."

Khaine threw the piece of braided cloth at her feet.

She glared at him. "I never lied to you."

"You took my b-brother from me!"

His expression pained, the humid air seemed to gather his words and hold them. His brother? Silence crept into the woods.

Khaine spat blood from his mouth and winced as one of his ribs cracked under the skin. His eyes were glued to her, black seeping into their murky depths. His hair matted to his chiseled face with black veins pulsing under the surface.

Khaine's expression was one she hadn't seen before.

"What brother?" she asked. He never mentioned family. Then again, he never said anything to her that wasn't a command of sorts. In his defense, she never asked.

Because he would never acknowledge anything to her! What was the point in trying? What was the point in asking the demon anything?

He groaned and twisted his face. "B-bind your wrists."

Exactly. No answers, just more demands.

Skye gritted her teeth. "That's not lying. I *never* lied to you, which is exactly what you did to me. You haven't told me a single thing since you kidnapped me from my home, from my family. You despise me without cause, call me a disgusting breed, and constantly command me to do this or that. You held me against my will."

"B-bind—"

"You couldn't even be bothered to get me shoes when you spent so much time perfecting your damn wardrobe! You have no care for me, for my family." She held back the tears and cleared her throat. "Caden could be dead. My *sister* could be dead, and none of that matters to you. I'm glad I'm not your mate. I would rather *die* than be mated to you!" She took a breath and narrowed her eyes on him. "I hate you."

Khaine fell to his knees. He caught himself, palms digging deep into the soft mud. He tried to stand and fell against the ground face first.

She waited. This was another one of his stupid tricks, another ploy to make her feel bad about berating him. Any second, he would stand up and give her one of his demeaning comebacks.

He didn't move.

Any second.

Nothing.

Skye leaped forward, sliding to a stop beside his limp body. Adjusting her dress, she spread her knees and used all her strength to turn him over. She heaved and managed to roll him into the bush behind him.

Unconscious. His face had dug into the dirt and was covered in mud. She cleared what she could from his eyes. Perhaps he had hurt himself more than she thought. Could a fall like that kill him? He wasn't a purebred demon. Could he die from mortal wounds?

Skye shook him. Still nothing.

She shook him again, hard. "Hey, wake up!"

He wasn't moving, *at all*. Bending down, she positioned her ear to his mouth and waited. Her heart dropped an octave lower in her chest. He wasn't breathing. She frantically shook him, not caring about the internal damage she might cause. "Khaine! Khaine, wake up!"

She pressed her hands to his chest and threw her body into what she hoped was CPR. One of his ribs cracked under the pressure. Oh, God. Blood covered her hands, black and warm. His blood. *Lots* of it. It flowed from under his body, mixing with the mud and moss against her knees.

Skye stood on shaky legs and backed away, holding her trembling, blood-soaked hands in front of her. Holy shit, she killed him.

Chapter 18

Caden stared at the broken glass around the cars. Blood littered a few shards along the pavement, discarded under a tall lamppost. Bullet holes riddled some vehicles along the tree line, and others looked like they were pushed aside with force.

Stopping beside a blue minivan, Caden leaned against the hood as another dizzy spell raked her. They were coming less frequently, but even with Mckenzie helping her through them, she was still slowing them down.

"Was she here?" Caden said, pulling a knife from the sheath on her leg and digging it into the van's hood for support. She didn't think the owner would care about a little knife hole when the back end of the vehicle had been smashed in.

Didn't care, either.

"I smell her. She went inside that bar."

Mckenzie pointed to an illuminated sign across the parking

lot. Temptest strung across the front in bold letters. It was an immortal nightclub, the largest in the area. Why the hell would Khaine bring Skye to an immortal nightclub in Evanston?

"Why the fuck would he bring her here?" Mckenzie said.

Caden huffed at her remark and checked that the bandage was still in place on her head. She'd checked over a hundred times since leaving their hideout. It was absolutely...fucking...ridiculous. This damn blood condition was starting to control her life.

"It looks like there was a fight," Mckenzie said, running her hand along a piece of blood-soaked glass.

"Agreed. Can you tell where they went from here?"

"This way."

Caden pushed herself off the van, grabbing her knife from the hood. Mckenzie didn't have to tell her to tread carefully. Everything about the scene around them said wrong. Broken glass, both from the vehicles and now the bar as they passed. Blood everywhere. She couldn't tell if it was mortal or immortal. Mckenzie would be able to smell it to know, but Caden didn't think it mattered, right now. There were even two sets of tire tracks leading away from the front entrance, burnt rubber stuck to the boardwalk as though several *someones* had made a hasty getaway.

They didn't need to go inside to see if Skye was there. Mckenzie walked around the side of the building, following the stone pathway beside the docks to where the tree line opened into thick woods. Caden took measured steps beside Mckenzie, half for support should she have another spell and fall, and half as backup in case whatever caused the mess out front was still around.

Mckenzie stopped.

"What is it?"

Caden wasn't immortal. She couldn't see in the dark as well as Mckenzie could.

"Elite."

Caden pulled her sword from its sheath and assumed her battle stance.

"They're already dead, Superwoman. Put the sword away."

Caden smirked. "I think I'll hang on to it. Keeps me from getting ambushed like some people."

Mckenzie shot her an annoyed look, a faint glow from the lighting sky reflecting off the water. "I wasn't ambushed. The damn demon was already in the bar when he attacked."

Caden walked around Mckenzie and knelt beside one of the bodies. They were definitely Elite soldiers.

Dead ones.

"Being in the place you're ambushing tends to help," Caden said absently.

She could practically feel Mckenzie rolling her eyes behind her as she examined one of the soldiers. Deep gashes wound around his neck, claw marks that made cavernous pits.

"Khaine."

"I was thinking the same thing," Mckenzie said.

Another soldier's head was smashed in, and several had no head at all.

"This doesn't look good. Pick up their trail. We need to find her."

"Working on it," Mckenzie gritted.

"Well, work faster."

Caden wiped her bloody hands on her leather catsuit and

stood.

"They headed south, doubled back around, and then..."

"And then?" Caden asked, urging her on. The faster they found Skye and the demon, the faster they could kill that fiend for kidnapping their sister. With this many Elite soldiers in one place, that meant Leclain had been here, too. They could handle the demon. A half-crazed vampire in charge of an entire military force? That was another story.

"The trail goes cold."

"What do you mean it goes cold?" Caden sheathed her sword and turned to Mckenzie looking out into the woods, congratulating herself for not spinning too fast and falling. "You're a Sylph, there's no such thing as a cold trail."

"I mean, it goes cold," Mckenzie grated, turning back to Caden with a scowl. "They're not in this dimension, anymore. I can't track them, here."

"Then get us to where you *can* track them."

"I'm afraid that's not possible."

Both turned toward the male voice. Caden watched Mckenzie glare at the stranger with her eyebrows high. This was new. For Mckenzie to glare at someone instead of chopping their head off for the intrusion wasn't normal.

"Castello."

Caden searched her mental bank for that name. She turned to Mckenzie and smirked. "Castello? Would this be the infamous Cas?"

Mckenzie shot her an evil look. "Stuff a sock in it."

Castello smiled. "You told your family about me?"

He was wearing a green shirt that clung to his broad shoulders, green pants that molded themselves to his hips, and dark shoes trimmed in green. His medium-length curly hair, dark and shining in the morning's early bursts of light, swayed over his shoulders as his green eyes regarded Mckenzie.

A Dryad.

What did Mckenzie gain from being associated with a Dryad? The way she sneered at him said it wasn't a friendly association, and yet Castello still lived.

What the hell?

"What I did or didn't tell my family is my business," Mckenzie said. "What are you doing here? Following me?"

"I was giving you space, just as you asked. How is Sophie?"

"You ask about a nine-year-old girl after spending the night in a place like this?" Mckenzie ran a hand along the blades under her skirt, her curly, brown hair bouncing around her shoulders. "How many orgies did you participate in? One? Five? One hundred?"

Castello drew back his lips and snarled. "Jealous?"

Crossing her arms, Caden cleared her throat, loud. They looked at her. This was ridiculous. Skye was now in a dimension Mckenzie couldn't track—which didn't make any sense because a Sylph could track across planets—with a demon that might or might not kill her, and these two thought it was an appropriate time to settle some personal pissing contest?

"What happened here? And what did you mean by not possible?"

Castello kept his eyes on Mckenzie. "Khaine came for Asha. I'm guessing the amulet around her neck had value to him. It opens another dimension, one only accessible with the amulet. The Elite stormed the place for a Hovard."

"Where's this amulet?" Caden asked.

Castello turned to her and his eyes softened. "Khaine took it with him when he followed Skye into the portal."

Shit.

"Don't you mean *forced* Skye into the portal," Mckenzie said.

"No," Castello corrected. "Followed. She was trying to leave him behind, I assume. She seemed angry with him for kissing the Hirx."

"Why would a demon kissing a Hirx make her angry?"

Castello eyed Caden, one of those dark brows rising. "You tell me."

He fished a folded paper out of his pocket and handed it to her. Caden took it, barely keeping her arm steady when another dizzy spell swept through her. She needed to sit down but would be doing no such thing in the presence of an immortal she didn't know, especially one Mckenzie didn't seem fond of.

And not with so many dead bodies around.

Mckenzie eyed the note in Caden's hand. "What is it?"

"Skye asked me to give it to you," Castello said. "Said she may have found a way to solve her problem."

Caden unfolded the paper and read it.

I'm safe. I think I found a way to prevent the vision. Tell Caden I'm sorry if she's alive. Don't try to follow me. I'll be alright.

Caden handed the note to Mckenzie. "How do we know this came from her?"

Castello cocked a brow, his voice amused. "I don't write like a girl." He steeled his expression. "The demon didn't seem to mean her harm."

Caden and Mckenzie scoffed in unison.

"It doesn't matter if he—"

"Shh."

Caden stopped talking, Castello's face going ridged. Mckenzie stiffened beside Caden, her hair jostling as she scanned the perimeter with her immortal eyes. The look on her face said they weren't alone.

A man stepped from behind a tree and stalked cautiously toward them, a leather shoulder bag slung across his chest. There didn't seem to be a single gun tucked under his silk, maroon shirt, so not an Elite soldier. The crop of dead bodies didn't seem to faze him either, so not likely mortal. At least, not a mortal unaccustomed to death. His blue eyes scanned the carnage around them before masking to a visage of indifference.

Castello stepped forward and glared. Roots snaked from beneath the stone boardwalk, cracking it and intertwining together. They wove like a braid into a circle around the stranger. Caden tensed as the roots began to build themselves upward around the man. A warning.

"Easy," the man said. "I mean no harm."

Mckenzie sidled up to Castello. "That's an unknown variable. What do you want?"

"I overheard the name Khaine. You're looking for him."

It wasn't a question, but Caden suspected honesty might speed things along. "He kidnapped our sister."

"A Guardian? Not blood related I suspect." His eyes narrowed.

He knew about Guardians?

"What's it to you? He took her; we want her back."

Castello tightened his hold on the roots, molding them together like molten iron. "How do you know Khaine?"

Before Caden could comprehend the man responding, Mckenzie unsheathed a knife from her thigh and launched it at the intruder. It embedded itself in the man's left arm only seconds before his eyes faded to a glossy black. Black blood seeped from the wound.

Castello sneered, snatching the stranger around both wrists with his vines and forming one into a noose around his neck. "Demon."

The demon grated his sharp teeth, not able to remove the knife from his arm. Caden tightened her grip on her sword. She should kill the bastard. How many half-breed demons were out there? Tiny beads of sweat erupted on her forehead, somehow finding their way to the palm of her hand. She needed to calm herself before she dropped her sword. Fuck this damn disorder, she thought. As soon as Skye was safe, she was finding a cure.

"Speak," Caden said. "I'm losing my patience."

Mckenzie launched another dagger, this one embedding in the demon's right thigh.

He clenched his jaw and snarled. "My name is Bastian Bahr. I'm a friend of Khaine's."

Another blade stuck above his heart.

Bastian grunted at the same time a small trail of black blood escaped his lips. "You need my help."

Castello's eyes blazed a brilliant green as his muscles contracted under his shirt. The noose around Bastian's neck constricted what little air Castello had allowed him, leaving the demon with none.

"That's another unknown variable," Castello said.

Caden eyed Castello wearily. Who the hell was this guy? Better question, who was he to Mckenzie? Having him on their side appeared to be a plus, but with immortals, there was no telling how long that would last.

Mckenzie reached for another blade. It seemed all that time *not* enacting revenge was catching up to her. A demon was a demon in her eyes.

"I can take you to your sister," Bastian choked out.

Mckenzie gripped her dagger but held it. "How?"

Instead of answering, Bastian coughed, spitting blood from his mouth. Caden rolled her eyes at the silent battle between Mckenzie and Castello before Castello finally loosened the vines around Bastian's neck. It seemed he would have no problem using them to pinch the demon's head off. The knives were still entrenched against Bastian's bones, leaving the wounds to bleed freely. They would start to heal as soon as Bastian pulled them out. *If* he pulled them out.

Bastian took in a hoarse breath and cringed. "You can't enter the dimension without the amulet. I, on the other hand, can take you there."

"How?"

"My runes connect me to Khaine." He twisted his body as if trying to point to the tattoos crawling up his neck. "Wherever he goes, I can follow."

"Elaborate," Castello said.

"I can reopen the dimension, letting *us* in."

"He said she's his mate," Caden said. "What's to say he'll even hurt her?"

His black eyes actually *darkened*. "His mate?" He spat blood from his lips and clenched his fists. "If Khaine has your sister, he'll kill her. I could persuade him not to."

"Why would you do that?"

"Guilt is a dangerous drug."

Mckenzie looked at Caden. Waiting for her decision? She could gut this bastard and find another way to Skye, or trust there was no other way and follow this demon to an unknown realm. Fuck! She really detested those odds.

What other choice did she have?

"I can't guarantee your safety with them." Caden pointed to Mckenzie and Castello. Both shrugged. "But if you can get us to Skye unharmed, your chances might improve."

Bastian seemed to contemplate his situation, then nodded as much as the vines would allow.

Grumbling his displeasure, Castello released the demon. Bastian promptly pulled the knives from his arm and thigh and tossed them back to Mckenzie who caught them. He jerked the one from his heart and pitched it back to her as well.

"Be a good little demon or I'll give them back to you," Mckenzie said, waving a dagger in front of her.

Caden couldn't help but smile. She knew nothing was harder than Mckenzie relinquishing a kill.

"Open the portal," Castello said. His vines retreated into the ground, but his tone said he would bring them back if needed, and his illuminated eyes said he hoped that would happen.

Bastian dropped to his knees and rolled his sleeves up high above his elbows. Tattoos intertwined themselves along every inch of visible flesh, dark and intricate patterns that meant nothing to Caden. He hung his head and hovered his right hand over a symbol on his neck. It glowed as he spoke a few words in a language Caden didn't understand. Dirt and wet leaves scattered along the boardwalk with the wind, seemingly caught up from some other place. He pressed his hand over the glowing symbol and said one last word. The air itself appeared to evaporate around them as a tall spherical portal materialized out of the ground. It dangled above the earth, suspended by nothing and yet something. Thin and rippled in the center, it resembled the portal back at their hideout, but without the stone columns holding it in place.

Caden paused. What was to keep this demon from sending them to Hell? Mckenzie glanced at her, the same thought creeping along her face.

"I'll test it," Castello said.

They sheathed their weapons, Caden's sword feeling like a million pounds on her back, and followed Castello up to the portal.

Mckenzie fingered the blades now tucked back along her thigh. "If he dies, you die," she told Bastian.

A small smirk engulfed Castello's face. "The flattery is all mine." He stepped up to the portal and disappeared. Mckenzie followed without hesitation.

Shit and double shit. Caden stepped close to the portal, trying to see inside. The surface was like a mirror, only reflecting her own distorted and damaged appearance. This was *not* how she envisioned this rescue. Not wanting to give the demon beside her any reason to think her weak, she lifted her foot and marched through the void.

Chapter 19

No, no, no. This couldn't be happening. Khaine's lifeless body lay slumped in the mud, twisted and broken. Skye steadied her breathing and wiped her hands on her dress. He was dead. Something in her stomach clenched. No, he couldn't be dead. He was immortal. He would come back, he had to.

Why do you care?

There was no reason for her to want him alive. No reason for her to feel sorrow for him. So why the hell was she fighting back tears? He was a demon. Her kind killed demons.

Skye brushed her moist eyes with the back of her bloody hand. She stumbled to the river and dipped her hands in the water to wash them, then rubbed her eyes again. Bile rose in her, tickling the back of her throat. Swallowing several times kept it down. She should move his body, or try CPR, again. Maybe he wasn't dead after all and demons couldn't be killed by mortal means.

Why was she hoping that were true? Because she wanted to kiss him? More?

"Get a hold of yourself." He was gone. She should move his body someplace animals wouldn't get to it and…and what? Go on about her journey like he was never a part of it? Good God, she'd gotten too used to him being around. Arguing with him. Taunting him. Thinking about him in ways she never thought about another man. There was no future to be had with Khaine, and that realization didn't stop her from pondering being his mate.

"You weren't his mate. He could never love you." And that was the point of it, of her not accepting him. But how could a man that showed no compassion, care so deeply about a single goal? She had no idea what that goal was, but he cared for it. Was willing to die for it.

His brother. He'd mentioned family. Had mentioned her stealing his family from him. Was that his goal? Was finding some brother she knew nothing about what this journey was to him? And if that were the case, didn't that prove the demon could love something other than himself?

"Stop it!"

Skye finished rinsing her hands and dried them on a cleaner part of her dress. It didn't matter, anymore. Why beat herself up over what could or couldn't have been?

Standing, she took stock of her knees and cringed. Mud and moss and blood had molded to each crevice, clinging to her like glue. She'd just cleaned her hands, it could stay there, for now. She needed to move Khaine's body.

Thrashing leaves in the distance caught her attention. Skye

turned to follow the sound. Thin bushes beside a set of thick trees rattled their limbs. Something large moved behind those bushes, shaking them. Skye ran back to Khaine's body and forced him onto his side. His sword was gone. He must have lost it when he fell. She righted him on the ground and searched his pockets. A small box was in his right. That wouldn't help her. She put it back. Running her hands down each leg turned up no other weapons.

Fuck!

The sound of bark being scrapped from one of the trees stopped her, nails digging into the wood. Snarls followed the sound. Definitely an animal. Maybe it was a friendly one?

An enormous horned beast broke from between the trees forty feet in front of her. Large green eyes locked on her position beside Khaine. Curved claws, larger than its paws, gripped the ground and flexed. It was gray with silver highlights and black undertones, enhancing its green gaze. Dense spikes shot from its mane, combining into larger groups around its front shoulders.

The creature shook itself and pawed the grass under its feet.

Maybe if she didn't move, the beast wouldn't acknowledge her as a threat. Skye gripped Khaine's torn shirt above his chest and tried to will the creature to see her as small and harmless. The more minuscule she thought herself, the less of a threat she posed. The serrated rock beside the river caught her eye. She could lunge for it, but that might startle the animal into attacking. A limb from the nearby tree could be used as a spear, but breaking off one large enough would take time and anything smaller would no doubt snap the moment she tried to stab the thing.

The smell of Khaine's blood could have lured it in. If she slowly stepped away from him, the animal might disregard her. And leave Khaine to be eaten by that thing?

Skye grimaced. She couldn't do it; leave Khaine to be food. All she wanted to do was cry angry tears and kick Khaine in the ass for dying before she could finish berating him.

What other choice did she have? He was already dead. She was in this thing's territory. Why fight it if she didn't have to?

Mercenary Code 101: Pick your battles.

Skye uncurled her hand on Khaine's shirt and pressed her palm into him for leverage.

Her hand *moved.*

Skye snapped a glance at his eyes. They were closed. Not an inch of his body had changed position.

Her hand rose, again. He was breathing!

Holy shit, he was breathing. Her mind immediately told her how bad that was. Breathing. Wounded. He was a buffet waiting to be eaten.

The animal gnashed its teeth, one long, forked tongue slipping from its mouth. She was sitting by its lunch.

Right, fuck mercenary code. She'd trained long and hard enough with Caden. She was kicking this thing in the ass.

Skye leaped for the serrated rock a second before the creature burst into a run, pummeling through bushes and over downed logs. Its paws hammered on the ground with each step toward her, deep booms radiating from its large frame as it hit the hard dirt. It landed in the soft mud as she snatched the stone from the riverbank. Skye ducked as the animal jumped the flowing water in one smooth motion, its two front feet touching down in the mud on her side of the water and its back legs spinning it to face her. Stabbing its shoulder as it turned, she rolled with the movement to come up on the other side and flank it. Instead of acknowledging her, the animal swung its head and sank its teeth deep into Khaine's leg.

Khaine didn't move. Even with the creature's teeth locked in his flesh, Khaine's body lay motionless in the mud. The wolf-like animal whipped its head and pulled Khaine toward a nearby tree.

Oh no, you don't, she thought.

"Hey!" Skye picked up another rock and threw it at the beast. "Let him go!"

It disregarded her, dragging Khaine away from her and the river at her back.

Skye jolted up and dove for them both. Landing on the animal's back, she plunged the sharp rock into its right shoulder and shouted as it flung her away from it. It twisted, its large head trying to reach the rock, trying to dig it out with its teeth.

She didn't waste a second waiting to see if it would succeed. She funneled her arms under Khaine's and heaved with everything she had. Her feet slid over the damp grass under her, making it hard to get traction, and her dress tangled around her bottom.

Khaine moved an inch. Skye strained her muscles and pulled. Another inch.

"Come on!"

The creature flopped onto its side, rubbing against the ground to remove the rock. It twisted in the dirt, snarling and howling. Skye grunted against Khaine's weight as she dragged him another inch away from the beast. Then another. Each pull seemed harder than the last, but he was moving. All she cared about was getting him away from the creature long enough to deal with it.

Skye stopped dragging Khaine and tried not to panic in the silence surrounding them. No howling. No snarling. Damn.

Skye looked up and into the creature's saw-like teeth. Drool dripped from its lips and onto her shoulder. The rock was gone.

The animal sliced its claws along her left arm, cutting deep before she could twist away. She ducked, narrowly missing its teeth as its jaw snapped toward her head. Khaine was on top of her legs, pinning her and preventing her from moving. She needed to get away from him before she blasted him out of fear. She could feel her emotions skyrocketing to dangerous territory.

The beast chomped at her head again and she ducked, pushing at Khaine with everything she had in her, trying to move the large demon enough to get up. He was heavy, pushing her back into the ground with each move of her arms tucked under his. The creature lunged for her, catching her ear with a single claw before she could move her head.

Skye screamed, the sound echoing through the woods and bouncing back at her. That was it. She'd fucking had it! Everything that had happened in the last however long she had been with the demon, came crashing to a head. Angry and frustrated, she managed to get her right leg free and blocked the animal's next attack with her forearm to its throat. Her left leg came free next, giving her enough leverage to grip the beast's spiked fur and simultaneously pull herself from Khaine's body and wrap her arms tight around the animal's neck at the same time. Her legs dug into its side as she squeezed.

It shook her, thrashing her body into the ground trying to untangle her limbs from its back. It could thrash all it wanted. Skye was done! Done being weak. Done being afraid. Just...done!

She held on, locking her forearms together with a grip she refused to loosen. The beast bayed in her arms, thrashing her against trees and bushes and choking as she cut off its airway. She squeezed even harder, funneling any fear into pure rage, its neck muscles indenting under the pressure. She could feel the thick cord under her arms snap as its head lulled to the side and it crashed to the ground on top of her.

She couldn't breathe. Her lungs were on fire and suffocating her under the weight of the creature. Adrenaline fueled her. Twisting her body, Skye unlodged herself from the creature and rolled to a standing position beside it, her stance low and ready for another attack.

She took several deep breaths as she stared at the beast, waiting.

It didn't move, its head hanging against the ground at an odd angle. She gasped for each ragged breath that followed and tried to calm the thunder in her chest; tried to calm her breathing. She waited a whole minute for her adrenaline to crash and her stance to waver.

She'd killed it. Snapped its neck. Skye took another deep breath and slowly stood up.

Khaine's body lay under a tree a few feet away, slumped on his side over a rock. She looked down at herself, too stunned to see much. Blood covered her dress from dragging Khaine as far as she had, mixing with the blood from her arm and ear. It took another whole minute for her to register the claw marks that had sliced her. She fingered her left arm; touched her ear. They didn't feel bad.

Skye stared at the creature's lifeless body. She'd done it! Killed it with her bare hands! Caden would be so proud!

A knot formed in her stomach. Caden had better be alive, because if she had to relive this day to her sisters without Caden...

She looked back toward the tree where the demon lay motionless. Skye limped to Khaine and knelt beside him, then eyed the beast she'd killed. There could be more things like that creature out there. She pressed her hand to Khaine's chest and sighed. He was really breathing. Not caring to examine why that made her feel relieved, she hooked her arms under him and began pulling him toward a set of rocks in the distance. If she was lucky, there would be a cave for them to hold up in, perhaps give Khaine time to heal.

And then what?

Nothing had changed. He'd still lied to her about being his mate, and she still had only days to live. Skye brushed her hair from her face and tried to focus on one thing at a time; getting Khaine someplace where nothing could eat him.

Chapter 20

Khaine ran through the woods, Pine trees towering overhead and blocking the fiery night sky. There was an animal inside him begging to be set free, but he was afraid the beast would take over his mind and his people needed him.

No, not again. He didn't want to relive this moment, again.

Faster he ran, his hands clenched into fists and his jaw tight. By the Gods, he could make it! Another presence. Sounds of footfalls driving into the damp Scottish soil. One on his left, another on his right.

"Can ye see it?" Bastian's voice rang in his ears.

Then a more familiar sound. A voice that sent pain shooting through his heart.

"Nay! Keep going, tis not far. I can see the lights."

"Tis not your fight, brotha! Go back!" Khaine roared.

I should never have done this to you. Forgive me.

"These are my people too, Khaine."

"Raiden!"

Raiden picked up speed, bursting through the line of trees. Bastian followed him, leaving Khaine the last through the void. They stood in a row in the clearing, stopped by the flickering lights across the meadow.

"Fire," Raiden breathed.

Khaine remembered this scene all too well, had prayed he would never have to see it again, and still, his mind betrayed him. Still, his mind played out every moment anew.

Red streaked the sky with flashes of yellow and orange breaking through the heat. Screams echoed out over the field, women and children yelling for their loved ones, the men shouting for water, shouting for mercy. Shouting for the gods to save them. The fire spread through their village, each hut drawing it in as if begging to become ash. Burning. Their village, their home...burning.

The smell of charred wood blanketed the surrounding field, carried by the fire's breath. The smell of death laced the air, choking him.

Raiden bounded forward toward the village. Khaine tackled him from behind, pressing him into the Hazel brush. Fire lapped at his skin, his body breaking out in a sweat. "Stop!"

Khaine rushed to stand beside his dream image. Never let him go, his mind roared. "Hold onto your brother, you fool!" This was the moment, the moment Khaine betrayed them all. The moment Raiden decided Khaine could no longer be trusted to protect their kind. Not this. Not this, his mind churned. "Make it different!" he shouted to himself. "Change it!"

Bastian helped them both to their feet, Khaine releasing

Raiden. "Tis done," Bastian said. "Nothing we can do, here."

"Tis a lie and ye know it!" Raiden yelled. "We can help them." He gestured to the village engulfed in flames, desperation radiating from the stiff lines of his back, sweat dripping into his eyes.

"Nay," Khaine said. "They are gone, brotha. Gone!"

"He's *not* gone, you fool! Save him. Save your people!"

Raiden glared at him, his eyes digging daggers into Khaine's heart. "Ye did this." His voice was a whisper, no more audible than their people dying. "T'was you that brought this upon us! Ye killed them all! Set them free. Your own kind." He glared at him and spat on the ground. "Demon!"

Khaine cringed at the sound of demons bellowing in the dark- ness, at their people crying out for help.

Yes, all his fault. He was the one that set them free. If not for him, their father would be alive. If not for him, Leviathan would know no realm but Hell. If not for him, their people wouldn't have burned in their skin right before his brother's eyes. Khaine wiped the sweat from his face, wanting to retreat, but knowing his mind would allow no such reprieve.

"Nothing can be done for them, now. Nothing can save them. Leviathan played his game, and he played it well."

"Ye know what's down there." Bastian gripped Raiden by the shoulders and shook him. "Look at me!" He did. "Leviathan got his revenge, and so too shall we. Tis not over. We will—"

Khaine stared out across the shortened field. The heat of the fire swelted across his face. He watched their people trying to escape the burning huts, each one caving in on itself, straw and hay feeding the fire's greedy appetite. Bastian's words were far away, too far for him to hear or comprehend, but the torturous cries of his people burning alive seemed too close. His body glistened with sweat. Adrenaline. Pain. Determination. Regret. He didn't know where one ended and the other began.

In the middle of their village, people fought for their lives. One caught him, standing still amongst the chaos, his smile molten iron. Distorted. Wicked.

Leviathan.

Next to him came another, dragged to the center by one of Leviathan's demon spawn.

Khaine turned his head to Bastian and Raiden. Their muted conversation was miles away and neither of them noticed. Then to his dream self, staring out at the village in horror. If he'd had the strength to rip out his eyes, he would have. Instead, the dream played out before him as he turned his gaze back to the pair. "Jonah."

Leviathan worked his arm into a noose around Jonah's neck, tightening...tightening. Khaine watched himself ball his hands into fists, each nail piercing his flesh. The demon smiled as Jonah fought in his hold. Leviathan's eyes glued to Khaine's, but Jonah couldn't see him, the eyesight of a mortal no match for a demon.

"Come and get him," Leviathan said.

The faint realization of a ceased conversation didn't break their connected gazes. Bastian and Raiden moving to stand beside him didn't break their connected gazes. They'd heard that voice, the demon of destruction calling them out.

"Jonah," Khaine breathed. Another shooting pain stabbed at his chest, the intensity of it staggering.

"Nay. We canna help him, now."

Khaine moved next to his dream self and punched the air where he stood. His fist sailed through his dream body. "How did you know! You didn't even try!"

"Doona presume to know that. We have to try!" Raiden said.

Yes, he thought, urging his past to see reason. Fight for them.

If Khaine's eyes could kill with a single look... His demon stirred like never before, clawing at the inside of his mind. Bastian stood beside him, seeming to feel the same, shifting in place, anxious. There was no way Raiden could see what they saw, hear what they heard. His necklace prevented that.

Khaine's eyes held on Leviathan, an unspoken promise of revenge lingering in the air. Jonah, his father's most trusted friend, an uncle to them all, was going to die. Not because none of them cared to intervene, but because Khaine was no fool. He knew they'd lost.

Khaine swung his arms at himself, slicing the air. He punched and pleaded, screamed and scorned. He sank to his knees and gripped his head, closing his eyes and begging his mind to end this, to let it stop.

"Nay," Khaine's dream self said. He growled low in his throat, pounding his demon into submission. "They're gone."

Raiden turned to Khaine, finally breaking his gaze from the fire. "Ye do nothing! Ye stand there and let them destroy our home, and do nothing. Stand there as they kill our friends, and do nothing. Perhaps ye are more demon than man, brotha."

Khaine forced his eyes to Jonah, fingers gripping his hair tight. It wouldn't end until he looked. It never did.

Leviathan clutched Jonah by his tattered shirt and shuffled him to the edge of a burning hut. Jonah twisted and thrashed in his hold, then stillness. His feet bordered the edge of oblivion, his mouth clamped in a thin line on his face. Pain broke through the corners of his eyes, and still, he stood.

Leviathan smiled at them, at Khaine, and stretched his arm out wide. Jonah's feet tipped into the blaze and the fire engulfed his body. Inch by inch it climbed, and still, he stood. Not screaming. No, he would never give the demon that satisfaction.

Khaine screamed. He screamed for Jonah. He screamed for Raiden. He screamed for his mind to give him peace, to release him from this nightmare. He screamed for his own stupidity as Jonah's body was consumed by the flames. He screamed until Jonah was gone, until Leviathan was gone, and still, he screamed until Raiden's words silenced him. His dream had never reminded him of this moment. He closed his eyes.

Raiden turned to Khaine. "Ye are no brotha o' mine." His gaze was daggers, his words a poisoned needle. He ripped the necklace from his neck, his demon awakening under the surface. "I will avenge them. If it means travelin' to Hell, I will avenge them. You're dead to me, brotha. Ye hear me! Dead! Ye died when your demon began to live." He threw the necklace on the ground and walked back into the woods.

"Aye, brotha. So did you."

Skye watched Khaine. His body was sweating, the blood from his wounds still crusted along his sides. He'd been sweating for the last hour and shaking against the hard ground. Every now and then, small tremors would rack his body. She could only hope all those things meant he was healing. The scrapes on his chest were gone and his bones no longer felt broken, but she didn't know how much damage he sustained when he fell.

She scooted over to his leg and hiked the material up his calf. The teeth marks from the animal trying to drag him away were still visible. Small scars indented his skin, red and angry. There was no doubt they would be gone come nightfall, which seemed hours away, but she thought they should have healed already. She took a closer look. Around the teeth marks were small signs of something oozing out. She smoothed his pant leg back in place and returned to staring at him.

Why wasn't he waking up?

Was it possible the creature's bite was poisonous? Maybe working through being poisoned took longer to heal than physical wounds.

She sighed and eyed his chest. All those muscles, perfectly honed. His black shirt had been shredded, leaving blood-stained skin peeking through in several places. His tattoos ran down his arms, over his chest, and dipped below his jeans.

She bit her lip. He was unconscious. He would never know if she took a quick peek. She'd checked his leg, but what about the rest of him? Skye inched her fingers up Khaine's motionless body. She was only going to check the rest of his wounds, she told herself.

Hooking a finger under his shirt, Skye lifted the material up his stomach. Several abrasions slashed across his skin from the fall. They were almost completely gone, not even an angry red mark left behind. Just small indentations. Even at rest, his muscles formed thick abs across his midriff. She brushed his skin and examined the symbols there. He was hot to the touch, and each caress sent a jolt through her arm. Her body reacted to his, much like it did back in the woods when he pinned her to the grass and ground his hips against hers. She licked her lips, sliding the material higher up his chest. His nipples were two rosy-pink circles she found herself wanting to tongue.

Get a grip!

His nostrils flared and his body shifted. Was it possible she affected him, too?

A laugh escaped her. "Not his mate, remember." But there had to be some level of attraction if he'd asked to kiss her. Or had that been another part of his twisted plan?

Her eyes drifted to his full lips, cast in a thin line. Caden would cart her off to some mental hospital if she knew Skye was fantasizing about a demon. It was too absurd. Too forbidden. His eyes darted behind his lids and his body shivered.

Skye let his shirt drop and inched a few feet away. How could a demon affect her so much?

Maybe it had nothing to do with him and she was simply adjusting to a new place. This dimension was starting to wear on her. It felt like they had been here for days, but night hadn't yet come, and the sun was still high in the sky like it didn't plan on falling for some time. She twirled a stick in the sand. Her stomach growled.

She turned her head away from Khaine and caught a glint of something on his wrist. Light from overhead bounced off his watch and sent a reflection onto the wall beside him. She narrowed her eyes, not trusting herself to get closer. It wouldn't matter, anyway, she could see the cracked face of it from where she sat.

His watch was broken.

That wasn't something that would normally unsettle her, but a broken watch combined with Jade's words made her chest seize and hands tremble. She'd mentioned a broken clock. Was Khaine's watch what she had seen? And time that wasn't the same? She'd heard of other dimensions where time moved differently than earth.

It *did* feel like a day had past since she landed in this world's desert. Did Jade's vision follow the path of earth's time, or this time?

Why was she waiting here? Khaine wasn't going to die. She should continue her journey, and if he caught up to her, then so be it. She was wasting time sitting here, playing in the damn dirt with a stick, ogling a demon.

Skye chucked the stick and watched it crash against the tall rock behind Khaine, tumbling to the ground in pieces. Drawing things in the sand wasn't going to save her life. An image of Khaine, of his face when he mentioned his brother, played in her mind and wouldn't go away. The look in his eyes had spurred more questions than he would likely answer, but telling herself that was the only motive for sticking around seemed to give herself a reason.

Something ticked in her stomach. It was *not* because she wanted to know why he'd lied. It had *nothing* to do with not being his mate.

Besides, there was no telling if another of those beasts would come sniffing around the second she left. How could she live with herself knowing she left a defenseless being alone? Her sisters would comment that her actions defied the mercenary code.

"Screw the code," she said. It wasn't like she wanted to be a mercenary, anyway. She had more hopes of designing clothing.

Her stomach gave another cry of hunger.

Skye sighed and checked the strip of cloth on her left arm. She'd torn off more of her dress to wrap a piece around where that creature had clawed her. It had stopped bleeding and no longer pained her, but she checked it to be sure.

Her eyes drifted back to Khaine.

At least she could wait for him to wake up, berate him for lying to her, then tell him how done they were, and if he thought to follow her, he had best learn to come back to life faster. *Then* be on her way. She wasn't going to die in the next few hours. She had a few days left, at least. Plenty of time for that deity to give her answers.

Another hunger pang. She needed food. Khaine would need something solid as well for his body to continue healing. Did demons eat? She'd never been around one long enough to find out. Didn't matter. She was starving and there was a perfectly good dead animal out there waiting to be roasted. Skye stood and dusted the dirt off her knees.

She'd tucked Khaine between a few rocks and had covered one side with a large tree limb. The rocks appeared too tall for an animal to climb down from overhead, and the end of their makeshift cave was too small for anything larger than a domestic cat. If she secured the branch over the only accessible opening, nothing would likely disturb him. She'd build a fire, then find something to carve meat off that creature. Surly the meat wasn't poisonous.

Chapter 21

K haine shifted, his mind foggy and limbs stiff. The smell of burning wood wafted to his nose and his eyes popped open. He scanned his surroundings but didn't see a burning village, just a small fire surrounded by large rocks. He sank back onto the ground and forced the rhythm in his heart to a calmer pace. He could still hear their people screaming, could still see Leviathan pushing Jonah into the fire.

And Raiden. He closed his eyes, trying to remember every detail of his brother's face.

It was all a dream. One day, he told himself, he wouldn't have to suffer the nightmares, anymore. He'd find rest once Raiden was home.

"You've been out for hours."

Khaine jolted and searched the cave. He found Skye sitting by the fire, a leaf of meat in her lap. His mate. She was here? He leaned onto his side, wincing as a sharp pain stabbed his chest.

232

His ribs were still bruised. It would seem they had healed from being broken, but bruising was always the final step.

"Your shirt was shredded so I used it to start a fire."

He ran one hand over his bare chest before looking down. No blood. No cuts or deep gashes. They must have healed while he slept. And she'd undressed and cleaned him? He forced his lips not to curve even as he smiled inside. Her hands had run over him while he'd slept.

Khaine cleared his dry throat. "You stayed."

Not only had she stayed, but she must have dragged him to this cave. He surveyed the rocks towering on either side of them. Smaller rocks staggered themselves in an alcove behind him, sealing off whatever entrance had been there at one time. No, not a cave he realized. There was no ceiling overhead, but an opening between the rocks that showed a clear, blue sky. No clouds.

A slight breeze broke through what looked like a makeshift door, a large, leafed tree branch blocking the opening between the rocks.

Skye groaned and shoved another piece of meat into her mouth before standing. She discarded the leaf of food beside her and picked up another. A stick suspended chunks of roasted animal over the fire. His eyes narrowed. She'd found and cooked food?

It should have been *him* providing *her* with food. Instead, he'd been comatose and useless.

There was a pile of leaves on the ground next to the fire, bunched together in what looked like a bed.

How long had he been out?

Had she slept?

Skye seemed to battle with herself as she held the leaf, then walked toward him and set it on the ground by his feet. He watched her every move, the sway of her hips, the swell of her breasts. She'd cut the dress he'd given her to just above her knees, leaving creamy skin he could picture himself running his hands over. He shuddered.

Her dress was dirtier than the last time he remembered; with blood he couldn't place the smell of littering the dark material. The flowers embellishing the top half were no longer bright and vibrant, and a cut piece of cloth had been tied around her left arm, covering what looked like a scratch.

"Wasn't sure if you ate food, but I was hungry, and the thing that attacked you looked well enough to eat."

She stood beside him, waiting. Khaine furrowed his brows and reached for the leaf, folding it so the slice of grayish meat wouldn't fall off. He hefted it to his lap and studied it. "Thing that attacked me?"

Searching his mind gave no clues to her statement. All he remembered was finding her by the water, washing her feet in the stream, then her berating him before he passed out from his wounds.

What had she said to him?

Khaine lifted a piece of meat to his nose and smelled it. The aroma of fresh venison hit his stomach and he took a bite.

Skye scrutinized him as he took a few bites in silence. Something in her jaw ticked, the same look she'd been casting his way the past twenty-four hours consuming her face. She was angry with him. Her blue eyes blazed with a storm under the surface.

"You collapsed. You weren't breathing."

So, the fall *had* killed him. He'd suspected it would, and still he'd tried to leap the canyon like an idiot.

Her eyes grew distant and her words low. "I didn't think you would come back." She turned her head to the side, avoiding his gaze.

Khaine stared at her, a chunk of meat poised in one hand, halfway to his mouth. "You thought I was dead."

"You *were* dead," she snapped as she turned back to face him. "You weren't breathing." Her lips twisted into a grimace as she glared at him.

He let that sink in. He hadn't been *dead* dead. "And this angers you?"

"No!" she huffed.

No, not anger. Had she grieved him? Had she thought that he would never wake up? Khaine twirled the slice of meat in his fingers. Had his death affected her?

Skye sighed and took a step back. "It *didn't* anger me," she said, running one hand through her blonde hair and cringing when it got stuck. She pulled several strands out before dropping her arm. "I just thought beheading a demon was the only way to kill it."

Khaine set the piece of meat back on the leaf. So, was she angry because he hadn't died for good, or was she angry because he'd died at all?

"Beheading a demon is the only way to kill it. I may die from being wounded, but I won't stay dead unless someone cuts off my head." And there was no reason in the world for him to tell her that, so why had he?

He watched her, trying to gauge her response to his statement. Skye toyed with her dress and averted her eyes. Her creamy skin was mostly clean, but blood had long since ruined the dress he'd given her and settled in her hair.

"Oh," she said.

Oh? Khaine's heart leaped in his chest. He got to his feet and was in front of her before she could back away, the pain from his bruises forgotten. His death *had* affected her. Just when he thought he had her figured out, she did something that surprised him. He had been sure that she would kill him given the chance or abandon him at the earliest opportunity. Instead, she'd cleaned him, prepared him food, and watched over him while he'd healed. As if that wasn't enough, she claimed he'd been attacked by some animal.

Khaine stilled himself in front of her, not trusting his actions. Not trusting his demon's anger. Had she fought this animal for him? His demon half rumbled, the idea of her alone and defenseless flashing in his mind. She could have been killed and he wouldn't have been able to stop it from happening!

Tension radiated through his shoulders. He balled his fists and tried to reason with himself. "What of this animal?" He did little to conceal the anger in his voice.

Her eyes shot to his, but whatever fear he thought he saw on her face was quickly masked by confidence. She straightened her shoulders and stood her ground. "Like I said, you collapsed. This creature tried to drag you off and eat you. I stopped that from happening."

"And you killed this creature?"

She narrowed her eyes at him. "What do you think you're eating?"

Khaine took a step back. She'd protected him? Stopped some creature from dragging him off, then killed said creature and fed it to him? Before he could stop himself, Khaine smiled. His woman was ruthless, and dare he think it, protective. Of him?

Uncertainty flashed in her blue eyes and a heady aroma of honey surrounded her. "Why are you smiling?" Her breaths became uneven, her chest rising and falling in tune.

—Claim her—

Khaine's cock shot to attention in his jeans, painfully and suddenly hard. The smile on his face vanished and something in his eyes had her backing away from him, all aura of confidence diminished. His smile had aroused her. He could smell it in the air. And this caused her fear?

Skye stopped beside the fire and hefted her chin, her feet clad in torn material and leaves as she planted herself in the soft dirt. "Let's get one thing clear. I only stayed to make sure you didn't get eaten by some animal, and long enough to make sure your wounds would heal. As soon as I'm done with my food, I'm gone."

If any other person would have spoken to him in her tone of voice, he would have cut their head off without hesitation. In her voice, with her lovely, full lips speaking the words, all it did was turn him on more. The thought of her defying him made his demon half squirm with anticipation. To kill, or to claim?

Claim!

Then her words registered in his mind. He frowned. "Gone?"

"Yes, gone. You've tossed me around long enough." Her voice dropped so low that if he weren't a demon, he wouldn't have heard her last words. "And if you try to follow me this time, I'll kill you."

Khaine glowered at her. Now she was threatening his life? Tension boiled up his back and down his arms. His demon half remained caged.

"You lie. You care nothing for the lives of others," she went on.

Her blonde hair had more blood in it than when she'd gotten in his car. Black. His blood?

The memory of her scolding him by the river settled in his mind. That was the second time she'd commented on him not caring for another person. She could never understand how much family meant to him. How far he was willing to go to bring Raiden back from Shrodah.

I'm glad I'm not your mate, she had said. A declaration of what she would rather be than be mated to him flashed across his subconscious.

"Your words," he said.

"Have merit if you would just listen to them."

Khaine scowled. "You said you were glad you weren't my mate. Explain."

Skye laughed, her chest rattling and forcing her breasts to jostle in the dress. His eyes glued to them before he could steel his focus. He'd seen those breasts before.

Her laughter was sinister, a bout of hysteria instead of joy. It echoed in the small enclosure. He found her eyes again as her laughter died.

"Me?" she yelled. Her voice rose another octave higher and bounced around them in the tight space. "Explain? You want *me* to explain?" More laughter burst from her like a wave. "That's cute."

"Cute?"

Her laughter fizzled to nothing as her eyes shot daggers at him. Smoke from the fire circled the room, the meat she'd discarded over the pit crackling under the flames.

"Drop the act. I know I'm not your mate."

"Why would you—"

"I saw you with her."

Her whispered words dangled in the air, waiting for his mind to reach out and catch them. His chest tightened, his demon half scurrying to some dark corner. Khaine limped forward, a pain in his leg reminding him it had been severely broken. None of that mattered. The pain he could stand. The look on Skye's face was another story.

Khaine fought the dryness in his throat. "What did you see?"

"You. The Hirx. Asha was her name, right?"

His palms glistened with sweat. "What did you see?"

Fire danced over Skye's heated face. Her stormy eyes radiated a hurricane inside.

Her lips thinned. "You kissed her. I saw her on your lap with your tongue shoved in her mouth. You bargained for a kiss from me, then went off and got all cozy with another woman. How the hell does that signify me being mated to you? Mated men wouldn't do that. Mated men would be incapable of tossing their woman aside..."

Khaine glared at her. Tossing her aside?

"...in such a way. That just proves that you don't care. You're incapable of caring because I'm *not your mate.*"

His demon half bounded to those steel bars inside him. His legs stiffened. Fuck the pain! "You should stop talking." He scrubbed at his bare chest; his forehead creased.

Firelight danced across her features. "And what purpose

could you have had in making me believe I was mated to you? Did you think I would spare your life just because we were destined to be together?" She smirked at him. "What went through your head?"

He narrowed his eyes. "That you were my mate."

"That you were a demon and me a Guardian and that if you professed to some unbroken bond between us that I wouldn't kill you for being what you are?"

"Woman," he warned.

He was nearing his breaking point. She needed to stop talking. His muscles tensed in frustration.

"Well, I see through your lies, Khaine. I know I'm not your mate, and if you think—"

Khaine closed the distance between them and grabbed her by her arm. His mind snapped, her lack of reason taunting him and exciting him at the same time. His demon half gnashed those steel bars and he was helpless to deny it what it wanted. Khaine wrapped his arm around her waist and molded his mouth to hers.

Chapter 22

Skye felt her legs bow beneath her and tried desperately to keep herself from collapsing under the rush of sensations. His mouth locked over hers, his lips hot and demanding. A flutter of electrical jolts swirled in her stomach, intensifying with every touch of his tongue to her needy lips. His mouth demanded hers to open for him and she was powerless to deny the demon anything. She parted her lips and he growled into her open mouth, his tongue tangling with her own.

When she pulled back, he probed deeper. When she demanded more, he let her take it.

Skye laced her fingers through his shoulder-length hair. Her hands curled into fists, dragging him harder against her greedy mouth.

Didn't know it could be this good!

Gods, yes. This was what she wanted, what she *needed*.

She'd kiss the damn Hirx from his lips, make it to where he

never thought of her again.

Khaine uncurled his arm from her back and smoothed both hands down around her waist. Another blast of flutters hit her stomach as he slid his palms lower, cupping her bottom and lifting her from the ground. She instinctively wrapped her legs around his hips and held on.

Skye ground her core against him, urgently wanting something she knew nothing about. His bare chest, those perfectly formed muscles, caressed her breasts. Tantalizing. Taunting.

She probed deeper with her tongue, molding her mouth to his as hard as she could.

Her mouth was on fire, her head on the verge of dumping her into darkness. Too many sensations. Electrical currents shot between them. Did he feel them, too?

Khaine made an animalistic sound in her mouth, vibrating her entire body. Yes, he felt it.

His tongue did a figure-eight dance around her own and she moaned in abandon. Khaine soaked up the sound. A distant realization of them moving made her unlace her fingers from his hair and grip his shoulders. Urging him on. Wanting him to stop. The pressure was building, her body floating. She could come like this, her core rubbing against his groin at the same time he rocked into her. The hardness against her womanhood sent dizzying shivers up her spine.

Skye whimpered into his hot mouth as her back hit something hard, her breathing momentarily forgotten. She rocked into him, rocked her core against his hard shaft, his breath feeding her the oxygen she wasn't sure she needed at that moment. One of his hands snaked under her dress, worked over her bottom, cupping and kneading, then traveled higher to her waist, lifting her dress with it. Then higher still, to her side. She let out a hushed moan in his mouth as his hand hit home, brushing against her taut nipple.

She broke their kiss to throw back her head. She tried to pull him closer, tried to mold her body into his.

Something in her brain was screaming at her to stop this, to find reason, but Skye was so far gone she wasn't sure she remembered what reason was.

Khaine leaned forward and trailed his tongue up her neck. The warmth sank deep, traveled lower. Her hands moved back to his hair and tingled.

Tingled...

Her body was a thunderous wave, ready to crash...to explode.

Skye shot her head forward, not caring when her forehead connected with his. Tiny electrical currents were gathering in her palms.

"Stop," she breathed. Skye untangled her hands from his hair and pushed at his chest, a dazed look swirling in those black eyes. "Oh, god. Put me down!"

The warmth in her stomach churned into a sense of desperation. Panic rose to the surface as she desperately tried to calm herself.

Khaine gripped her harder, some battle working inside his brain and seeming to play out in his hands. She forced her feet to the ground and shoved at him, again. He released her.

Skye bounded to the other side of the cavern and knelt by the large rock. Her hands felt like shock waves building toward something dangerous, and she knew exactly what that dangerous was. How could she be so stupid!

"What—"

"Don't speak," she cried. She needed to calm herself and hearing the demon's husky voice wasn't going to help her. She closed her eyes tight, blocking out the world around her, trying desperately to pretend that Khaine wasn't standing only feet away.

Skye fisted her hands together and held them in her lap. "Breathe..." One...two...three. "Just breathe." ...four...five...six.

The currents in her palms eased to a manageable degree, but her heart was still racing. Gods, how could she be so selfish? How could she forget herself like that?

"Are you—"

"Stop. Just give me a minute."

...seven...eight...nine.

Skye took a deep breath and felt the currents wash away. She took another, filled her lungs so full her heart was forced to slow, then let it out. She could have killed him! Her emotions might not have gotten the better of her while fighting off that creature, because she had felt powerful at that moment, but that didn't mean they were in check.

And still, she wanted to be back in the demon's arms. Wanted to be kissing him, again. A sense of coldness swept over her where the demon's hands had been. The feel of him against her, of his hands and mouth expertly working over her flesh. She wanted that.

It could *never* happen.

That boy, the only other person she had ever kissed, hadn't affected her this much, and *he* had *died*. Another breath.

...ten...

Skye took one last deep breath and opened her hands. She looked at them. No currents. No tiny shockwaves leaking from her palms. No building orb in her hands or twitch in her fingers ready to be turned into a portal. She flexed each one and then smoothed them along her dress.

There was no avoiding Khaine forever. Skye eased her head up and locked eyes with him. He was too beautiful, too tempting. His hands were tight balls hanging at his sides and his forehead creased. Those black eyes bore into her, promising things she could *never* experience with him. The fire cast a sensual flicker of light over his bare chest. She'd touched that chest, felt those muscles. Ran her hands along those tattoos. An emptiness worked into her bones.

Skye forced her legs to move and stood, dusting her knees as she went. Her legs felt like they were going to give out, but she compelled them to hold her weight.

Khaine stared at her. She rubbed her sweaty palms down her dress, realized it was hiked above her waist, and promptly pushed it back down. Her face flushed. *Say something, coward!*

Like what?

She hung her head, refusing to meet his gaze. "I'm sorry."

Gods, why couldn't she be normal?

Khaine's rough voice bounded around her. "Sorry?"

His footsteps echoed between the rocks and her eyes snapped back to him. "Don't!" She slid along the large boulder, putting more distance between them, her palms guiding her against the rough surface.

He stopped. Stood. Seemed to assess her. "What did I do wrong?"

"Nothing. You didn't do anything wrong."

"You *are* my mate."

Skye closed her eyes.

"I don't care about the fucking Hirx!"

He seemed so honest. She *wanted* to believe him. And that kiss?

"Then why—"

"I only wanted the damn amulet! I couldn't kill her or risk both our lives."

That made sense. Skye forced herself to look at him, to gauge the truth from his words. Oh, she believed him. He thought she pulled away because of the Hirx?

He growled low in his throat. "I needed to bargain with her, get her to give it to me without a fight. She's a sexual creature. Nobody has ever denied her."

"Not even you," she managed to say.

"I *did*."

"No, you didn't. I watched you kiss—"

"Not then. Before. That wasn't the first time I've ever been to Temptest." Khaine sank back to the rock behind him and dropped to the dirt floor, leaning against it with his legs outstretched and arms crossed over his bare chest. His eyes had faded to their normal brown, hints of gold flickering behind them. "I went there once before, shortly after coming to the states. She tried to entice me, to get me into her bed, but I'd heard rumors of what happened to men who had sex with her. None of them could eat, let alone piss or shit without begging to be back there, and that was *if* they lived. She strips you of any will you have and devours it, all while making you think you're having the best fucking lay of your life.

"I didn't fuck the Hirx. I walked away before she sank her

claws deep. I thought that if I gave her a taste of something she wanted, something she had lost when I left, that she might return the favor and give me the amulet. At least let me borrow it for a time."

Skye eased herself down against the rock and crossed her legs. "The one that got away."

"Exactly."

"Then you didn't...you know..."

His lips quirked, a smile playing in his eyes. "No, I don't. Do explain."

She rolled her eyes and tsked. "Like kissing her. Did you like kissing her?"

"No."

That one deep, disgusted word hit her heart and stuck. She glanced at him, surprise seeping into her voice without her consent. "Not at all?"

His lips drew back as he smiled. Skye forgot how to breathe. The demon smiling was an all-night erotic show at dawn that left you begging for just one more look before it ended, one more dance. Anything for another glimpse of the seductive display.

"You were jealous."

"Was not."

"Was," he said with a laugh. His brown eyes lightened as he watched her.

"Not," she gritted. She sighed. "Just looked like you were enjoying yourself, and mated men wouldn't—"

"I wanted to rip her throat out and feed it to my demon for dinner." His eyes seemed to suddenly darken at the thought, just like they had while kissing her. "Kissing the Hirx was like kissing a sewage pipe fresh from the ground." He looked at her under his lashes and lowered his voice to a dare. "You *are* my mate."

"Okay." Something in those fierce eyes, in the desperation of his voice, told her he was telling the truth. She *was* the demon's mate. Was she relieved? Frightened?

The warmth in her body started to build again, so she took a breath and tried not to think about how she really felt.

The silence stretched. This was the most they had said to each other since he kidnapped her from her home and forced her to follow him.

"Why did you stop me?"

No anger. No promises of retribution. His question hung in the air, a simple question he wanted answered. Skye couldn't deny what they had done, how it had made her feel. How was she to tell the demon he would never be able to kiss his mate? How could the two of them together feel so right in one moment, and be so wrong in the next?

You're a Guardian, him a demon. It could never work.

Skye stood and walked to the branch guarding their little nook. "I need a drink." She held out her hand when he started to get to his feet. To her surprise, he didn't try to follow as she moved the leaves aside and stepped out into the woods. If only she still had the strength to run. What the fuck was she supposed to do with him?

Khaine eased himself back against the wall and let her go. He twisted and massaged his sore leg. The bones were healed, and in another hour, he wouldn't even feel it. Like nothing had happened.

He brushed his fingers over his lips and smiled.

Smiled.

She was becoming fire to his ice, burning him from the inside out, and he couldn't get enough. The way she had responded to him, moaned in his mouth. He wanted her hands on him, again. Wanted her to touch him like she had. Grip his hair as hard as she had and demand him not to stop.

What the fuck was he going to do with her?

Raiden needed him. Khaine needed his mate. Deep down, he knew he could never have both. Saving Raiden meant killing Skye. Keeping his mate meant never seeing his brother, again.

Khaine stood and paced between the rocks. He stoked the fire and added a few more logs Skye had left beside it. He paced some more. He would find another way to bring Raiden back from Shrodah. The deity would know a way. She could help him save them both.

And if not?

Fuck!

Khaine punched the stone wall beside him, the rock crumbling under his fist.

If not, he knew who had to come first. His brother. Bastian would never forgive him for giving up this opportunity. Hell, Khaine wasn't sure he would forgive himself. That was a decision that would haunt him for the rest of his miserable existence.

And killing his mate wouldn't?

Khaine stood by the fire. The dirt under his feet had been shuffled aside, two bare paths marking the ground beside Skye's makeshift bed. How long did it take to get a drink?

He glanced at his watch, realized it was broken, and stalked to the entrance of their little makeshift cave. She'd been gone too long. He froze in his tracks. Had she run? His heart dropped.

Khaine reached for his sword. Gone.

He must have lost it when he fell. The hell with this. He would go find her, demand to know why they were not still kissing, and then drag her back here and bury his cock inside her. The deity could wait.

Chapter 23

Skye knelt by the water and scooped the cold liquid to her lips. She sucked it into her mouth and swallowed, repeating the process several times. The overbearing demon had talked to her. Actual words that didn't constitute demands or trickery. Was this a new side of him?

She shook off her wet hands and sighed. There was no reason for her to torture herself with thoughts of Khaine...of that kiss...

"Get a hold of yourself."

But, what a kiss!

There was no denying that she was attracted to him. There was also no denying that that attraction could never become anything. Not only would that be bad for everyone, but what if she developed feelings for him? Her sisters would never accept him for what he was. A demon.

Her stomach somersaulted at the thought of his lips brushing against hers, the feel of his hands sliding under and up her dress. How close she had come to losing control!

How could someone that made her agitated beyond reason, also make her feel like she was the only person in the world?

"Doesn't. Matter," she gritted to the trees.

The forest around her sang with animals and birds she had never heard before. Not knowing what lay hidden behind rocks and tall shrubs, or lived high in the canopy, almost unnerved her. The whoosh of rushing water gave her something to focus on, something to ease herself. Skye took stock of her clean hands and the line of dirt circling her wrists. How long had it been since she'd bathed? She fingered her hair and winced at the blood and grime that had matted it into knots.

At least the woods were warm and humid, making the cool water a welcome retreat. Skye slipped off her dress and discarded her underwear on a fallen log, leaving on her makeshift shoes to keep any scratches on her feet from reopening. Her feet didn't hurt anymore, but she thought it was better safe than sorry to leave the leaves tied in place. The strip of fabric around the cut on her arm was next. She untied the material and glanced at the wound. It had already scabbed and seemed like it wouldn't open again, so she dropped the temporary bandage on the grass. She tip-toed into the river, the water reaching her calves, and sank to her knees.

Skye let out a blissful sigh.

Whatever feelings she thought she was having toward the demon were simply a product of kissing him.

But you were having feelings for him before!

Yeah, ones of pure aggravation.

Skye groaned. That attraction to him hadn't changed.

When it came down to it, if she didn't stop her feelings from progressing to more, she would have to choose either her family or the demon.

Skye wasn't sure she would be able to make that choice. She loved her family more than anything; the people who had been there for her when no one else had, but thoughts of Khaine kept bulldozing their way into her traitor head. She needed to keep her mind off of him, her hands off of him, and most *definitely* her lips.

The thought of accidentally blowing him up should give her enough motivation.

How could she be so stupid!

The water running along her arms and down her back felt heavenly. Skye used her hands to remove the worst of whatever blood, dirt, and grime had settled on her skin, then lay back in the stream and ran her fingers through her hair under the water. Remnants of blood flowed away from her, cascading over colored stones and loose moss.

Every few seconds, she found herself glancing at the trees around her, trying to see through their large bodies to what may lie beyond. The thick foliage didn't offer much in the way of sight, so hefty and so dense that it was hard to see anything but shadows, but the last thing she needed was to get caught off guard by one of those monstrous creatures, naked no less.

The brush surrounding the trees actually offered a sense of privacy. Skye relaxed in the flowing stream, her head back as she leaned against the stones on the bank. The clear sky overhead taunted her. It was calm, serene, not like her emotions with Khaine.

The water rippled along her body, down her sides, and over

her breasts. Her mind toyed with her desires, memories of Khaine's hand following the same path. She found her hand mimicking the motion of the river's caress, smoothing over her stomach and down to her...

She jolted. Twigs snapped in the distance and brought her limbs to an upright position, her eyes scanning the bushes and trees. The sound of retreating birds filled the still air. Water sloshed down her back and whipped across her skin from her hair. She instinctively covered her breasts, then frowned and let her arms drop. Her eyes didn't pick up any movement, but the lack of singing birds or bugs chirping seemed to unsettle her even more. What had scared them away?

Skye stood and wrung out her hair with both hands, her cautious gaze never leaving the darkness between the plants. She fixed her damp hair into a braid all the way up her head and then tied it off with a sliver of green stem she pulled from a bush. It curled and knotted perfectly around the end of the braid like a strip of fabric. Stepping onto the bank of the river, she shook out both feet and reached for her dress. There was no way she was putting the underwear back on. They had been rubbing against the core of her for days, now, and didn't look like the cleanest material. She could go without.

She took the dress and quickly dunked it into the water, wringing it out before putting it on. At least it was cleaner than before.

The feeling of eyes on her remained all through her dressing. Those tiny electrical jolts she had felt with Khaine were working their way up her back. She half expected to find the demon standing behind her when she turned, but nothing.

Skye undid the material and tucked a fresh set of leaves

around her feet, using the same piece of torn cloth to secure them. The scratches weren't as deep as she'd thought.

The silence of the forest began to gnaw at her. She turned in a circle, unsure if she should heed the feeling and head back to Khaine. Mountains in the distance caught her eye. They peeked through the towering limbs of green. Could they be floating? Could there be a cave among them?

The hair on her arms stood up, something making her feel off. Not wanting to be alone in a forest she knew nothing about, with the feeling of eyes on her everywhere, Skye picked up the first serrated rock she found and started her trek back to the shelter. They needed to find the red water that Asha had mentioned.

They?

She stopped.

Was she really planning on continuing with Khaine? The demon wasn't in any danger of dying, so there was no need for her to stick around, but they were heading to the same place. It might be for different reasons, and she might not know what his reasons were, but a strong, totally not sexually charged at all, demon could prove useful. Those tattoos all over his body were intricate spells that could help them on their journey, couldn't they?

And there it was, again. *Their* journey.

Skye gritted her teeth and threw her head back, cursing whatever higher power thought mating her to something like him was a grand idea. She needed to be focused, not fantasizing about a demon.

This was fucking absurd.

The blue sky above her flashed and she slammed her eyes

shut against the bright light. It blinded her, knocking her to the ground with her hands outstretched and gripping chunks of wood and grass. A wave like a sonic boom hit her in the chest, but not from any sound. It only took a second to realize her heart was beating a million times too fast and thudding against the walls inside her.

Just as suddenly as the flash had appeared, it disintegrated into the sky, taking all the light with it. She opened her eyes to clinched sticks in both hands and tall blades of grass threading through her fingers.

"Are you hurt!"

Khaine's deep voice had her bounding to her feet and back-tracking to a large tree trunk behind her. Startled, she stood in the darkness. It didn't take long for her to find Khaine, his legs battle stance and eyes black.

Her heart skipped several beats and it seemed to take twice as long for her lungs to fill with air. She outstretched one hand to keep him at a distance while she composed herself.

Khaine scanned the woods in all directions before his eyes locked on her, again. "Are you hurt?" His voice was calmer in her ears this time, not the thunderous roar she'd first heard.

"No." She took another breath as she relaxed. "How did you get here so fast?" Before the question was out, she found herself narrowing her eyes on him. A reddish tinge played over the sculpted muscles of his chest, those intricate tattoos dancing over his tanned skin. "Have you been here long?"

He turned his head away from her. "You shouldn't be out here, alone. You're mortal."

"And that makes me weak?"

His head whipped back to her just as fast as he'd looked away.

"You're my mate. I'm supposed to protect you."

"I never asked for your protection!" And that's where they differed. She had no desire to be anybody's burden.

He glowered at her.

Skye returned the look. "I can take care of myself. I don't need looking after. I get enough of that from my family and I don't need it from you. I'm not an object you own!"

Khaine took a half-step forward, his hands fisted like he wanted to pummel her, then stopped. He showed her those impeccably white teeth that had elongated into slight fangs and snarled, the vibration working up from his stomach to his chest and rolling over her in the darkness. His demon hovered under the surface, black veins streaking through his face. He twisted his neck and seemed to tuck himself into something more human.

"I'm...sorry."

"Do what?" Skye forgot the meaning of words for a moment. "What did you say?"

He growled, then stood to his full six-foot-two-inch height and unclenched his fists. "I said, I'm sorry."

She stumbled over her words. "Right. Well, right..." Skye mentally shook herself, jumbling her thoughts back to a whole. "I mean, of course you are. You *should* be."

"Don't push me, woman. Apologies are not something I do well."

Skye rolled her eyes. "Obviously."

His shoulders hunched as he scowled at her.

This wasn't like him. Apologizing. She needed to focus on something else before she read too much into it or murdered him for watching her bathe. He could deny it all he wanted, but his eyes held the truth.

Skye twisted in place, taking in the sudden change in scenery. The sky was full black over their heads, not a single star shining. A single red moon hung above the trees, large and menacing. All around them, the trunks of the forest were glowing with blue and green mushrooms that hadn't been there before. If they had been there, she was sure she would have noticed them. Slithering creatures she didn't want to ponder came out of one crevice or another, some glowing, some blending into the darkness around them. She hastily lifted a foot as one scurried by, not wanting to see if it would bite her.

"What happened?" she said.

Khaine moved beside her, his eyes taking in the scene. "I don't know. Each dimension is different. Perhaps this one has no gradual change from day to night or night to day. Anything is possible."

"So, you're saying that flash could happen again at any time and it would be daylight?"

"Yes."

"Fantastic," she said.

Khaine pointed to the river. "Look."

Skye turned and glanced at the flowing stream she had been bathing in only moments before. She almost gasped. The moon overhead reflected in the stream, casting a subtle red glow over the surface, but it wasn't the reflection that caught her attention. Several of the stones under the water were glowing with an eerie red tinge, so dull she almost thought she was imagining it. Every few seconds they seemed to pulse a brighter hue, illuminating the water in a red strobe effect. She followed the river upstream with her eyes where the trees parted in a wider path away from it. The further away the water flowed, the brighter the red reflected in the surrounding woods.

"Red water," Khaine said.

Was that all it was? Not actual red water, but tiny stones that seemed to give off a red light? If that were the case, wouldn't any body of water in this place be red? At this point, there was no telling.

Khaine shifted to stand in front of her, his muscled back blocking her view. She tried not to stare. *Really* tried.

"We should follow it," he said. "There's no telling when day will come or if the river forks."

She licked her lips. "Uh-huh."

Khaine faced her. His eyes faded, leaving a tremor low in her belly. Tiny flecks of gold sparkled in his black eyes.

Her cheeks flamed. Skye cleared her throat and pretended she hadn't been pondering sinister things. "What if the rocks don't mean anything? It could be a coincidence."

His eyes shifted back to an arresting brown, and he tilted his head. "I see no other option. We follow the river."

"Right." Skye wrung her hands, refusing to make eye contact. "We should get moving." She stepped around him and took the lead, leaving him a few strides behind her and radiating heat against her back.

"Just focus," she whispered to herself.

"What?"

"Nothing."

Follow the red water, the sky cave is the way. Sounded simple enough. Now, if she could just get there without killing the demon, and not on purpose.

Chapter 24

Caden scrubbed the sand from her eyes for the hundredth time, trying to pace herself with normal movements around the dead bushes. At least her head didn't feel like it was spinning, anymore. If only her limbs would join the club.

Night had fallen in this dimension with an angry red moon towering over the desert. What shrubbery blanketed the rolling hills glowed with a hint of red. It was just enough light for her to see without tripping over her blasted feet. The others would have no problem. Immortality had its perks.

Bastian knelt in the dirt, his blue eyes calculating and leather satchel slung over his shoulder. All of them had traveled in a general North direction when they first stepped through the portal. Now, they had been standing in this same damn spot for the last ten minutes while everyone gathered themselves.

Ten. Fucking. Minutes.

Mckenzie sniffed the air with Castello's eyes devouring her

every subtle move. The Dryad appeared fascinated with her ass. Caden would be sharing words with Mckenzie about the man as soon as they were back at their hideout, Skye with them.

"Which way?" Caden asked.

Bastian took off walking East, the sand downgrading on a slight hill.

"Where do you think you're going? Their trail heads North." Mckenzie fingered her blades. "We don't need you anymore, demon. I'm a Sylph. I can track them from here."

Stopping, Bastian cocked one of his thick brows. The moon cast a disturbing visage over the demon, his short black hair lowlighted with streaks of its red haze. "My runes sense their presence to the East. North could take us miles in the wrong direction."

"And we're to trust a demon? Following his tattoos, no less?" Mckenzie scoffed. "You're welcome to go East, but we're going North. In fact," She unsheathed one of her daggers and held it, her brown eyes daring the demon to make a move, "I insist."

Castello sidled up to Mckenzie, his hands at the ready. What good would a few dead roots serve? It wasn't likely the Dryad could hold a demon that way. Nothing in this dimension looked alive.

Bastian tilted his head, the expression on his face calm. "If Khaine has mated to your sister, he will do all in his power to keep you away from her. You need me to convince him to let her go."

Caden dangled her sword in the air. "We have that covered." They'd convince the beast with death.

Bastian's blue eyes regarded them. "Very well," he said after length. "We go North." He began walking.

Castello grabbed Bastian by his throat as he passed. They glared at each other. They were almost the same height, with Bastian a couple of inches taller. Both were built like tanks, but Bastian had a more fluid grace to his muscles, while Castello looked like he could simply pummel the demon into the ground with his fist. She imagined it would be entertaining to watch the men fight. Who would win, she wondered?

"Enough," Caden spat. "We follow Mckenzie." She glanced at Mckenzie and raised a brow. "All of us."

"Drop the demon," Mckenzie gritted.

"Giving me orders, Love?"

Mckenzie rolled her eyes, her curly brown hair dancing about her cheeks. "Hardly."

Castello released his hand from Bastian's throat. The demon didn't even bat a lash, just kept walking North with Mckenzie taking the lead and Castello tight behind her. Caden would have to be blind not to notice where Castello focused his eyes. An epiphany played out in her head, one she kept to herself.

Castello dropped back far enough to walk side by side with Bastian. The red of the moon coated his green attire, making it appear brown. "What's in the bag?" he asked.

"The Raudskinna."

Before Caden could contemplate movement, Mckenzie had turned, her dagger still in hand, and launched it at Bastian's chest. He twisted at the last second, the blade embedding itself in his shoulder. He gritted his teeth and snarled at Mckenzie, subtle black veins streaking through his face.

Castello shot vines from the dirt as Bastian shifted to demon form, his eyes solid black. He bounded after Castello, sharp claws slicing through the roots in his path. Tackling the Dryad with a sickening thud to his chest, Bastian's claws sank deep into Castello's sides.

Caden moved to stand by Mckenzie as Castello and Bastian tumbled over themselves in the sand. Punches were thrown, claws swiped across flesh, roots forming knots around the two. Caden rolled her eyes and crossed her arms. Neither of them attempted to intervene. Watching proved to be more entertaining, and Castello's outburst seemed to verify her suspicions.

"He's your mate," Caden said.

Mckenzie nonchalantly shrugged her shoulders. "I have no need of one."

That sounded about right. Mckenzie didn't like having others around to cramp her style. The only reason she tolerated the rest of them was because they didn't push her, accusing her of not being able to do things on her own.

Bastian cut a smooth line across Castello's side. His blood soaked up the moon's rays, making it appear darker. Castello reciprocated the attack with a fist to Bastian's face as a single root twirled around his ankle, tripping the demon. Bones cracked.

"Should we stop them?"

Mckenzie stood for a half-second, seeming to battle with herself, then turned and walked toward a cliff. "Let the boys settle their differences."

Caden cocked a brow at the men before she followed, taking stock of their current predicament. What did she care if one killed the other?

Stretching over two hundred feet across was a deep canyon, the rocks jagged on either side and several holes sunk in the walls where some had broken free. Down below was a rapidly flowing river, barreling over high boulders and plunging down steep ledges. It was tinted red as it flowed from between the cliffs and emerged in the forest below. Every now and then it seemed to glow a brighter hue like a pulsing vein.

"They crossed."

Caden pondered their options, which were few. "How do we get to the other side?"

She ripped the bandage from her head, ready to be rid of the damn thing—her injury felt scabbed enough to not start bleeding again anytime soon—and let it drop over the side. Across the ravine was a thick green forest and a cooler temperature. Glowing plants were protruding from enormous trunks, lighting the darker patches between trees. Despite the night's shaded temperature, her leather suit was starting to stick to her in the desert's hot air. She could feel cool air emanating from the other side as if there were two separate dimensions inside this one.

Vines shot from the cliff's ledge, braiding themselves into wide bands as they worked their way to the other side, digging deep into the grassy dirt. Caden turned as Castello formed several more into slats that ran horizontally with the others, his eyes green and face bloodied.

Bastian waited beside them in silence, his nose broken and bruises disappearing along his throat. His demon was tucked away, again.

Neither one looked any worse than the next. She absently wondered again which would win in a fight, and not a testosterone-filled battle, but an all-out war for death.

Castello finished forming the bridge and swung his arm out across it, motioning for Mckenzie to take the lead. Green eyes contrasted the blood all over his face. "After you."

Mckenzie tilted her head to the side and curved her lips in a sexual show. "I bet you say that to all the girls." She stepped out onto the plaited vines.

Caden couldn't help but snicker at the Meat Loaf reference. Castello followed Mckenzie—big surprise!—and Bastian crossed next. Caden went last, figuring if any of them fell she would have more time to react. Being human could have its downsides, she mused.

"How do you know about Guardians?"

Bastian slowed his pace when they reached the other side and glanced at her. Despite being a demon, he wasn't hard on the eyes. She imagined women throwing themselves at him. *Other* women. She didn't need a man in her life. She fingered the top of her head, running her hand over the scab there. Her tight ponytail would keep it in place. There was sure to be a lot of blood to wash out, though. Skye was no doubt blaming herself for what had happened. The sooner they found her, the better.

"Wasn't always a demon."

For a moment, Caden couldn't comprehend what he was implying, then it sank in, hard. "You used to be a Guardian?"

"Khaine as well. There was a time we killed our kind. Still do when given the chance."

"Do you know anything about people having visions?" Caden asked.

Mckenzie's ears twitched. She seemed to be waiting for his

response just as much as Caden. Castello growled beside her and Mckenzie dropped back, raising her eyebrows in an innocent gesture. "I can have other interests," she said.

"Not with men," Castello gritted.

"Seers," Bastian said. "They have visions of the future. Our people used them for guidance, to predict bad omens and plan for war."

"Have their visions ever been wrong?"

"No."

He didn't even have to think about it?

"And there has never been an instance where they were successfully altered, either. Some tried, they all failed. Some claimed the future was already set in stone and that nothing could change it. The path might deviate, but the outcome would always be the same."

Caden hung her head, refusing to acknowledge that Skye's destiny was to die. None of them would stop trying to save her. Ever.

"You have a Seer among you? What vision have they witnessed?"

"If what you say is true, it doesn't matter."

Bastian nodded his head in agreement, deflating her hope all the more. She would *not* let herself believe Skye was lost to them. There had to be a way, and that way was getting her away from Khaine and back home where she was safe, surrounded by her sisters.

"Time in this dimension feels strange," Castello said. "We should move quickly. We could be days behind them."

Mckenzie turned her head and locked eyes with Caden. Was she thinking the same thing? Would Jade's vision follow this dimension's time frame, or theirs? If the vision stayed true and being in this dimension upped the ticking clock, that meant Skye could die before they got to her.

"Are you good, Cad?"

Caden took a few seconds to gage her body's condition. The spinning had stopped and her legs no longer felt like rubber. Sudden movement would still render her useless, but she could work around that. Anything for Skye.

"I'm good," she told Mckenzie. "Let's just find her."

Mckenzie took off at a jog, the others tight behind her.

Chapter 25

K haine tore his eyes from her ass for the millionth time.

Raiden. Raiden. Raiden.

He needed to find his brother. The woman in front of him meant nothing. Mate or not, if the deity didn't have an alternative to sacrificing her, she would die anyway. How quickly she had altered his goals. Finding a portal and opening it had been at the top of his list.

Skye could open portals at will.

He should hate her for keeping that secret, but her ability would prove useful. A twinge of guilt seeped into his bones. He didn't want to use her.

Perhaps he should just ask...

Khaine cringed. That would mean revealing who he really was. All his fucking mistakes.

He still toyed with that possibility.

Bastian said he would have the rune needed to allow Raiden

passage home. It was hidden deep in the Raudskinna's pages. Bastian would uncover it and have the book and page ready. Khaine didn't doubt that for one second. If Bastian said he was going to do something, he did it.

With all those problems solved, there was only one goal left toward bringing Raiden back from Shrodah. He needed to find a way to sacrifice something else. *Anything* else.

Watching Skye bathe in the river had sent his cock to an achingly hard position in his jeans. The need to stroke himself had almost been irresistible. Her hair had pillowed around her shoulders while she lay in the river, her full breasts crystal clear under the surface and taut nipples peeking above the waterline. When she ran her hands over herself...*madness*. Had she been thinking of him? He'd watched her fingers trace down her sides and over the sensual curve of her hips. One of her delicate hands had dipped between her legs and she'd stroked herself under the water.

His cock jerked in his pants at the memory.

He'd imagined her thinking of him at that moment. And that nest of perfect hair between her legs?

Khaine groaned. Was she thinking of him, now?

Skye stumbled over a low branch and jerked to face him at the sound. Her stormy, blue eyes regarded him with such interest he couldn't help but smile. Yes, she was thinking of him, of their kiss. Was she thinking of more? She faced forward and continued walking, the smile on his lips fading to a frown.

Her long, blonde hair had been washed clean, now dry and swaying against her back. A few more inches and it would graze the top of her ass, much like he imagined his finger doing. A little further down and he could imagine his cock grazing something far sinister.

Thoughts of burring himself between her legs had been playing out in his mind for the last couple of hours as he followed her in silence. They hadn't spoken, and the lack of her voice was starting to drive him just as mad as his sexual fantasies. He hadn't had a conversation with another person in years, perhaps centuries. Speaking to her had felt like a drug he couldn't pass up, her voice a soft melody to his demonic ears. And if conversing with the Guardian meant kissing her again? He would grit his fucking teeth and tell her anything she wanted to hear.

For a Guardian, his mind mocked?

Khaine bashed those thoughts into a corner of himself, locked them inside a safe, and vowed never to reopen it. He didn't fucking care what she was! *Mine*, his demon roared.

Ours, Khaine corrected.

Guardian or not, she'd saved his life. Had battled for him. Were her feelings toward him changing? *His* feelings toward her had been derailed. Had he really seen her as naive, too arrogant about the world to so much as care for herself?

He'd been *wrong*.

Skye was every bit as strong as him. She hadn't run from a fight that could have killed her, hadn't tried to save herself, but instead stood her ground and battled a creature she knew nothing about, to save a man who had shown her nothing but spite. Khaine had been wrong in thinking she wasn't worthy of him; *he* wasn't worthy of *her*.

Khaine maneuvered around a large trunk by the leisurely running water, following Skye's every footfall. His hands clenched and unclenched several times, wanting to touch her.

Wanting her in his arms.

Wanting to speak to her...

"When did you learn you could open portals to Shrodah?"

He wanted to learn about her; anything and everything he could.

She stopped and turned, the red glow of the rocks beneath the water pillowing around her soft face. "Is that where they lead?"

He cocked a brow.

"I mean...I already knew that." She continued walking, ignoring his first question.

Stubborn woman!

"I know you know nothing about yourself."

No response.

Khaine clenched his jaw and scowled at her back. Her very nice back. A very nice back that dipped to a very nice rear.

"Not speaking to me? Why won't you admit it?"

"Now you *want* to speak to me?" She sidestepped an encroachment of mud. "What happened to me being naïve? And what else did you call me? A disgusting breed with no honor?"

He winced. *Had* he called her those things? Dammit, that wasn't what he meant! Even if it was, he didn't mean it now.

"Why should I say anything to you at all? It's not like you've confessed anything to me about yourself. You made it clear from the beginning that you hated me..."

"I errored."

"...and if you had a choice, you would have nothing to do with me. I don't even know why I bother," she said under her breath.

Khaine revolted at the reminder of his words. He'd said

many hateful things to her. "That was before."

What was this sudden change in her? He thought they had reached an understanding of sorts back at the cave.

Skye twisted and speared him with her hurricane eyes. "And now? Am I supposed to believe that something changed? That you suddenly feel differently about me and my family? You told me you could never love. You hated me before ever getting to know me and wouldn't even tell me why."

This was not the outcome he'd been hoping for. He wanted to talk to her, not have her yell at him. Again. Yelling didn't lead to kissing, and he really wanted to be kissing her.

Khaine stood in a confused stupor, watching her walk away and wondering what it would take to get her to open up. He was not used to conversation. The give and take. Back in the cave she'd made for him, after she'd saved his life, he'd revealed a little about his past. She'd seemed interested, and not yelling at him like usual. If he told her something about himself, would she do the same?

Khaine caught up to her and weighed his options. What could he tell her about himself?

Again, he entertained the idea of telling her about Raiden.

No, that was a subject he didn't want to delve into if he could help it. What would his mate think of him, then? He'd betrayed his people, his own father and brother. It wasn't something he wanted to remember.

The red-tinted water beside them rippled over a few rocks, descending into another patch of trees below a ledge. She scaled the hill with ease, using the branch from a nearby bush to help her down. Light from the glowing mushrooms filtered over her braided hair and Khaine fisted his hands to keep from reaching out and touching it.

Something else. What else could he tell her?

"I lived in a village...with people." He cringed. Khaine vaulted the ledge and wrung his hands on his jeans, staring at the ground as he walked. "When I would sleep, I would have nightmares about demons attacking our village, of them killing our people. My father's friend, Jonah, taught me the sleeping rune to help me rest. He was a good man and he died and I—"

Skye stopped so abruptly that he slammed into her. He grabbed her arm to keep her from falling and then released it. He retreated a few feet away from her, the bewildered look on her face filling the space between them. Skye brushed her teeth along the smooth line of her bottom lip. Her eyes measured him in the darkness, calculating.

Khaine forced himself not to move, to let her come to him on her own accord. How would she respond? Would she yell at him again? Accuse him of lying? Would she laugh at his attempts? Did she have some other reminder of things he had said, things he wished he could take back?

Skye seemed to battle with herself before groaning and shaking her head. "How did he die?"

The silence taunted his beast, begging it to answer.

"Demons attacked our village, burning it to the ground. He burned to death while I watched."

Her face twisted. "That's horrible."

And it was all my fault, he thought.

Her tongue ticked across her teeth as she shifted in place. After a length, she sighed and rubbed her arms. Without the sun baking through the trees, the temperature had dropped to a shivering low. Her dress didn't appear to be keeping her body warm enough, and still looked damp from being washed.

There hadn't been time to rebuild the magic he had lost before entering this dimension, or he could have fashioned her something to wrap around herself. They would need to stop soon so Khaine could gather enough magic and at least reform his sword. Not having his blade at his back was starting to weigh on him.

"I didn't know I could open portals."

Khaine tore himself from his thoughts. She was watching him, waiting for something. He clamped his teeth down on his tongue to keep himself from calling her a liar. Even he recognized the lure she was casting out, and he would have to be foolish not to catch it. "Until Temptest?"

Was she lying?

Skye bit her lip and nodded her head. "My emotions can cause me to explode on occasion. Literally," she laughed, the sultry sound of it dancing around him. "It's mainly fear and only when I'm extremely afraid. I never knew why. Caden helped me learn to control it better, helped condition my fears into something manageable," she turned and continued walking, following the riverbank. "But it meant staying away from people and things that might cause me to get worked up. It meant not going to that party or not having that relationship because any one of those situations could have gone wrong without me being able to stop it.

"I stayed home, did my job as a Guardian when the time came, which was rare, and spent the rest of it huddled in magazines or bent over my sewing machine."

Khaine kept himself glued to her side as they walked, his

hunger for her masked. "You make your own clothing."

Her face lit up and Khaine found himself unable to breathe.

"It's what I love to do. If I could outfit the entire Province, I would."

"Then why don't you?"

She shrugged her shoulders and turned away from him, continuing along the river's rocky edge. "Running a business means interacting with people; leaving the comfort of my home. It wasn't a risk my sisters were willing to take."

"Imprisoned." Khaine nodded his head beside her. "They imprisoned you."

"I never thought about it like that, but I guess in a way, they did. I would train with Caden," she cringed and corrected herself. "*Do* train with Caden. She's been teaching me how to use a sword. How to defend myself. One day I'll be able to take mercenary contracts and help them provide for us. As soon as I'm not a threat to people."

"Why would you take mercenary contracts if making clothing is what you love?"

"All my sisters are mercenaries. Well, except Jade. That's how we buy the things we need."

"Then sell your clothing."

She snickered beside him. "I don't think anyone would want to buy it."

"Have you tried?"

Skye looked at him. "Selling my clothing would mean interacting with immortals. It wouldn't be wise."

Khaine puzzled over that. A mortal interacting with immortals could be a deadly thing, but if it was what she loved to do. "You should do it. Sell your designs."

"You think so?" she asked. "I suppose I could design a few things and talk to the others about it." Her smile illuminated the darkness around him. "Mckenzie *loves* the skirts I make for her, and Caden's catsuit was something I came up with because she somehow finds herself in tight situations. Bulky clothing would get caught, and then of course, black helps her go unnoticed at night. I also had to design something that she could easily wash blood from." She shrugged her shoulders. "I suppose that's a given, though."

Skye furrowed her brows, her tongue running along the edge of her teeth like a window into her thoughts. There seemed to be a question in her mind, one she desperately wanted to ask. When she slowed her pace and faced him, he straightened his shoulders, eager to answer her.

"How do you know so much about Guardians?" she said. "Were the demons that attacked your people being hunted by them? Did they teach you?"

Khaine's lips thinned. "No."

"Then how?"

That wasn't the question he was anticipating. The answer was simple, and the first step toward his mate learning about him being a failure.

"I...wasn't always a demon," he said.

"I know. You said that. What does that have to do... Oh." Her wide eyes seized on him. "You mean, you used to be..."

"A Guardian."

Chapter 26

Skye tried to process that information. In the back of her mind, it made sense. Some other part of her didn't believe it to be true, though. It had to be some ploy by the demon. Some tactic to get information from her, about her kind.

She tried to keep his pace as Khaine moved faster along the muddy path by the river. His tense shoulders and fisted hands told her this wasn't a subject he liked. If he had been a Guardian in his past life, then why despise their kind, now?

"My village protected others against the demons. Those who were too weak or didn't know of their existence. We dedicated our lives to ensuring the portals between realms remained closed."

"We? How many of you were there?"

"Hundreds. Thousands."

Skye skirted a tall bush and pushed several branches out of her path. "That many?" Where had they gone?

"Before the Guardian line was wiped out, there were twelve other villages like ours all over the world. Each one protected a portal to Shrodah, the Hell dimension where demons are born."

"What happened to them?"

There was an edgy hint to his shoulders, the ridged line of his back straightening. He fisted his hands—in anger?—and continued along the river, leaving her to follow him.

Was he telling the truth? Had he really been a Guardian before becoming a demon? All the prominent muscles along his arms and legs said he'd been a man of strength. A warrior.

Yes. Deep down, she knew it was true. How else did he know so much about her? More than her or Jade even knew about themselves.

Khaine walked in silence, the strain in his body rolling off him and slamming into her. The mood between them had shifted, and Skye wanted it to go back to how it had been before, when they had been talking about her making clothing.

"Khaine?"

"They died," he snapped.

"All of them?"

He turned on her so fast that she stumbled and fell to the mud, her bottom colliding hard against the ground. Her hands dug into the soft soil beside the water as she stared up into his black eyes. He towered above her, the dark lines of his face hiding something ominous under the surface.

"No," he said. "Not all of them." His face curled into what looked like hatred. "You're here, and your sisters. A constant reminder of what I was."

Why wouldn't he want to be reminded of his old life?

"I'm sorry," she said, and genuinely meant it. There was a lot of hurt in his black eyes and Skye wanted to take it away. She shouldn't feel that way, but staring at the demon, how could she not?

He scoffed at her and turned, but didn't continue walking. Whatever happened to the Guardians, the demon felt strongly about it. It was clear he didn't want to talk about it, and Skye would have to be stupid to press him.

She bit her lip and tried to change the subject. "Did you ever meet someone like me? With my power, I mean?"

Khaine glanced back at her and frowned. His black eyes shifted back to a soft brown as he stuck out his hand. Skye laced her mud-coated fingers around the demon's large palm and let him help her to her feet. The muscles in his arms rippled as he pulled her up. He could crush her without another thought, kill her before she could even think to stop him. She should fear him.

Perhaps she was naïve, after all.

"Once," he said, "though our people didn't know what she was."

Skye trudged to the river and dipped her muddy hands under the surface, rinsing them in the cold water. The glowing rocks laying against the riverbed made the dirt she washed away look like blood as it rushed downstream.

"One night there was a loud bang in the village," he said as she dried her hands on her dress. The red water rippled a soft hue over his bare chest. "Our campfire had been scattered and caught one of the huts on fire. A little girl was standing beside it. I couldn't have been more than fifteen." His eyes narrowed, a distant look overtaking him. "The whole village gathered around her, asking her what had happened. There were too many people talking for me to hear what was said.

"The next day, our father told us she had some power inside her that could hurt our people. Said she had been sent away before she could destroy us and that it was for our own good. Her mother and father kept to themselves after that, never speaking to anyone or joining in celebrations."

"They didn't just let her go," Skye guessed.

He looked at her. "No. I suspect not. Years later, we overheard a rumor that she had been killed and her body dumped in the lake by our village." He tilted his head at her. "I always wondered what power she had possessed. Why they thought she was such a danger to our people."

Skye stood, her face grim. "She could open portals."

Khaine kneeled and washed the mud from his hand. "I think so."

When he got to his feet and turned, she followed him along the river. Perhaps in his time, she *would* have been deemed too destructive to live. It had taken her years to get her fear to a manageable level. If not for Caden, she had no idea where she would be. Perhaps like the little girl; tossed in a body of water for something she couldn't control. People have a funny way of wanting to destroy things they fear.

Khaine cocked his head and studied her as she sidled up next to him, those beautiful brown eyes catching the light and taunting her with sinister things. His deep blonde hair darkened in the shadows and danced in the glow. Maybe immortals feared him because they didn't understand him.

"How did you learn about yourself?" he asked. "Who told you about portals and how to protect them?"

"My mother." Skye smiled at the hint of disbelief on his face. "When I was twelve, my mother admitted herself into an asylum. She would have visions of the future."

"A Seer," he said.

So, that's what they were called.

"Yes. But her visions became too much to bear. When she was lucid enough, she would tell me about portals and demons, and would write in a journal with symbols she said would protect other people like us. She told me once, before she died, of a portal that I needed to find. Said that it was my duty to keep it safe." Skye tilted her head at Khaine and smiled. "Though I guess I failed."

"It would seem so," he said. No hatred or glaring. There was a hint of playfulness in his tone that shook her.

"What happened to your mother?" he asked after length.

"She killed herself."

Khaine grimaced. "I am...sorry. It was often that way with Seers in our village. The older they got, the more their minds failed them."

Khaine held back a bush for her to pass. She skirted past him and forged on. "Right, well...Caden and I managed. When I was fifteen, we set off on our own to find this portal. I don't know, maybe to honor the last thing she ever asked of me. It's not like I knew what to do with the portal when we found it." She stopped and closed her eyes. The smell of damp leaves and rain hit her nose. "I remember the first night the portal opened. It had never been a problem before and it was just the four of us, Mckenzie, Caden, Brooke, and I. Jade wasn't around then. We fought all night until it closed at dawn, and I'd destroyed more than a few pillars and chairs from the fear of it."

When she finally opened her eyes, he was staring at her, something in the demon's gaze coaxing words from her lips.

"Every year after that it would open. And then there came a year when it didn't. After that, it seemed to be random. McCain never mentioned the portal opening." She looked at Khaine, standing along the river beside her. "Why is that? Why was it always random and not at all for the longest time? What causes the portals to open?"

"The portals open every year on the Winter Solstice," he said, his voice deep and hypnotic, "the longest night of the year."

Skye nodded her head, already knowing that much.

"The children were taught in our village that the demons increased in power throughout the year and used that power to gain their freedom."

Khaine smiled at her, one of the first real smiles she'd ever seen on his face. She almost lost her breath. As if grasping what he had done, he masked his features and carried on. It almost ashamed her, wanting the demon to smile again.

"The only way to prevent their escape is to inscribe a set of runes on the portal."

Runes? "I never inscribed any runes on the portal."

Khaine scratched at the stubble forming along his face. "You never drew on the portal or around it?"

Realization dawned on her. "I would practice drawing the runes from my mother's journal in the dust around the portal." She frowned. "But I never did it on the Solstice."

"It's likely the runes remained long enough to be of use before any dust could consume them. Our people feared that happening and would only send a single person to inscribe the runes on the portal hours before the Solstice, just to be sure nothing disturbed it."

That made sense. When they had first found the portal, they had cleared the debris from around it and cleaned the stone. They had probably washed away the remains of any runes that were left behind, and then when they decided the dust was too much to keep away from the portal, she began drawing in it at random.

"Were you ever chosen?" she asked. "To inscribe the runes?"

His eyes faded and his mood dropped. "Once. Our father forced us to do it as a punishment."

"Us? Do you mean your brother?" Skye regretted her question the moment she asked it.

Those black veins streaked across his face, there one moment and then gone. "We should keep walking." All manner of friendly conversation was washed from his face, the overbearing demon sliding back into his normal caged demeanor.

He left her standing in the mud by the river, the moist soil seeping into the cracks in the leaves around her feet. They were starting to ache, had been growing more bothersome with every step she took for the last hour. The more she walked on them, the more the universe reminded her they were still healing, but there was nothing she could do about it, now. They had to keep moving. There was no telling how long the sun would stay down in this place.

If Khaine didn't want to talk to her about his brother, that was fine. She wouldn't push him. There were subjects about her past that she would rather avoid as well.

Skye told herself to focus on the task at hand, to forget the demon. Easier said than done. The sooner they made it to the deity the better. If they were lucky, night would last as long as day. And if they weren't lucky, her time could run out before they got there.

She followed Khaine, all his eagerness to answer her questions washed away like the mud from her hands. She kept his pace and let him be, trying not to ponder the change in him. His eyes had held the aura of a pained man, one desperately trying to gather his broken pieces and glue them back together. What had happened to his brother? What did her demon feel so strongly about?

She contemplated that last twisted thought in silence. *Her* demon?

Chapter 27

Khaine grieved their people in quiet, the memories of his past seeping into his mind and blocking out everything else. Skye hadn't said anything to him since he left her by the river. The silence consumed him. He curved his head to the side to see her rubbing her arms, crossing them against the chill. His demon side kept the frigid air from seeping into his bones. The further they walked along the water, the lower the temperature dropped. She was cold.

Khaine stopped and ushered her to a clearing between several large trees. Their giant bodies would block most of the night air wafting between them. "We'll stop here for the night."

Skye examined the brush around her, kicking a pile of dead leaves and limbs aside before falling to her bottom with a thud. "What about the red water? We don't know when the sun will rise, which means we can't know how long those rocks will continue to glow. We could lose track of it before we make it to the deity."

"The river carries on for miles. We'll follow it as far as it goes."

"And if it splits?"

"We'll deal with that if it comes. You're cold and you need to rest."

She rubbed her arms and yawned.

Khaine regarded her, her braided hair pillowing against her back and blue eyes shadowed with undercurrents of fatigue. His mate, tired and cold. He couldn't explain away his need to comfort her, and he also knew Skye wasn't likely to welcome such care from a demon. From him. He left her sitting in the dirt, hugging herself between the trees, and forced his mind to a task, any task that might comfort his mate.

"I'll build a fire."

"I can help," she said, getting to her feet and glancing out to the trees.

"No. I can do it."

"Why is it so hard for you to accept help from people?"

He scowled at her. "I'm supposed to provide for you."

She gathered a few sticks and dropped the stack by a pile of rocks, then began arranging them into a pit. "How old are you?"

Khaine rose a single brow in bewilderment, puzzling over her question. His age had been lost to him over the years and not something he regularly celebrated. He ran through a few calculations. "Four-hundred-and-thirty-seven. Give or take a few years."

Skye made a choking sound in her throat and cleared it, the twigs by her feet forgotten. She pierced him with her wide eyes.

"*Four-hundred-and...* You're ancient!"

Khaine cringed. "I wouldn't put it quite like that."

She continued stacking wood inside her makeshift firepit. "Well, I don't know how women did things back then, but in this day, we take care of ourselves."

He smiled and shot her words back at her. "Why is it so hard for you to accept help from people?"

The sudden curve of her lips stopped his heart. "Do it again."

"Do what?"

"Smile. You have a beautiful smile."

Her cheeks flushed, but she ignored his comment. Instead of push, Khaine left her by the circle of rocks and gathered several larger logs, placing them by the sticks. Her smile was like the sun against his face on a winter day. He could stare at it for hours. Skye seemed to busy herself with arranging everything into a neat pile, her smile gone.

She turned to him. "Do you know how to spark it? Some of these leaves and sticks are wet. The humidity in this area is high," she said with a sigh. "What about one of your runes?"

"My magic is depleted." Khaine knelt by the rocks and gathered a few sharper ones by his knees. He cut them across each other with smooth, hard strokes. A handful of sparks shot from between them. It took several minutes of him banging them together and her blowing a light breeze over the leaves before they lit. Khaine stacked the leaves in the pit, scattering them amongst the dryer patches of sticks, and watched the fire spread. When he was sure the fire wouldn't go out, he placed a few of the larger logs on top.

Skye warmed her hands against the flames, her body plastered as close to the fire as the heat would allow. "I thought your runes worked whenever you wanted." Her breath frosted the air and she scooted a few inches closer.

"Witches have such a power, able to pull energy from the electrical charges around them. I can only pull on that energy while meditating, and it's gone when I use it."

"Must be nice, being able to produce magic whenever they want."

"Yes, must be nice."

The shivers along her body started to subside and he watched her settle in against the fire. Her pale face soaked up the flames and left a warm glow on her cheeks. She already looked better. Khaine relaxed across from her, one arm propped on his knee.

"What did you do for your people?" She cupped her mouth as she yawned. "Somehow, I don't see you as the type to sit in a hut, teaching children or brewing tea."

Khaine laughed.

Skye shot her eyes to his at the sound, more heat flooding into her soft face.

He cleared his throat. "No, none of those things. I was a fighter, a warrior, trained at an early age to protect our village and others from demons."

"I can see that." She motioned to his arms, to his muscles.

Khaine smiled as her gaze darted back to the fire. The flames reflected in her blue eyes.

"What about after...you know..."

"After I became a demon," he finished for her.

"Yes. After you became a demon. What did you do then?"

He couldn't mistake the way she'd called him a demon without cringing. Perhaps his mate was getting used to him. He'd already tossed her background in a pile and set it on fire. He didn't care what she was. She was more than he could ever hope for in a mate. Kind. Strong. Determined.

"Many things," he said. Like watch his brother be sucked into Hell, his village and people die because they were too proud to accept help from a demon, and his world as he knew it crumble.

"I mostly drifted. Not many job opportunities for a demon." Khaine winked at her.

Her smile lit the darkness like a beacon to his heart. "No, I guess there's not."

"After I came to the states," he continued, "I took contract jobs to keep myself busy."

"You became a mercenary?"

"Of sorts, though not attached to the mercenary organization. I took private jobs from people that didn't care how the job was handled. They paid well and I got to do what demons do best."

Skye pulled her knees to her chest and rested her head on one, staring at him. The color had returned to her lips, the cold in her finally washed away by the fire. She seemed content. At ease.

A slight curve stole her lips, a hint of mischief in her eyes. "You mean like kill things?"

Khaine smiled. "Yes, like kill things."

"Who taught you to fight?"

"My father taught me to wield a sword," he said. "Those that didn't have abilities like the rest, but were born stronger than others, were called protectors and tasked with guarding our camp. If the runes along the portal couldn't keep it closed, it was up to us to keep the village safe and ensure our people's survival."

"Those that didn't have abilities?"

"You said your mother kept a journal. Did she not leave it to you?"

Skye hung her head, shielding her eyes from him. Out of shame?

"Yes, she gave it to me, but not a lot was understandable."

"Surely she told you about your kind when you visited."

Skye sighed. "I wasn't able to visit often, and when I did visit, she wasn't always there mentally. What notes she left were mainly about her own ability and had nothing to do with mine. It was Caden that helped me the most.

"We met in foster care. I guess we bonded because we were different."

"Both Guardians," Khaine said.

Skye chuckled. "Actually, just Jade and I are Guardians."

Just the two of them? He'd thought for sure her sisters were like her. Well, except for the Eabrith.

She shrugged her shoulders. "Mckenzie is a Sylph, Brooke an Eabrith, and Caden... Well, she has this rare blood disease that's slowly killing her." Skye grimaced. "The doctors don't know what it is or how to cure it, probably because it's not a mortal disease."

She paused for a moment and shook her head. This subject bothered her. Not that he couldn't understand why. If there was something slowly killing someone he loved, it would bother him, as well.

"Anyway," Skye said, continuing on. "Caden didn't want

to be some experiment to the mortal doctors, so told them to piss off. I suppose me destroying things wasn't all that strange to her, or maybe she decided she would help me since she couldn't help herself.

"She taught me what she knew about immortals and the Province and supported me when my emotions started destroying things. The people caring for us threatened to kick me out, but Caden wouldn't let that happen. And if for some reason I was moved from one foster care home to another, Caden would always come up with a way to go with me, either by damaging property or threatening to murder the couple in their sleep."

She laughed. "I guess the foster care organization finally decided sending me without Caden wasn't in their best interests."

"Did you not have other family? A father?"

"No," she said. "My father left my mother before I was born. I never knew him. And if I did have other family, my mother was never quite coherent enough to tell me about them."

"That's why you know so little."

Skye nodded her head at him.

It made perfect sense. She'd been forced to grow up in a world she didn't know, with powers she knew nothing about. The fact that she survived all on her own astounded him. Her sisters had helped her, yes, but he felt certain that if she had to do it all again with no help, she would succeed.

He didn't think he could be prouder to have her as his mate.

And knowing that about her past made other things clearer. She'd been sheltered and afraid because of her growing power, a power she had little control over. That blast she had rocked him with back at the tomb, had nearly killed him.

Khaine grit his teeth and shifted on the ground. The question he really wanted to ask was burning him inside. He had to know why she had pulled away from him back at the rocks. Why she was so afraid to acknowledge what her body wanted.

"Are your emotions the reason you're still a virgin?"

Khaine fisted his hands, urging himself not to reach for her. His demon half thrashed, desperate to have her any way it could get. He wanted her in his arms, his lips locked on hers. He wanted her body splayed under his own, his cock buried deep inside her.

Skye's eyes shot to him as she flushed, her cheeks red and prominent in the fire's flames. A mortified expression filled her face. She tucked her hands into her lap, ducking her head as if trying to hide from him.

"Have you known no man?" he asked.

She whispered her response, so low the fire almost consumed it. "Yes."

Khaine stiffened. "Yes, you have known no man? Or yes, you have?"

Just when he thought her cheeks couldn't inflame more than they already had, another wave of red washed over her as she looked at him. "Yes, I have."

He ground his teeth as his demon half roared inside him. He'd kill the fuck! Rip him to shreds. And her? Hadn't she lied to him? She'd said she was a virgin.

Before he could stop himself, the accusation burst from his lips, his voice coarse and bouncing between the trees. He called her on her lie. "You said you were a virgin."

Not that it bothered him. He didn't give a fuck if he wasn't the first person to have her, just as long as he was the last.

So, why is it bothering you?

Khaine growled.

Skye glared at him, all the heat in her face extinguished and replaced with a different kind of fire. "I *am*," she said.

Khaine released his tight shoulders and forced himself to be calm. "Then how—"

"Just because I'm a virgin doesn't mean I've never been with a man," she snapped.

Khaine stared at her. He lowered his voice and tried to be patient. "Isn't that the definition of being a virgin?"

"I was with a man, once. It never got that far."

He narrowed his eyes. "I don't understand."

She sighed. "My emotions have a mind of their own, as you know. Sometimes they make me react in certain ways."

"Like blowing things up."

She nibbled her bottom lip and nodded. "Or opening a portal by accident."

What did that have to do with anything?

Skye picked up a stick and poked at the fire, stirring the flame back to life. Embers crackled and rose into the night sky.

"I met this boy at a club when I was sixteen," she said. "Caden allowed me to go with her that night, as long as I stayed close to her. We were celebrating her first real mercenary gig and the party ended up following us home."

"The boy, too," he gritted, trying to keep himself calm and let her finish.

"We were getting a little hot in my room and my emotions were all over the place. A combination of nerves and excitement."

Khaine froze as his heart dropped. "You didn't..." How horrible that must have been; to explode in a moment like that. A mortal boy wouldn't survive.

"No, nothing like that. It was worse. Instead of my emotions blasting out, they created a portal. A demon got free before I knew what was happening. It killed him."

"I'm sorry," he said. To be in that position, unsure of what you had done.

Had he not been in the same place? When he accidentally inscribed the wrong rune on the portal and let Leviathan free on earth... He hadn't known how to fix it, how to make it right. He froze like a coward, and his father paid the price.

"Caden killed the demon and managed to get the portal closed, probably because she tossed it right back where it came from."

At the time, it hadn't made sense to Skye, but after she threw that Elite soldier into the portal... She guessed that was *one* way to close them. Or maybe tossing something into them only worked on portals *she* opened.

Skye sighed. "After that day, well..."

"She decided you shouldn't go out, anymore."

She nodded. "I can't trust myself to control it. There's no telling when it could happen. I'm sure that with time I could learn to handle my power. I didn't even know I was going to open a portal outside Temptest, but it happened. I can't put myself in a position like that knowing how it could turn out."

Khaine fingered the box in his pocket, the box Bastian had given him before he left. His brother was everything to him, and getting Raiden back meant more than he could ever express, but just when he thought he would never be given another chance at happiness, the higher powers gave him a mate. He'd hated her, at first, for being what she was, but he knew without a doubt that if given the chance, she could mean just as much to him, if not more.

"If you didn't have your power, would you have stopped me?"

Khaine didn't have to explain what he meant. He could see on her flushed face that she understood. Her stormy eyes roamed his body as she played with the cut edges of her dress, folding them between her fingers. Lust filled him. He could feel her gaze raking over his bare chest and down his sides and his cock was helpless not to respond, surging in his jeans. She seemed to notice the bulge between his legs.

Her voice a low rasp, she shook her head. "No."

Never had he wanted something more. He suddenly wasn't sure if he could give her up just to have Raiden back. He wasn't sure he could give her up for anything. He liked conversing with her. He liked her drive. She was good and kind and everything he wasn't.

Khaine stood and gave her his back. It was that or bed her by the fire, consequences be damned.

"Get some rest," he said over his shoulder.

He found a spot close by between another set of large trees and sat on the ground with his legs crossed. Khaine closed his eyes and tried to focus on rebuilding his magic, thoughts of Skye swirling in his head and tempting him. The box Bastian gave him was still tucked in his pocket, safe.

For now.

Chapter 28

Skye rolled onto her back and stared into the bright, blue sky. The sun breaking through the trees warmed her face and arms, leaving the dead fire beside her forgotten. The hair on her arms prickled with a shiver of warmth.

She jolted to a sitting position.

Warm.

Sun.

The river was crystal clear. No red glowing rocks. No mushrooms swelling from the tree trunks around them. No black sky hovering high above, seeming to suck all the light from everything else. The forest was once again coated with a fresh swath of green, the bushes and tree limbs covered in bright leaves. Even the rocks along the river, the ones that fell too close or were sucked in by the water, were encased in thick, green moss that molded itself to every groove, smoothing out even the most irregular of surfaces.

She could actually *see* the moss.

Blinking her eyes several times adjusted them to her bright surroundings. How long had she been out? God, she knew she'd been exhausted, but she didn't feel like she had been asleep long. Her back was stiff, her neck kinked, and the slight hum of sleep bouncing in her head told her she couldn't have been lying on the hard ground for more than a couple of hours.

The fire beside her had dwindled to nothing, burnt logs still smoking in the cooler air. The temperature was rising by the second, the humidity of the forest expanding to form tiny droplets of perspiration on her forehead. No cackling sounds or smoldering embers were left inside the circle of rocks, and a low fog was forming with the mix of hot and cold air.

Skye canted her head. The forest was once again alive. Birds sang in the treetops around them as small animals rustled in the bushes. Most of the creatures in this realm were things she had never seen before. If she focused on it too much, all it did was alarm her. So far, they hadn't posed any threat. She would let them go about their business as long as they kept to themselves.

Khaine sat with his legs crossed in the dirt, each hand propped on one knee. His back was straight, his thick hair shielding half his chiseled face, and his beautiful brown eyes were shut tight.

Meditating.

The tattoos curving up the demon's sides and chest, and stretching over the muscles on his arms, were pulsing with every breath he took. He'd said he needed to rebuild his magic to use all those runes caressing his bare skin. He'd started the process right before she'd passed out, so he couldn't have been at it long. Even so, she needed to wake him.

There was no telling how much time had past, and she didn't have much time left to begin with. His broken watch had been a sullen reminder of that fact. It was still buckled low on his wrist, the face of it shattered. They needed to get moving; follow the river as far as it took them and find the sky cave. Time was already off in this dimension.

Skye reached for the ground beside her, ready to stand and wake the demon. Her palm cupped over something hard. The edges of a square box pressed into her hand and she picked it up. No longer or wider than a card, and no thicker than a piece of granite, the box felt light in her hands as she turned it over and examined it. Had Khaine placed it beside her while she slept? He was meditating when she'd fallen asleep, but he could have easily been pretending.

It looked like an ornate jewelry box. Intricate markings were engraved on all sides and burned into the dark wood. Who else could have placed it next to her? They hadn't encountered another living being—well, besides that cat-like creature that tried to drag him away for supper and all the other creepy crawlies skittering about—but no other person. Looking closer, Skye recognized the box as the one she had pulled from his pocket before he was attacked.

It had his smell to it.

Suddenly as giddy as a schoolgirl, Skye flipped the box back over and fingered the small latch. She opened it carefully, the wood radiating with an old-world flare. A satin-lined interior, the color of wet coffee, rested beneath a single piece of silver. Skye pulled out the small oval, gasping when a long chain came with it.

A necklace.

She looked at Khaine. He was just as still as before, bare-ly moving. His chest rose a hairbreadth at a time when he breathed, but the rest of him was cold and hard. Had the demon given her a necklace? She narrowed her eyes at him. Why would he do that?

The small silver pendant boasted tiny markings all around its oval body that bled into the chain and wrapped around the long, twisted metal. She couldn't explain it, but holding it calmed her. They were the same markings that were on the portal, the same markings as his tattoos, though different in subtle ways. It had to be embedded with some form of magic.

Should she accept the gift? *Was* it a gift? Was it possible for the demon to care? She already suspected that was true. The way he'd looked at her when he spoke about his people told her exactly how much he could care. He loved them.

Oh, just stop. You know you're going to wear it.

She sighed. There was no arguing with herself. She couldn't deny that the necklace was beautiful, and for Khaine to give her something, anything, touched her heart in an odd way. She kind of liked this thoughtful side of him.

So, wear it!

It's not like she couldn't give it back, later. If she was still alive, she reminded herself. Or, maybe this was supposed to be a testament to how he felt and if she wore the necklace, he would take that as a yes toward being his mate.

Don't you want *to be his mate?*

God help her, she kind of did. He'd lost so much in his past. She'd thought him nothing more than a barbarian of a man, a demon with no thought or care for other people. She couldn't have been more wrong. There was still so much about Khaine that she didn't know, but she wanted to find all that out and more. He'd cared for his people, in such a way that she knew he had to have loved them. She was beginning to suspect he actually hated himself more than he hated her.

She wanted to find this deity and save her life, even if just to start something new with Khaine.

Skye unhooked the clasp of the necklace and put it on, letting it drape between her breasts. The cold silver felt good against her humid skin.

Deeper meanings be damned. She liked it and she wanted to wear it.

Skye closed the box and locked the hinge. She didn't have any pockets and the wood seemed too old and too valuable to leave behind. She got to her feet, dusted herself off, and walked over to the demon. She set the wooden box in his lap and started to wake him, but pulled her hand back. If he was rebuilding his magic, that was something they might need. She should let him be for a moment, give him a little more time. She turned to the forest. She could relieve herself, get a baring on their location, then wake him.

Skye trudged into the forest and a few moments later, with her stomach no longer feeling like it could explode at any moment and her leaved shoes and hair revamped, she climbed to the top of a shorter tree to see how far they had gone. She toyed with the necklace on her chest, swinging it back and forth with a smile.

In the distance were those same mountains she'd seen outside while bathing. Now that they were closer, she could also tell that they were suspended in the air, hovering above smaller cliffs and rocks. They looked like they were floating with an eerie fog encasing them.

Sky caves. There had to be a cave hidden amongst them. Perhaps her luck was changing after all.

Pivoting as best as she could, while trying not to fall from her position atop the tree, Skye followed the river as it sloped, weaving in two separate directions. Both led to the massive rocks soaring in the air, their towering cliffs suspended by nothing on all sides. There was no telling what path they needed to take. Either direction could lead them to the deity.

Them?

Something about the demon had gotten under her skin. Khaine was sunk deep in her head. She wasn't sure she had a good reason to continue fighting the feeling. She already acknowledged wanting to see where things could go with him, so why lie to herself? What would Caden think of her, now?

Skye hooked her foot on the branch below her and heaved herself down. She climbed, one large limb at a time toward the bottom. When the same rustling sound she heard outside their makeshift cave echoed from a direction not far in front of her, she froze.

Bushes jostled in the still air. The chirping of birds and tells of smaller animals, that had livened the forest when she woke, skittered along the ground and over rocks, but this sounded larger. She really hoped it wasn't the thing that attacked Khaine.

As if on cue, a mass of needle-tipped thorns poked above a group of rocks.

Skye tilted her head to the clear sky and mouthed a silent, sarcastic thanks.

She shifted in place and tucked her body into the tree, molding herself to the enormous trunk. The cat meandered from behind a thick encroachment of rocks, one heavy paw after another beating against the ground as it walked. Its hair was a silken, black frame of spikes along its body, unlike the lighter gray mane of the one before, and those deep green eyes were prowling the dirt in front of it.

Skye moved to see what it was doing but sucked herself back again when another stalked from the shrubs to join it. Then another. And another.

Four of them.

Fuck.

There were four large, beastly animals roaming the dirt beneath her, on the hunt. She was trapped. How was she going to get back to Khaine?

Could these cats climb? It didn't seem to be possible with their broad shoulders and high hind legs. She could keep to the trees, could get back to Khaine by jumping from one to another. She could do it. They weren't that far apart, and their rounded bodies would give her something to hold onto when landing.

All she could think about was waking Khaine before these animals found him. They were headed in his direction. She didn't know much about rebuilding magic, but if Khaine was dead to the world around him at that moment, he wouldn't be able to defend himself. No matter how she felt about the demon, watching him die wasn't on her list of options, anymore. Been there. Done that.

Didn't like it.

Skye crept back up the tree, careful not to step on anything that might make a sound. If praying to the higher powers was a surefire way to help her right now, she would. As it stood, they couldn't even be bothered to guide her toward a path that meant living. All they could muster was a gnawed bone behind steel bars in a hell-zone with no food. She'd take her chances with the tree.

The trunk was too large at this level for her arms to get a solid grip. If she could maneuver toward the top, she might be able to wrap around the other trunk when she jumped. It was either that or gamble with the ground and four to one didn't seem like good odds.

There was always option C; wait for the creatures to find Khaine, let the demon and frankenstein cats battle it out, then climb down and continue their journey.

Skye mentally scolded herself. She was *not*, and never would be, a damsel in distress.

The limbs of the tree stretched all around its body from bottom to top, with thick, massive leaves like those from a Catalpa tree. They were shaped like a Pine, soaring into the sky, some touching where clouds would hover. She heaved herself to a wide branch and peaked at the search party underway below. They were still prowling the ground, getting dangerously close to the tree trunk. Could they pick up her smell? Did it linger on the tree? She'd touched it when climbing up.

Grunts and snarls streaked the silence around her. All four cats were momentarily distracted sniffing the middle of a tall bush. Skye took the opportunity to pull herself up another leg and assess her landing zone across a four-foot gap.

Doable.

A shrill cry drifted through the branches under Skye's feet, forcing her to stop and look down. She immediately regretted that decision. One of the larger creatures was directly below her, hunched back on its hind legs with its two front paws digging into the tree. Their eyes locked.

Holy shit.

Maybe the cat wasn't actually looking at her.

Right, and maybe the earth wasn't round. She adjusted her feet to keep herself from falling, still holding onto the large trunk as if ready to jump. If she held still enough, the creature might disregard her. She still wasn't sure if the blasted thing could climb. God, she hoped it couldn't climb.

As if she needed a dose of reality, the large cat dug its claws into the bark and hoisted itself upward. The three other cats chose that moment to start circling the trunk, no doubt coming to their companion's call.

Skye shifted her eyes to the tree beside her, ready to make her grand escape. She could get back to Khaine, he could help her. Two against four had better odds.

Images of Khaine being dragged away by one of the animals made her pause. Sure, Khaine was a demon. Sure, she had no rational reason to keep him safe. So, why the sudden dread at the idea?

No, she had no desire to lead these things back to him while he was unaware and watch him die. God help her, she didn't want the man to die at all. Her heart somersaulted at the thought right as her inner diva chastised her for calling him a man.

Get a grip, she scolded herself. Demon or not, he was still a man. Could still die.

Skye glared at the creature now halfway up the tree. "I can call him a fucking man if I want to!"

Right at her outburst, the three cats on the ground sunk their claws into the tree and began to climb, one after another, up the enormous trunk. Her heart pounded.

Super smart, Skye!

There was no way she could let her fear win. Not now.

Skye glanced again at the branch she intended to land on. If she jumped, the creatures would follow her, likely faster than she could run. That familiar pit, the one she had begun to detest with a fervid force, crept into her stomach and churned. That blasted signal that told her she wasn't doing well to control her emotions. She clutched a branch of the tree and closed her eyes.

Deep breaths. In. Out.

All she could do was wait for the blast to knock through her. She would fall. As soon as her fear gave way, the limb she stood on, the branch she was clutching to keep herself steady, would crumble and drop her to the forest floor.

Twigs snapping drew her eyes open and straight to the animals, now so close she could smell their putrid scent. Her heart hammered in her chest as her sweaty palms threatened to slip. There was nowhere to go, nothing she could do.

She was going to die.

Fuck trying to be the strong woman.

"Khaine!"

Skye yelled his name, hoping to God he would hear her. The creatures climbed higher. She glanced at her hands, confused. Why was nothing happening? Why was her fear not blasting her from the tree? She was terrified, her chest so tight she was fighting for air.

Skye could practically hear Caden in her head, yelling at

her to pull herself together like she had before Skye unraveled. Still, there was nothing. No blast. No portal. And no time to contemplate any of that.

The cat closest to Skye leaped onto the branch level with her, now in striking distance. Disregarding her plan to jump from tree to tree, and with no time to wait for Khaine, she peered straight at the ground. Maybe the creatures would be so taken aback by her course that they wouldn't follow.

Fuck!

Skye closed her eyes and jumped, landing on the branch below her just as one of the beasts swatted a claw in her direction. She jumped again, lower still. There was no getting to the branch under her. One large creature was poised above her head, the others climbing up below her. Skye gauged the distance to the ground and contemplated her next move.

Before she could come up with a solid plan, one of the cats reached the branch she stood on, jostling her. There wasn't time to regain herself before she fell.

Skye screamed as she hit the ground hard, knocking the breath from her lungs.

Chapter 29

K haine came to with a jolt, something waking him from his meditation. He hadn't rebuilt enough magic. It coursed through his veins once again, his tattoos swirling with the added fuel, but he shouldn't be coherent yet. Scanning the surrounding trees with a frown, he noticed more than he wanted to. The fire was no longer burning, the sun was up, and Skye was gone.

He bounded to his feet, intent on charging headfirst in whatever direction he sensed Skye, but stopped himself as the clattering of a box drifted through the still air. He glanced down at the wooden case that held Raiden's necklace. He'd told Bastian to destroy it. He had never wanted to see the damn thing again. It reminded him too much of the past, and the past hurt.

Then Bastian had informed him that he would be needing something of Raiden's for his brother to be returned from

Shrodah, and that he'd kept it because he thought Khaine might want it back one day. And then Skye...

Maybe the higher powers were finally starting to take his side.

After Skye told him why she could never be with him, well...for what he and his demon half seemed to want from her, Khaine felt compelled for her to have the necklace. He had tried to tell himself that it was only because he wanted to fuck the Guardian beyond reason, but he couldn't deny that fixing her problem, any problem, would bring him joy. He didn't care what he got out of it. She could yell at him for trying to help her, and he would still do it. What more could he do for the mate that saved his pathetic life?

Khaine frowned.

He just wanted to see her happy.

None of that answered the question at hand. Why was the box now laying at his feet? Had she denied the gift?

Khaine took a breath, trying to ease the sudden fear in his chest. Her denying the necklace would be the same thing as denying him, would it not? His demon half growled at the thought. Placing more of those damn steel bars in place, Khaine reached down and grasped the intricate wood. All around him, the forest had come back to life. Birds chirped at the heated glow of the sun overhead. Animals he had never seen scurried from bushes to trees. It was as though the forest were mocking him, laughing at his ridiculous attempt to apologize. Telling himself that it didn't matter, that there was no reason to open the box for proof of Skye's refusal, he unlatched the lock and opened the lid.

He couldn't *not* look.

Under the ornate, wooden cover, the inside of the box was lined with brown silk, the material indented in the middle.

It was gone. She'd accepted his gift.

Khaine's lips curved as that fear in his chest eased into a different kind of pressure, one he hadn't felt in a very long time. Hope.

His forehead creased. Where had she gone? Surely she hadn't left him, again. She'd seemed accepting last night as they sat around the fire and spoke. Actually spoke. He couldn't deny that he liked their conversations. He wanted to think that he was finally wearing her down, but it was *her* that was melting *him*.

The scream bounced through the trees a millisecond before his feet were moving, the empty box being tucked in his pocket. There was no mistaking Skye's voice, no mistaking the desperation in that sound. Khaine bounded through the thick trees in the direction of her scent. The forest on either side of him came alive with the squawking of birds overhead, their distinct sound of danger emanating through his bones. This realm was starting to wear on him. Nothing here seemed right. He poured every ounce of energy he had into getting to Skye, wherever she was.

The forest seemed to constrict him, closing in on his chest as he ran faster than his body wanted. He didn't give a damn that his muscles were fighting back, trying to give out as he poured more energy into every step. Didn't care if his lungs were on fire and he couldn't breathe. As long as he got to Skye before something happened to her.

Coming up on a large tree, Khaine noticed her scent only moments before the scuff marks on the ground. All around the enormous trunk were footprints dancing against the dirt, some human, some not.

It was the 'some not' that had his heart sinking.

"Skye!" He roared her name into the forest.

She'd been here, he knew it without a doubt, could scent her all over the tree, but she wasn't the only one. Something else had been here with her. Several somethings by the look of the disturbed ground. The tell-tale signs of a struggle had his chest tightening. Bushes lay smashed and contorted, their dense bodies bent and broken.

Seconds passed as he spun in a circle, trying to catch her scent. Where was she?

Her voice rang through the forest around him. "Khaine! Khaine!"

He tore off after the sound, pushing past limbs and shrubberies, small animals he hadn't a care for scurrying under rocks and logs. The birds he had heard were long gone, Skye's screams likely alerting them to the danger they wanted to avoid; the danger Khaine desperately needed to get to. There was no telling what had caused her alarm. The ominous sound of silence around him, of the birds and animals making themselves scarce, threatened to throw him into a panic.

He raced through the forest, skirting enormous trunks and hurtling over ragged boulders. Just when he thought the deep expanse of woodland was out to punish him, to keep Skye tucked in its thick embrace where he would never get to her, the trees seemed to thin as more of the sun's rays drifted through the canopy. Coming to a halt in a clearing, Khaine searched the tree line for signs of Skye.

And then he found her, and all the blood drained from his

face.

Several yards away on his left, Skye stood by a cliff, her back to the edge. His brain seemed to short-circuit, not wanting to comprehend the danger his mate was in.

Four large beasts circled in front of her, their thick, black manes shaking as they lunged for her and then retreated. They were larger than any cat he had ever seen, with dark black fur and claws that could decapitate a person in seconds. With each step the creatures took, Skye took another step back. *Closer toward the cliff.*

She stood with her feet spread as if to keep her balance. In her right hand was a large branch that she waved in front of her, keeping the creatures at a distance, but that would only last so long, and the look on Skye's face said she knew it.

The creatures seemed to be toying with her, knowing she had nowhere to go but not wanting their prey to fall. Beyond her, on the other side of the cliff, Khaine could see the desert they had entered when first arriving, but there was no ravine, just a wall of rock his mate currently stood on the top of. If she fell...

He might come back to life, but his mate would *die*.

Skye seemed to notice him, her eyes alight as she wailed the large stick between her and the four creatures. Her feet shuffled in the rocky dirt, balancing between each other as if she could gain more space.

Khaine assessed the creatures. There had to be a way to get them away from his mate safely. If he charged them, she could fall. There were four of them, and only him and Skye. They were severely outnumbered, and he didn't have a fucking clue how strong these beasts were.

None of that mattered. He would kill them for threatening Skye. Would rip their heads off for thinking they could harm his mate. He would crush them between his arms and relish in the feel of their lives being cut short. His demon purred.

Khaine ran his hand over one of his runes, the magic he'd rebuilt drifting through him in waves. His muscles vibrated with the intensity of his anger. He wasted no time gripping the black onyx of his blade as it formed in his hand.

Pure rage funneled through him. Sweltering heat from the desert realm washed over his face as he took several strides toward the creatures, his blade gripped tight in both hands. He couldn't charge them, but he could get their attention. All he had to do was get them away from Skye. As long as they were focused on him, she could get away. She would be safe. His life was meaningless. Better he risk death than her.

Khaine growled low in his throat, the sound hanging in the empty space between him and the creatures. Two of them turned their heads to regard him. *Yes, fight me!*

They shifted in the hot dirt and focused on him. Two of the creatures were still holding Skye against the cliff, but two was better than four. He needed to get her to safer ground and away from the cliff.

"Hold on!" he told Skye. He would get to her. He *would*.

Skye swung the branch in her hand across the expanse in front of her, backing the other two beasts a couple of paces away. Sweat glistened on her pale skin. It dripped into her eyes before she wiped her hand across her face.

Khaine focused on the two creatures stalking toward him, their front claws digging into the hard ground. He held his sword tight and pointed it in their direction. They seemed to slow, gauging what kind of threat he was.

A big one, he thought.

"Khaine, be careful!" Skye was inching her way to the side, steering the two beasts toward the clearing. Clever woman, he thought.

"Watch your step," he called to her.

If she fell... There was no telling what he would do.

Likely dive after her.

He started to do the same; steer the creatures focused on him in a direction that would put him closer to his mate.

Skye swung the branch and took another step to the side, her face determined. "Don't worry about me," she gritted. "Watch their teeth. I think they're poisonous."

Poisonous? Khaine narrowed his eyes at the animals in front of him. "And you would know this how?"

A murderous thought crept into his head. One of the beasts focused on him lunged in his direction. He cut it back with his blade and snarled in warning.

"Did you fight one?" The anger in his voice resounded all around him. Was this the thing she said had attacked him?

Skye screamed as one of the creatures leaped in her direction, driving her closer to the edge. She was making progress in steering them toward the clearing, ushering them toward Khaine. A few more steps and she would be standing beside him. Khaine twisted and herded the other two to the side.

"One being the key word there," she said, exasperated.

Khaine smiled. He didn't care if it was one or one hundred. His mate had fought one of these things? For him? Just when he thought she couldn't surprise him more.

She had won that fight, but she could have been hurt. What

if he had woken up to her dead? What if these creatures had taken her from him? She'd saved his life and that thought warmed his heart, but the demon in him had other thoughts.

This was his chance to get revenge. His demon was prowling its cage, begging to be let free. He would be stupid to deny it.

Khaine opened the cage, letting his demon out in a wave of fury. His muscles locked him in place as pure madness engulfed him. The feel of his body shifting had him rolling his shoulders in anticipation. This was what he was. Death. Violence.

Just a few more steps, he told himself. Skye was almost in a position where she wouldn't fall over the cliff if she lost her footing. The closer all four creatures were to him, the further they were from his mate. Khaine turned his head to see if she was making progress, just as the two creatures circling in front of him decided to attack.

It would seem they viewed his demon as a predator and not prey.

One leaped for him, swiping at his shoulder as it tumbled beside him. Its claws cut clean to bone before he turned and bashed the hilt of his sword into its head. The sound of Skye screaming caught his attention and he turned. She was on the ground, rolling to stand as the two animals lunged at her.

"Skye!"

She sprang back to her feet and rammed the branch into the side of one, the animal howling as it stumbled back. Before it could right itself, Skye was on top of it, her arms circling its neck. She let out an animalistic cry as she squeezed. The other prowled beside them as though waiting for the right moment to help its comrade.

Khaine fell to his side as one of the creatures knocked him off his feet. He spun, his sword outstretched, and connected with its head. It lulled to the side, his sword cutting deep enough to send it careening back, but not deep enough to kill it. He righted himself just as the other animal's teeth dove for his leg. Khaine kicked the beast in the side and swung his sword down on the other, severing its head from its body. He sank his claws deep into its ribcage and snarled as he plucked its heart from its body.

Warm blood splattered his arms and face. He licked his lips, the metallic taste pure bliss in his mouth. A howl of triumph broke from his lips as he pulverized the heart in his hand.

He chanced a glance back at Skye just as she crushed the creature's neck. For a single moment, there was nothing else. All he could see was his mate, her braided hair swinging around her face as she twisted and crouched beside the other creature in a low stance. Her stormy eyes were ablaze under the bright sun. She looked like a wild woman. Strong. Resolute. The animal with the crushed neck seized against the ground, its windpipe broken, starving it of oxygen. Skye didn't seem to care. There was no hesitation or fear in her untamed gaze, just pure hatred as she eyed the other creature in front of her.

A wicked grin spread across Khaine's face. His mate was ruthless. To crush an animal without mercy...

"Khaine, focus!"

Her words startled him back to reality just as thick claws dug into his side. Khaine roared at the pain and grabbed his sword, pummeling the creature over and over again as it gnashed its teeth toward his arm.

"Khaine! Sword!"

Without another thought, Khaine gripped his sword and tossed it through the air. Skye caught it and swung wide, dissecting the animal across the stomach. He didn't stop to see if she would finish it, just returned his gaze to the animal in front of him. Khaine gripped it by its thick mane and tossed it across the clearing. It toppled over itself in the air and crashed against the ground with a thud. The creature righted itself and shook off the dirt.

It charged for him, faster than any animal could move. He didn't fucking care how fast it moved. Khaine sank his claws into its side the moment it was within range, then gripped its neck and twisted. He relished in the feel of bone cracking, in the sound of agony as the creature bayed under his grip. He waited for it to stop moving before he plunged his claws into its flesh and ripped its heart through its chest.

Khaine dropped the heart and pivoted, intent on finishing off the other two creatures. Skye stood only yards away, her breaths long and hard. The tip of his sword was stabbed through the beast's neck she had crushed. The other creature lay only feet away, its head no longer connected to its body. Skye pulled the sword from the creature's neck, rested the tip against the ground, and leaned on it.

She'd killed them.

He tucked his demon back in its cage, his breaths coming in waves against his chest.

Blood was once again running along Skye's face and arms. She didn't seem to care, just peered at his sword with a frown.

He moved to stand in front of Skye so fast his sides revolted. "Are you hurt?"

He wasted no time assessing her. Her breathing was labored,

her hair matted with fresh blood, and her dress was torn in a few more places, but she otherwise seemed unharmed. A few scratches here or there. Nothing serious.

Instead of answering him, she continued staring at his sword.

There was uncertainty in her eyes when she looked at him. "You tossed it to me."

Khaine rubbed his hand down his face and tried to reason with himself. She was fine. She wasn't hurt. She took care of herself. Rather fucking well if he was being honest. She'd just killed two large creatures in a matter of moments.

Khaine assessed his own damage. There was a deep gash on his arm and one on his stomach, but other than that, he would live. The cuts were already starting to heal. He shifted to the side and slowly held out his hand for his sword. She was still staring at it with a funny look on her face.

"Like, you actually tossed it to me."

Confused, Khaine slowly took his sword from her hands and hefted it over his shoulder, encasing it in a sling with another of his runes. The feel of it at his back eased him. "This bothers you."

Before she could respond, he spotted Raiden's necklace hanging against her chest. It was there. She was wearing it.

Khaine reached for it, his hand shaking despite him trying to remain calm. When his fingers touched the pendant, he sucked in a breath and caressed the jewels. She was really wearing it. She'd accepted his gift. His mind struggled to believe what was right in front of him. The sight of it dipping just above her breasts caused his chest to swell. He'd never wanted to see it again, but this... Khaine smiled.

Skye looked down at his hand, then seemed to peer at the dead creatures beside her and the other two littered around the clearing. Her frown deepened. "Something's wrong."

Chapter 30

Skye reached for the necklace as Khaine dropped his hand, twirling it back and forth on the chain around her neck. Several thoughts were plaguing her.

The first thought? Khaine had given her his sword. Like, actually tossed it to her when she'd asked for it. She'd thought for sure she was a goner, those creatures backing her to the cliff. The second she had looked over the edge, her heart had dropped. Then Khaine showed up, revealing his sword and *tossing it to her*. The man couldn't confuse her more. Maybe he really didn't see her as naive anymore. He'd said he didn't mean all those nasty things he'd told her. Could the demon be starting to trust her?

Her stomach did a little somersault. This couldn't happen. She couldn't get used to him. God help her, if accepting Khaine's presence was any indication of the feelings she was starting to get for the demon...

What her sisters would think of her, now.

Skye scrunched her face as another thought crept into her head. Her stomach had been in knots as she'd raced from the large tree to the cliff trying to get away from four murderous beasts. Then standing at the cliff, her heart in her throat.

Staring at four enormous creatures about to make a snack out of you, or worse, toss you hundreds of feet over a cliff to your death, did things to one's emotions.

Like make you terrified.

She had been beyond scared at that moment, so why had nothing happened? She had desperately tried to calm herself as she'd swung the only weapon she could find in front of her, a measly stick she had hefted from the ground as she ran, but nothing had worked. Then Khaine showed up and the fear of him possibly being hurt had sent her into a panic. All she could think about was his lifeless body as that creature had tried to turn him into a meal. She'd warned him about their poisonous teeth, but what if he had been bit, again? What if he had died, *again*?

Something was wrong.

Khaine eyed her, his bare chest glistening in the afternoon sun. Did he have to be so beautiful? Even covered in dried blood, she wasn't sure the demon could be more tempting. They stood in a clearing at the edge of the forest where the trees could no longer block the light. The sun was beating down on them in waves, the coolness of the forest almost beckoning her back. She couldn't focus on any of that, right now.

His eyes were regarding her with worry. "What's wrong," he asked.

Skye had a feeling the necklace he gave her was no ordinary

gift. She suspected it to be imbued with some form of magic, from the symbols that looked like runes on the box and then again on the necklace itself, but she hadn't guessed it for sure.

Now, all she could do was wonder. If she was right, the possibilities that opened...

She twisted the necklace between her fingers. "Where did you get this?"

Khaine's demeanor changed from worry to something else, the lightness in his eyes fading as his face went blank. "We should keep moving."

He turned his back to her and started walking toward the forest, dismissing her question. As if nothing had changed between them. As if he still didn't trust her. No, she knew better. He couldn't shut her out, not after everything they had already been through. Not after he'd actually told her bits about his life.

"Khaine."

Skye held her ground, letting his name hang in the sweltering heat. She wasn't moving until he gave her answers.

All around her were the sounds of animals coming back to life. They must have gone silent when their fight broke out, not wanting to draw attention to themselves. Her skin felt like it was blistering under the hot sun. She wiped a bead of sweat from her face. Even the rocks under her leaf-covered feet were starting to wear on her, and still, she wasn't moving.

Khaine stopped, his bare back glistening with sweat. The deep breath he took emanated in the stiffness of his shoulders. When he turned back to her, his face was hollow.

"Where did you get it?" she repeated. She braced herself; took a shot in the dark. "Was it your brothers?"

Khaine's eyes shifted to a deep black so fast that Skye cringed. It was stupid; her reaction. He would never hurt her. She didn't know how she knew that, but she did. She had seen his demon more than once now, but it wasn't the sight of him that caused her to pause. Her question had angered him somehow, and that realization saddened her. Standing in the heat of the sun, with his bare chest streaked with blood and face grim, he didn't look like a demon at all. He looked like a wounded man.

Skye walked toward him, cautious, afraid that if she moved too fast she would scare him. He let her, standing still with his fists tightly clutched at his sides. Tension rolled in his shoulders. Skye stopped in front of him, so close that she could feel the warmth of his breath. She stared up into his dark eyes and waited. She wanted him to open up to her, wanted to know what he felt so strongly about. Maybe she could help him. Maybe she could ease the pain she saw.

She'd learned what pain was when she lost her mother. The demon had lost a lot over the years. To carry all that hurt and regret changed a person.

Long moments passed with his black eyes roaming her. His blonde hair fell into his face, almost shielding the hollowness. Skye didn't move, just waited.

When she was sure he wasn't going to respond, sure she had somehow overstepped, Khaine gritted the single word through his clenched teeth. "Yes."

He didn't say anything else, just stood with his muscles tight and his lips pressed into a thin line.

He'd given her his brother's necklace? He obviously had strong feelings for his brother. She already suspected that this journey of Khaine's had something to do with him. Why give it to her if it mattered so much to him? She wanted to ask him, but he already seemed on edge. She would leave that for later.

"What does it do?"

His shoulders seemed to ease as his eyes faded back to a coppery brown. He reached out and took the necklace from her fingers, rubbing the jewel against her chest. "It cages one's abilities. It was created to take away the side effects of a certain race. For instance, if a Witch were to wear it—"

"She wouldn't be able to do magic."

"Exactly," he said, dropping the necklace. "And if a Lykae were to wear it, they wouldn't be able to shift. It doesn't take away one's immortality, just dampens their power."

Skye thought about that for a moment, her heart in her throat.

"So if one were to explode when their emotions showed any fear?"

Khaine smiled at her. "It would prevent that from happening."

"And if one were to open portals?"

Khaine shook his head, a back-and-forth motion that seemed to settle low in her stomach.

She forgot how to breathe. Skye clutched at the necklace and stared at him. Was he serious? Not about the dampening of one's abilities. He actually gave her something that meant she could have a normal life? She didn't know what to say. Her life had been consumed with being careful, with being sheltered and hidden.

"How long does it last?"

"As long as you're wearing it."

Her mouth fell open. She couldn't accept it. She had to give it back. She couldn't even comprehend the thought of a normal life. There was no way he'd had the answer to all her problems in his pocket this whole time.

Well, not all her problems. There was still the issue of her life possibly ending soon, but holy shit! Why had this solution never been a thing? Why hadn't Caden or Mckenzie had such a thing made for her? Why hadn't she had such a necklace this whole time?

Skye couldn't keep it. Even if only for the simple fact that it meant so much to her and it was Khaine that seemed to just solve her biggest problem. As if she wasn't already melting toward the demon, he had to go and do this.

"I don't understand." She couldn't think of anything else to say. "Why?"

Khaine's forehead creased. "Why?"

"Yes, why?"

He scrubbed a hand over his face. "Magic is said to be infinite. I'm sure the spell could be replicated, though the Witch that created the necklace was very old and powerful. Anything made by someone without that knowledge would likely deteriorate over time, though I assume it would still have the same—"

"No," she said. "Not why does it last so long. Why did you give it to me?"

Khaine took a step back as though her words stung him. "Because you're my mate. Because it's my job to care for you. Because I want you to be happy." He paused. Took a breath. "Because I know what it's like to hate what you are."

"You hate yourself?"

Khaine's lips curved into a smile. "No. I used to, but not anymore."

Skye dropped her hand. "And your brother?"

His shoulders tensed, but his eyes didn't shift or fade. "He hated being a demon. He hated what we had become and what that meant."

"I don't understand," she said. Why would his brother become a demon if it wasn't what he wanted?

Sweat dripped into her eyes and she wiped it away. Khaine watched her, then reached out and grabbed her arm, lightly ushering her toward the trees. She tried to fight his hold on her, but he tightened his grip.

"What are you doing?"

"You can't stand here forever," he said. "You'll get dehydrated. We need to keep moving."

She didn't give a damn about getting dehydrated! There were so many questions she wanted to ask him. So many things she didn't know.

How could a demon that seemed to hate her very existence, turn around and show her more care than he wanted to show himself? If he didn't hate her anymore, what *did* he feel for her?

Khaine held her elbow and steered her toward the forest. She wanted to ask him what he meant about his brother, why becoming a demon bothered him so much, but she would have to be stupid not to see that Khaine was done with answering her questions.

The tightness in his grip, his ridged shoulders, even the way his face was set like stone. This was a subject he didn't like.

Instead of arguing with the demon, she let him lead her back into the trees. He was quiet as they walked, and she didn't want to push him too hard. Something in her just knew, if she started asking more questions, she was certain to do just that.

The cool breeze really did feel like heaven against her hot skin as they walked toward the river. Khaine finally dropped her arm and let her follow beside him. She took a moment to relish in the lack of the blistering sun overhead, the tight canopy of the woods blocking most of the rays. As soon as they were back by the stream, Skye bent down and scooped water into her mouth, then rinsed her hands and face. The sight of blood washing downstream should have alarmed her, but she was getting used to being covered in blood.

Khaine did the same beside her, bending down to the water and rinsing his face.

Skye took her time, trying her best to get rid of the gore that seemed attached to her skin these days. The dress Khaine had given her was destroyed ages ago, but it's not like she had anything else to change into, so she focused on getting the blood off what she could. The second she was home, and this curse was no longer a problem, she was going to make herself a catsuit just like Caden's.

The thought almost made her cringe. Not the thought of being home, but of what that meant for her and Khaine. That would be the end of anything between them. It would be either that or leave her sisters. Skye knew they would never accept him, even if she wanted them to.

Rather than get lost in her dark thoughts, Skye shifted to sit on the bank of the river and eyed Khaine. He continued washing the blood from his skin. Unlike her, he hadn't bathed in how many days? She'd taken the short time after their kiss to clean herself, and although she had washed his bare chest while he was asleep and healing, that only went so far.

Khaine cupped water into his hands and splashed it against his chest. She watched him. It was hard *not* to. Water ran down his sides, mixing with dried blood and turning a deep shade of red. Her stomach danced at the sight of him; at all those tattoos curving over his tan skin. When he shifted himself to wet his hair, then comb his fingers through it so it lay flat against his head, she almost forgot the questions she was burning to ask.

He dipped his hands into the water, then combed them through his hair several more times. It didn't get all the blood out, but it was enough that she barely noticed it anymore. He was silent as he washed himself. She let him be, not wanting to upset the demon more than she already had. The silence threatened to drive her mad, though.

The slight stubble was back on his face, running along his jaw and cheekbones. He'd shaved it at some point before getting to Temptest, but it was already growing in. Skye found that she liked the scratchiness of it. When he'd kissed her back at the cave, the roughness of his face as his lips had molded to her own was like heaven.

Khaine righted himself and paced a short distance away. He hadn't looked at her since they got back to the river. Maybe there was something she could say to get his good mood back.

Skye got to her feet and followed Khaine. He sat with his back against a large trunk and propped his elbow on one knee. His eyes looked hollow. His demeanor broken.

Make it better, her mind was screaming.

Before Skye could think to say anything, Khaine shifted in the dirt and groaned. His eyes darted between black and brown before settling on a deep shade of coal. He looked at her, his teeth bared and the hint of a demon slithering in his veins.

The sudden change in him took her back. "Are you okay?" She sat in the dirt in front of him, unsure of what else to do. "I didn't mean to push or upset you."

Khaine looked away. His voice clenched, he said the last thing she expected to come out of his mouth. "I killed him."

"What?" Surely he didn't mean... Something inside her churned. She almost didn't want to say it. Of all the things he could have said, admitting to something like that. He felt so strongly about his brother, she knew that.

Skye shook her head, unsure of how to respond. When he didn't elaborate, she felt like he was waiting for her to ask. He was going to make her say it?

"You...you killed your brother?"

Khaine finally looked at her, a weariness on his face she had never seen before.

"No," he said after length. "I killed our father."

Chapter 31

Khaine heaved a breath and did his best to tuck his demon away. He twisted against the trunk, wanting to be anywhere but where he was, with his mate looking at him expectantly.

What was he supposed to say? He just admitted to killing his own father. He didn't think anybody could come back from that. She must think he was the worst person to ever walk the earth.

Scratch that. He wasn't even a person. He was a demon. How little she must think of him. He'd told himself she never had to know about his past, about how much he had failed, but that wasn't true. He wanted her in his life. What kind of man would ask a mate to accept them without that mate knowing how far they had fallen?

How fast she had come to matter to him.

He was no good for her. He should have let her go back

to her sisters. He should have shielded her from himself. His problems, his hate, that wasn't something his mate needed or deserved.

His mind seemed to choose that exact moment to remind him that Skye would have to die. Unless this deity could give him an alternative, he needed a Guardian to sacrifice for Raiden to be allowed out of Shrodah. He had entertained the idea of sacrificing one of her sisters instead, but that was before. Skye would never forgive him. *He* would never forgive *himself*.

He would find a way to keep her alive *and* get Raiden back. How could he not when Skye came to mean so much? And there was the problem. If she meant so much to him, he had to come clean. He had to tell her.

Khaine cleared his throat, the tightness in his chest making it hard to breathe. Skye sat across from him, her blonde hair still twisted in a braid and flowing over her right shoulder. Her eyes seemed to bore into his soul.

"Do you want to talk about it?" she said.

Her voice was like a flood of emotions to his ears. As if all the pain and regret were finally catching up to his pathetic self. The softness of it warmed him, but it couldn't melt the dread he felt.

Khaine looked at the trees surrounding them, anywhere but at his mate. "No," he said. Then he shook his head. "But you deserve to know."

When he looked back at her, her stormy eyes were regarding him with a kind of sadness he wanted to remedy. Khaine scrubbed at his bare chest as though he could gouge out the pain.

"You don't have to," she said. It was almost a whisper, like she was pleading with him.

As though she wanted to make *him* feel better. Khaine stifled a laugh.

No, he saw the way she had looked at him by the water as he washed away what blood he could manage. He pretended not to notice, but her eyes had held a touch of mischief. He found himself wanting to bury his cock in her. Her breathing had been awash with lust, he could smell it in the air. He was going to fuck his mate senseless, knew she wanted as much, but he couldn't do that before she knew what she was getting into.

If he claimed her, he knew for certain he would never be able to let her go. He would never forgive himself if he didn't give her the chance to run. Oh, he would chase her. He would do whatever it fucking took to convince her he was worthy, too.

Are you?

Khaine rubbed a hand down his face and sighed. "I want to," he told her.

He *needed* to.

"Okay. Whatever you did, I'm sure it was an accident."

"An accident." Khaine let out a harsh laugh. "I told you about our village picking one person to inscribe the rune on the portal before the solstice?"

She nodded her head. "And you were chosen?"

Khaine looked away. "We both were, my brother and I. I was young, senseless. I told Raiden I would finish the stupid task myself so we could go back to sparring."

"Raiden is your brother?"

"Yes," he said. "We were sparring in a field when our father told us it was our turn to inscribe the rune. I didn't give a damn about the portal at that moment, just wanted to get back to what we were doing. Instead of taking my time and inscribing the right rune, I inscribed the wrong one."

His father probably thought it would help them understand and accept their duty to their people. How wrong one person could be. It was hard to believe how much one person's selfishness could cost them everything.

He looked at Skye, wanting to make sure she understood how bad his actions were.

His voice dripped with anger and shame. "I crossed a line or missed something, I don't know, but instead of sealing the portal I *opened* it."

Skye took a breath. "But you were able to close it, right? You did so back at the hideout when I accidentally destroyed the portal. You know how to close them."

Frustrated with his own stupidity, he yelled at her. "No! I fucked it up!"

That was the point of it. It was his fucking fault. Everything that had happened was all on him, and he couldn't take it back no matter how many nights he prayed to do so. He needed her to understand what kind of man he was.

He cringed at his thoughts. He wasn't a man. He was a demon, and a pathetic excuse of one.

The sudden jolt in her had him taking a breath to calm himself. She didn't deserve his anger. The cool air did little to ease him, but he managed a semblance of human.

"It wasn't a normal rune I inscribed," he said when he was sure his demon was securely in its cage. "There are several levels of Hell within Shrodah. Most of those levels only house lesser demons, but some are the prison to Gods. The rune I inscribed opened the portal to a level that housed a demon prince. Leviathan.

"I knew my mistake the moment he walked out of the portal's surface. They don't look the same. They look human, but a demon prince lives for nothing but death and destruction. Lesser demons may kill a few people, but a demon prince would rather wipe out an entire society.

"I yelled for help as I drew my sword. Raiden had gone back to the village to wait, and our father... I didn't know it then, but he had followed to make sure we did our job. I was knocked to the ground and when I came to... When I came to, our father was on the ground and Leviathan was standing there with our father's heart in his hands."

Khaine clenched his fists and closed his eyes, trying desperately to rid his mind of that sight. How could he be so fucking stupid! Why didn't he just take his time? Why!

He took a breath, then another. When he opened his eyes, Skye was kneeling in front of him, her face stricken. He hadn't even heard her move.

She reached out to him and he tensed, but she didn't stop. Skye grabbed his hand and squeezed it. "It wasn't your fault."

How could she be so good? So forgiving?

Because she didn't know the half of it.

"It was," he gritted. It was all his fucking fault!

Khaine tried to look away, tried to hide his shame, but her eyes, those beautiful blue eyes he could stare into for hours, held him so thoroughly in her grasp that he couldn't find a way out. The river flowed behind her, dancing tiny sunrays against her skin. She looked like a goddess sent to strike him down. The worst part? He would probably let her.

Skye's eyes hardened. "It wasn't. You didn't kill your father. Leviathan did."

"But I was the one that set him free. I was the one that caused it all."

"That doesn't mean you killed him. That boy that died, the one that I was with, does that mean I killed him?"

Khaine revolted. "No, never. That wasn't your fault."

"You see," she said. "It wasn't your fault either. It was a mistake. An accident. You never meant for your father to get hurt."

She seemed so sincere.

"You don't know that."

"I do," she said, her voice laced with so much will that his chest seized at her words. "You care about your family. You love them. You would never do anything to intentionally hurt them."

The silence between them stretched as Khaine just stared at her. Her face was full of so much pride? Love? Determination? How could she not hate him? How could she not think less of him after he just admitted to causing his own father's death? Maybe he didn't deal the blow, but he caused the outcome.

"You really should run from me," he said, his voice pained. "I'm no good for you."

Skye reached out and cupped his face in both hands. "I'm not going anywhere."

His heart swelled. Khaine hitched his breath and held it. Her face was flushed and unshed tears hung at the corners of her eyes. Gods, he didn't deserve her. Didn't even think he deserved getting Raiden back.

"You don't understand," he said as she dropped her hands.

He needed her to understand just how much he had failed. "It wasn't just our father. I killed them all. My people." Khaine corrected himself. "Our people." Because hadn't he killed hers as well?

"After our father was dead, Leviathan tore through the surrounding villages. They all died, didn't even stand a chance. He even managed to free other lesser demons to help in his war against us. The people in our village blamed me for all of it."

"And your brother? Did he blame you?"

Khaine's lips quirked into a smile. "Not at first. He wanted revenge. We all did. But there was no defeating Leviathan. He was too powerful.

"It's like it was a game to him. I think that's why he let me live after he killed my father. To watch us all suffer. And there was nothing we could do about it. We couldn't stop him."

Skye sat back on the cool ground. A small smile curved along her face, lighting her eyes. "That's when you became a demon."

As if he was some hero in this story.

"It wasn't that simple. Becoming a demon requires drinking the blood of a pure demon before you die, and not everyone survives." Khaine sighed. "My brother and our good friend Bastian came to, and myself, but there were two others that didn't make it." And he didn't even have time to mourn them.

"Raiden hated what we had done. Hated himself. Hated how things had turned out because of me. It was hard for him to accept what he was. I think he expected to die with the others."

In fact, Khaine often wondered if that was what he had wanted all alone. Maybe he wanted to die but didn't have the courage or strength to deal the blow.

"Our people abandoned us for what we had become. Raiden tried to warn them about Leviathan, but they attacked him. They called him foul things and shunned him for being a demon. I couldn't take it back. I couldn't fix it."

"So you made the necklace."

Khaine nodded. "We thought it would make it better, found a Witch that could help, but he still had so much rage for what had happened."

Khaine looked at the necklace around her neck, then back at her eyes. "Do you know how to kill a demon prince?"

Skye shook her head.

"You can't," he said, practically spitting the words. "We tried and failed, and when Leviathan found out what we had done to ourselves, he burned our village to the ground while we watched. My father's friend, Jonah, the one that taught me the sleeping rune, burned to death in front of us. All our people. Dead.

"Raiden renounced me as his brother. He threw the necklace on the ground before me and walked away. He blamed me for all those deaths because I didn't do anything to stop it. He vowed he would avenge them, would send Leviathan back to Hell where he belonged."

"And did he?" Skye tilted her head, a few strands of hair swaying in tune with the trees around them. "Did he send Leviathan back?"

Khaine hung his head. "He did, but it came at a price. When the portal to Shrodah lay open before us, the anger my brother felt at me, at what we had become, at our people being slaughtered right in front of us, finally hit home. He let his demon take charge. Instead of pushing Leviathan through the portal, Raiden grabbed him and jumped. The portal closed behind them."

Skye cleared her throat, her stormy eyes misted. "I'm sorry."

Khaine fisted his hands and stood. He paced in front of the water, all the pain in his chest threatening to break free. He walked to the nearest tree and punched it, relishing in the bark as it cut his knuckles. Splinters fell to the dirt around his feet, but he didn't care.

Skye didn't move, just watched him. He could *feel* her eyes on him. When the forest stopped closing in on him, he moved to the river and washed away the blood from his hand. Then he stood there, his back to Skye, not wanting to face his mate.

He took several deep breaths. Gods, he wished he could just go back. Wished he could fix everything he had fucked up.

He stood and stared out at the thick forest. "I learned there might be a way to bring Raiden back," he said. "I just had to find a portal and wait for the planets to align in the right formation."

The sadness in her voice drifted behind him like a knife. "And I took it from you."

He turned to face her. "It wasn't your fault. I scared you. Again, it's all on me."

He had blamed her at first, but the truth was, she did nothing wrong. It was *him* that burst into *her* home. *Him* that kidnapped *her*. None of it would ever be her fault. He *never* wanted her blaming herself.

She moved so fast. One minute she was sitting and the next she was standing in front of him, his back to the water as her eyes bore right through him. The anger in her voice made him cringe.

"Stop it," she yelled. "It wasn't your fault. Not your father's death. Not the death of your people. Not your brother being sent to Hell. And not me destroying your chance to get him back. None of it was your fault."

He closed his eyes and inhaled the scent of her. He wanted to believe her, he did, but it was so fucking hard when he had spent most of his miserable existence telling himself otherwise.

Skye grabbed his hand and squeezed it. "That's why you're here. You're searching for another way to bring Raiden back."

Khaine opened his eyes and gave a curt nod. "Nothing will ever matter more. I'll find another portal. I'll—"

"*We* will," she said. "We'll find another portal and bring him back."

Something inside Khaine seemed to finally break. She could never understand what she was saying. She should hate him. She should think him unworthy. Yet here she was, determined to help him.

"Why," he asked. There was no reason for Skye to want anything more to do with him. Why did she care? He couldn't understand.

Skye quirked her lips in the most seductive curve he had ever seen. "Because I'm your mate. Because it's my job to care for you. Because I want you to be happy."

Khaine stood in stunned silence, and then he laughed. For the first time in what felt like centuries, he threw his head back and laughed in abandon. He let himself go, poured everything into the laughter. It was either that or crumble inside.

When his laughter finally subsided, he peered at Skye and smiled. "You stole my line."

She wrinkled her nose at him. "Yeah, well it *was* a pretty good line."

Before Khaine could stop himself, he reached out and wrapped his arms around Skye, pulling her to him. She felt so good against him, like holding onto her could make all the pain just disappear. He wanted to stay like that forever. Wanted to forget about everything else and just be like this, with her. She slid her arms around his back and buried her face in his chest. Bliss. That's all he could think about. His failures no longer mattered. His mate was tucked against him, her braided hair brushing his cheek as he bent down and nuzzled her head.

Skye breathed deep against his chest, her hands stroking up and down his bare back.

Then the scent of her shifted.

Khaine tensed around her, his eyes darkening. "We should get moving."

Skye broke his hold on her and stepped back. He watched as she reached out and caressed the necklace around her neck. "Is that what you want?"

Her voice... Gods, her voice almost had him lunging at her in desperation. That's the farthest fucking thing from what he wanted. What he wanted was to wrap his hands around her hair and pull her mouth to his. What he wanted was to caress her between her legs and drive her just as mad as she drove him. What he wanted was to bury his cock inside her and forget about everything wrong in his life.

"No." The single word came out harsh and strangled. "That's not what I want," he said.

Chapter 32

Skye stepped back and wrung the necklace between her fingers, her heart pounding. How could this demon drive her so utterly mad in one moment, and then make her feel such desperation the next? She wanted to hate him. She wanted to blame him for kidnapping her and turning her world upside down.

She couldn't. None of it was his fault.

Would she not do the same in his shoes? Everything he blamed himself for...she would have burned the world to the ground if anyone hurt her family. Had she not been a part of his hurt? Had she not destroyed the one thing he needed to get his brother back?

How would she ever make that right?

She'd been so wrong about Khaine. She thought him just a demon that didn't care for anyone but himself, but he wasn't. He was a man that cared more deeply than she would ever know. The hurt in his eyes over everything he had lost almost crushed her.

He'd shown her a different side to himself. If all the demon wanted from her was to have sex with her and leave her broken, then why give her the necklace? He could have been cruel and treated her differently, and maybe his actions in the beginning were less than kind, but he didn't have to care for her or care for what she wanted in life. Giving her the necklace, wanting to make that part of her life better...

Skye toyed with the necklace. Being so close to the demon as he had hugged her and pressed his face to her head, did funny things to her stomach. The feel of him; hard and warm against her. The smell of him; like cinnamon and whiskey. She'd told him she would never be with him.

Then, it became she *couldn't* be with him. She dropped the necklace and stepped closer to Khaine. He'd changed that. He'd made it possible to want him, and holy shit, did she ever.

He wanted her, she knew he did. He could have forced himself on her. He could have not cared about what she wanted or didn't want. He respected her wishes and let her come to him on her own, backing away whenever she told him to stop.

His midnight eyes roamed over her body, making her stomach twist with anticipation.

Khaine didn't move, didn't speak, just let her look at his bare chest. Did she affect him like he did her? She reached out, slow and careful, and brushed her hand against his stomach.

He clenched his teeth and sucked in a breath.

Oh yeah, she affected him.

"Skye..."

Her name rolling off his tongue caused her body to respond.

His eyes were obsidian, gold flecks dancing in the swirling darkness. There was a weariness to him that made her feel more powerful than she ever had in her life.

"What do you want?" she asked him.

Khaine reached for her hands and stilled them. "You don't have to."

Skye broke free of his hold and ran her hands up and over his chest.

"Woman," he pleaded. "If you don't stop…"

"Please," she said. She didn't know what she was asking for, but she knew she wanted it to be Khaine that gave it to her. She wanted to know what it would be like to lose herself in the demon. Consequences be damned.

If she did this, there was no turning back. She would never be able to let him go. Skye knew without a doubt that the demon would ruin her for everybody else. There would be no other.

I don't care!

Khaine reached up and cupped the back of her neck. His touch was light, like he expected her to back away, as his dark eyes bore into her. His body shifted, black veins forming along the ridges of his face.

"You get one chance to say no," he said, "or I'm never letting you go."

She didn't think she could ever tell him no.

Skye bit her bottom lip and moaned his name. "Khaine, please."

He came to life so fast that her heart seized in her stomach. Khaine gripped the back of her head and molded his mouth to hers.

Gods, yes!

He groaned in her mouth, then twined his tongue with hers in a circle. Skye tried to keep up, tried to get closer. She didn't know what she wanted him to do, but she knew she wanted *more*.

"Khaine."

Khaine growled her name back to her, then kissed her so deep she wasn't sure she would ever come up for air. Her mouth was on fire as his lips brushed against hers in a sensual caress. First soft, then with more force. She matched his movements, then ran her hands along the hardness of his chest.

He ground against her, the firmness of him pressing into her thigh. He worked her mouth against his own and sucked on her tongue.

Warmth pooled low in her stomach as she twisted her tongue with his, then danced her fingers over his nipples.

A sound of desperation escaped him and he pulled back, breaking their kiss. Skye wanted to scream and tell him to keep going, but the look of pure agony on his face made her pause.

"Do it again," he choked out.

Her breathing labored, Skye brushed her fingers against his nipples.

Khaine groaned and grabbed for her waist, ushering her away from the water and toward a large tree. The moment her back hit the trunk, his mouth was on hers, kissing her so deeply she forgot how to breathe. His hands roamed down her sides and grasped the hem of her dress, lifting it over her waist.

Skye released his nipples and slid her hands over his shoulders and up his neck to his hair. She twisted her fingers against his scalp and tried to pull him closer, tried to kiss him harder.

A pressure was building in her stomach, one she thought she would never find release from.

Pressure.

It ebbed and flowed inside her.

Skye pulled back from his mouth. "Wait."

Khaine brushed his hands against her stomach and peered at her, his face tight. "It's okay. You can't hurt me, now."

But what if the necklace didn't work this time? What if she lost control?

She desperately tried to calm her breathing enough to respond, but Khaine shook his head. "Let me show you."

His hands stilled against her, waiting. The wildness in his deep voice threatened to do her in. He waited for her to respond, was asking her if she wanted him to stop.

Good god, she wanted him. She didn't think there was any way to calm the thunder in her veins. Make him stop? She trusted him. Trusted that Khaine was right. She had to because there was nothing else left. She was lost.

Skye nodded and bit her lip, unable to say anything around the rush of sensations.

Khaine smiled, the curve of his lips revealing sharp fangs. It should have unnerved her, but all it did was light her on fire.

Khaine pushed her dress higher, over her breasts and head, then dropped it to the ground.

The cool breeze raked her hot skin, sending tiny shockwaves through her body. She tried not to cover herself as his eyes danced over her breasts. The look on his face seemed crazed. If he looked at her like that any longer, she thought she might burst. The pressure between her legs was almost too much.

"Khaine." She moaned his name, pleading with him.

He sank to his knees before her and eased her thighs apart. With his demonic eyes glued to hers and darkness growing in his veins, he brought his head forward and kissed her.

Skye let out a harsh sigh. He smiled and kissed her again, this time licking the core of her. Her insides burst as she cried out, but he didn't stop. Khaine alternated between licking and sucking, driving her excitement to a dangerous high. She wanted him to stop. She wanted him to keep going. She wasn't sure where one thought ended and the other began.

The pressure between her legs built, threatening to do her in. The stubble along his jaw scratched at the inside of her thighs, leaving delicious jolts vibrating throughout her body. Skye reached down and gripped the top of Khaine's head, threading her fingers in his thick hair to keep herself still. She threw her head back and closed her eyes, trying not to lose herself in the rush of sensations. Just when she was about to fall into oblivion, the warmth of his tongue against the core of her disappeared.

Skye shot her head forward and opened her eyes, whimpering at the loss of his mouth.

Khaine got to his feet and took a step back, a wicked grin on his face. Then his hands reached for the waist of his pants. He undid the top button, his fingers drawing her attention. Skye watched with a wild fascination as he unzipped his jeans. His gaze fierce, he kicked his shoes off, his pants following.

Skye just stood there, all the heat in her belly spilling over. Holy fuck, she thought. Why did he have to look so good? Her eyes widened at the sight of him exposed, wondering if she could take him.

Khaine stalked to her, his cock jerking under her intense

scrutiny. The second he stood in front of her, his mouth devoured hers, any doubts immediately washed away.

His hand trailed down her stomach and she moaned, breaking their kiss. He eyed her as his hand slid lower between her legs, cupping her.

She squirmed against his hand, rocking her hips in a slow back-and-forth motion against his palm as she gripped his biceps. He watched her, let her work herself against him, then pressed his other hand to her side and held her still.

Skye wanted to protest, but then his hand shifted and one of his fingers entered her. She threw her head back and cried out. Yes, more!

Khaine gritted his teeth beside her ear. "Hold still."

She tried to still herself, but the feel of his finger deep inside her made her hips rock of their own accord. She was so close.

Then his finger was gone.

Skye looked at him and scowled. If he stopped right now, so help her, she would attack him.

He rested his forehead against hers, his breath hot against her face. "I'm sorry," he said, "but I don't want to hurt you."

"You won't," she pleaded.

"Just be still."

His finger was back, stroking inside her in a slow rhythm. He shifted his hand and inserted another. Skye gripped his arms tighter as the pressure in her built. He worked his fingers in and out, her body clenching firmly around him. Then his hand shifted again, and a third finger pressed against her. The pressure turned into a slight pain. He caught her mouth in his, soaking up the sounds of her soft cries. His fingers stretched her, the sharp pain replacing everything else. She tried to shift her body to accommodate his fingers, give him more room.

"Easy," he said, breaking their kiss.

The more his fingers moved inside her, the more the pleasure began to build again. Khaine watched her, his fingers dancing in tune with her heartbeat. Skye held onto him. The feeling was almost too much, but she wanted more.

"Khaine."

Then his hand was gone. Khaine shifted himself and lifted her to his waist, the tip of his cock pressed against the core of her. She traced her hands up to his shoulders to steady herself. Khaine rubbed his shaft between her legs and molded his mouth to her lips. Within moments, warmth spread between her legs, spurring her on.

Khaine gripped her bottom. The tip of his cock pressed against her opening, sending another jolt of pleasure through her body. He broke their kiss and leaned back, his black eyes holding her immobile.

Then he sank his cock deep inside her.

Khaine couldn't move. The feel of her around his cock was too much. One stroke and he would be done. He stilled himself, trying to recover while letting Skye get used to the feel of him.

Fuck, he could stay like this forever.

"Khaine."

The desperation in her voice made him groan.

He moved one hand low behind her back, in between her and the trunk, then slid his cock out and back in slowly.

Her head fell back against the tree as she moaned. Khaine pulled out and thrust back into her, gritting his teeth against the tightness. Her breasts bounced with his movement, steeling his gaze. He thrust into her again and again, faster and harder as her cries filled his ears. His body tensed as his demon relished in the feel of his mate wrapped tightly around his cock, driving into her with more force.

Her core seized around him as she shouted her release. Khaine captured her mouth in his, swallowing the sound as he continued to pound into her, driving his release to a staggering high. He backed her away from the tree and held her bottom tight as he thrust with more vigor.

Skye wrapped her arms around his neck, holding on as he neared his own orgasm. She kissed him, rubbing her clit against him as his cock drove into her over and over again.

Khaine growled into her mouth as he let go, pumping his release deep inside her. She yelled his name, another orgasm vibrating through her body along with his own. He kept thrusting into her, though slowed his pace as her head fell against his shoulder.

When his mind cleared enough to focus, Khaine turned himself to the tree and eased them into a sitting position with Skye on his lap. He bent his legs out, giving her enough room to rest against him. Her head didn't move, but she kissed his neck, her hot breath rushing over his skin.

He rubbed her back as he desperately tried to catch his own breath. They stayed like that, gathering themselves.

Skye lifted her head and peered at him, a wicked smile on her face.

Before she could say anything, Khaine grasped her mouth and kissed her.

"You're mine," he said when he finally let her go.

He was never giving her up. There was no distance she could run, no place she could hide. If she ever decided she didn't want him in her life, she would have to kill him. His chest swelled as he looked into her stormy eyes, trying to find the words to tell her how he felt.

As if she understood where his mind had gone, Skye leaned forward and slowly brushed her lips to his.

She eased herself off his cock and sat back. The loss of her wrapped around him almost had him pushing her to the ground, wanting to be back there. Instead, he let her go, helping her to sit beside him in the dirt.

"You might have a fight on your hands," she said. "I don't think my sisters will approve."

"I'll win," he said, matter of fact. Whatever he had to do to convince them that Skye was his, he would do it.

He was never letting her go.

Skye chuckled, the sound forcing a smile from him. Khaine reached out and took her hand, easing her to her feet as he stood. He walked her to the river before he let go, then trudged to the center of the flowing water. When he peered back at Skye, she was tiptoeing in after him, mischief in her eyes.

Chapter 33

Caden eased beside an enormous tree and tried to stop the woods from spinning. They had been jogging at a steady pace for the last hour. The sun had risen shortly after they stepped foot on the other side of the ravine into a thick forest, and that made something in her stomach twist. Nothing in this dimension made sense. Time especially.

Bastian sidled up beside her. "Your injury should have healed to a manageable degree, by now." His blue eyes held a questionable glow.

Caden shot the demon a smirk. "What's it to you?"

"I can fix it," he said, his tone matter of fact.

She cocked a brow. "You're not putting your claws on me."

Castello snickered. He stood by Mckenzie, duh, as she surveyed the ground by the water.

"Feeling lonely, demon?" Castello leaned back against a tree with his arms crossed over his chest. His dark, curly hair rustled in the cool breeze.

At least the air inside the forest was a million times cooler than the scorching air in the desert they arrived in.

"Hardly," Bastian said. "She's not my mate. Perhaps you should focus on your own." He turned his gaze back to Caden. "I can speed up your healing."

"And why would you do that?" Caden asked.

"You're slowing us down," he said.

She unsheathed her sword in one swift move, ignoring the sudden dizziness it caused, and pointed the tip at Bastian's throat. "Was that too slow for you?"

Mckenzie stood and adjusted her skirt. "Might not be a bad idea, Cad. These marks on the ground look like a fight. Khaine's blood is all over this area, so at least it appears he lost."

Castello nodded his head toward the animal carcass on the ground; the reason they had stopped. "It's been torn into. Someone or something took chunks out of it."

Caden lowered her sword and glared at Bastian. She didn't want him pulling any hocus-pokus crap on her, but if he was telling the truth, she wouldn't have to pretend to be alright, anymore.

"Fine," she said. "But if you try anything stupid, you'll regret it."

Bastian's blue eyes lightened as he lifted a brow. "Counting on it."

He rolled up his right sleeve and ran his hand over a small tattoo that looked like a circle with hieroglyphs. Whispering under his breath in a language she didn't understand, the tattoo started to glow a subtle hue of green.

Fan-fucking-tastic.

"Hold still," he said.

She did her best not to flinch as his hand moved to the top of her head and around to the back. He didn't touch her, just seemed to hover a few inches from the surface. A tingling sensation replaced the headache she was starting to get used to, then even that began to fade. When he dropped his hand and stepped back, Caden titled her head.

The dizziness eased until the trees around her were no longer spinning in place. The headache was gone, which was a relief all on its own. It had been getting hard to see around the pain. She lifted her hand to the back of her head and probed the scab. It still hurt to touch it, but she wasn't doubled over.

Bastian shifted the satchel over his shoulder, his demeanor that of a businessman that had just sealed a deal. "You're welcome."

Caden sheathed her sword and narrowed her eyes. "Watch it. I've still half a mind to kill you where you stand. You're only here because you might prove useful."

She turned to Mckenzie. "Can you tell where they went?"

Mckenzie fingered the blades along her thigh and started walking in an Eastern direction. When they came across a crack between two large boulders, Mckenzie wasted no time ducking between them.

Inside, the air was warmer, the slight wind rustling through the woods blocked on all sides. Against one large stone wall was a pile of rocks, stacked neatly into a firepit. A large branch was strung out across the pit, held in place by smaller sticks that propped it up on either end. Dried meat hung from the middle of the branch, black and charred.

"At least we know where that creature went," Castello said.

Mckenzie moved to the pit with Bastian beside her. A makeshift bed was strewn out over the dirt beside the rocks, fashioned from leaves.

Bastian lowered his hand over the coals. "They're still warm," he said.

Mckenzie eyed Caden. "They can't be far."

Kneeling by an indentation in the soft dirt, Bastian assessed a patch of black marks on the ground. "Khaine's blood."

Mckenzie shot him her best sad face. "Going to cry?" She mimed wiping a tear from her eye, then hardened her gaze.

Caden smiled as Castello glared at Bastian.

If Khaine was anything like Bastian, perhaps Skye wasn't in too much danger. It didn't escape her that Bastian, Khaine's own friend, had said otherwise.

And it didn't matter.

By the looks of the scene outside, and Khaine's blood on the ground in here, if Skye hadn't already killed the demon, Mckenzie would take the lead. There was no changing her mind against a kill when she decided it was the best course of action.

And after what happened at Lesters, Mckenzie had decided that a long time ago.

Bastian's face changed from worry to indifference as he stood. "We should go."

"You're not in charge," Mckenzie said, but she got to her feet and headed for the opening between the rocks.

Caden tried, *really* tried not to roll her eyes as Castello followed Mckenzie. If that's what having a mate was like, Caden hoped to God she was never unlucky enough to be one.

She caught up to Mckenzie, leaving Bastian taking up the

rear. She did her best to drop her voice so the demon wouldn't hear. "Do you think Skye is alright?"

Mckenzie sighed, her voice hushed. "We'll find her, Cad. We're going to kill Khaine and bring her home."

Caden turned to look at Bastian. He cocked a brow in their direction. If he had heard their conversation, he made no indication of it. Killing Khaine could prove to be a challenge if the demon decided to intervene. They would cross that bridge if needed. With Castello, and hopefully Skye on their side... Let's just say, four against two seemed like good odds.

Skye followed Khaine into the river, sighing at the cool water as it ran up her calves to her knees. Khaine snatched her waist as she got closer and planted a deep kiss on her lips.

Moaning, she opened her mouth, letting Khaine delve his tongue inside as he teased the tips of her nipples. When he pushed her lower into the water, she let him, tangling her fingers in his thick hair so their mouths wouldn't part.

Khaine rubbed his hand between her legs, small electric shocks working through her body as he cleaned her. Skye broke their kiss to look at him. His dark eyes threatened to consume her in ways she could only imagine. How could one man tempt her so thoroughly?

She felt more alive than she ever had. Why couldn't it be like this? Why couldn't they just stay here and forget everything else?

That could never happen. As much as she wanted to explore his body, run her hands over his tattooed muscles and touch him in places she would likely never touch another man, this had to stop. If she didn't push him away now, Skye was certain she never would.

Khaine growled his protest as she nudged at his chest, easing him away from her. All she could do was smile at the agony in his eyes. Instead of getting lost in those treacherous waves, Skye untied her hair and let it fall over her shoulders. He watched her as she dipped her head back in the river and washed away any remaining blood and grim from their previous battle.

His eyes roamed over her, stirring her body without even touching her, warming her in ways she needed to not dwell on. Skye was starting to think she would never be able to let him go. Her feelings toward the demon were shifting. It alarmed her, how fast he had attached himself to her life.

She sat up in the water and wrung out her hair. If this deity didn't know of a way to prevent the vision from happening, she would die. That was her destiny. As much as she wanted her future to be with Khaine, that likely wouldn't happen.

The look of pure satisfaction and contentment on his face made her want to scream.

As if the demon could sense the change in her mood, he frowned and reached out to her, grabbing her hand and kissing it. "What's wrong?"

Watching the cool water as it rippled around him...

Skye took a breath to steel her thoughts. How was she supposed to break it to the demon? How was she to tell him that his mate, the one thing immortals waited centuries for, might die? The pain in her chest almost broke free, but she held it back.

"There's something you should know," she said.

He came clean on what he was after and why; it was time she did the same.

Easier said than done!

Telling Khaine about the vision would be like accepting it would happen, and she hadn't accepted that. Not now. Not ever.

Steadying her hands against the bank of the river, Skye hoisted herself out of the water. She found her dress discarded by the tree Khaine had backed her into, using it as an anchor as he pleasured her. Memories of his hands and mouth roaming her body made her stomach dance.

The sound of Khaine getting out of the water drifted to her ears as she put her dress back on. When she finally got the courage to turn around, he was shoving his legs into his pants, an uncertain look on his face.

"Did I do something wrong?" he asked.

"No, of course not."

The last thing she wanted was for Khaine to assume he had hurt her somehow. The fact that he cared warmed her heart.

The leaves wrapped around her feet were only hanging on by the corners, so she focused on retying the fabric. The bottoms of her feet didn't hurt anymore, but walking around barefoot might change that fact, and even a thin strip of protection was better than nothing.

"You didn't do anything wrong," she said when she could find her voice. "It's me."

Khaine shoved his feet into his shoes. "There's nothing

wrong with you."

Why did he have to sound so sincere?

Maybe she could just dig a hole in the forest and disappear there. Skye busied herself with rebraiding her hair, trying to find the right words to say.

"You know how my mom used to have visions?"

Khaine moved to kneel in front of her, his elbows resting on his knees. He gave a curt nod.

"Well, about a year before she killed herself, she had one of her visions. She was hysterical, talking about the portal and a demon killing me."

Khaine flinched, but she kept going, afraid that if she didn't get it all out now, she wouldn't say everything she needed to.

"It never happened, obviously. But then Jade..."

"Your sister?"

"Yes. She also has visions. Before you showed up at the hide-out, she had a vision of a demon killing me, just like my mother. She was hysterical, sobbing and rocking back-and-forth. When she finally came to, she told me that she saw a demon killing me, that a strange man was going to show up and..."

Khaine held up his hand to stop her, horror shadowing his features. "I'm that strange man?"

Skye nodded. "I think so."

His eyes darkened to a deep black as he set his jaw. "What else did she say? Tell me everything."

The anger in his voice made her want to cringe. She bit her lip. "She said she saw a broken clock and that time didn't feel the same. She said I wasn't there at the hideout, but somewhere else."

"I don't understand. What does the clock mean?"

Skye pointed to his watch and he followed her movements. She didn't think his eyes could turn a deeper shade of black.

"I noticed your watch was broken back at the rocks," she said.

Khaine stood and backed away. His face had gone pale, but his demon was beginning to show in the undertones of his veins. The trees towering behind him did little to quell her uncertainty. She thought the admission would bother him, but there was something odd about his demeanor.

"What else did she say?" he asked.

Why did he sound so angry? It was *her* life on the line, and while she might be his mate, she didn't expect anger to be his reaction. Sadness, maybe, but not anger.

"There wasn't much—"

His voice dropped an octave lower and rumbled in his chest. "What. Else. Did. She. Say?"

Skye glared at him and stood, dusting her hands on her dress. He had no right to speak to her like that. They were past him being demanding, at least she had thought.

"You don't get to order me around, anymore. That's not how things—"

"Just tell me," he said. "Please."

The sound of desperation in his voice made her pause.

"Ten days," she said. "Ten days after the strange man comes, a demon will kill me."

Khaine looked stricken. He scrubbed his hand over his face and took a breath. His demon retreated, leaving only the paleness of his skin and eyes that looked more hollow than she had ever seen. A distant feeling emanated from him as he looked away, rubbing a hand over his bare chest.

"Jade has had visions before, but never something like that. Besides, my mother had her vision years ago and nothing ever came of it. Maybe it's all just a coincidence."

The shift in him was making her heart ache. Why did he have to seem so concerned? Why did she have to open her mouth and say anything at all? She could have just left things as they were. All she wanted to do now was ease the troubled look on the demon's face.

"I thought maybe this deity could tell me how to stop the vision, if it's true."

When Khaine eyed her again, he seemed calmer, but a sense of coldness had overtaken him. "We should go."

Instead of waiting for her to say anything, he began walking along the riverbank, leaving her standing there confused.

Skye waited two whole beats before she was jogging after him. His long strides were making him move at a pace she couldn't keep up with.

"Khaine, slow down! We don't even know where we're supposed to go. The sun is up. The river forks up ahead. What if we take the wrong path?"

Khaine stopped so abruptly, she slammed into him. She took a step back as he turned on her.

"We've been in this dimension for days. If time isn't the same here, how long has it been back in our world? Ten days could be next week, or tomorrow." He gritted the last word like she didn't already understand the seriousness of her situation.

He said nothing else before he continued walking.

Argh! Aggravating demon!

"We can't say the vision will happen," she called out to him.

His only response was clipped and full of anger. "A Seer's

visions are never wrong."

"Khaine!"

What had gotten into him? She understood that the prospect of losing his mate might not sit well, but that didn't mean he had to shut her out. They were in this together, him to get his brother back, and her to save her life.

Skye hurried after him, trying to catch up while she dodged rocks and skirted bushes. "Khaine, wait."

Khaine stopped and turned on her, catching her shoulders this time so she wouldn't slam into his chest. His hands gripped her arms and held her as his voice dipped and vibrated through the air, echoing around her.

"Enough!" he yelled. "We're going to find this deity. We're going to fix this. We don't have time to ponder what might or might not be. Do you understand?"

Skye stared at him, too shocked to say anything. His anger resounded around her, making her insides reel back as though hit with a devastating blow. She glanced at him and nodded, fighting the tears she felt building in the corners of her eyes.

Khaine released her without saying anything else and left her standing by the water. She didn't know why this affected him so much, but she had no desire to argue with him when he seemed like he was about to explode.

Skye trudged behind him, keeping her distance.

Chapter 34

K haine helped Skye over a boulder, easing her down on the other side. Enormous rock cliffs hung in the air above them, towering over a flat, green meadow. Grass spread out over small hills that seemed to roll far into the distance, shimmering several shades of green under the cloudless sky.

This dimension made no sense. There should have been a desert to their right, based on the location of the cliff Skye had stood in front of and the fact that the river hadn't veered too far to the left. Instead, the forest butted up against the bank of the water on either side of them, with the river splitting in opposite directions.

He assessed the stream. This portion of the realm wasn't as warm as the desert was, but still a few degrees higher than the woods they came out of.

Fuck!

Which way were they supposed to go?

Both bodies of water didn't seem any different than the other, and both seemed to veer toward the rocks hanging in the air. There was nothing suspending them, which unnerved him more than he wanted to admit, but it wasn't the strangest thing he had witnessed in this place. There had to be a cave hidden deep in one of those mountains above them, but *which one*?

And how did they get to it?

Skye waited beside him, still quiet. She hadn't said a single word to him after he snapped at her. Her demeanor had frosted, the annoyance in her set shoulders driving him mad. Not that he could focus on that, right now.

The vision. Her words replayed in his head like a bad omen, because they were. He had never heard of a Seer's visions being stopped, but that's exactly what needed to happen. Bastian had told him he would need to sacrifice a Guardian for Raiden to be set free, and then Skye informed him that her mother *and* sister both had a vision of a demon killing her.

Khaine took a breath; tried not to lose his mind.

He would find another way to bring Raiden back *and* find a way to stop Skye from dying. Wasn't it simple? If Khaine decided *not* to bring Raiden back from Shrodah, then the vision of Skye dying at the hands of a demon would never come true. Unless the vision was about another demon and not himself.

He couldn't take that chance. If he wasn't the one that killed Skye, then her life could still be in danger. They needed to get to that deity and *now*.

As if he had already decided that Skye would be the one he saved and not Raiden...

"Are you going to make a decision?"

Skye's clipped tone had him peering at her. Her hair was still damp, braided once again against her back, reminding him of things he couldn't focus on. It was the fire in her eyes that had him questioning his entire existence. Why did her anger have to affect him so much?

Khaine tried to reason with himself, telling his inner conscious that it didn't matter how upset she was.

He failed.

"I'm sorry," he said.

Skye cocked one of her luscious brows. "For?"

Stubborn woman!

"For getting angry. Your sisters' vision worries me."

And just like that, she smiled.

"It worries me, too," she said. "We'll get your brother back and we'll figure out how to stop the vision. It's going to be okay. None of this is your fault."

He wasn't so sure about that. He wasn't fucking sure of anything, anymore.

"So...which way?" she asked.

He hadn't the slightest clue. They could wait for nightfall, but that could put them that much closer to her death and—

"Hey! Wait for me!"

Khaine and Skye turned their heads at the same time. His brain tumbled over itself as the sight of a female crested over a hill in the distance.

Skye sidled up next to him. "Um...somebody you know?"

They hadn't seen another person in this dimension since they arrived, and nobody had followed him through the portal as far as he knew.

"No," he said.

The woman waved her hand excitedly at them, dragging a large bag behind her. Her neon red hair fell to just above her shoulders, with black lowlights swaying around her pale face. They both stood in stunned silence as the woman dragged her bag along the thick grass and up to the river in front of them, but it wasn't the person itself that had Khaine taking a step back and reaching for his sword.

The woman's white shirt was cut short, showing a tiny portion of her stomach over a set of pink running shorts. Across the front of her shirt was the word 'Honey' in bold, orange letters. She wasn't wearing any shoes and didn't seem the least bit concerned about the fact.

But none of that made him step back and reach for his sword, either. It's what slinked up to the water beside her.

Skye offered Khaine a glance, the look of confusion and a touch of fear in her eyes mixing with his own uncertainty.

Beside the woman was a large cat-like creature, its paws bigger than his hand and black, spiked fur running along the length of its back.

"Khaine..."

"I see it," he said, bracing one arm out in front of Skye in case that thing decided to lunge, one hand still on the hilt of his sword.

This was the same creature they had fought back at the cliff; the same creature they had killed *four* of. It stood beside the woman, panting with its tongue handing out.

The woman hefted her bag into the air and slung it over the creature's front shoulders, not even batting an eye. "George, sit!"

The cat sat.

Without warning, Skye burst into laughter beside him. Damnit! Now his mate had lost her mind.

She braced one arm across her stomach and gave in to the laughter, only seeming to calm herself when she couldn't breathe. Khaine removed his hand from the hilt of his sword, but kept his stance at the ready.

Skye wiped at her eyes. "You named it George?"

"I was going to name him Spike, but he didn't like the reference."

Khaine looked at Skye and shook his head.

"Buffy?" Skye asked the woman.

The woman's face lit up, her blue eyes dancing with several colors like a rainbow. "You know the show? I *love* Buffy! George and I just finished season four. We're waiting for the next season to come out."

Skye chuckled. "Um...it's already out. That show has been over for years. There're seven seasons."

The woman made a dramatic show of throwing her hands in the air and wailing. "You're kidding? I'm always behind on this stuff." She adjusted her shirt, not that pulling it down did much. "No bother. We're going to watch *all* the seasons. Caden loves watching it with us, even though she sometimes gets a little dramatic and starts yelling at the picture box."

Skye came to life at the mention of her sister. "You know Caden?"

"Well, not yet, dummy. But we're all going to be the best of friends."

Skye furrowed her brows and canted her head to the side. "I don't understand."

Khaine cleared his throat, certain that if he let them go on much longer, he was going to explode in frustration. He hadn't the slightest fucking clue who or what Buffy was, and didn't give a damn, either. Nor did he care about this woman becoming friends with Skye or any of her sisters.

"You're the deity," he said.

There was no other explanation. This had to be who they were looking for.

"In the flesh!" Her voice was the epiphany of cheerfulness. She leaned over the river on her side and dropped her voice to a whisper. "Though who knows for how much longer."

How much longer what?

She seemed to pause like a television for several seconds, then perked back up. "You can call me Honey," she said.

That seemed to warrant another laugh from Skye.

"And you're Skye and Khaine. I've been waiting *ages* for you." She rolled her eyes, seeming to emphasize how long the wait had been. "I was here a year ago, but I get my times a little mixed up. I thought for sure I would miss you!"

"You knew we were coming," Khaine said. It wasn't a question. Of course, she did. A deity that saw into the past and future wouldn't only know they were coming, but why. Maybe she'd had time to find a solution to their problems.

"Then you can help us," he said.

Skye elbowed him, causing him to glare at her.

"Don't be rude," she said under her breath.

Honey patted the cat, George, on its side. It crossed the water with Honey following until her and the creature were standing at the edge of the forest in front of them. The contrast of the woman and the cat, backed by a set of towering cliffs suspended in the air, had been fucking with his head. At least his mind found the sight of them standing against the forest easier to handle.

"Help? I can do more than that. The combination is sixteen, twenty, and three. You *have* to turn it to the left first."

Neither of them said anything. Khaine was starting to wonder if this deity could help them at all. She didn't seem all there.

Skye scrunched her face beside him. "I think you have us confused with someone else."

"Do I?" Honey tapped a finger to her lips. "Well..." She leaned forward. "What is it you wanted? I could have sworn you needed the combination to Hitler's safe."

"No, why would we—" Skye shook her head. "Wait, you know that?"

"Well duh, silly. How else was I supposed to get the bomb on the airplane?"

Skye shook her head, visibly confused. "What bomb?"

Khaine gritted his teeth and fisted his hands. "It doesn't matter. We need your help." If this deity didn't focus, and fast, he was going to kill her. His demon rattled its bars in approval.

Skye touched Khaine's arm as if she knew where his mind had gone. The gesture actually calmed him.

"We're trying to get his brother back," she said to Honey, "and my sister had a vision I would really like to avoid."

Khaine tensed. Gods, if this deity couldn't help them, there was no telling what he would do. He'd come this far to get Raiden back, further than he ever thought possible. There was no measure of how much farther he was willing to go to reach his goal.

And Skye? There was no way in hell he had found his mate

just to lose her. Wouldn't fucking happen.

Honey seemed to short-circuit, standing completely still and not speaking. Her eyes didn't move, didn't even blink as she froze in place. Khaine waited with zero fucking patience. It was like she had disappeared and was somewhere else. Skye waved a hand in front of Honey's face, but nothing.

Without warning, Honey jolted back to attention, startling Khaine and making Skye jump.

"Sorry, where were we?" The deity planted both hands on her hips. "Right! You needed to know the best way into the theater with JFK."

Wrong. Fucking. Century.

Khaine snarled at the deity and scrubbed a hand over his face, his patience nearing its end. "No! I need to know the best way to bring my brother back from Shrodah!"

Honey peered at Skye. "He sure is a grumpy one."

Skye nodded her head beside Khaine, the smile on her face aggravating him even more.

When the deity finally turned her attention back to Khaine, it was all he could do not to strangle her.

"That's easy," she said. "All you have to do is let your mate take care of everything. She opens a portal, she dies, you get your brother back, it's a win-win." She paused just long enough to wink at him. "But you already knew that."

He was going to kill her. He was going to strangle her with her own fucking shirt. Twist her insides into a ball. Carve out her eyes and then show them to her corpse.

Skye turned to him. "Khaine? What is she talking about?"

Skye watched Khaine, his lips pressed tightly into a thin line and his eyes darkening by the second. Tension filled his muscles, his tattooed arms and shoulders rolling with what seemed like rage.

The silence all around them threatened to consume her. No birds. No animals. No cat-like creatures trying to kill them. Though, the last was presently sitting on its haunches just staring. Skye's heart dropped several inched toward her stomach.

"What is she talking about?" Skye said.

He wasn't looking at her, refused to meet her gaze. The deity's words played on repeat in her head.

"Did you know?"

Did he? Did he already know about her death? Did he know that she was some key to getting his brother back from Hell?

"Of course, he knew," Honey said. Her voice changed to a deeper tone as if mimicking another person. "The book depicts the sacrificial stone... What kind of sacrifice?" She outstretched her arms. "A Guardian."

She smiled. "Did I do a good impression?"

If Skye could kill the demon with just a look, he would be dead.

"Who said that to you? Was that your plan all along?"

Khaine finally looked at her, his eyes narrowed. "No!"

"Bring me here, seduce me, then get me to open a portal and kill me to get your brother back?"

Khaine's face dropped, his eyes shifting back to their arresting brown. Sadness seemed to fill him, but she knew better. How stupid could she be? Skye suddenly felt like the dumbest person to ever live. She knew that trusting the demon was a mistake. She knew that falling for him wasn't a good idea. And yet, here she was. Trusting him. Falling for him.

Her chest began to ache even as it dropped, churning low in her stomach.

"Was that your plan? Did you know that bringing your brother back meant sacrificing me? Are you the one that kills me?"

That couldn't be right. The vision had depicted a demon that was more purebred than human.

Khaine scrubbed at his bare chest. "You don't understand. It's not like that. I came here to find another way."

"You lie," Skye yelled.

She wouldn't cry. She wouldn't.

Anger threatened to consume her. "Did. You. Know?"

Khaine seemed to revolt at her words. He clenched his jaw and gritted the single word. "Yes."

As if the admission could make her feel any worse. Instead of letting the tears that so desperately wanted to flow free, Skye balled her fists and punched Khaine in the chest.

Stupid. Stupid. Stupid.

How could she be so stupid!

She punched him again, relishing in the feel of her fist connecting with his hard body.

"I did something wrong," Honey said beside them.

She hit him again, and again, all her anger and frustration finally coming to a head. She backed him toward the trees with each blow until his back hit a large trunk.

Skye focused all her hate on Khaine. "You never once cared about me, did you? Just admit it. You planned to kill me!"

"You're wrong!" he said. His eyes were deep coal now, boring into her. "I would never hurt you."

"All you want is to get your brother back. It doesn't matter to you that I have to die for that to happen."

"Woman."

Skye stared at Khaine, a hole forming in her chest. Why did it have to hurt so much? Why did the realization that he never cared for her, that his only goal was to kill her to get his brother back, have to cut so deep?

"Don't lie to me!" she said as she hit him again.

Khaine's face faded as he took her punches, the dark veins under the surface making him look like the demon he was. A demon that only cared about himself.

"Why didn't you just kill me back at the hideout? Why did you have to carry this on so long? Why let me fall for you just to take it all away?" She yelled at him as she punched him, unable to do anything else. "What was the point!"

His eyes narrowed. "Fall for me?"

Skye took a breath and stilled her hands. Screaming at him wasn't making her feel better. Punching him only made her feel bad, which made her want to cry even more. The hole in her chest seemed to keep growing. Her voice echoed all around them, bouncing off the trees and bulldozing its way back to her ears. Khaine stood against the tree, not moving, not speaking, his face tight.

"What was it you said to me?" she asked, her voice calmer. "Nothing will ever mean more to you than getting Raiden back? I guess that includes the death of your mate."

Khaine's face paled around his dark eyes. "That was before."

"Are you the one that kills me?"

She had to know. She had to know if it would be him. If he planned to kill her from the beginning.

"I would never do anything to hurt you," he gritted through clenched teeth.

"Liar!"

Skye couldn't take it anymore. She'd had enough. It didn't matter if he would be the one to kill her or not. He would obviously have a hand in it. His brother mattered more to him. He couldn't have made that more clear to her. This whole journey for him had been about getting Raiden back. And her? She'd been the key he just decided to bring along until he'd had the means to carry out his plan. It's like her fate was sealed the moment he learned she could open portals on her own. It was a win-win for him. He didn't need to find both a Guardian to sacrifice and a portal to open when they had been presented to him in a package deal.

Skye tried to reason with herself. If he really planned to kill her to get his brother back, and she was the portal he needed to carry out that plan, why ask the deity where to find one? The other part of her mind said it didn't matter. He'd lied to her. He'd kept a secret from her when it had to do with her life.

How little she mattered.

She speared him with her angry gaze. "All you've done is lie to me."

"You should move to the side," Honey said, her voice barely registering.

Khaine finally moved, gripping her shoulders. "Listen!"

Before he could get out another word, a single knife pierced the air beside Skye, burrowing deep in Khaine's chest.

Honey shrugged her shoulders. "I told you to move."

Skye stepped back as another blade sank into Khaine's shoulder. She jerked her attention to the trees, her heart a thunderstorm in her chest when she spotted the source.

"Caden! Mckenzie!"

Two men walked up behind them. One she didn't know, but the other she remembered from back at the club. Castello. It would appear he had gotten Skye's message to her sisters, just like he'd promised.

Mckenzie grabbed another blade from her thigh and tossed it, this one hitting Khaine in the leg. He sank to one knee and groaned, but didn't make a move to retaliate.

Skye didn't care. They could pummel the demon with as many daggers as they wanted.

She disregarded Khaine and bounded into a run, tackling Caden with so much force there were sure to be bruises. "You're alive!" Tears filled her eyes. "I thought I killed you."

Caden hugged her, wrapping her arms tight around Skye and squeezing. "Takes more than a little explosion to kill me."

Skye got to her feet and hugged Mckenzie next, not caring when Mckenzie kept her eyes on Khaine.

"How did you get here?" Skye asked.

Mckenzie motioned to the guy standing next to Castello. "The demon helped."

Demon?

Caden stood, unsheathing her sword and pointing it at Khaine. "We're taking our sister back."

"She's mine," Khaine growled, pulling the knife from his

chest.

The man she didn't know walked over to Khaine. With short, dark hair and a slight stubble along his face, he wasn't hard on the eyes. His maroon shirt was tucked into black slacks that he had rolled at the sleeves. Tattoos ran up both arms, almost identical to the ones Khaine had all along his body.

His voice was curt as he helped Khaine to his feet and not so gently pulled the knife from his leg. "Let it go."

He was a friend of Khaine's, that was clear, and judging by the way he held himself and all those tattoos, and Mckenzie calling him a demon...

"You're Bastian," she said. Khaine had mentioned him. There were only three that survived the turn, and since Raiden was currently in Hell.

"A pleasure," Bastian said, turning to her with a smile.

Honey walked into the middle of the group and clasped her hands in front of her chest. "I just *love* family reunions!"

Castello nodded to Honey, his shoulder-length hair swaying about his shoulders and green eyes calculating. "And you are?" He regarded George sitting on the ground but didn't seem concerned there was a large cat presently holding a duffle bag on its shoulders.

It's not like that was the strangest thing in this situation. Caden and Mckenzie had teamed up with a demon?

Honey walked over to Castello and held out her hand. "I'm Honey, your soon-to-be sister-in-law."

Sister-in-law?

Mckenzie snatched a dagger from her thigh and pressed it to Castello's throat. "Getting married?"

"Not unless you're offering, love"

Love?

Argh! Skye threw her hands in the air. What the hell was going on? She'd had enough of everything. All she wanted to do was go home, forget the vision, *forget Khaine.*

Khaine called to her. The pain in his voice almost sounded genuine. "Skye."

She took a deep breath to calm herself. No. Not again. She knew better. There was no way in hell she was falling for another one of his tricks.

Skye glared at him, and in a voice that spit venom, said, "No. We're done." She then turned and walked into the trees, leaving everyone behind her.

Chapter 35

Khaine stalked into the forest, sinking his fist into any-thing he could find. The trunk of a tree, a rock, even the hard-packed soil was no match for his frustration. He tore bushes from the ground and tossed them into the air, then shredded more with his claws.

He needed to fix this. He wanted to chase after Skye and demand she listen to him, but he knew he didn't deserve that.

He wanted to march over to her and kiss her so thoroughly that she didn't care he was fucked up beyond repair. He didn't deserve that, either.

In fact, he didn't deserve Skye at all.

She was more than he could ever hope to have in his pathetic life. Kind. Caring. The person that had saved him when he wasn't even sure he would save himself.

He wanted her back. He wanted to prove to her that she mattered to him, that he didn't want to kill her.

Don't you?

Khaine roared into the trees and scrubbed a hand down his face.

No, he didn't want to kill her. If killing Skye was the only way to get Raiden back, his brother could rot in Hell for eternity.

Khaine eased himself down on a rock and hung his head. The pain in his chest seemed to keep growing, his demon half stalking the bars in his mind, desperate to get to her. He didn't know what to do or how to fix things with her, he just knew there had to be a way. If he had to live the rest of his immortality without her, he would rather die.

He took a deep breath at that thought. Didn't he feel the same about Raiden? He loved his brother, would do almost anything to get him back, but he was willing to destroy the entire world if it meant Skye would accept him, because he loved her more.

As if the universe could feel the darkness growing inside him, the sky flashed with a sudden white light, then plunged into a deep, black abyss. The forest went silent as the glow of plants emerged from the trunks of trees around him.

He didn't fucking care.

Khaine propped his elbows on his knees and held his face in his hands. Maybe if he stayed like this long enough, death would finally find him.

Footsteps sounded between Khaine and the trees in front of him. The thud of something hitting the ground barely registered in his mind. He knew it was Bastian that had followed him, could sense the demon, but he didn't care. Nothing else seemed to matter to him.

When the footsteps retreated into the distance, he let his mind wander. His thoughts were consumed with Skye. Her legs wrapped around his waist as he drove into her. Her laughter as she stood before Honey, one arm braced across her stomach. Her stormy eyes anytime she glared at him, or the way they became brighter when happy or aroused. The conversations they had with each other, both aggravating and calming.

Her smile. Gods, he could get lost in her smile.

"You know it wasn't right."

Bastian's voice rumbled around him, the vision of Skye disintegrating in his mind. Khaine lifted his head. Bastian dropped a pile of wood on the ground and began arranging the logs into a neat stack, crossing them into a pyramid shape.

"Sacrificing your mate just to get Raiden back... You would never forgive yourself," Bastian said.

Khaine's demon slithered to the surface. Did Bastian really think so low of him? Yes, maybe he had entertained thoughts of killing her, but those had been so brief that Khaine wasn't sure they counted. When it came down to it, he could never hurt her. He might contemplate strangling the aggravating woman, but he would never do it. He would rather kiss her into submission. Or just kiss her, period. Actually, he would gladly let her have her way, just as long as his mouth was molded to hers.

Anything. He would give her anything. The amount of power she held over him was almost alarming.

Don't care!

"I wasn't going to hurt her," Khaine growled.

Instead of responding, Bastian busied himself lighting the fire he built. The stubble on his face had grown into the semblance of a light beard since Khaine had last seen him. Khaine brushed at his own face. He hadn't shaved in days. Tiny hairs scratched his hand and he sighed.

With the fire finally supporting itself, Bastian eased onto the ground and looked at Khaine. "What was your plan?"

"Find a portal and bring Raiden home," Khaine said. He didn't want to have this conversation with Bastian. What he planned to do or not do with his mate wasn't something he wanted to talk about.

"Did you find anything?" Khaine asked instead.

Bastian hefted a shoulder bag over to him and opened it, pulling out the Raudskinna.

"You brought the book?"

"I thought it might be needed." Bastian set the book in his lap but didn't open the cover. "After you left, I thought I might follow you in case you needed help. I tried to catch up to you in Pembine, but you had already left."

That didn't answer his question. Khaine lifted a brow, trying to be patient.

Bastian sighed. "This book is strange. The language seems to change every time I open the cover. It's not like anything I have ever seen."

"You can't read it," Khaine said. Not that it mattered. There was no use in finding a portal or the rune if he didn't have a Guardian to sacrifice. Besides, Skye *was* a portal.

And he couldn't bring himself to use her.

Even if he found another Guardian, even if he fell so low that he was able to kill an innocent person to sate his desire, Skye never asked for her power and barely knew how to use it. He could never ask her to do the one thing she despised herself for.

As if his mind wanted to torture him more, the scent of Skye wafted to his nose. He breathed deep and relished in the smell of lilies and fresh oranges. She wasn't far.

"I can't," Bastian said.

Khaine looked at him. "Can't what?"

Bastian cocked a brow. "Your mind is wandering. You miss her."

He gave a curt nod.

Bastian set the book aside and added another branch to the dwindling flame.

"I told you I wouldn't be able to find another portal. I thought that I could study the book more and that maybe I could eventually read it, but I couldn't. You need that portal if Raiden is to come home."

Bastian had no idea that his mate *was* the portal. Khaine groaned.

"We'll figure something out," Bastian said. "In the meantime, I was able to uncover the rune."

Khaine watched as Bastian pulled a paper out of his pocket and held it. He didn't hand it to Khaine, instead, he just stared at him as though he knew everything Khaine was thinking. The fire danced over Bastian and the paper in his hand, the sight a reminder of everything Khaine had lost.

He should have felt happy that Bastian had deciphered the rune. He should have felt happy that getting his brother back was still a possibility. Instead, Khaine felt hollow inside.

"What do you want to do?" Bastian asked.

The shame in Khaine almost consumed him. He had Skye who was able to open a portal for him, who had Raiden's necklace around her neck, *and* she was the sacrifice needed for

Raiden to come home. Bastian having the rune didn't matter. He hung his head and sighed. "Nothing."

There wasn't a damn thing he was going to do about it.

Skye tucked her knees to her chest and stared at the fire. Night had fallen, seeming to reflect her current mood. Caden, Mckenzie, Honey, and Castello had followed her after she'd walked away. Khaine and Bastian had gone another route.

Why did that make her heart ache even more?

She did her best to hold herself together when all she really wanted to do was cry. And scream. And find Khaine so she could punch him, again. Or kiss him. She missed the demon.

There was no reason for Skye to want anything to do with Khaine, but she couldn't shake the look of torture on his face when she'd told him they were done. Was he telling the truth?

He'd said he would never hurt her; had sought out the deity to find another way of getting Raiden back. The pressure in Skye's chest was building to a dangerous degree. She wanted to believe him, she really did.

Then believe him!

If only it were that simple.

He'd kept a secret from her. The fact that he didn't trust her to tell her what he knew, cut deeper than any plan he did or didn't have.

Honey scooted closer to Skye and patted her back. When she

first met the deity, her smile had been infectious. Now? All it did was make Skye want to bury herself in a deep hole and stay there. How could everyone around her seem so happy when she was crumbling inside?

"There, there," Honey said. "You'll work it out."

Was she serious? "Work it out? He wants to kill me."

It's not like there was any coming back from that revelation. Caden's brow rose.

Honey cocked her head, her red and black hair swaying to the side. "Well, you don't have to be so dramatic about it." George lay at her feet, snoring in a way that made the creature seem less menacing.

Instead of arguing with the deity, who was actually starting to grow on her, Skye sighed and continued staring at the flames as they danced shadows all around her.

Mckenzie sat on a log Castello had pulled closer to the fire and ran a file along the length of a blade, sharpening the rim to a paper-fine edge.

"We'll leave at first light," she said. "Maybe we can backtrack and find a way out of here."

"Don't worry," Caden said to Skye. "That vision isn't happening. Khaine can't hurt you."

As if Caden thought Khaine would be the one to kill her. Yes, the demon might want her dead, but it was for reasons none of them would understand, and Skye was too frustrated and tired to explain.

Castello hung in a hammock he had fashioned out of vines from his hands. Being a Dryad seemed to have its perks. His arms were folded behind his head. "Why not ask Bastian? He got us here, maybe he can get us out."

Mckenzie glared at Castello. "We don't need the demon's help."

"No need to get feisty, love. You're in charge." He winked at Mckenzie who just rolled her eyes and went back to sharpening one of her knives.

If Castello kept calling Mckenzie love, there were going to be a lot of questions in a really short span of time. Skye peered at Caden. She had been with them for a while, maybe she knew something.

Caden shrugged her shoulders at Skye and mouthed the word 'mate'.

What? Castello and Mckenzie were mates? When did that happen?

Whatever, it didn't matter.

Skye glanced behind her into the dark woods. Even with the glowing plants slithering up some of the trees, she still couldn't see that well. There looked to be an orange light that came to life a couple of hundred yards to the south, but there was no telling if that was another fire, or if it was Khaine and Bastian sitting around it. There were too many trees and bushes blocking her view.

She wanted to talk to the demon. Maybe he was telling the truth. Maybe he never planned to hurt her. Maybe he really had been searching for Honey so he could find a way to save both her and Raiden.

Caden and Mckenzie wanted to take her home. She would never see Khaine again if they had their way. She knew they were just trying to protect her, but they had all been trying to protect her for years. Wasn't it time she took care of herself?

Caden shifted in the dirt and cast her a look that said she

knew what Skye was thinking. There was a dark patch of what could only be blood that had matted on her head, making Skye feel bad. She knew she was the cause of it. At least Caden was alive. She didn't seem too bad off, either. Maybe Skye's fear hadn't done that much damage.

"Don't tell me you miss the demon," Caden said.

The dread in Skye's stomach worked its way to her throat. She didn't want to hurt her sisters. She knew all of them, even Brooke and Jade, would never approve if she told them how she felt about Khaine. She didn't want to hurt them by disappointing them.

"I'm going to use the bathroom," Skye said, getting to her feet and making a hasty retreat.

Caden narrowed her eyes. Honey stroked George's thick fur. She winked at Skye as she disappeared into the darkness.

When she was sure nobody had followed her, she changed direction and started walking toward the orange glow she had seen, veering around enormous trees. The closer she got, the more her insides twisted into knots. Maybe she shouldn't have yelled at Khaine. Maybe she should have listened to him.

She knew he cared deeply for his brother, cared even more for the family he lost. How could someone who cared that much be a bad person? If she could just find him, talk to him, get his side of the story. Yes, he wanted to bring his brother back from Hell. Wouldn't Skye want the same if it were Caden? Or Jade? Or any of her sisters? She wasn't sure she would be able to do the right thing if it meant getting them back. To her, getting them back *would* be the right thing.

And the level of trust and kindness he had shown her? She could tell herself that the change in Khaine was only because he wanted to seduce her, but deep down, she knew that wasn't true. She wanted to believe he cared for her, because God help her, she definitely cared for him.

Skirting around another tree, Skye held her stomach. Everything she felt, about her situation, about Khaine, seemed to be colliding inside her.

She drew nearer to the faint glow; the flickering of a fire now clear in front of her. She stayed in the shadows, watching her footing as she eased closer. Khaine was sitting on a rock, his head hanging low with his elbows propped on his knees.

Bastian sat in front of him on the ground, adding a log to the fire. She kept her footing light as she slunk behind a tree and peered out. Neither of them noticed her, both seeming too deep in conversation. They were yards away and Skye found herself straining to hear them. She didn't want to interrupt, wasn't even sure if she should talk to Khaine or not. The uncertainty about what she should or shouldn't do seemed to swell inside her.

"What do you plan to do about it?" Bastian asked.

Khaine seemed consumed with the dirt under his feet as he answered. "Nothing."

Khaine's blonde hair reflected the dancing flames while his black eyes soaked up the light around them. Smoke drifted into the air, spiraling in the same way Skye felt inside. She took a step forward, intent on clearing the air with Khaine, but his words stopped her.

"I can't let her go," he said. He shifted himself on the boulder. "If Raiden coming back from Hell means Skye has to die, then Raiden can rot in Hell for eternity."

Skye froze. He couldn't mean that.

Khaine seemed to cringe at his words at the same time Skye's heart dropped. He would rather his brother suffer in Hell than bring him home? He'd known her death was the means to bringing Raiden back. Did he really not plan on killing her? Did he really plan to choose Skye over Raiden?

"You think you've made the wrong choice," Bastian said. It wasn't a question, but it hung in the air like one.

Khaine lifted his head, his voice clipped. "Haven't I? Raiden is my brother. He means everything to me."

"But Skye means more." Bastian rubbed his face. "We can find another way to bring Raiden back."

"Not before the planets align," Khaine said.

"No, but one day is better than not at all. Raiden isn't going anywhere. Killing your mate..." Bastian paused and shook his head. "There's no coming back from that."

"I care for her."

"You love her," Bastian said.

Khaine paused, not saying anything, then nodded his head.

Skye forgot how to breathe. He didn't... He just... He loved her? The warmth in her heart swelled, then turned to ice in her veins.

Bastian got to his feet and walked to Khaine. Skye twisted herself behind the tree so he wouldn't see her.

"Then choose Skye. We can find another way to get Raiden back; you can't replace your mate. You deserve happiness."

Khaine groaned. "Do I?"

Yes, Skye wanted to scream!

Her mind raced. Khaine had just admitted he loved her. He was willing to choose her over his brother. The unease in her stomach began to grow. She couldn't let him do that. He might be able to live with that decision, but what about her? How was she supposed to look at him knowing how much he gave up? Yeah, maybe they *could* find another way to bring Raiden back, but what if they couldn't? What if this was his only chance?

Skye closed her eyes and tried to calm herself. What she was contemplating was insanity. When she opened her eyes, she had to do a double take.

Standing amongst the trees behind Bastian and Khaine, several yards away where the glow from the trees barely illuminated her face, was Honey. Her arms waved frantically in the air as she darted her eyes in a 'come here' gesture.

Skye glanced behind her. Hadn't Honey been back with the others? Hadn't she been *behind* her?

Not that it mattered, right now.

Skye slunk over to Honey, careful not to draw attention to herself as she skirted the thick bushes around Bastian and Khaine. She shook her head as she neared the deity, confused.

"What are you doing here?" she whispered.

She grabbed Honey by the arm and led her further away from Khaine and Bastian, afraid they would see or hear them.

Honey rolled her eyes as they walked. "Solving all your problems, of course."

George wasn't with her, which seemed odd, but nothing about Honey was exactly straightforward.

"I don't understand," Skye said, ushering Honey into the woods and behind a tree where the soft glow from the mushrooms didn't touch the darkness.

"What's to understand? Nothing makes sense. That's the beauty of it."

Skye filled her lungs with air and held it for one beat...two, letting it out slow and easy. The smile on Honey's face was about to drive her mad.

"Do you know of a way to get Khaine's brother back?"

Honey smiled.

Hope filled Skye. "You do, don't you." It wasn't a question. The look on Honey's face said all Skye needed to know.

"The question is," Honey said, "are you willing to do it? Because you already know how to get him back."

"I have to die."

"Bingo!"

All the hope in her chest seemed to shrivel. The world around Skye was too bright and cheerful to coexist with the dread inside her. Not that she hadn't already been contemplating doing just that; getting Raiden back on her own. How could she not?

"Is there a way to stop my death from happening?"

There had to be a way to save them both.

"No. If you stop it from happening now, it will only happen later. Fate is fate. What's meant to happen will happen whether you bake the cake or not."

Cake?

Skye disregarded the last statement. "You're saying that either I die now and Raiden comes back, or I die later and Khaine still lives without his brother. Either way, I die."

Honey's eyes shifted to a brighter hue, rainbow colors dancing behind her eyelids. "Exactly. Four cups sugar. One cup peanut butter. One and a half—"

Skye snapped her fingers in front of Honey's face. She couldn't lose her sanity, now. She needed Honey to focus. If what she said was true and there wasn't a way to stop the vision from happening, only a way to alter the when and how, then Khaine giving up the chance to get his brother back was pointless. Why sacrifice a part of his happiness only for Skye to die later anyway?

"Honey, please," she pleaded. "How do I bring Raiden back?"

Honey seemed to freeze in place, not breathing, not blinking. When she finally came to, her eyes were hollow and her voice flat.

"Place the offering before the portal and inscribe the rune. Present the sacrifice before the doorway closes."

What rune? What offering? Skye tried not to panic. Her insides felt like a weight was crashing down on her and there was nothing she could do to stop it. She rubbed her hands down her dress.

The offering had to be something simple, something that would signify—

She was an idiot! Skye fingered the jewel around her neck. It had to be Raiden's necklace. Why else would Khaine have had it on him? The offering most likely had to be something from the person you wanted to free, otherwise there was no telling who or what you would let loose from Hell.

Honey's voice shifted back to a resemblance of normal; bright and cheerful. "Do I give you the paper, now?"

"Paper?"

She pulled a paper from a pocket in her shorts and handed it to Skye. Without wasting any time, Skye unfolded the paper and peered at the scribbled drawing. Several lines interspaced a tight set of circles and seemed to be encased by an arch. The rune. The deity had had it in her pocket this whole time?

Skye closed her eyes. It was either that or bellow her frustration to Honey, and the deity didn't deserve that, no matter how difficult she might be.

"Perhaps it's time to go home?" Honey asked.

Skye peered at the faint glow of the fire where Bastian and Khaine were still sitting. He wasn't likely to forgive her for making this decision without him, but at least he could have a semblance of happiness with his brother back in his life. She couldn't let him choose her. She couldn't let him make a choice that would mean losing his brother *and* his mate. At least this way, he would get to keep one.

She turned back to Honey and nodded; her mind set. It was time to go home.

Chapter 36

S kye stepped over the threshold, her brain momentarily hitting the pause button. She couldn't comprehend where she was as she stepped onto the stone floor and looked around. Wood covered an expanse of stone with dishes stacked neatly on top. In one corner, a hole had been knocked into a rock wall, a cooking pot sitting in the middle over a fire. The smell of something roasting in the pot hit her nose and made her stomach growl.

Home.

It should have made her feel warm inside. Instead, Skye felt nothing but unease. She should have said goodbye to Khaine. Should have told him how she felt or that she hoped he found happiness. Why couldn't she have stopped for a few minutes and thought about how the demon might feel?

Because she knew, if she said anything to him at all, she wouldn't be able to go through with her plan. And if Khaine knew what she intended to do? He would have bound her in some cage and kept her there for eternity. She couldn't let him choose her.

Who would have thought that the deity could have sent them back at any time? It's like she knew what needed to happen and waited for the right moment.

Of course, Honey knew. She was supposed to know everything, even if not coherently at times. It had only taken her a few seconds to open a portal for Skye, and Skye even less time to walk through it.

The faint sounds of a television in the next room filled her ears. Brooke and Jade were chatting about the clothing choice of someone on the screen. She could hear the voices of her sisters as they argued over who picked the better outfit. Skye carefully stepped out of the kitchen and down the hall, passing their makeshift living room without so much as a swish of her hair. She spotted a little girl she had never seen before sitting in between Brooke and Jade, but didn't have the time to ponder who it might be.

She wanted to stop and tell Brooke and Jade that she loved them. She wanted to hug them and talk about fashion. She wanted them to know that it was her choice, that Khaine had nothing to do with it. Instead, she continued down the hall.

First things first; she needed to know what day it was.

Skye made her way to the generator room. They always kept newspapers in there or magazines that Caden brought back, and when they were done reading the latest issue of the outside world, they put them in the pile. She shuffled through the stack, placing each date to the side and counting how long it have been since she left. When she came across the most recent date, her stomach dropped.

She should have known she would find it; Jade was never wrong when it came to her visions. And Honey? She must have known what day it was. Still, looking at the date on top of the newspaper, had her trying not to laugh.

If the date was right, she'd been gone exactly ten days.

If her death was tied to getting Raiden back, that meant it was now or never. She swiped a knife off the rack where Mckenzie kept her blades and forced herself to move.

Skye jogged to the stairs leading into the basement and down the steps, her anxiety building. By the time she reached the bottom step and walked into the room where the portal used to be, her hands were slick with sweat. She rubbed them down her dress, not caring when flakes of dried blood dislodged from the material and stuck to her palms.

She should have been afraid that her fear would boil over, but the necklace around her neck, Raiden's necklace, kept that from happening.

The debris from her blasting the portal to pieces had been swept to a corner of the room in a tight alcove. Larger stones still lay in a pile where the portal used to be. Skye made her way over to them and dropped to her knees. It was almost dark outside, the mirrors around the space barely catching the fading light.

Taking a deep breath, she placed the knife beside her and pulled the paper Honey had given her from between her breasts. She laid it out on the dusty stone, smoothing the corners. All she had to do was draw the symbol, place Raiden's necklace next to it, and open the portal. At least, that's what she thought needed to happen. She wasn't sure of anything else after that. The vision said it was a demon that killed her, so it had to be Raiden that did the deed, didn't it?

"Present the sacrifice before the doorway closes," Honey had said.

She supposed just being here could be the same as presenting herself. She hoped she didn't have to be the one to carry out the final step. If she had to kill herself, she wasn't sure she could do it.

She took a breath and held it, trying to calm her nerves. Maybe she was being selfish. Maybe she *should* have let Khaine decide what he wanted.

Don't be a coward!

There was no turning back, now. She'd made up her mind and needed to stick with it. This was her way of taking back control of her life. This was her way of showing Khaine how she felt. She was going to die one day anyway, why not die helping someone she loved?

Because God help her, she *did* love Khaine.

Skye unfolded the paper and glanced at the symbol inked across its surface. She used her hand to brush an even path of dust over the ground, then pointed her finger in the powdery mess and began to draw the rune. She did her best to copy the image exactly as Honey had drawn it, careful to keep the lines the same size and circles as perfectly round as she could manage. When she was done, she sat back on her heels and listened to the pounding in her chest.

Skye took another breath to steady her racing heart, then another for good measure. She eased the necklace off her neck and placed it on the ground next to the rune, trying not to let her fear win. Without its power, she needed to keep herself calm and under control. Causing an explosion wasn't what she wanted to do. She had spent the last however many years trying to keep herself from accidentally opening a portal, so it seemed ironic that that's exactly what she wanted to do in this moment.

She just wasn't sure *how*.

Skye sighed and wrung her hands together. She'd done this back at the club. If she could do it once, she could do it again. She stared at her hands and imagined the tiny currents she had felt. She imagined the color of the portal and the feeling of electricity in her hands.

Nothing.

Frustrated, Skye tried to remember what she had been doing at that moment. Khaine had been surrounded by Elite soldiers with Leclain standing behind her. She hadn't been afraid, just desperate to make something happen.

Skye peered at her hands and thought about Khaine; about how much he cared for his brother, for her. She willed the pressure in her chest to expand, gasping when it tingled in her fingertips before fading.

Skye closed her eyes and let her emotions take hold. She could do this. She was strong enough to save Khaine's brother. Khaine was willing to sacrifice so much for her, there was no reason she couldn't do the same for him.

She let everything she felt for Khaine grow inside her, funneling it into her palms.

The feel of him against her flesh.

The frustration when he tried to be demanding.

The stutter of her heart when he'd said he loved her.

Skye took it all and molded it into pure energy in her hands.

She tried to picture it building and swirling around itself. The energy worked its way down her arms, forming into a ball she could feel herself holding. She gasped as it tingled, the energy building with tiny electric jolts. Skye added to it, shaping the energy into a larger version of itself, fueled by thoughts of Khaine. Fueled by her own need to help the demon she had come to love.

She let it build until she wasn't sure she could hold it anymore, and let it go.

The result was instant; a spherical burst of energy hanging in the still air as it expanded around itself. Her chest pounded as she stared at the portal she'd created. It grew, backing her away as it morphed and solidified into a larger doorway. The thunder in her heart grew with it, unsure of what would happen next.

What if demons started coming through the glassy void?

Damnit!

She should have thought about that before she opened the portal.

Just as the fear churning in her stomach was about to explode, Skye held her breath. Claws emerged from the swirling void. A single gray hand snaked out of the surface, razor-sharp claws protruding from each finger. The fear in her chest threatened to break free, but she held it back, thoughts of Khaine grounding her.

Skye backed away several more paces, scooting along the hard floor.

An arm connected with the hand, breaking free as the image of a shoulder and chest followed. It didn't look anything like a human, more like a purebred demon with gray skin and black veins streaking through its body. The creature was tall, so tall that Skye craned her neck up as its head slithered from the portal's surface.

Skye tried not to scream as she looked into its eyes, so black they seemed to not exist at all. Its cheekbones were high and sharp, with dark lips pressed into a thin line. The hair on its head was long and tangled around itself. Corded muscles covered the expanse of exposed skin, bulging as the creature stepped one foot, and then another, out of the portal in front of her.

This didn't look like Khaine's brother at all. Skye found herself trying not to panic as whatever it was dislodged itself from the portal and fell to one knee.

Skye stared at it, her mouth open and a scream posed on her lips.

It had to be Khaine's brother, had to be Raiden, but it was so hard to see anything human in whatever had come through. One thing was certain, it was definitely a demon.

The demon bowed its head and struggled for breath. Skye twisted on the ground, unsure of what to do next.

"Raiden?"

Her voice echoed around the chamber, making her cringe at the sound.

The demon's head shot forward, its black eyes boring into her.

Its mouth curved back, showing pointed fangs. "Who are you," it ground out, its voice so gravely it sounded like the scratching of stone.

Holy fuck!

This had to be Raiden. This had to be Khaine's brother.

What the hell had happened to him?

Behind him, the portal began to shimmer.

Started to *fade*.

Skye threw herself in front of Raiden and gripped the blade, holding it out to him. The portal started to sway in on itself, the corners imploding as it grew smaller. Desperation filled Skye. They didn't have much time.

She shook the knife in front of Raiden and willed him to look at her, his eyes hollow and pained. "You have to kill me!"

Raiden shook his head, seeming unsure of what was happening. Damnit! There wasn't time for her to explain. If Raiden didn't kill her right now, he would be sucked back into the portal and lost forever.

"Raiden," Skye screamed, grasping his shoulders with so much force she thought she might break something. "You have to kill me. It's the only way for you to stay here."

"I don't—"

"Khaine sent me to save you." She pleaded with him; tried to get him to comprehend what needed to be done. "You have to kill me or the portal is going to take you back. Do you hear me," she cried.

She shook him violently, desperate to get him to listen. The portal behind him was growing smaller by the second. If he didn't kill her now, there wouldn't be another chance. She thrust the blade in front of him, begging him to take it.

"You. Have. To. Kill me," she said, grinding the words out in a way she hoped he would understand.

Please.

Raiden shook his head again but seemed to be coming around. His black eyes regarded her with a kind of weary sadness.

"Khaine?" he said.

"Yes! Your brother, Khaine. He sent me to save you."

Raiden pushed himself to his knees, his limbs seeming to protest his every move. "Who are you?"

"Someone that cares for your brother and wants you to get back to him. Please," she said. "You have to kill me."

The portal behind him was almost closed. Panic coursed through her veins, making her crazed. She desperately tried to calm herself, but nothing seemed to be helping. Skye clung to the knife in her hand like it was meant to save her and not Raiden.

Raiden glanced at the blade, then at Skye. She noticed it in his dark eyes; the moment he decided he wouldn't do it. Skye's stomach dropped.

"Please," she said.

Raiden shook his head, the portal behind him seconds from being gone completely.

Skye wanted to reason with the demon but knew she would lose. She didn't know if Raiden didn't want to kill her because he thought it was wrong, or if he didn't want to kill her because he didn't want to be free. Frankly, she didn't care. There wasn't time for him to have some moral dilemma. Khaine needed his brother. It was time for Raiden to come home.

Skye thrust the knife into Raiden's hand, and before he could pull away, she sank the blade deep into her chest.

Raiden pulled his hand back and bellowed, but it was too late. The deed was done. The portal behind him shimmered into nothing, closing as if it never existed.

And still, he was there. That meant she'd done it. The portal was closed, and Raiden was still there!

Skye tried to smile at him, but her face didn't seem to respond. The pain in her chest consumed her, and still, she didn't care. Khaine was getting his brother back. Raiden was getting his life back.

She groaned as Raiden twisted her on the ground, easing her into his lap. The horror in his eyes almost made her regret her decision, but she reminded herself that it was meant to be this way. She tried to speak, tried to tell him that it was fine, that everything would be okay, but no words came out. Her vision faded, her eyes closing several times without her consent.

When warm liquid was poured inside her mouth, she hardly noticed the metallic taste of it, or where it had come from.

The only thing she could think about was Khaine and how much she loved him. She hoped that Khaine and Raiden found happiness. She hoped that her sisters would understand. As everything around her faded into darkness, she hoped she found them all again, in whatever life came next.

Khaine stood and paced in front of the fire. He knew Bastian was right. He knew they could find another way to get Raiden back without Skye having to die. He couldn't lose her so soon.

Bastian added another log to the fire.

"We'll find a way home at first light," he said. "Perhaps you should speak to her."

"And say what?" Khaine groveled. "I fucked it up just like everything else."

Bastian shook his head. "You tell her how you feel."

"You don't understand," Khaine said. "I was cruel. I called her things I didn't mean. I didn't tell her about getting Raiden back because I hoped I could find another way."

Khaine thought things were going well between him and Skye. He'd apologized and tried to do better. He should have told her sooner. He should have told her that he would never hurt her and that this whole fucking journey was his desperate attempt at saving both her *and* Raiden.

He rubbed his face and paced faster, his feet digging lines in the dirt. He should have known he could never have both.

"If she cares for you, she'll understand," Bastian said. "You know I'll help you any way I can."

Khaine stopped before the fire and nodded. Bastian had always been willing to help; always did the right thing.

He hung his head and sighed. "I'm sorry for pushing you away." When he looked at Bastian, one eyebrow was cocked.

"I think having a mate will be good for you," Bastian said. He leaned over and pushed the Raudskinna back in his shoulder bag, then stood and swung it over his chest.

"Don't push me," Khaine said, but he couldn't keep the smile from his face.

It was good to have Bastian here, he thought. Perhaps there was still hope to fix the friendship he'd pushed away.

Bastian walked to him, and before Khaine could refuse, clasped his arms around Khaine. Khaine paused for a moment, too stunned to move. When his mind finally reset, he hugged Bastian, wrapping his arms around him as if his friend could take away all his frustration and pain. Khaine fought the tears in his eyes and nodded as Bastian stepped back to peer at him.

"Now, let's go find your mate," Bastian said. "Perhaps talking to her would be a good start."

Khaine gave a curt nod and turned toward the trees behind him, a knot in his throat. He focused on putting one foot in front of the other, intent on marching right into Skye's camp and telling her exactly how he felt. It didn't matter if she believed him or not, she needed to know. He had to try and make this right with her.

Khaine rounded a large trunk and came up short.

Honey waved her hands at them, the smile on her face making Khaine groan. The amount of happiness this deity threw off was enough to fuel an entire army of depressed immortals, and all Khaine wanted to do was throttle her.

"Boys! Oh, boys!" She waved her hand frantically as she got closer.

Fine, he would see what the hell she wanted, *then* find Skye.

Chapter 37

Khaine stopped in front of the deity and glowered at her, Bastian beside him.

"What do you want?" Khaine said.

Honey's red and black streaked hair bounced around her shoulders, barely catching the light from the oddly glowing plants around them. Her white shirt seemed to consume the green and blue hues, making it even more jolly.

She pressed a finger to her lips as though she were thinking. "Well, it *would* be nice to find a bone large enough for George, but then there's the problem of throwing it." She paused, the rainbow effect of her eyes becoming more prominent. "I met a giant one time that died of an allergic reaction to flowers; his bones would have been perfect! But the cookie I fed the squirrel didn't bounce on the water."

Khaine shook his head and skirted around Honey. It seemed the more you talked to her, the more she didn't make sense.

"I don't have time for this," Khaine said. "I need to find Skye."

Bastian followed close behind him, pushing his way through the bushes. Khaine stepped over a downed log and walked faster. The sooner he found Skye, the sooner he could apologize and explain things.

"That's what I'm here for, dummy," Honey called behind them. "She went to get Raiden."

Khaine jolted to a stop, then turned. "What did you say?"

The deity ran up to them, the smile never leaving her face. Khaine must have misheard her.

Honey clapped her hands and laughed. "Skye went home so she could open the portal and bring Raiden back. Aren't you excited!"

The blood drained from his face. Khaine shifted on his heels and started running through the woods, his chest tight. His mind shut down, not focusing on anything but the orange glow he could see in the distance. He knew Bastian was running beside him, but he didn't care. Trees blurred as he raced through the forest. The dizziness from moving so fast threatened to do him in. Panic engulfed him like an inferno.

Khaine moved quicker than he ever had in his life. When the forest finally broke and the fire came into view, Khaine only ran faster. The clearing wasn't large, more like a tented canopy of trees and bushes with a soft patch of dirt in the center. Khaine barreled into the middle, his mind counting the people there.

Mckenzie and Caden sat around the fire. Castello lay in a hammock of sorts, braided together by vines. They all peered at him, Mckenzie getting to her feet first as Bastian joined him in the clearing.

No Skye.

"Where is she?" Khaine roared.

His body shifted; his eyes sure to be turning. He didn't fucking care! If his demon wanted to come out, let it.

The other two bolted to their feet. Vines shot out from the ground, wrapping around Khaine's ankles and snaking up his legs. Several things pointed in his direction at once. A dagger held by Mckenzie. A sword held by Caden.

A curved stick held by Honey as she came into view.

"This is interesting," Honey said. "Is this how you play Cops and Robbers?"

Khaine twisted his legs, frantically trying to free them from the tight vines.

Bastian moved in front of Khaine, his arms suddenly caught in another set of vines and held in place.

"Wait," Bastian said. "We're just looking for Skye."

Caden moved in front of them, her sword steady. "You have no business with our sister."

Khaine gritted through his sharp teeth. "You don't understand," he yelled. "Honey said she went home to save my brother. Where is she!"

Gods, please let the deity be wrong. If Skye went back to save Raiden, if she opened the portal to set him free...

Caden got in Khaine's face and narrowed her eyes. "Explain."

They didn't have time for this! He needed to find Skye.

Khaine fought against the vines, his muscles straining. When his movements only made the vines close tighter around his caves, he gave up.

"Please," he pleaded. "Is she here or not?"

Mckenzie flipped the dagger in her hand, tossing it end over end. "She went to use the bathroom. Now tell us why you're so concerned for our sister."

They all stared at him, waiting.

Bastian nodded his head at Khaine. "The faster you get to talking, the faster we find her."

Khaine gritted his teeth and addressed Caden. "My brother got trapped in Hell. The only way to free him is to open a portal and present a sacrifice. The sacrifice needs to be a Guardian."

A knife shot forward, embedding itself in Khaine's shoulder. He clenched his jaw, black blood running down his arm. At one point the pain would have calmed him, now it enraged him more.

"I wasn't going to kill her," Khaine gritted.

Mckenzie pulled another dagger from her thigh.

"Honey said she went to get my brother back," Khaine continued, trying to steady his voice. "We need to find her."

Caden's eyes bore into Khaine as she drew her sword and held it tight against his chest. "Why would she do that?"

His lips thinned. He didn't know why. He wanted to believe that Skye cared for him, but there was no reason for her to sacrifice herself to get Raiden back. It wasn't her fight! He could live without Raiden. He couldn't live without Skye!

Caden watched him, her face not giving anything away.

Without turning her head, she addressed the deity. "Honey? Did Skye go home to save Khaine's brother?"

Honey dropped the curved stick, pouting. "So, we're not playing a game?"

"Honey," Caden repeated, still staring at Khaine as though he were about to be murdered.

The deity rolled her eyes. "Fine. Yes, your majesty. She went home."

Caden looked like she was going to be sick, finally glancing at the deity and lowering her blade. "How did she get home?" she demanded.

Honey shrugged her shoulders. "I opened a portal for her, duh!"

Khaine glared at Honey, his fangs barred and claws ready to slice her in half. "Open it again," he said.

The vines around Khaine and Bastian disappeared as Mckenzie walked over and pulled her knife from Khaine's shoulder.

Khaine was in front of Honey so fast nobody could have seen him move. He gripped her shoulders and shook her. "Open it!"

George poked his head between them, the flicker of the fire dancing across his teeth. Khaine reluctantly stepped back, desperation consuming him. He held the deity's eyes, pleading with her. He would get on his fucking knees if that's what it took!

Honey patted George on his back. "Don't you worry, he's just a grumpy old man." She sauntered a few paces away and raised her hands, clapping them together before stretching them wide. "All work and no play."

In an instant, the shimmering of a portal hung before them. Khaine wasted no time, moving quickly toward the opening. Caden stopped him with a blade across his chest. He grit his teeth at the intrusion but didn't move.

"If Skye dies, you die," Caden said. If her voice alone could kill him, it would have.

Khaine looked at Caden, trying to tuck his demon away. This was Skye's sister. Caden had been with Skye from the beginning. He knew Caden cared for Skye just as much as he did. He knew she had more rights to his mate then he ever would in a thousand lives. While he would have killed the woman when they first met, he couldn't do so now. Skye loved her sisters. He could understand wanting to keep Skye safe. He could understand Caden's rage toward him, since it seemed it was going to be his fault that Skye died after all.

Khaine nodded. If Skye died, he would gladly let any one of her sisters take his head just to follow her into oblivion.

Caden lowered her sword.

Without a word, Khaine burst through the portal and landed in a stone room. A fire was heating a cast iron pot in one corner, the smell of roast wafting into the air. The others emerged from the portal next to him, but Khaine was already moving in the direction of Skye's scent.

He rounded a corner into a smaller room, with a television playing in the center of one stone wall and a couch positioned in front of it. Two women sat on the couch with a young girl between them. They turned their heads at him and simultaneously jumped to their feet.

"You!" the two older females yelled as one.

One of the women, short black hair spiked on her head, narrowed her eyes at Khaine. "What the hell are you doing in—"

He didn't let her finish, just backed out of the room and continued down the hall. He stopped at every entrance and briefly peered inside, looking for stairs that would lead him down into the portal room.

"Keep moving," Caden said behind him. "End of the hall!"

Khaine found the stairs and took them three at a time, his legs on fire. Footsteps echoed behind him. Several people were in close pursuit. Voices he couldn't focus on bounded to his ears in the tight space, but his mind refused to comprehend their words.

Move...fucking...faster!

If he didn't get to her in time... If he didn't reason her out of this madness...

Khaine hit the bottom of the steps and blasted into the underground chamber. When his mind stopped spinning enough for him to gauge what he was looking at, Khaine froze.

Several hard thuds pounded into his back as everyone behind him stopped too late. Khaine kept his stance steady as he tried to reason with the image in front of him.

Skye lay on the stone ground, her blonde hair spilling out from her braid, blood underneath her. A knife protruded from her chest, the sight of it making his heart stop.

Above her, with one hand grasped around the blade, was a tall figure with black blood covering its gray skin. It wasn't human, but it wasn't a demon either. Its features were too human-like to be a purebred demon, but too demon-like to be a half-breed or prince. Khaine willed his mind to focus and looked closer. His insides screamed at him.

It was the eyes that gave the figure away as it looked at Khaine in horror.

Raiden.

Caden pushed past Khaine and with her sword drawn, bolted toward Raiden. Khaine and Bastian moved as one, intercepting her path and knocking her away. She bounded to her feet, but Bastian held her back as Khaine peered at Raiden.

"Wait," Bastian yelled to Caden.

What the hell had happened to him? This couldn't be his brother.

His demon half roared inside him, recognizing Raiden even if Khaine couldn't.

Before Khaine could think to move, vines shot from the earth, breaking the stone into pieces around them. They clasped Raiden in a vice and held him as he roared, the sound so deafening and full of pain that Khaine cringed.

He didn't care. The sight of Skye's body tore through his conscience.

Regaining his senses, Khaine sank to his knees over Skye. She wasn't moving. The knife in her chest glistened with a red hue that made bile rise in his throat. Khaine gripped the knife and pulled it free, then tilted her with his hands gently under her head.

"Skye!"

Please, wake up.

She wasn't responding.

"Don't do this to me," he cried. "Skye!"

Caden skidded to a halt on the other side of Skye, pressing her hands hard into her chest where the knife had been. Skye wasn't breathing. Her chest was so still that Khaine felt sick inside. The warmth in her body was fading, a stiff coldness taking its place.

Khaine looked at Caden, pleading with her to fix it. Fix Skye. Make her come back. She met his gaze, but the sadness and hatred she shot back at him had him shaking his head.

He didn't know what to do. He didn't know how to fix this. His runes could heal small wounds, but this was death they were talking about!

"You did this," Caden said.

Khaine looked down at Skye, his heart crumbling in his chest. Blood pooled in Skye's mouth, black and warm.

He focused on the blood, his mind seeming to reset. He looked at her mouth, then back at Raiden. His brother was standing several paces away, vines covering him to hold him in place. He wasn't fighting, and the look in his brother's eyes – God's, his brother! – told Khaine all he needed to know.

Khaine gently set Skye's head back on the stone, then pushed Caden to the side. He thrust his hands over Skye's chest and began pumping them up and down in quick succession. Her blood soaked his hands, but he kept going. He pressed his lips to hers and breathed into her lungs, then went back to the same steady compressions.

"Stop," Caden yelled at him. "Haven't you done enough? She's gone! You killed her!"

Caden got to her feet and gripped her sword.

"She's not gone!" Khaine yelled. He pumped his hands faster into Skye's chest. "He gave her his blood."

He didn't know if what Raiden had done would work, but it was the only hope he had left. Only pure demon's blood could turn her. Whatever had happened to Raiden in the time he was trapped in Hell, perhaps the change in him was enough. It had to be.

Please! He pleaded with her, pleaded with whatever higher power would dare listen to him. *Come back to me.*

Caden pushed Khaine off Skye. He landed on his leg with one arm braced behind him. Her questioning gaze bore into him.

The room around him seemed to disappear, the walls of his guilt and pain closing in on him.

"She can come back," Khaine said, his voice hollow.

She had to.

Caden stared at him for one beat...two...then yelled across the room. "Brooke!"

"I'm here," came the weak reply.

Caden clenched her teeth. "Zap her."

The room grew quiet.

"I can't." The woman's voice was stricken.

Khaine looked at the woman who spoke, long red hair flowing down her back. As if his mind decided to let him focus, the entire room came back into view. Bastian stood by Raiden, but the vines no longer held him in place. Castello and Mckenzie stood by the two women he'd seen in the television room, their faces grim. The little girl was nowhere to be seen. Honey stood by George, petting his shoulders as though she found the scene before her boring. Not smiling.

The sickness in Khaine's stomach began to grow.

"Brooke," Caden yelled.

The woman, Brooke, shook her head, her face pale and eyes full of tears. She wore a white shirt over a long black skirt that swayed around her as she moved closer, apprehensive. When she was finally within reach of Caden, Caden pulled her down over Skye. She crashed to the stone floor on her knees.

"Brooke," Caden said in a soothing tone. "You have to help her."

Brooke looked at Caden, then at Khaine. Her face held a touch of panic.

Khaine tried to smile at her, tried to reassure her. If she could help, all she had to do was try.

"Please," Khaine said.

Brooke bit her lip and nodded. Her eyes shifted to a blinding white as she moved her hands over Skye. Currents shot from her fingertips. The arc began to grow under her palms as it coiled and collided in place. She let the static charge build, white light emanating throughout the dark chamber, then cringed as she pressed her electric-fueled hands into Skye's chest.

Chapter 38

Skye opened her eyes and rolled onto her back. The soft blanket tucked around her body tangled with her movements, making her finger the baby blue material. She stared at the stone ceiling overhead. The room was dark except for a faint glow of light adding to the fogginess of her brain, but there was a familiarity that seeped into her mind as she took stock of her surroundings.

Blue comforter. Stone ceiling. She turned her head and peered to the side; a sewing machine.

This was her room.

"You're awake."

The familiar voice echoed along the rock walls of Skye's bedroom. She shifted in her bed and sat up.

Caden eased out of Skye's blue armchair in the far corner and walked over, sitting on the edge of the bed. The table lamp positioned at an angel on Skye's dresser illuminated her small room, but her eyes were oddly having no problem seeing into the dark corners.

"How do you feel?" Caden said.

Caden's hair had been washed, no more dried blood scabbing in her high ponytail. Her pleather catsuit had also been discarded for a pair of suede, Powerpuff Girl sweatpants and a white t-shirt.

Skye pushed back her blue comforter and assessed herself. No more ugly dress that had been shredded and soaked with blood, now replaced with blue shorts and a black shirt, ones she had made herself. She fingered her hair, which seemed to have been washed recently, and tried to reason with herself.

She felt confused more than anything, but there was an inferno of pent-up energy coursing through every inch of her. That was new.

"I feel—"

Skye scrunched her face at the scratchy sound of her voice. Something sharp poked her tongue as she spoke, making her reach a hand out to finger whatever it was.

Fangs.

There were fangs in her mouth!

Her heart sped to a dangerous roar in her ears. "Caden?"

Caden scooted closer and pulled Skye's hand away from her mouth. The look of worry on her face wasn't making Skye feel any better. She had to calm her breathing!

"Don't freak out," Caden said.

Right, because *not* freaking out was what someone did when they were told not to freak out.

Skye closed her eyes and counted to ten, taking long, deep lungfuls of air. She'd already blasted Caden with her dangerous emotions once, she didn't need to do it again.

She quickly reached for the necklace around her neck. A moment of panic filled her as she noticed it was gone.

"It's okay," Caden said. "They said you might feel a little different for a while, but as long as you stay calm, your demon won't feed off you and you know, freak out too."

Her eyes flung open. "Demon?" Skye squeaked.

"Shhh," Caden said. "Everything's fine."

But the sarcastic tone of her voice said everything was *not* fine.

Skye took several deep breaths and let them out as slowly as she could. Something slithered inside her, like a foreign being had taken up residence and wanted out. She briefly entertained the idea of being possessed by a demon and that she was going to need an exorcism pronto, but the rational side of her brain said that likely wasn't the case.

Demon?

This was fine, she told herself. Everything was fine. So what if she now harbored a demon, or *was* a demon – who fucking knew at this point! – that didn't mean she was going to start acting demonic, right?

Right. Don't freak out...

"I don't understand," Skye said, taking another slow, deep breath.

"At least you won't have to worry about blowing things up, anymore," Caden said.

What? Did she mean her power was gone?

Right, because becoming a demon changed a person.

Her. A *demon...*

She inhaled and exhaled several more times, trying not to focus on herself. It was either that or acknowledge that she really *did* feel different. The thing inside her – demon or whatever – retreated into the shadows of her mind.

"I don't understand," Skye said, again.

Caden gave a half smile, the corners of her lips curving. "When you opened the portal to save Khaine's brother and he stabbed you—"

Actually, Skye stabbed herself, but she didn't think that fact mattered right now.

"He gave you his blood before you died. I guess he saved your life in a way, even if it almost didn't work. Brooke had to zap you a few times to get you back."

"What? Brooke zapped me?"

"Well, it was either that or let you die," Caden said, her voice exasperated. "I suppose being turned into a demon is better."

Skye was too focused on the fact that Brooke had brought someone back to life by zapping them. She'd only ever tried on small animals.

Then Caden's words seemed to finally take hold.

Turned into a demon. *She was really a demon.*

"You don't sound too happy," Skye said.

Caden sighed. "We all love you, Skye. It's your life and we can't tell you how to live it. Just didn't see it coming." She shifted one leg to rest on Skye's bed. Her tone shifted, becoming almost flat. "Why did you do it?"

Skye closed her eyes. This was it. This was the moment she knew would come whether she wanted it to or not. How was she going to tell her sisters that Khaine, a demon that kidnapped her and planned to sacrifice her to get his brother back, actually mattered to her? How was she supposed to tell

Caden, the one person that had been there for her almost her entire life, that she actually loved the stubborn, thick-headed, man-that-wasn't-a-man?

Words died in her throat. She didn't know what to say. She didn't even expect to be sitting in her bed, right now. She was supposed to be dead. Not that she had a death-wish or anything, it was just unexpected.

Caden hung her head. "Do you love him?"

Skye wrung her hands in her lap. "Please don't make me choose," she whispered.

Because she wouldn't choose her sisters.

How had things come to this? She was supposed to hate Khaine, and she did, at first. All that had changed, though. Now, all she wanted to do was talk to him.

Caden lifted her head and peered at Skye. She narrowed her eyes, but ultimately smiled. "You know I would never make you choose," she said. "I just...don't understand."

Skye tilted her head and smiled uncertainly at her sister. "That makes two of us."

"Look," Skye said. "I know Khaine is...is..."

"A dick? A bastard? A pig-headed, no-good, two-timing, son-of-a-bitch?" Caden offered.

"A lot," Skye corrected. Ugh, why did this have to be so complicated?

"I know he's a lot to accept, but it would mean a lot to me if you did." Skye took a breath, let it out. "He matters to me. He matters a lot. I don't want to choose between the people I love."

"So, you admit you love him."

Skye punched Caden in the shoulder. "C'mon, please." Skye

took another breath. "I do. I'm sorry."

The laugh Caden let out almost melted Skye in place, washing away whatever fear had been building inside her.

"I'm just messing with you," Caden said. "I already told you; I won't make you choose. I don't like him, but I love you and will support whatever decision you make." She scrunched her face as she rubbed her shoulder in the dim light. "Just don't go decking me like that. You're a lot stronger now."

Oh, shit! She didn't even realize.

"I'm so sorry," Skye said, reaching over as if to rub away the punch.

Caden shook her head. "Don't worry about it. I imagine you're going to have a lot to figure out now that you're...different."

That was putting it mildly.

"Besides," Caden continued. "It's not me you have to convince. You know Mckenzie has been waiting for the opportunity to kill Khaine."

Some inner part of Skye beat against her — the demon? — threatening to kill Mckenzie if she laid a hand on Khaine. There was so much rage inside her, she didn't know where it was coming from or why.

"She's held back so far," Caden said. "But I'm not sure how much longer that's going to last. The side-eyes are getting intense."

Probably because Mckenzie wanted to kill Khaine for what he did at Lesters.

Shit!

How could she forget?

Skye jumped up from her bed, knocking Caden to the side

as she scrambled to her feet.

"How long have I been out? Where is Khaine? She hasn't hurt him too bad, has she?"

Oh, God. What about Raiden? And Bastian? If Mckenzie decided all the demons in a ten-mile radius deserved a slow death, that's exactly what they would get.

And Skye would kill her. She would kill Mckenzie if she laid a single hand on any of them.

"Whoa, slow down," Caden said. "The last I seen, lover-boy was still alive in the living room. The damn neanderthal refuses to leave."

He was here?

Skye forced herself to take a breath. What the hell was she thinking? Kill Mckenzie? That's not what she wanted. Mckenzie was her sister. She would never harm her sisters.

It had to be her demon.

She couldn't focus on that right now.

Skye slipped her feet into a pair of blue slippers. She needed to see Khaine. And Raiden? What happened to him? He didn't look so good when he came out of the portal. Was he doing okay?

Caden twisted on the bed and smiled. "Okay, fine. Go save Khaine. But know this. If he so much as makes you cry, I'm still siding with Mckenzie and helping her hack him into tiny pieces."

Caden lifted her brows and shrugged her shoulders. "Or, you could probably handle him fine yourself now, seeing as how you're immortal and all."

Holy fuck!

Skye froze. She hadn't even thought of that! Immortal?

She looked down at her hands and cringed at the black claws protruding from her fingertips. She closed her eyes. Taking a deep breath and holding it, she counted to ten. When she opened her eyes again, the claws had receded.

Blowing things up because of her emotions was one thing, but claws?

This was going to take some getting used to...

"I think the only thing that's saving Khaine right now, is the look he had on his face when he found you in the portal room."

The look on his face? Had he mourned her? Losing one's mate wasn't an easy thing, but Skye knew that wasn't the only reason her death would have affected him so much. He loved her. He'd told Bastian as much. Skye rubbed her chest as her heart expanded ten-fold. She peered at Caden.

Caden rolled her eyes. "Well, go save him, then."

Right. Save the demon.

Skye walked over to Caden and hugged her sister. "Thank you." Caden could never know how much her accepting Khaine meant to her, even if that acceptance had stipulations.

Before she got caught up in her emotions, Skye made her way to the door and opened it. Her heart hammered in her chest, nervousness setting in.

She hadn't exactly spoken to Khaine since yelling at him. She never told him of her plans to bring Raiden back. What was he thinking? Would he be angry? Would he still love her, knowing what she now was?

Yes, he was a demon, but that didn't mean he would want to be mated to one.

That didn't mean he would still love her.

The hall was quiet, but faint voices echoed down the stone

corridor. She followed the sound, innately aware of the cold draft wafting across her warm skin. While she would have rushed back to her room and donned a sweater, she didn't need to.

She was also aware of the constant dripping sound coming from behind the stone. She could hear the small clatter of water as it fell.

Could actually *hear* it.

Skye tried to focus on putting one foot in front of the other. If she concentrated on her new heightened senses for too long, she would likely go mad.

Before Skye could round the last corner, the voices emanating from down the hall seemed to register, but it was Khaine's bellow that sent shivers down her spine and had her running the rest of the way to the sound. The first thing she noticed? Khaine plucking a dagger from his chest and tossing it back to Mckenzie.

The second thing?

Mckenzie reaching for another one.

Khaine's deep voice echoed in the small confines of their living room. "I'm not leaving!"

Skye snapped.

Before she registered thinking, Skye found herself standing in front of Mckenzie, Khaine at her back, with one of Mckenzie's daggers in her hand. She held it in a firm grip and shoved it in Mckenzie's face. There was an inferno inside her, one she didn't know what to do with. All she wanted to do was hurt Mckenzie for hurting Khaine.

"Anybody stabs the demon and it's going to be me," Skye said.

She heard Khaine's voice behind her, but it sounded far away despite the warmth of him seeping into her. "Skye..."

Mckenzie lifted a brow. "You going to stop me?"

Skye tried to steady herself, tried to lower the dagger in her hand, but anger seemed to consume her every thought. "If I have to."

"Skye," Khaine said. He placed a hand on her shoulder, and everything went wrong.

Skye clutched at her chest as it felt like it was about to explode. Fire spread through her body. Claws shot out from her hands as she felt her bones shifting under the surface. She took a step to the side, unsure of what to do. Pleasure mixed with pain pulsated through her, making it hard to breathe.

She tried to swallow around the fangs in her mouth as her panic started to swell.

Khaine came into view, breaking through the haze around her. "Easy," he said. His deep voice resonated all the way to her core. "Just breathe."

"I don't...I don't know what's wrong," Skye said.

Khaine's face hardened. "It's the mating bond. Just breathe."

She couldn't. Skye desperately tried to calm herself, but the energy inside her was skyrocketing. She shook her head, unable to voice that she most certainly *couldn't* breathe.

Khaine gripped Skye on either side of her head and held her face close to his. "Just look at me. Everything is fine. Breathe."

She gazed into his black eyes, a reflection of her own staring back at her, and forced air into her lungs. Every breath she took felt like it was on fire.

"There's no danger," Khaine said. "You're fine. I'm fine. Just breathe for me."

The sound of Khaine's voice seemed to give her enough strength to take several more deep breaths. There was a roaring sound in the back of her mind that seemed to scream at her over and over again.

—Mine—

Skye focused on Khaine, on the feel of his hands touching her. The fire in her chest seemed to ease, allowing her to breathe at a somewhat normal pace.

Holy shit. If this was what Khaine felt when he learned she was his mate, no wonder the demon kidnapped her. Skye wasn't sure if she was about to murder everyone in a ten-mile radius or drag the demon back to her room and claim him.

Khaine smirked as he released her face and stepped back. Skye wanted to grab for him, but several things registered all at once. Mainly, several people as she took stock of the room.

Caden stood by the doorway to the living room, Brooke and Bastian beside her. Honey shot her an ear-splitting smile from one of the recliners with George sitting by her feet, making Skye wonder if she had been there the whole time.

And Mckenzie? She was currently glaring at Skye from the far wall by the television.

Heat flooded Skye's face. She hadn't meant to upset Mckenzie. "I'm sorry," she said. "I didn't mean to threaten you. I just..."

"Was going to give me back my blade?"

Skye looked down and realized she was still holding one of Mckenzie's daggers. She twirled it in her hand like it was a foreign object she'd never seen before.

"Yeah," she said. Skye tossed it back to her sister and offered a weak smile.

Mckenzie narrowed her eyes but ultimately smirked. "Fine. You deal with the demon." She walked out of the room without saying another word.

If Skye didn't know Mckenzie so well, that would have made her feel about two feet tall, but this was Mckenzie. For Mckenzie to just walk away, meant she'd accepted that Khaine wasn't going anywhere.

Caden's voice broke through the silence. "Honey, out."

Honey gave a mock, pained expression as she slid from the recliner. "Ah, but this is the best part."

"You got dishes to do if you plan on staying." Caden offered Skye a smile and followed Honey out of the room, George behind them.

Bastian chuckled as he also turned to leave. "I'll see to the girl."

The girl? What girl? There was a faint memory of a little girl sitting on the couch in the living room when Skye first made it back, so figured it had to be the Guardian Mckenzie had gone after.

The moment everyone was gone, Skye felt the silence closing in on her. She peered at Khaine, but the expression on his face was filled with tension.

His brown eyes roamed over her, his lips thin. "Are you okay?"

Skye thought about his question. "You mean, how do I feel now that I'm a demon and I have no clue what that means?" She smirked. "Not too bad, I guess."

As long as she didn't focus on that fact for too long or contemplate murdering her family because they threatened her mate.

Because Khaine was actually her *mate*.

The tension in Khaine's shoulders didn't ease. "Good."

That's it? Good?

When Khaine didn't say anymore, Skye shifted in place.

"How's Raiden?" she said.

Khaine's eyes faded to black and then lightened back to their coppery brown. "Gone," he gritted. "He talked to Bastian and then left."

"I'm sorry," Skye said. "We can find him. We'll do whatever—"

"I should have told you," Khaine interrupted, his deep voice rebounding in the room.

Skye stood in place as Khaine brushed a hand through his hair. "I should have told you when I found out there would need to be a sacrifice. You could have died." His face twisted and paled. "You *did* die. I'm sorry. I never planned to hurt you."

"I know," she said, her voice a whisper.

"You don't understand. I held your lifeless body. I cradled you in my arms. Your blood—"

Khaine took a deep breath. He stuffed his hands in his pockets, his demeanor grave. His clothes had been changed, now wearing dark-blue jeans and a tight, black t-shirt. She hadn't noticed when she first entered the room, but looking at him now, it was hard not to. His medium-length, dark-blonde hair dusted his shoulders as his eyes peered at her with a kind of uncertainty. He'd shaved since she last saw him. She had liked the stubble on his face and made a mental note to tell him so in the future.

"Why did you do it?" he asked, breaking the silence.

Skye glanced around the living room and tried to think of what to say. He seemed angry with her. Was he mad at her for bringing Raiden back, or upset because she had died doing it? Her eyes found Khaine again; her mate.

Gosh, would she ever get used to that?

The way Khaine's shoulders were hung and face flat of emotion, she thought her death might be the reason for his irritation.

Skye gave him a faint smile. He really did care for her.

But did he still love her? Even after what she had done? What she was?

"I overheard your conversation with Bastian."

Khaine froze, his eyes not giving anything away. Skye twisted her feet on the ground and then moved closer to stand in front of her mate.

"I couldn't let you pick me over your brother. I could never live with that."

"I could," he said.

"Honey told me that it didn't matter if I saved Raiden or not. The vision would one day happen. She said there was no stopping it, so either I saved Raiden and died, or I died for nothing. Why not die doing something for the person I love?"

Khaine's eyes darkened. "You love me?"

Skye gave a nervous laugh. Was that it, then? Was all the tension in his shoulders because he thought she still hated him?

As if to solidify her assumption, Khaine gave her a wicked smile.

"You don't hate me?" he said.

Skye shook her head. "I would do the same if it were my

family."

His shoulders eased as he smiled even wider, then frowned. "I don't think your sisters will ever forgive me."

"They will," she said. "They have to. You're my mate."

Darkness seeped into Khaine's eyes as a wicked grin slid across his face. The look he gave her sent shivers down Skye's spine.

"Good, because I'm not going anywhere." Khaine cocked one of his sexy brows, a mischievous glint in his eyes. "But there's something we need to settle between us."

"And what's that?" Skye asked.

"I do believe you promised me a kiss."

Skye's heart sped up. "A kiss?"

He gave a quick nod. "You promised to kiss me if I told you how I learned the sleeping rune."

Skye smiled, the memory of them standing outside the nightclub in nothing but Khaine's T-shirt coming back to her. "A time and place of your choosing?"

He gave a curt nod. "I mean to collect."

His voice was matter-of-fact. Something in Skye told her that the demon needed this. Needed to remind himself that she was alive.

And Skye? All she wanted to do was bury herself in the demon and stay there. She wasn't sure if that was because she loved him or because her demon was demanding she take him back to her room and claim what belonged to her, and at this point, she didn't care.

Skye eased closer to Khaine, her body vibrating with her own kind of need, one she wasn't sure would ever go away. "If you insist."

Khaine reached out and grabbed her waist, pulling her into his chest. The second their bodies touched, her fingers twisted into claws as that voice in her head said *mine.*

She wasn't sure Khaine could seem happier, could smile wider. Skye gave into the feel of his hands on her, sighing as his fingers dipped lower. When his mouth finally molded to her own, she opened to him instantly.

He broke their kiss, almost making Skye want to scream.

Khaine's black eyes bore into her own. "I love you," he said.

Her heart swelled as she stared at her demon.

"I love you, too."

Then his lips were back on hers.

Skye deepened their kiss, demanding and taking all at once. She held onto his shoulders as he lifted her to his waist and began carrying her down the hall. God help her. If anyone tried to stop them now, she was bound to rip them to pieces, because she was never letting the demon go.

Epilogue

Skye walked into the living room, trying not to spill the bowl of popcorn in her hands. She sat next to Khaine on the sofa and smirked as he grabbed a handful and stuffed it in his mouth. Caden hit play on the DVD remote before falling back into her chair.

Happy. Skye felt happy.

Khaine had given her back Raiden's necklace to keep her demon in check. His brother had left it when he departed. They would find him. She still didn't understand how Raiden's blood had saved her. Khaine had said only pure demon's blood would work, but Khaine also said his brother had been...different. Whatever the case, she never got the chance to thank him before he left. Perhaps being in Shrodah *had* clouded his mind. She didn't think coming back from Hell could be easy. Maybe Raiden just needed time to adjust.

Skye could also use some time. The necklace helped keep her

demon side at bay, but she wanted to learn to live without the necklace, wanted to learn how to deal with the rush of new senses. Caden and Khaine agreed they would both help her learn to control that part of herself. It's like she was starting over, but at least she was starting over with her mate by her side.

Bastian sat with Sophie, the little girl Mckenzie had found after Jade's vision, and pointed to symbols in a book. Turned out the little girl was a Scribe, as Bastian and Khaine had called it. It was nice of the demon to try and help the little girl with her abilities, even if his own had been lost to him after becoming a demon. It didn't appear that Bastian would be leaving anytime soon. The fact didn't seem to bother anybody. Both he and Khaine had proved useful over the last week, busying themselves with repairs around the hideout. It was actually nice having them around.

Brooke and Jade sat next to Khaine, arguing over whose outfit Skye was going to finish first. She'd finally decided to take Khaine's advice and start her own clothing line for immortals. It wasn't like she had to worry about being weak, anymore. Being immortal could have its perks.

Mckenzie had finally stopped glaring at Khaine, but maybe it was because the demon smiled at her anytime she did. All Skye could do was laugh. She loved Mckenzie and could understand that Khaine had some making up to do, but she was certain it would all work out.

Castello had left shortly after Skye had woken up and learned she was a demon. She felt certain it was Mckenzie that had sent him on his way. Now that Skye had a mate of her own, she couldn't fathom how Mckenzie managed such a thing.

Send Khaine away? The thought made her feel sick.

Perhaps Mckenzie and Castello would settle their differences.

Khaine grabbed Skye's hand and held it, the feeling of his palm against her own warming her. Something was bothering her, though. Ever since the blast that had knocked Caden to the ground and caused her blood condition to spike, and whatever Bastian had done to her to help her heal faster, Caden had been off. The dizzy spells were coming more frequently and keeping Caden from taking any mercenary contracts. If they didn't get better, Skye knew Caden would have to find out what was wrong and how to fix it. That would mean dealing with the Elite, and that wasn't something she wanted Caden to do.

Skye didn't want anything to happen to any of her sisters, especially Caden.

Instead of dwelling on things she didn't have any control over, Skye squeezed Khaine's hand and smiled at her demon.

"Are you sure you're ready for this?" she asked him.

Khaine grinned. "I'm sure I'll live. How bad could this movie be?"

It would appear he had a lot of learning to do, but there was time.

Skye leaned over and planted a kiss on Khaine's lips, trying not to get lost in the excitement that flared low in her belly. "Well, if you can handle women screaming at a TV and like being disappointed with how things end, I'm sure you'll do just fine."

Khaine laughed, the sound sending butterflies straight to her stomach. "I'm sure I can manage."

Oh, boy. Yeah, he had a lot to learn.

433

Author's Note

Thank you for taking the time to read the first book in the **Immortally Forbidden** series. Writing this book was such a joy and nothing makes me happier than getting it into the hands of those who love paranormal romance as much as I do. If you enjoyed **Demon in the Dark**, consider leaving a review on the site where you purchased the book, and watch for **Caught by Desire**, the next installment in the **Immortally Forbidden** series.

Turn the page for a special preview of the next book
in Amber Knightly's edgy Immortally Forbidden Series
featuring Darren McCoy and Salean in

CAUGHT
BY
DESIRE

Immortally Forbidden Series book two

WHITE CARDINAL
PUBLISHING

Chapter 1

S alean flipped the dagger in her hand, back and forth between the handle and the blade. She sized up her target, her brows furrowed as she concentrated on where she would strike first. The throat? The thigh?

Releasing her hand, she sent the dagger flying. It stuck deep in the practice dummy's left shoulder, right where she intended for it to hit. While it didn't sail straight through the hay material, her aim was spot on. She'd take what she could get.

Salean glanced to her right and sighed. A cool breeze wafted through the doors on the second floor, but she kept them open. It helped to not feel like a prisoner.

Not that she was a prisoner, she reminded herself. Her Aunt Diane and Uncle Morgan had been more than kind to her over the last twelve years, but not being able to leave the villa was growing on her. It didn't matter how large the estate was, or how often she was able to traverse the eighty-acre property. Seeing the same sprawling gardens with the same animal-trimmed hedges and stone pathways, only succeeded in making her feel trapped. All she wanted was a change in scenery.

And maybe a little revenge.

She straightened and grabbed another dagger from her bedside table. She had set up the practice dummy in her bedroom, behind a folding divider where nobody could see. The villa guards couldn't hound her about being out before nightfall and zero distractions meant she could focus on her aim.

Salean tsked as she bounced between one foot and the next, the purple, shag carpet soft under her bare feet. Pulling back her arm, she aimed the dagger right at the dummy's nipple. It was a small target to hit, and one that would prove her aim the most.

Running her tongue along an incisor, she adjusted her footing and let the dagger go. It hit dead on, slicing the dummy's nipple in half.

Yes!

She twirled in place, throwing her arms in the air in quiet celebration. Her aim had more than improved! If she kept this up, maybe her aunt and uncle would finally believe she could take care of herself.

And maybe, just *maybe*, she could finally avenge her parents.

Oh, she'd tried. More than once. But she was young and naïve then, and trying to go after the Elite at fifteen wasn't the best decision to begin with. Heck, she didn't even make it off the villa grounds before she was caught by the villa guards.

The clock on the far wall started to chime as bright lights filled the growing darkness outside. Salean rushed to the double doors of her balcony and peered out. The flashing neon lights of the outdoor pool confirmed that the sun had finally set, which meant Diane and Morgan would be in the kitchen soon. If she could catch them before they left, they might let her tag along.

One could only hope, anyway.

Tonight was the vampire and Lykae alliance meeting. They met every year to discuss boundary issues and territory. This meeting was important. The deer and elk around the area had decided to deviate from their normal migration pattern, which meant Salean's aunt and uncle no longer had enough blood to sustain their House. If the Lykae didn't agree to shift the vampire territory, Diane and Morgan would be forced to take drastic measures.

She'd never been to an alliance meeting before. The thought excited her. At least she would be able to leave the villa.

Salean closed the balcony doors and hurried to stash her daggers. She tucked them in the top drawer of her nightstand and then walked across her bedroom to slide the divider back in place, disregarding the blades still stuck in the practice dummy. She glanced at the clock.

Maybe if she gave her aunt and uncle a few minutes before she started begging, they would be more inclined to let her go with them. There was still plenty of time before the meeting was set to start.

If she could just leave the villa, just for a couple of hours...

She was growing restless, and not just with thoughts of avenging her parents. Salean busied herself by brushing her red hair, then adjusted her white, silk shirt. She rubbed her palms along the fabric of her jeans and then laced her black sneakers on her feet.

She took another peek at the clock and sighed. Well, that killed all of two minutes.

Groaning her frustration, she paced the length of her bedroom, careful not to knock over the divider.

She was twenty-four now, that was more than old enough to take care of herself. The Elite, the mortal military unit created by Gregory Hues that tortured and studied immortals, and led by the vampire Leclain, hadn't found her in the last twelve years. They came close a couple of times, but Salean was safe. Morgan and Diane made sure of that. Nothing bad was going to happen to her. All she had to do was plead her case and remind them that the Elite didn't know where she was or how to find her.

Even if they *did* find her, wouldn't that allow her the opportunity to pay them back for everything they did to her family? Again, not that they would find her. Not here, anyway.

The villa was situated in a secluded area outside Pembine, Wisconsin, and since it was patrolled by vampires on one side, and inside the villa walls, and Lykae on the other, the Elite wouldn't be getting anywhere near her.

She just had to convince her aunt and uncle that attending the alliance meeting wouldn't end with her back at some Elite compound being dissected by a bunch of mortal scum.

And that she wasn't going to run off on them and try to *track down* the Elite.

Should be easy enough.

A vampire and Lykae meeting meant plenty of other immortals around. She wouldn't be alone. There would be plenty of eyes on her the whole time.

The clock on her nightstand flashed as another minute passed.

Argh!

Salean gathered herself and took a breath. If she stood pacing in her room for another second, waiting for the right opportunity to ask if she could go to the meeting, she would likely implode. Or grab her daggers back out of the drawer and shred the dummy, which she didn't want to do.

Here goes nothing!

Salean trudged to the door of her bedroom and stepped into the hall. A soft, red carpet extended the length of the hallway with cream-painted walls and white balusters. All the lights in the villa were on, set on automatic timers that illuminated the main building right at dusk. The smaller outbuildings, the cottages where the other House vampires lived, were starting to light up outside the stained-glass windows as she passed, walking with a brisk speed. The entire property was coming to life.

Sometimes it sucked being one of the few vampires that didn't die at sunrise and that could go out during the day. The vampires that had found their Lifebloods and were no longer controlled by death sleep, were stationed as daylight guards in the villa. Salean wasn't controlled by death sleep, and she also hadn't found her Lifeblood, but being a half-vampire, half-mortal hybrid meant the sun had never bothered her. Why did that suck? Because the daylight guards weren't exactly the best company, and sometimes she found it hard to sleep when the sun was up.

Her aunt and uncle were mated, which meant the sun didn't bother them either, but it was easier to run a vampire House if you slept when most vampires slept.

She turned a corner as seaside paintings, hung in red picture frames, began to line one side of the corridor. Aunt Diane loved the ocean, having grown up in California. The paintings reminded her of home. Living in the middle of the woods, surrounded by trees on all sides that were only broken by strategically placed gardens, walkways, and a pool, didn't really boast the same feel of coastal life.

She'd had the villa designed to mimic an oceanside retreat. Some might think it unnerving, the contrast of the stucco walls and modern fixtures against the country backdrop, but for Salean, it was the only home she had ever known.

At least, the only one that counted. Her stay at the Elite's compound for those twelve years after she was born, wasn't a place she would call home.

She picked up her pace, eager to get to the kitchen before she lost her confidence. By the time she arrived at her intended destination, she was damn near running.

Salean rounded another corner and barreled into a large figure standing in the doorway. She yelped at the change in motion, the sudden stop startling her.

"Whoa there, Pipsqueak," a male voice said.

Salean let her breathing calm and stepped back. Christian Blake eyed her, standing in the arched doorway with a smirk on his face. His silk shirt was tucked into an immaculate pair of gray slacks, with his short, black hair freshly washed and combed.

"Sorry," she said. "I didn't see you standing there."

Christian laughed. "Evidently, seeing as how you bulldozed into me. What's the rush?"

"Give her a break," Holly said, meandering into the kitchen with her compound bow slung over her shoulder.

"Holly!"

Salean burst into a run, tackling the vampire mercenary with enough force to knock her back.

Holly Stanton was the best mercenary around, according to Salean. She was definitely the deadliest with a bow. She never missed a shot and could kill her target from over five-hundred yards away.

If only Salean could be that good with her blades.

"Well, it's good to see you too," Holly said with a laugh. Holly's bow dug into Salean as she hugged her, the lean curve of the wood draped across her chest and attached to the quiver of arrows against Holly's back.

She wore her customary camo half-tank with black cargo pants that always made Salean think of an Amazon warrior. She was a deadly woman that could more than handle herself if needed. The feathered end of each arrow sticking out of the quiver could attest to that. The arrowheads were laced with Holly's special poison recipe.

Christian skirted the large island counter and grabbed a few glasses from the cupboard. "I would be offended, but I'd go for the person with the bigger stick too."

Salean chuckled as she untangled herself from Holly. "I'm equally excited to see both of you!"

Holly walked to the fridge and grabbed the pitcher of blood, handing it to Christian. "Watch yourself," she said. "Wouldn't want Morgan thinking you're corrupting her."

Salean hefted herself onto a stool in front of the kitchen island. "I know what a dick is."

"Salean!"

Holly whirled on her as Christian chuckled.

"What?" she said. "I'm not fourteen, anymore." She may be sheltered, but she wasn't *that* sheltered. In fact, it was probably Christian that taught her the word dick. Well, maybe she looked it up after hearing him say it, but anytime he was around and talked about the trips he took to immortal nightclubs, Salean couldn't help but tune in.

Christian busied himself by pouring the pitcher of blood Holly brought him into three glasses. Holly sneered at him but grabbed a cup, sipping the contents. She reached for another and handed it to Salean, sliding it across the marble countertop.

"Are you both here for the meeting?"

"Wouldn't miss it," Holly said.

Christian took a drink of blood, the sleeves of his silk shirt rolled to his elbows. "Morgan wanted me around in case the Lykae decide to cause trouble."

He was a House messenger. One of several. His job was to carry written correspondence between the Houses. If one House needed to call for aid, it was Christian's job to deliver the signed letter. It was easier to trust a vampire with the task than the mortal mail system, or a call that could be made from anyone. Sending a letter through certified mail could still get lost, but a vampire ensured the message was received without incident.

Well, usually without incident.

Salean pondered what it meant to have both Christian *and* Holly attending the meeting. Did her aunt and uncle think the Lykae wouldn't renegotiate terms? If the vampires were forced to break the truce and hunt on Lykae land, that meant a war between them was certain. It would be up to Christian to deliver the letter to the other Houses asking for help, and having a vampire mercenary around that never missed a shot would definitely come in handy.

Salean was starting to think she didn't stand a chance at asking to attend the meeting at all. She drank her breakfast that Holly handed her, her mood turning sour. *Fudge.*

"What about you?" Holly asked. "What's got you up so early?"

Um, the fact that the sun didn't dictate her sleep schedule?

Salean sighed and took another drink. "I was going to ask if I could go to the meeting."

Christian whistled through clenched teeth as he cringed. "Yeah, not so sure that'll go over well, Pipsqueak."

Salean glared at him. "I'm not a pipsqueak anymore and I can take care of myself."

"Nobody is doubting that," Holly said, her tone careful. "We just know how valuable you are and that Morgan and Diane wouldn't want anything to happen to you."

"Nothing is going to happen," Salean said. "The Lykae have always been kind to us. Morgan and Diane are probably worried for nothing. I would be fine. It's just one little trip out of the house."

"Yeah, and after all the other trips out of the house you tried to take?" Christian said.

"He's got a point," Holly chimed in. "You're not planning on going after the Elite again, are you?"

Well, she was, but they didn't need to know that. She wasn't planning on sneaking off at the meeting. She didn't even know how or where to find the Elite.

Salean shrugged her shoulders. "While I still want to avenge my parents, I really just want to get out of the house for a little while. I'm not going to run off. It would be no big deal."

"What's no big deal?"

Salean turned as her uncle's voice filled the large room. Morgan walked into the kitchen, his long, black hair falling over his shoulders and contrasting against his blue dress shirt. He patted her on the back as he moved around the island counter to stand by Christian.

Her Aunt Diane came in next. She was wearing her usual attire, though today's dress was a flourish of green that complemented her brown hair. The smile on her face anytime she noticed Salean, always warmed her.

"What did I miss," Diane said. It was clear she'd heard Morgan's comment. Of course she did. Vampires had excellent hearing.

Salean just wanted to fold in on herself. They probably heard her talking about leaving the villa. How was she supposed to ask them to attend the meeting? She'd only ever left the property a couple of times, and not because she was trying to sneak away. And both times? The Elite had almost found her.

Morgan leaned against the counter as his wife moved to stand beside him.

"Salean was discussing a trip," he said.

Great. So her uncle *had* heard what she said.

"I was just thinking that I'm older now, and I've been training hard—"

"Training with who?" Diane cut in, her eyebrows raising.

Oh, no. "Nobody," she quickly added. "Just working by myself in the gardens."

They didn't need to know that she stole one of the practice dummies from the weight room. Or that it was currently in her room behind a divider. *Or* that it had daggers she took from the armory stuck in it while the other daggers lay stashed in her dresser drawer.

Salean clasped the cup of blood and eyed her aunt and uncle. "I've been watching a few of the guards training in the weight room—"

"Watching others train is not the same as training yourself," her uncle interrupted. "There's no reason for you to train, anyway. You're not still thinking about going after the Elite, are you?"

Well, yes!

"No," Salean said. "Of course not."

Fudge. She hated lying to her aunt and uncle.

"I just don't want to depend on people anymore."

She looked to Holly as if she could help her. When all the mercenary offered was a smile, Salean tried Christian.

"Don't look at me," he said. "I'm staying out of this one."

Argh!

"And what one would that be?" Diane asked. She was still smiling, but the look on her face made Salean's heart sink. It was like her aunt knew exactly what she was going to ask.

Salean took a breath and smiled at her aunt and uncle. "I was wondering if I could go, tonight." She wasted no time in trying to plead her case. "I won't get in the way. I'll stay to the side and keep my hood up so nobody will see me. I won't cause any trouble at all, I promise. I won't try to take off. I'll just attend the meeting and then come home. I can even stand next to Holly. She can watch out for me."

"Whoa," Holly said. "I'm also staying out of this one."

Salean glared at the mercenary. *Thanks a lot!*

Before Salean could turn back to her uncle, his deep voice filled the kitchen. "No," he said.

"It's not a good idea," Diane said as if trying to make her uncle's answer hurt any less. "There are too many risks."

Yeah, like the risk of them not trusting her.

"There are no risks," Salean all but whined.

Great. How was she supposed to sound strong when she was practically begging?

"Even if you don't try to go after the Elite," her aunt said. "We still don't know the extent of your abilities."

They had all but confined her to the villa after the last close call with the Elite, arguing that until they knew more about her abilities and she was able to defend herself, it was best if she stayed close to her family. How was she supposed to know more about her abilities if nobody was willing to let her experiment?

And how was she supposed to learn to defend herself if nobody would train her?

"Because you won't test my abilities," Salean said. All they wanted to do was remind her about how different she was.

"I stopped aging years ago according to Dr. Hartly, and my cells regenerate just as fast as any other vampire."

"Yes, but the mortal part of you is still there," Morgan said. He broke into his fatherly tone as if he could make her see reason. "Being one of a kind means there are a lot of things we still don't know. There's no telling if you're immortal or not."

There it was. That was the sole reason she'd been cocooned in the villa and kept hidden from the Province. That was the only reason they wouldn't help her avenge her parents. They all liked to tell her it was because the Elite could find her and take her back to one of their compounds, but that wasn't the *real* reason. The *real* reason was that nobody could tell her if she was immortal or not.

"Please," Salean pleaded. "I promise, I'll be alright. Just this once. I won't cause any problems."

Diane softened. "The last time we took you out of the villa, the Elite almost found you. We just want to keep you safe."

The last time had been a fluke on Salean's part. Some stupid mortal had caught eighteen-year-old her on camera, jumping higher than a mortal should be able to jump, all in the name of getting some stupid balloon a little girl had lost to the rafters. Yes, she'd made a reckless decision, but the Elite only showed up because the mortal posted that video to social media, and they didn't even know it was Salean they were after. All they knew is that an immortal had been caught on camera in a public place, and they thought themselves high and mighty for trying to control the situation. And by control, that meant confiscating the mortal's phone and trying to kill any immortal involved.

It could have happened to anyone.

A couple guards that went along with them had seen the Elite show up. They had all been gone before the Elite even knew who they were looking for. Salean was still upset they didn't stick around long enough for her to get the revenge she wanted.

"This is different," Salean said. "It's an immortal meeting.

There won't be mortals around and there will be plenty of people there to keep me safe. Pleeaassee."

Diane turned from her to Morgan.

Morgan sighed. "This is no simple meeting. No decisions will be made toward the alliance until after, but if things get tense, I expect you back at the villa immediately. I'm trusting you. Understood?"

Salean perked up. "Understood. I promise, I'll come right back. I won't go anywhere else. You can trust me."

Diane turned to Holly. "You'll look after her?"

"Of course," the mercenary said. "I won't let her out of my sight."

Right, because *now* she wanted to help.

Holly winked at Salean.

Salean glared at the mercenary, then smiled. She was really going. Her first alliance meeting! She didn't care if she had to hide in a box chained and bolted with padlocks and only a tiny window to look through, as long as she got to leave the villa for a couple of hours. Nothing bad was going to happen.

About the Author

Amber Knightly considers herself a demigod, wrecking havoc in the lives of her immortal peers. When not living that fantasy, she's a motorcycle loving mother and reader extraordinaire.